Catherine Cookson was born in Tyne Dock, the illegitimate daughter of a poverty-stricken woman, Kate, whom she believed to be her older sister. She began work in service but eventually moved south to Hastings where she met and married Tom Cookson, a local grammar-school master. At the age of forty she began writing about the lives of the working-class people with whom she had grown up, using the place of her birth as the background to many of her novels.

Although originally acclaimed as a regional writer – her novel *The Round Tower* won the Winifred Holtby award for the best regional novel of 1968 – her readership soon began to spread throughout the world. Her novels have been translated into more than a dozen languages and more than 50,000,000 copies of her books have been sold in Corgi alone. Fifteen of her novels have been made into successful television dramas, and more are planned.

Catherine Cookson's many bestselling novels established her as one of the most popular of contemporary women novelists. After receiving an OBE in 1985, Catherine Cookson was created a Dame of the British Empire in 1993. She was appointed an Honorary Fellow of St Hilda's College, Oxford in 1997. For many years she lived near Newcastle-upon-Tyne. She died shortly before her ninety-second birthday in June 1998.

'Catherine Cookson's novels are about hardship, the intractability of life and of individuals, the struggle first to survive and next to make sense of one's survival. Humour, toughness, resolution and generosity are Cookson virtues, in a world which she often depicts as cold and violent. Her novels are weighted and driven by her own early experiences of illegitimacy and poverty. This is what gives them power. In the specialised world of women's popular fiction, Cookson has created her own territory'
Helen Dunmore, *The Times*

BOOKS BY CATHERINE COOKSON

NOVELS

Kate Hannigan
The Fifteen Streets
Colour Blind
Maggie Rowan
Rooney
The Menagerie
Slinky Jane
Fanny McBride
Fenwick Houses
Heritage of Folly
The Garment
The Fen Tiger
The Blind Miller
House of Men
Hannah Massey
The Long Corridor
The Unbaited Trap
Katie Mulholland
The Round Tower
The Nice Bloke
The Glass Virgin
The Invitation
The Dwelling Place
Feathers in the Fire
Pure as the Lily
The Mallen Streak
The Mallen Girl
The Mallen Litter
The Invisible Cord
The Gambling Man
The Tide of Life
The Slow Awakening
The Iron Façade
The Girl
The Cinder Path
Miss Martha Mary Crawford
The Man Who Cried
Tilly Trotter

Tilly Trotter Wed
Tilly Trotter Widowed
The Whip
Hamilton
The Black Velvet Gown
Goodbye Hamilton
A Dinner of Herbs
Harold
The Moth
Bill Bailey
The Parson's Daughter
Bill Bailey's Lot
The Cultured Handmaiden
Bill Bailey's Daughter
The Harrogate Secret
The Black Candle
The Wingless Bird
The Gillyvors
My Beloved Son
The Rag Nymph
The House of Women
The Maltese Angel
The Year of the Virgins
The Golden Straw
Justice is a Woman
The Tinker's Girl
A Ruthless Need
The Obsession
The Upstart
The Branded Man
The Bonny Dawn
The Bondage of Love
The Desert Crop
The Lady on My Left
The Solace of Sin
Riley
The Blind Years
The Thursday Friend

THE MARY ANN STORIES

A Grand Man
The Lord and Mary Ann
The Devil and Mary Ann
Love and Mary Ann

Life and Mary Ann
Marriage and Mary Ann
Mary Ann's Angels
Mary Ann and Bill

FOR CHILDREN

Matty Doolin
Joe and the Gladiator
The Nipper
Rory's Fortune
Our John Willie

Mrs Flannagan's Trumpet
Go Tell It To Mrs Golightly
Lanky Jones
Nancy Nutall and the Mongrel
Bill and the Mary Ann Shaughnessy

AUTOBIOGRAPHY

Our Kate
Catherine Cookson Country

Let Me Make Myself Plain
Plainer Still

HANNAH MASSEY
&
THE FIFTEEN STREETS

Catherine Cookson

PATHWAY

TRANSWORLD PUBLISHERS
61–63 Uxbridge Road, London W5 5SA
a division of The Random House Group Ltd

RANDOM HOUSE AUSTRALIA (PTY) LTD
20 Alfred Street, Milsons Point, Sydney,
New South Wales 2061, Australia

RANDOM HOUSE NEW ZEALAND LTD
18 Poland Road, Glenfield, Auckland 10, New Zealand

RANDOM HOUSE SOUTH AFRICA (PTY) LTD
Endulini, 5a Jubilee Road, Parktown 2193, South Africa

Published 2001 by Pathway
a division of Transworld Publishers

HANNAH MASSEY
Originally published in Great Britain by Macdonald & Co. (Publishers) Ltd.
Copyright © Catherine Cookson 1964

THE FIFTEEN STREETS
Originally published in Great Britain by Macdonald & Co. (Publishers) Ltd.
Copyright © Catherine Cookson 1952

Copyright © The Trustees of the Catherine Cookson Charitable Trust 2001

A catalogue record for this book is available
from the British Library.
ISBN 0593 049918

Printed in Great Britain by
Mackays of Chatham plc, Chatham, Kent.

HANNAH MASSEY

Catherine Cookson

PATHWAY

Contents

The Arrival

As she came slowly through the doorway into the snow-covered street she paused for a moment and put her hand against the wall near where the cards that gave the names of the flat-dwellers reposed in three slots one above the other. But, as if becoming aware of the proximity of something dirty, she snatched her hand away and put it in her coat pocket, then went slowly down the street.

She was a tall girl with very long legs, a flour-white face topped with thick, dark auburn hair, which had been cut to bouffant style but which now fell from jagged partings over each side of her high cheek-bones. She had large, slightly slanted grey-green eyes, and a wide straight-lined mouth, but what could have been a set of perfect features was marred slightly by her nose which was a little too long and a little too thin. Altogether she looked rangy. She was wearing a knee-length brown coat with a broad belt that swung loosely below her buttocks, and she carried in her hand an open-woven basket; she didn't look adequately dressed for the weather, she looked like a young woman who had slipped out hurriedly to do some shopping. And this was apparently her intention.

Walking slowly past four Victorian houses, similar to the one she had just left, she came to a row of shops.

9

The first was a baker's. She passed this without looking in the window, but by the butcher's shop next door to it she paused for a moment before going on. She paused again in front of a chemist's shop. But thereafter she did not stop until she reached the large all-purpose store at the end of the block. Here again she paused and scanned the contents of the window before entering. Her journey down the street had been slow, even leisurely, and her whole attitude, if judged by her back, could have been one of boredom; yet immediately she was within the store her manner changed. She did not pause at any counter, but walking hastily around the perimeter of the store she made for a side exit, and having gained the street once more she took to her heels and ran.

The street opened into a main thoroughfare thick with traffic, but she made for the other side of the road with the assurance of someone used to London's traffic. Once across, she left the main road and cut down another side street, not running now but hurrying at the point of a trot. Ten minutes later she stopped outside a small pawn shop and stood for a moment inhaling deeply before entering.

There was no-one in the shop except the man behind the counter. He was in his fifties and looked unusually spruce to be in a pawn shop. Pawn shops were dusty places, even those like this one that sold new stuff such as silver and rare china. Men who worked in pawn shops seemed to take on the patina of their surroundings and it usually gave off a dull sheen, but even this man's smile looked clean and bright.

'Good morning, madam,' he said.

'Good morning,' she answered. Her voice sounded

rough, almost rasping, as if she had a bad throat or her mouth was dry.

'What can I do for you?' He inclined his head towards her, as if he had known her a long while and wanted to be of service to her.

She groped into the single deep pocket of her coat and brought out a ring, which she placed on the counter.

He did not immediately touch the ring but looked at her. He watched her swallow twice, then waited for her to speak.

'Could you . . . could you give me ten pounds on it?'

'Ten pounds!' His eyebrows moved up slightly towards his smooth hair. He picked up the ring and reached out for a small black eye-piece. After a moment he looked at her again; his expression had changed. It could have been the expression of a man who had found something out, something detrimental about someone he loved. He said again, 'Ten pounds?' His words were a question, and in answer she moved her head.

He looked at the ring once more; for an eternity he looked at it, and she grew old the while.

'Yes.' He let out a long breath. 'Yes, I can give you ten pounds on it. Yes. Yes. Well now, would you like to sign?' He pulled a book towards her and offered her a pen. As it passed from his hand to hers it fell to the counter and he apologised, saying, 'Oh, I'm sorry,' although they both knew it wasn't he who had dropped the pen. When she had signed her name he turned the book towards him. 'Rose Massey,' he read aloud, then glancing up at her he proffered gently, 'You have forgotten the address, madam.'

She stared at the book for some seconds before writing

in it again. When the pawnbroker turned it towards him he studied it a moment before saying quietly, 'Eight Brampton Hill . . . Brampton Hill?' He put his head back on his neat shoulders and, looking up towards the age-smoked ceiling, said musingly, 'I can't quite recollect . . . Brampton Hill?'

'It's on the outskirts, Lewisham way.'

'Oh. Oh, Lewisham way.' He was nodding at her. Then he smiled, and picking up the ring he placed it behind him on a piece of glass, and from a drawer he took a bundle of new notes from which he pulled off the elastic band and counted ten out to her.

She folded the notes twice, then again, until they were a tube squeezed in her fist. 'Thank you. Good morning,' she said.

'Wait . . . you will want a ticket.'

'Oh, yes.' There was another eternity while she watched him write out a ticket, and when he handed it to her he smiled again as he had done when she came in.

'Thank you.' She did not return his smile but inclined her head.

'Thank . . . you.' There was deep emphasis on the words.

She was conscious of him watching her walking to the door, and her legs shook and her feet in the high stiletto-heeled shoes wobbled slightly. In the street she hesitated a moment, looked to the right, then left, then once again began to hurry towards the main road, but when, at the corner, she saw a taxi coming towards her, the 'For Hire' sign up, she hailed it.

'Can you take me to King's Cross?'

'Certainly, miss.'

'I mean could you get me there for about ten to one? The train leaves at one.'

'Ten-past twelve now . . . I don't see why not, if the traffic jams are kind to us. Hop in.'

In the taxi she sat bolt upright, gripping the handle of the basket on her knee with both hands.

When they were stopped by traffic lights for the third time she leant forward and asked, 'Will it be all right?'

'Eh?' he said.

'Will it be all right? Will there be plenty of time?'

'Yes, yes, we'll make it and likely twenty minutes to spare.'

She sat straight again, staring unblinking at the constant movement ahead.

'There you are,' said the taxi-driver. 'What did I tell you? Just two minutes out.'

Standing on the kerb she hesitated on his tip, whether to give him a shilling or two shillings. . . . She could make it two shillings, she'd have enough. Yes, she'd have enough.

She had just crossed the pavement towards the entrance hall when the taxi-driver's voice hailed her, and she turned towards him. 'You've left your basket, miss.' He jerked his head towards the back of the cab. She glanced downwards before running back, pulling open the door and grabbing up the basket.

At the ticket office she said, 'A single to Newcastle, please.'

She ran again, weaving in and out of the throng towards the platform. At the barrier she said to the ticket collector, 'How long before it goes?'

'Ten minutes,' he replied.

She withheld her ticket. 'I won't be a minute.' She turned from him and, running once more, went into the ladies and to the lavatory. She did not sit down but waited a few seconds before she left the basket at the side of the pan, then hurried out.

She was crossing the waiting room when a voice hailed her from the door. The attendant stood there with a large duster in one hand, the basket in the other. 'You forgot this,' she called.

Her eyes dropped again before she moved towards the woman, and taking the basket she said, 'Oh, thanks.'

As she approached the train she held the basket at an angle so that its emptiness would not be noticed.

After walking the length of the train she stood in the corridor. She had known she wouldn't get a seat, not this late. It didn't matter, it didn't matter. With the first shuddering movement of the train she leant against the partition and, her lids slowly closing, she allowed her muscles to unwind.

When a voice said 'Excuse me,' she opened her eyes and pressed herself back to allow a man with a suitcase to pass her, and when he looked at her and smiled his thanks no muscle of her face moved in response, but as he put down his suitcase and took up his stand against the door she moved slowly away. Walking down the corridor she crossed over the jangling connecting platform, and stood in the corner of the next coach.

It wasn't until the train reached Doncaster that she found a seat, and when she placed her basket on the rack it drew the attention of the two men and the woman sitting opposite. Time and again her eyes would lift to

14

the basket, incongruous between the suitcases, before dropping automatically down to the girl with the bright hair and the white face and the long legs, which she kept pressed close to the seat. She didn't look the type to travel with a basket.

When at Durham she was left alone in the compartment with one passenger, and he a man, she went into the corridor and stood looking out into the whirling darkness.

Before they reached Newcastle the man came out of the compartment, and as he passed her he looked at her with open curiosity. A girl was travelling with an empty basket and without a hat or a handbag . . . no girl ever travelled without a handbag.

Just before the train reached Newcastle she tore up the pawn ticket and put it down the lavatory, and when she left the train she left the basket on the rack.

Again she was hurrying, now into the main thoroughfare of the city. All the shops were still brightly lit, but most of them were closed, even the one that advertised late closing on Friday night was about to shut its doors when she entered.

'It's five to, we're closing, miss,' said the doorman.

'Please.' She looked up into his face. 'I won't be a minute, I just want a case.'

'All right,' he said, 'go on.' His voice was kindly, and broad and thick with the northern inflection, and told her she was home.

On a counter to the right of her were some suitcases. An imitation crocodile, priced at twenty-one shillings, brought her hand to it, and handing the money across the counter she said, 'I'll take this. Where are the hats?'

'On the first floor, miss.'

They had covered up most of the millinery in the hat department, but, glancing swiftly around her, her eyes alighted on a grey felt. Pulling it on and with hardly a glance in the mirror she said, 'I'll take this one.' The price was twelve and eleven.

As she turned to go down the stairs she saw a notice proclaiming 'The Bargain Counter'. A model with wire arms extended towards her showed a three-piece suit in charcoal edged with dull pink braid. It looked exotic, and therefore wasn't everybody's buy. The price had been slashed three times. The tag hanging from the lapel showed thirteen guineas in large red letters. This was scored out and underneath was ten guineas, then eight guineas, and now the black figures stated that the garment had been reduced to five guineas.

She said to an assistant who was watching her as she looked at the suit, 'What is the waist?'

The girl said, 'Oh, the waist? The hips are thirty-four.'

Before the assistant could pull the tag from the inside of the skirt to ascertain the size, she said, 'I'll take it.'

'There's no time to try it on.'

'I know.'

'You won't be able to get it changed, not at this price.'

'I know.'

The assistant was smiling as she whipped the suit from the model. 'I'm sure it'll be all right; you'll be able to carry it.' She smiled a complimentary smile.

After she had handed the girl the money, she took the parcel and put it into the case, and when she passed out of the shop the doorman said, 'I see you've got what you wanted, miss.' He smiled at her as men mostly did.

16

'Yes,' she nodded, but without answering his smile.

Once again she was walking back to the Central Station, without hurrying now. In the restaurant she bought a cup of tea, and from the bookstall a paper; then going to the booking office she asked for a single to Fellburn. Out of the ten pounds she had received for the ring and the pound she had in her pocket when she entered the pawn shop she had only a few shillings left, but it didn't matter, it didn't matter; she was nearly home.

Half an hour later she stepped out of the train on to the platform at Fellburn Station, and edging her way through the crowd in the station hall waiting for the buses she went out into the driving, skin-searing sleet. She had one more thing to do before she could go home.

She went down Marlborough Road. This cut off the main part of the town and the new shopping centre, for even at this hour the street would be thronged, it being Friday night and pay night for both the pits and the factories. Even if the shops were closed the coffee bars would be doing a trade, and the clubs . . . the clubs roared on a Friday night, and who knew who she would run into.

She came out near the park and past the road that led to Brampton Hill; Brampton Hill where the élite of Fellburn lived, those that were left of them; Brampton Hill, the name she had put on the pawn ticket. Why had she put 'Eight Brampton Hill' on the pawn ticket? Perhaps because she had heard of 'Eight Brampton Hill' since she had heard of anything. She passed by St Vincent's Catholic Church and the Convent, and next to the Convent the school at which she had attended until she was fifteen. Then she crossed the road and went down a dark alleyway. She had always been afraid of going down this alleyway, even as recently as two years ago; now she was afraid no more. What was it? It was just a cut between a factory wall and a railway siding. And the dark? The dark was no longer terrifying; it was something that you could lose yourself in . . . sometimes.

The alley led her into an open plane. Once or twice she slipped, her high heels slithering over the snow; but all the time she was making her way towards the faint blur given off by a lamp in the far distance. When she had almost reached the lamp she stopped and peered at the white-capped hills of builders' rubble. Stopping, she picked up a stone, weighted it in her hand, then discarded it as being too light. Then selecting a rough, chipped-edge house brick she laid it near her feet and searched until she found a similar one. When she found it she opened the case and took out the newspaper, and wrapping the bricks in it she put them in the bottom of the case, placing the bag containing the new suit above them.

The sleet, nearly all rain now, was full in her face and almost blinding her, but had she been blind she would have known the way to Grosvenor Road.

The houses in Grosvenor Road were large terraced houses; they were all old and looked respectable and dignified, even crowned with dirty melting snow as they were. Age alone had not brought these qualities to them; these had been built into the façade at the end of the last century. Each house had an iron-bound square of garden and the front door was approached by four steps, and number forty-nine, the third house from the top, was

18

unique in that its steps were made up of red and ochre-coloured tiles.

As she reached the top step she leant against the framework of the door for a moment. She wanted to get her breath, gather her wits together, say all the things she had rehearsed in the train. When there came to her the buzz of voices beyond the door, loud harsh voices, and the deep roll of laughter, she knew indeed that she was home. She straightened up and rang the bell.

PART ONE

ROSIE

Friday

When the door opened and Rosie saw her brother Jimmy standing there she did not move or speak, and he, for a moment, did not recognise her, for being six foot two the lights in the hall beyond him diffused its rays from the back of his head.

'Aye?' he asked. 'Who . . . ?' then bending forward he exclaimed in a quick, breathless whisper, 'Name of God! Is it you, Rosie?'

'Yes, it's me, Jimmy.'

She was in the hall now; Jimmy had one hand on her shoulder, the other still grabbing the door. As his voice, spurting up his long length like steam from a geyser, yelled, 'Ma! Everybody! Look who's here. Just look who's here,' he shook her.

'What is it? What's up?'

'No, no, begod! 'Tisn't true.'

'Rosie!'

'Where have you sprung from?'

'Rosie . . . Rosie.'

The hall was packed now, filled with men, all big men; and one woman, a big woman too. She came forward towards her daughter like a sleepwalker, her eyes wide and unblinking, and when she was a yard from her she flung her arms wide and gathered the girl into her embrace, crying, 'Rosie! Rosie! Aw, Rosie!'

23

Had Rosie wanted to speak she would have found it difficult for the breath was being squeezed out of her, but she, too, clung to her mother, hiding her face in her thick, warm, fleshy neck until she was pushed to a distance as Hannah Massey, looking round at her four sons, cried at them, 'Well, what are we standing here for like a clutchin' of dead ducks? Come on with you and into the room where it's warm. . . . But lass' – her hands were moving over her daughter now – 'you're wringin', absolutely sodden. In the name of God, have you walked all the way from the station?'

'I missed the bus.'

'Then why didn't you get a taxi?'

'I wanted some air; it's a long journey.'

'Aw, child . . . just to hear your voice again, it's lovely lovely.' Once more she enfolded her daughter in her arms; and now there was a derisive cry from one of the men.

'Away to the room she said, away to the room where it's warm. . . . Go on with you; go on, old 'un.' He put one hand on the massive back of his mother and one on the thin shoulder of his sister and pushed them amid laughter and chaffing out of the hall and into the sitting-room.

'Here, get that coat off you.' Hannah was behind her daughter, and when she had pulled the coat off her she stopped and surveyed her with surprise, as did the men.

As Rosie stood self-consciously pulling down the skimpy jumper over the tight skirt a trace of colour came into her face and she said, 'There was no time to change. I made up me mind on the spur of the moment. My other things are being sent on.'

24

'You haven't got enough on you to keep a rat warm, either in clothes or flesh.' Hannah was standing in front of her again, feeling her arms. 'And you're as white as a sheet, girl. Tell me, are you all right? I've never seen you like this in your life afore.'

'I've had the flu.'

'I can see you've had something, for begod! you look like a ghost. A puff of wind would send you flyin'. Come, sit yourself down here by the fire until I get you a meal.' She led her forward as if she was old or an invalid, then asked, 'How long you down for, lass?'

'Oh, a . . . a week or so.'

'You'll be longer if I get my way. . . . Just wait till your da sees you. Oh, begod! he'll be over the moon, over the moon he'll be.'

Hannah Massey now pressed her daughter into the easy chair by the roaring open fire, and with her hands resting on its arms she bent above her, her big broad face stretched and softened in tenderness, and she stared at her silently for some moments. Then reaching out and gently patting the white face she turned away, overcome with her emotion.

When their mother had left the room the four men who had been standing at a distance like spectators now gathered around Rosie and they chipped and teased her as they always had done; and to one after the other she put out her hand and touched them, and each of them returned her touch with a gentle pressure of their big rough hands, and their open affection blocked her throat and dimmed her gaze.

Of her nine living brothers Rosie knew these four the best. Jimmy, the eldest at home, who had opened the door to her, was thirty-three. He was tall and black and handsome. Arthur was thirty. He too was tall but had not Jimmy's bulk or looks. His hair was the colour of Rosie's, only a darker hue. Then there was Shane. Shane was twenty-eight and six foot, big boned and thin, and he took after his father.

Barny was the youngest of the eleven sons born to Hannah Massey; he was twenty-six but could have been twin to Rosie herself, who was three years younger.

As she looked at these men, the lads as she thought of them, the warmth that emanated from them became almost unbearable. Up to two years ago they had teased and petted her . . . and had been proud of her. Yes, they had been proud of her. But two years ago they had not appeared to her as they did now. Then she had secretly seen them as big, blundering, narrow-minded bigots. Then she had longed to get away from their deep laughter, laughter that the weakest joke could elicit. Then, God forgive her, she had looked upon them as common and coarse, men without a thread of refinement among them. How dared she have thought that way about them! . . . How dared she!

Barny, touching her wrist with his blunt, hard fingers, said, 'By, you've lost weight; you're as thin as a rake.'

'Well, you couldn't say she was ever fat.' Arthur pushed his fist gently against the side of her head. 'All thoroughbreds are lean, eh, Rosie?'

'Why didn't you let us know?' put in Shane, peering at her through narrow, thick-fringed lids out of a face that looked as Irish as his name. 'You been bad or something. . . . I . . . I mean afore you had the flu?'

'No. It was just the flu.'

26

'Just the flu,' said Jimmy, strightening up and adjusting his tie while he looked down at her. 'Just the flu. It's enough for, begod, it pulls you down. I should know: I had it, an' that bug, diarrhoea and sickness. It's been going mad round here. It was only four days I was down, but Christ!'

'Not so much of your Christing.' Hannah came marching in to the room with a laden tray. 'I've told you, our Jimmy, we're going to have less blasphemy round here . . . now mind, I've said it.'

The four men looked at their mother, a wide grin between them ,then turning to Rosie almost as one Barny and Shane cried simultaneously, 'Hear that, Rosie?' while Arthur put his head back and laughed; and Jimmy, bending above Rosie again, said in a mock whisper, 'Talk posh now; that's the latest. Live up to our best shirts.' He pulled at the front of his well-cut nylon shirt. 'Bloody and bugger and Christ's taboo . . . abso-bloody-lutely.'

'Jimmy!'

'All right, Ma, I'm only having you on.'

'Well don't.' Hannah Massey's back was straight, as was her face; her head was high, which brought it almost on a level with Shane's, who stood near her, and as she allowed her gaze to rest condemningly on Jimmy she spoke in an aside to Shane, saying in a tone of command, 'Fetch the dish out of the oven, you, and don't spill it.'

'OK, captain.' Shane pressed his shoulders back, made a salute with a wavering hand, winked broadly at Rosie, did a smart about-turn and marched, knees up, feet pounding the floor, towards the kitchen. This act brought great gusts of laughter from the others and a compressed smile to Hannah's lips. Then as she moved towards Rosie her face broke up as it were, and fell into soft warm folds, and she said, 'You see, they don't get any better, do they? They won't learn, not one of them. Brawn, that's all they've got. Could anybody on God's earth refine this lot? I ask you. . . . Now could they?'

'Oh, Ma.' Rosie smiled faintly and shook her head, and Hannah said, 'Come away, sit up; it's just something to be going on with. If you'd only let me know you were coming I'd 'ave had a spread for you.'

'Aye, begod you would at that.' Arthur nodded at her, his brown eyes twinkling. 'And we'd all 'ave been on our toes. Spit and polish it would have been for every one of us, an' sitting here like stuffed dummies waiting for your entry, like last time. Do you remember, Rosie?' He laughed at her. 'The house full of us all, like Madame Tussaud's we were, all set up. Here's one that's pleased, anyway, you've come on the hop.'

'Where's your things, Rosie?' said Barny now. 'If they're at the station I'll get Phil next door to pick them up in the car.'

'Aye.' Hannah, pressing Rosie into the chair at the table and, bending over her and looking into her face, said, 'I was just going to mention your things. Are they at the station?'

Rosie picked up her knife and fork. 'They're going to be sent on. I, I came on the spur of the moment, and just threw a few things into a case.'

'But . . . but that in the hall; that isn't your good leather case. Why did you travel with that thing? They'll bash the good one to smithereens on the railway, you know what they are. . . .'

'. . . And after meself paying nine pounds ten for it.' Arthur was leaning across the table imitating his mother's voice. 'You'll not get another present out of me; begod, you won't.'

Hannah struck out at her son; then cried at them all, 'Go on, the lot of you, and get going; you were almost on your way.'

'She's pushing us out,' said Shane. 'She's got our money.' He nodded to the other three. 'Friday night; she's got our packets and now we can get to hell out of it. She's got Rosie, so she doesn't want us. She wouldn't care if she never saw a hair of our heads . . . except on Friday nights. On Friday nights you're as welcome as the flowers in May to Hannah Massey's home.' He touched his trouser legs and went into a little jig, which his brothers applauded.

Hannah, ignoring the by-play, seated herself at the corner of the table opposite Rosie and heaving in a great breath she squared her lips as she said, 'Begod! I could cover with spit the amount I make out of you lot.' She nodded towards Rosie now. 'Rump steaks, fresh cream on their puddin's, suits at fifteen to twenty guineas a piece. And take their shirts now. Two pound twelve and six apiece I've to pay so's the sweat won't show at the oxters. Wouldn't you say now there's a fat lot left out of a pay packet when the bills are cleared?'

The four men, following a signal, now walked solemnly towards each other, and putting their heads together began to sing, 'Tell us the old, old story.'

The satirical chorus was broken up by Hannah remarking caustically, 'Aw, you're all flat, there's not a note right atween you. The only time you lot can sing together

29

is when you're three sheets in the wind. . . . Now' – her
voice held a note that Rosie knew from experience could
put a damper on the lads' rough humour – 'you've done
your piece so get yourselves along with you. I want to
talk to me girl here.' She winked at Rosie.

'Aw, there's no hurry, Ma. Me da should be in any
minute now.' Jimmy looked at his wrist-watch. 'I want
to see his face when he spots her.' He smiled towards
her and Rosie, with an effort, smiled back.

'Aye, me too,' said Barny. 'He'll be over the moon.
Aye, we'll all wait; so settle yoursel', old woman.' He
flapped his hand at his mother, which caused her to shake
her head widely as she lowered it to her chest like a bull
about to charge. Then before she could make any further
remark there came the sound of the back door opening;
and Shane, darting to Rosie, pulled her to her feet and
whispered, 'Get behind the door, go on.'

'Yes, yes, go on.' Hannah, her face alight once more,
signalled to her as she pulled herself up from the chair.

'Hannah!' The voice came loudly from the kitchen,
and she called back to it, 'Aye, I can hear you.'

'Where's them blasted slippers?'

'Coo! Mrs Massey.' Barny was whispering as he
poked his head towards his mother. 'Listen to him, Mrs
Massey; he's swearin'. He said blasted, Mrs Massey.'

'You wait, me lad, I'll give you blasted afore you get
out of the house the night. . . . Ssh!' She silenced them
all. 'Move round, don't look so guilty like, push yourselves about.' She pressed the door back, hiding Rosie,
then called, 'Have you found them?'

'No, I haven't, an' I'm not lookin' for them.' The
heavy padded footsteps came towards the living-room,

30

and Broderick Massey entered, growling, 'If you want me to wear blasted slippers then have them out for me.'

Hannah had her back to him and she busied herself at the long table in the middle of the room. She took a glass bottle from out of a large cruet and, shaking it, held it up to the light, ascertaining the amount of pepper in it, as she said, 'If I had three wishes in the world, do you know what I'd wish for?'

Broderick stopped dead on his way to the fireplace. He looked around his sons, all self-consciously doing nothing, then towards his wife's bent back and her great expanse of buttocks pressing her skirt up into a point above her thick calves. A sly twinkle came into his eye and a smile slithered over the grey dusty grime of his face, and he cast his glance towards Jimmy and winked. Then making his way to the chair by the side of the hearth, he sat down, saying, 'Begod now, let me think. The last time I heard that sayin' it pushed us all back over a hundred quid for the suite. You remember, boys?' He rolled his head backwards on his shoulders, taking in the amused glances of his sons. 'An' the time afore that it was spin-dryer, remember?' He jerked his chin upwards and his Adam's apple danced under the loose skin of his neck. 'And the time afore that, the time afore that was an electric mixer. An electric mixer, begod! You remember the schemozzle about the electric mixer? She couldn't mix another spoonful, rheumatics she had in the wrist you remember?'

The men were all laughing now; and Hannah, from the table, her back still towards her husband, said calmly, 'If I had three wishes, Broderick Massey, the first one would be to see my daughter in this very room. . . . And

31

the second one would be . . .' She straightened up and took a large knife and sawed off a thick slice of bread before continuing. 'The second one would be to see me daughter in this very room this very night. And . . .'

Before she reached the third wish Broderick was on his feet, and now he looked at her as she swung round, her face one large beam, crying, 'And the third wish would be to see me daughter . . .'

'Stop it, woman! Tell me.' He was walking toward her. 'She's comin'? Rosie's comin' home?'

The men were laughing out aloud now like lads at the climax of a joke they had prepared.

'She could be at that. Aye, she could be at that; she could be on her way.' She looked at him, at his thin, wiry body which looked puny against her breadth. She lifted her hand to his shoulder and turned him round to face the open door, and then silently she pointed.

He flashed his glance wide now towards her, then slowly he padded to the door and pulling it forward he looked at his daughter; and then they were in each other's arms.

After holding her for a moment in silence, words tumbled out of him. 'Aw, Rosie. Begod, Rosie. Aye, three wishes, three thousand wishes and every one that Rosie would be in the kitchen the night. Aw, lass. Aw, lass.' He held her from him and looked at her for a moment, then turning to Hannah who was standing to the side of him he said in awed tones, 'She's as thin as a lath.'

'She's had flu.'

'Flu, begod!'

'Aye, it's pulled her down.' They were talking as if

she was a child, a child who could not speak for herself. They murmured over her as they walked back to the middle of the room, and when Broderick sat down in his chair he still had hold of her hand and cried, 'Come and sit down on me knee, come on.'

'Don't be silly, Da.' Rosie shook her head. She was smiling more easily now but not laughing.

'Come here.' He pulled her on to his knee, and after holding her tight for a moment he pushed her upwards and looked at Hannah, saying, 'She's not the weight of a feather; you'll have to do some fatten' up here, missus.'

'Who wants to be fat?' Rosie touched his rough cheek, tenderly, lovingly, and he caught her hand and held it, his face crumpling almost as if he was going to cry, but he shouted, 'Who wants to be fat? Better than lookin' like death on wheels; you haven't a pick on you.' He felt round her ribs. 'Not a pick. Aw, we'll soon alter this. How long are you here for?' He squeezed her tightly now.

'A week, or so.'

'Make it . . . or so, eh?' He was about to go on when his attention was drawn to where Hannah, once again at the table, was now speaking to Arthur, but harshly, saying, 'You goin' to the club?'

'Aye,' said Arthur; 'of course I am.'

'Well then, wait for the others.'

'Aw, Ma.'

'Never mind aw ma-ing me. I told you what I'd do; and I mean it mind.'

'God in Heaven!' Arthur turned away and dashed out of the room, leaving the atmosphere changed.

As Jimmy and Shane exchanged glances, Hannah said

33

to them, 'You keep an eye on him, 'cos mind, I'm tellin'
you as I told him, if I see him with her once again I'll
go to her place an' pull her out and rub her nose in the
gutter. I will, so help me God. If anybody's going to
bring disrespect on me family it'll be meself, an' that's
the way I'll do it. But I'll take good care as long as I've
got breath in me body none of me own blood's goin' to
show me up.'

'If you'd let up, Ma, it would likely peter out.'

Hannah turned on Barny. 'Peter out, you say? It's been
going on for nearly a year now, and if her man comes
back from sea we'll have him at this door wantin' to
beat his wife's fancy man's brains out.'

'He's left her, Arthur's told you.' Barny's voice was
low. 'He won't come back.'

'Aye, he's told me an' I don't believe a word of it.
He'll be back when his ship's in. Women like that are
as bad as drugs to a man; they should be horse-whipped,
her kind.'

'Now, now, now! No more of this.' Broderick looked
towards his wife. 'Let the child get acclimatised again
afore you start. . . . Eh, Rosie?'

Rosie made no answer, but, pulling herself from her
father's arms, got to her feet, saying, 'I'll go up and have
a wash, Da.'

'You didn't finish your tea.' Hannah came quickly
towards her now, her face once again smiling. 'Look,
I'll get some more hot, there's piles of fish pie.'

'It's all right, Ma; I'll have something later. I'd rather
have a wash and tidy up. I feel filthy.'

'All right then, lass, all right.' Hannah stroked her
arm, then pushed her towards the door.

'I'll take your case up.' Barny followed her into
the hall, and Rosie said, 'It's all right, Barny; it's quite
light.'

'When did you carry a case upstairs?' Barny smiled
at her over his shoulder.

'Aye when!' Hannah exclaimed from the doorway
now. 'An' put on something nice,' she added. 'That
rig-out you have on isn't you at all.' She wrinkled her
nose, then smiled.

'Which room am I in?' Rosie turned from the foot of
the stairs.

'Oh, aye, begod, yes. Well, look.' Hannah pointed.
'Jimmy's on the landing now but I'll throw his things
back into the attic in two shakes when I get your da
settled.'

'No.' Rosie stepped down into the hall again. 'No,
please leave Jimmy where he is, Ma; I'd rather be up in
the attic. You know I always liked the attic; it's big, and,
well, I'd rather be there.'

'You mean that?'

'Yes. Yes, I'd rather be up there.'

'Aw well then, for the night. I'll make the bed up
later. And, Barny, you take up an oil stove now an' we'll
fix everything good an' proper the morrow.'

Rosie followed Barny up the stairs and on to the first
landing. It was a big landing with four doors going off
it and another flight of stairs leading from the far end.
They went up these and on to another landing with three
doors, and before they mounted the attic stairs Barny
stopped, and after switching on a light, said in a whisper,
'Notice anything?'

Rosie looked around her, then down to the carpet on

35

the landing. And glancing up at Barny, she smiled slightly as she said, 'A new carpet up here.'

He jerked his head. 'Oh, you don't know the half. All the bedrooms have fitted cord carpet now; no lino, not a bit of lino anywhere in the house except the living-room. She said she would do it, and she has.' His head jerked again. 'By, she's the limit, isn't she?' He laughed.

In the attic, Barny put the case on the floor, then stood looking at Rosie. 'It's nice to have you back, Rosie.'

'Thanks, Barny.' She turned towards him but didn't look at him.

'Are you all right?' he asked quietly. 'Nothing wrong?'

She lifted her eyes quickly to him. 'Wrong?'

'Well, you don't look yourself you know, nor sound yourself. I noticed it when you first come in. But the flu does pull people down. One of the fellows in our shop had it; he came back as weak as a kitten. He could hardly handle his machine.'

When she did not answer he strained his neck out of his collar, adjusted his tie, and said, 'They're over the moon down there, the pair of them. There'll be no holding her for days. You'd better put on your best bib and tucker to give her something to brag about. Jessie MacFarlane will know you're here within the next hour. And the Parkmans and the Watsons' – he nodded his head first to one side of the room and then to the other – 'will be advised' – he was now mimicking his mother's manner – 'of your arrival in very refeened tones to-morrow morning.' He pushed her gently as he laughed, then added, 'But I don't know about the Watsons, she'd had a do with them 'cos they rapped through about the

36

noise we made last Friday night. You should have heard her. Oh, she's a great lass.' He laughed again. 'Bye-bye then. See you later, Rosie. . . . Oh, I must get the stove.'

A few minutes later he came up with an oil stove, and when he had lit it for her she said, 'Thanks, Barny.'

'That's all right. Anything to oblige me beautiful sister.' He punched her playfully, then ran down the stairs whistling.

She was home. She sat down on the side of the single bed, the bed she had slept in in this room that had been hers from the time they had moved into the house when she was fifteen. They had come to it the same week that she had left school, and the grandeur of forty-nine Grosvenor Road had taken away some of the humiliating sting of not having got to the High School. She had failed her eleven-plus, and again the examination when she was twelve, and then at thirteen. Apart from her own disappointment about this, it was the blow to her mother that had affected her most. Only she and Barny had had the opportunity to try for the High School, but in Barny's case he didn't bother, for he was wise enough to know that he was destined for the pit the minute he left school. Dennis was the only one of the boys who had achieved scholastic distinction. Dennis was now a schoolteacher, but he had achieved this on his own and with the help of the Army. Her mother, Rosie had always maintained secretly to herself, had been hard on the lads, but she couldn't say she had been hard on her . . . never, for it had been the open desire of her life to see her only daughter get to the High School . . . and she hadn't. Yet this failure of her own to achieve success had not daunted her mother for long. She had not dragged her young family from a three-bedroomed bug-ridden hovel in Bog's End at the bottom of Fellburn, to a four-roomed cottage, then to a five-roomed house, from which she had jumped a great social gulf and landed them all triumphantly in Grosvenor Road, to be daunted by such a small thing as the failure of her daughter to pass an examination.

Rosie remembered the morning when Hannah had suddenly got into her hat and coat and said, 'Get your things on, I'm taking you to the Secretarial School. That's what you'll do; take a course and become a private secretary, and likely you'll end up running the firm; secretaries do.' She had smiled a conquering smile which effectively dissolved all protest. So they had gone to the Principal, and within a fortnight of leaving school Rosie found herself at school again, but with a difference. Instead now of wavering near the top of the class she was soon pushing towards the top; she knew she was . . . cut out for this. When at the end of the three-year course she came out top of her class both in typewriting and shorthand her mother had been borne skywards with pride. For days she floated, enveloped in a cloud of sagacity which had had its birth – so she told her family in her own words – the day it was revealed to her what her daughter was to be. And when the great moment of prizegiving came and Rosie was presented not only with certificates but with a medal, Hannah, sitting in the front row of the audience, made no outward or coarse show of her pleasure, but passed herself like a lady, born to see honours bestowed on her family. As she said cryptically later, 'When the thunder is rolling you don't get to your feet and shout, "What's that noise?'' ' The world knew that her daughter, besides being beautiful and with a figure that had none its equal in Fellburn, or any other town for that matter, was also a brilliant scholar.

And so said the papers the following morning. *Fallburn Weekly* had shown a photograph of Rosie being handed her medal by no less a person than the mayor. Hannah had bought half a dozen copies of the paper, and immediately despatched one to her eldest son Patrick who was in Australia. One to her next son, Colin, who was in Canada, and one to Michael, who lived in Cornwall, which could have been as far away as Australia or Canada for all she saw of him or his family. And she had thrust one at her schoolteacher son, Dennis, when he had paid her one of his infrequent visits just to let him see he wasn't the only member of her family with brains. And she had told him to show the paper to his Godless lady wife.

As the not-so-distant past came back to Rosie she twisted round and dropped her head on the pillow. It was all so ordinary, her past, at least the past that held its place in Fellburn. Nothing had really happened to her here; she had just been part of a large family, of which her mother was ruler and pivot.

Even the business of Ronnie MacFarlane seemed of little account now, although at the time she had thought it the worst thing in the world that could happen to anyone. For a man to go mad and tear the clothes off your back when you were just sitting with him holding hands on the fells on a Sunday night was shocking . . . and him a Catholic. That had made it worse. It had seemed the most horrifying thing at the time, that a

39

Catholic could be so full of lust as to lose control. How simple she had been. How naïve. And she knew now that if she had cared anything for Ronnie MacFarlane he wouldn't have had to pull the clothes off her. But you live and learn. The awful part of it was that you had to live before you could learn. And she had made Ronnie the excuse to leave home and find out about living. And she had done just that. The thought brought her teeth clamping into the pillow, and when the tears forced themselves from between her closed lids she pulled herself up straight and rubbed her hand over her face, saying to herself, 'Don't start now. Later . . . later. Take things quietly; it'll all work out. Go and get a wash and put on the suit.' Oh, the suit. Would it fit her? It would have to.

She went down the two flights of stairs again and into the bathroom. It was cluttered with cups, toothbrushes, toothpaste, hair cream, after-shave lotion and towels. It was a man's bathroom. But it was warm and it was . . . it was home. She had the silly feeling that she wanted to embrace it and ask it to forgive her, ask the whole house to forgive her. After she had washed herself her face looked whiter than ever. She had no cream, no powder or make-up, not even a lipstick, nothing. She smoothed her skin with her hand, she looked awful, then she stared at herself in the mirror as she thought there would be plenty in Karen's room. But no, she couldn't use her things without asking her.

Karen. She hadn't thought much of Karen. If she was to stay home there would always be Karen. Karen and she had never hit it off. Barny had often referred to Karen as a little bitch, and that's what she was, a little bitch.

40

It was difficult to realise that she herself was Karen's aunt because there was only two years between them.

Ever since she was a child Rosie had heard of Moira – her sister Moira. Beautiful, vivacious, fascinating Moira, who had been her mother's first child, and who, at the age of twenty-four, had died giving birth to Karen.

Even when they were children together Rosie knew that Karen resented her and the affection displayed towards her by the men of the family. So the dislike between them grew, and there was no-one Rosie knew happier than Karen when she had left home for a position – a grand position, in her mother's words – in London.

In the attic again she unlocked the case, and lifting out the wrapped bricks she went to the far corner of the room, and sliding back a piece of loose floorboard that gave access to a junction box she pushed the bricks far back between the beams. They had served their purpose; they had taken the emptiness from the case.

Now she tried on the suit. The skirt proved to be a little large but the rest fitted her as if it had been made for her.

Before going downstairs she locked the case, but stood hesitating with the key in her hand, then dropped it into a china trinket bowl. Her mother was not likely to go rummaging around until tomorrow, by which time she would have given her a reason why the case was empty.

On her way downstairs she went into the bathroom again and brushed her hair with one of the men's brushes, taking it upwards and back from her brow; then bit on her lips and pinched her cheeks. And when she entered the living-room her father and mother turned and gazed at her in open-mouthed admiration.

'Aw, that's more like my Rosie.' Hannah came towards her, pride wreathing her face. 'That's new, isn't it?' She touched the short coat. 'By, it's a smart set; I bet it knocked you back something.' She poked her head towards Broderick. 'Look at it, Brod.'

'Aye, it's real bonny. But it's the bonny lass that's in it that makes it out, isn't it? . . . I tell you what.' He sounded excited. 'We're not goin' to waste you on these four walls the night. You'll come along to the club with us. Just let me get meself changed and we'll all go and make a night of it.'

'Aye, that's the ticket,' cried Hannah. 'The very thing.'

As they looked at Rosie for approval the smile left their faces and Hannah said, 'You don't want to go, lass?'

'Not tonight, Ma; that's if you don't mind. I think I'll get to bed early. I . . . I still feel a bit shaky from the flu, and the journey was tiring.'

'Aye. Yes, of course.' Hannah nodded understandingly. Then almost dreamily she pushed her hand backwards towards her husband, saying, 'You away to the club on your own; I'm going to have a natter with me girl.'

'No, no, Ma, you go on. You always go on a Friday night.'

'Well, I'm not going the night and that's flat. Now that's settled. . . . Yet' – she held out her arms in a wide dramatic gesture – 'it's a shame to waste you, it is that, and you so bonny. Doesn't she get bonnier, Brod? Doesn't your daughter get bonnier with every year that's on her?'

'Aye indeed; but I'll like her better when she gets a bit more fat on her. I likes 'em plump.' He slapped at Hannah's buttocks.

As they laughed loudly Rosie smiled, and the front door bell rang and Hannah cried, 'That'll be Karen.' She nodded towards Rosie. 'She's doing a late turn at the exchange. I'll go and open it. She's been coming the front way 'cos it's shorter.

Rosie heard her mother's voice from the hallway extra loud and hearty, saying, 'I've a surprise for you. You'll never guess. Who do you think's come?' The next minute Karen was standing in the doorway.

'Hello, Karen.'

There was a pause.

'Hello. What's brought you?'

'What's brought her?' Hannah's voice was high. 'Doesn't matter what's brought her; here's one that's mighty glad to see her.' Her voice dropped now to a soothing tone. 'She's had the flu, she's come to convalesce.'

Karen made no rejoinder to this, sympathetic or otherwise. She moved forward but not near to Rosie. She never stood near to Rosie, to do so emphasised the difference between their heights and their figures, for Karen was five foot four and tubby. If she'd had a beautiful mother there was no sign of it on her. She looked over her shoulder towards her grandmother and said, 'I don't want any tea, I'm going to a dance.'

'You can't dance on an empty stomach,' said Hannah, still in a conciliatory tone.

'She doesn't dance on her stomach she dances on her feet, eh, don't you?' Broderick thrust out his hand

43

playfully towards his grand-daughter's cheek, but she ignored him and, turning slowly about, went out of the room.

Broderick, taking his pipe now from the mantelpiece and grinding his little finger around the empty bowl, said, 'Begod! I don't know who that one takes after; it's none of us, yet she was me own child's.'

'Oh it's green she is. Always has been, you know yourself, of Rosie here. An' the lads make more fuss of her when she's on her own. Yet she won't trouble you.' Hannah looked towards Rosie. 'She's never in the house five minutes, in and out like a gale of wind. She's going steady, I understand, though he's not much to crack on by all accounts. He's on a job on the new estate but has never reached more than fourteen a week yet. One of them that doesn't like overtime. Still, it's her choice.'

Rosie had always been puzzled at her mother's attitude towards her grand-daughter. She had never bothered about finding her a job, nor had ever timed her comings and goings as she had those of herself. With regard to intelligence, or having it up-top, as her mother would say, Rosie knew that Karen had much more 'up-top' than she had. With very little trouble she had got on to the switchboard at the telephone exchange. The criterion for such a job might not be brains, but Rosie doubted whether she herself would have been able to achieve this without her mother behind her; she wouldn't have had the nerve to canvass a councillor and to go round asking for references as Karen had done. Karen had the quality she herself lacked – initiative.

When Broderick went upstairs to change and they were alone, Hannah beckoned Rosie with a curl of her

44

finger as she whispered, 'Look, I want to show you something. Come into the front room, come on.'

Rosie followed her mother into the hall and across it, and when the lights were switched on in the front room she gazed at the new suite almost in awe before she murmured, 'My! What made you get this, Ma?'

'Well, I saw one like it in a shop in Northumberland Street in Newcastle after the war and I said to meself, "Hannah, you'll have one like that some day," an' there it is. I told 'em, the lads and him, it was just over a hundred pounds, but guess what?'

'I don't know.' Rosie was shaking her head.

'A hundred and forty-five.'

'No!'

'God's me judge.'

'Oh, Ma, a hundred and forty-five!'

'It's what you call a Parker-Knoll. Look.' She whipped off the cords that held the drop sides of the settee to the back. 'Look, they go flat. Isn't it magnificent?'

'Beautiful, beautiful.' Rosie's eyes narrowed as she looked into Hannah's beaming face, and for the first time since coming home a touch of humour came into her speech. She said seriously, 'What do the lads wear when they come in here, Ma?'

Hannah, smothering a gust of laughter, dug her in the ribs with her elbow. 'That'll be the day when I let them sit on that, or the chairs. They've been in once, but I had it covered over, every inch of it.' She ran her hand along the pale green tapestry and said almost reverently, 'There's never a day goes past that I don't come in and just stand and look at it. . . . Oh begod!' She flapped

45

her hand at Rosie. 'You should have been here the day it was delivered. Oo . . . h! The curtains. Every curtain in the street had the tremors. There they were, with their faces behind them, their eyes sticking out like pipe shanks. As for Jessie' – she thumbed in the direction of the wall – 'the green's still sticking on her yet. Oh, she's a bloody jealous old sod, that one.'

Somewhere deep within Rosie there trembled a quirk of genuine laughter – no swearing in the house she had said. Oh, her ma, her ma.

'It's always been the same since the days we were in place together. Determined to rise she was, and I said to meself, "All right, Jessie, for every step you take I'll take a jump," and begod, I have.' She nodded solemnly at Rosie. 'With the Almighty's help I have done just that. An' I'll go on doing it until the day I die. . . . But whist a minute.' She lifted her finger to Rosie's face as if admonishing her for interrupting. 'Wait till she hears me latest. I've got something up me sleeve.' She stretched the cuff of her woollen cardigan without taking her eyes from Rosie. 'An' she won't be the only one that'll be knocked off their feet with surprise this time. Aw, me lass. . . .' With mercurial swiftness her attitude changed yet again, and her big arms dropping to her sides, she stood before her daughter as if in supplication as she went on, softly now, her words hardly above a whisper, 'There's a saying, and true, that frock coats are not to be found on middens. That was true years ago but more so the day, for who gives a damn for you if you've got the wisdom of Christ and his parables but are living in Bog's End; who would listen to you from there, I ask you? No, you know yourself I've always said a man is judged by the cut of his coat an' a woman by the front of her house.'

As Hannah paused as if to allow her oratory effect, Rosie, shaking her head slightly, said, 'You're not going to move again, Ma, I thought you loved this place?'

'I am, we are, and I did.' She smiled widely now. 'But I'm going to move, girl. At least we are. And I did love this house, but everything has its allotted time and its place. . . . What have I been aiming for all me life since the first day I married? What's the place that's ever been in me mind? Think back, think back, Rosie.' She dug her finger into Rosie's arm. 'What did I tell you stories about as a child? Didn't I tell you about the fine rooms and the splendid furniture, and the luscious food that I meself cooked many a time?'

'But, Ma' – Rosie's eyes were stretching – 'you don't mean . . . ?'

'I do, I do. Number eight itself. Number eight Brampton Hill.' There was unmistakable reverence in her voice now.

'But the money! It'd be huge. You could never . . .'

'Hold your hand. Hold your hand.' Hannah held her own hand up warningly. 'They couldn't sell it outright, they wanted too much for it. Then speculators took a hand, and God so planned it that who should be one of them but Councillor Bishop.'

'You mean Mr Bishop from the church?'

'Aye, Mr Bishop from the church. That was another thing I learned many years ago. The more friends you have at court the deeper will be your carpet to walk on. Well, what are they doing but turning it into flats? When I first heard this it nearly broke me up. It was for all the

47

world as if a picture in me head had been smashed into smithereens. How, I said to meself, could I think of the old place and all its grandeur if it was in flats? And then the idea came to me, and I went along and I had a talk with Mr Bishop. . . . I was very good to his wife during the war, you know, when things weren't easy to come by, and he hadn't forgotten. "Cast thy bread upon the waters." There was never a truer sayin'. Well, as I was sayin', I went to him and got the inside information. Four flats they're turning it into, all with a separate entrance. And the two bottom ones have good bits of garden. It was the conservatory side I was interested in. There's seven rooms goes with that side. He showed me the plans. There they were set out afore me eyes. The drawing-room that was, together with the dining and breakfast-room, they're making into seven fine rooms, and the long conservatory thrown in. Oh, it's a fine sight, the conservatory. And a strip of garden, he says, a hundred feet wide and twice as long. Now what do you think?' She spread out both her hands, palm upwards, as if upon them lay the entire flat and she was offering it for her daughter's inspection and admiration.

But Rosie's face was serious. Not only serious; there was pity in it too. Pity for the restless ambition that was her mother's life force. 'But the money, they'll want the earth for it, and up on Brampton Hill! And then – Oh, Ma. . . .' She put out her hand and touched Hannah's. 'The lads, they'll never, well, you know them, they'll never fit in up there.'

The smile seeped from Hannah's face, and in its place came the defensive steely mask that Rosie knew well. Before the opposition to every move she had planned to a different house her mother had donned this mask, because before every move, someone, perhaps Dennis, or Michael, or even a neighbour, had dared to suggest, 'The lads won't fit in.'

'My sons will fit at Brampton Hill, Rosie, as they've fitted in to Grosvenor Road. There's no better dressed nor finer set up men in this town.'

They were staring at each other now, a veil of hostility between them. Rosie knew she had said the wrong thing, also that her mother spoke the truth, at least about one thing, for it would be hard to find better dressed men in Fellburn. But that fact would hardly count on Brampton Hill, for the lads had only to open their mouths and their measure was patent. They were working men; they would never be anything else but working men; and this woman, her mother, who would have died defending the fact that she loved her family, every single one of them, had made them working men and kept them working men.

It dated back more than two years ago since Rosie had discovered that her mother's thinking was slightly crooked. Her mother wanted prestige, and she went for it in the only way open to her, a bigger and better house. Truly she believed that a woman was known by her front door. That her ambition could have been achieved by the educational betterment of her sons she refused to acknowledge, and she had a reason for this particular way of thinking.

Rosie knew it was this fanatic and fantastic ambition of her mother's that had added just that weight to her decision to leave home in the first place. The term 'Keeping up with the Joneses' could hardly be applied in her mother's case, for Hannah did not desire to keep up with her neighbours but to march ahead of them, miles ahead of them. In fact, to walk in step with the Peddingtons who had lived in number eight Brampton Hill.

As her mother had said, she had been brought up on the stories of number eight Brampton Hill. They had been her fairy tales, and they had all begun with the day her mother had first set eyes on the house. It was in nineteen-fourteen, when Hannah was eleven, that she had come with her mother straight from Ireland. They had only the clothes they stood up in, but her mother had got a . . . position. She was to be kitchen-maid in the Peddingtons' establishment and to receive the vast sum of four shillings a week, living-in, of course. Her daughter, Hannah, was boarded with a distant relative in Bog's End. Her mother paid two shillings a week for her, until, in nineteen-fifteen, when labour was scarce, Hannah was taken into training . . . in the beautiful mansion. It was on her twelfth birthday, the fifth of May.

Hannah did well at the Peddingtons', until she fell for a soldier and on one half-day off became pregnant by him. She was not yet sixteen at the time. The man was a distant relation of the people she had stayed with. His name was Broderick Massey; he was a Catholic and therefore an honourable man. He married Hannah, and to the present day he considered it the best day's work he had done.

The Peddingtons, being broad-minded and aware that they had a good loyal servant in Hannah, took her on daily after her first child was born, and she stayed in their service, on and off between giving birth to babies, until nineteen-twenty-three when her fifth child was born dead. This Hannah took as a personal insult, and her spirits were very low until she became pregnant again. When her next child, too, was still-born, Hannah, who had decided years earlier that her main job in life was to bear children, realised that if she was to carry out this purpose she must go steady. So reluctantly she was available no more to the Peddingtons. Yet at times she visited . . . me lady, and her old friend Jessie Mulholland, the housemaid – who was now Jessie MacFarlane – and on each visit she sorrowed at the diminishing fortunes of the house. The scanty staff and the over-run garden touched her nearly as deeply as it did the owners.

So this was Hannah's life story, and Rosie had been brought up on it, and although it had been presented to her almost in the form of an Arabian Nights' story she had for many years assessed the tale at its true worth. Had her mother told her, two years ago, of her determination to live on any part of Brampton Hill, she would have greeted the proposal with, 'Oh Ma, you're mad; you'll be a laughing stock.' Yes, she would have dared say this, although it would have brought the house down about her ears. But now she was older, oh, more than two years older, twenty years older inside, and she had more understanding of everything and everyone. More pity for the mad things life led one to do. So she said softly, 'You would love to live there, wouldn't you, Ma?'

Hannah's face crumpled; it looked for a moment as if she was going to cry. 'Love it?' She shook her head. 'Lass, I would die of happiness.'

'It'll be very difficult all round.'

'Leave that to me.' Hannah was patting Rosie's cheek now. 'Leave everything to me.'

'What are they asking for it?'

'Hold your breath. Four thousand five hundred.'

'Oh, Ma!'

'Look . . . look at it this way. We paid seventeen for this house. 'We'll get three thousand for it like a hundred shot.'

'But houses are not selling, Ma. There's so much unemployment now; you know yourself the lads are lucky to be all in work.'

'I tell you, just leave it to me. There's a buyer for everything. But you're right. Houses are not sellin' the day; that is the two thousand pound ones are not sellin', for most of them go in for that price are finding it tight. . . . And don't tell me about the unemployed. I've had me share and I'm not goin' to cry over those whose turn it is now. Nobody cried over me when I was stretchin' a penny into a shilling. We'll sell this house, never fear, and what we get from it will be put down for the other. Then there's another thing, I'm not on me beam end either, I've got a bit put by.' She poked her finger into Rosie's arm. 'I'll show you the morrow; you and me'll have a crack. You leave all this to me. I don't suppose . . .' She paused and dropped her head slightly towards her shoulder and screwed up her eyes to pin-points before going on. 'I don't suppose you'd think of stayin' home, lass, would you, and gettin' a job here? Oh, me cup would overflow to have you home.'

Rosie was looking straight down towards her feet while moving her lips hard one over the other.

'Oh, all right, all right. It was only a suggestion like.

52

Mad I am at times with me plans. It's all right, lass. Now don't fret yourself, it's all right.'

Rosie lifted her head slowly. 'I've . . . I've been thinking about it, Ma, but – but there's Ronnie. I couldn't bear that to start up again.'

'Oh, but it wouldn't lass, it wouldn't.' Hannah's whole body expressed her excitement. 'I'm positive of that. He's married an' his wife's going to have a bairn. He hardly ever comes into Jessie's – well at least just pops in at the weekend to see her. . . . Aw, lass, would you? Would you?'

'Then there's Karen. She hates me being at home.' Rosie was looking into her mother's face now.

'Karen will have to take what she gets if she wants to stay here.' The aggressiveness slid from her voice and she murmured, 'As I said, she's goin' strong, and I'll do nothing to stop it, I'll help it on. Aw, lass, you mean it? You could get a job in Newcastle and be home at nights and I'll see your face every day.' She was upping Rosie's white face between her two brown-blotched, vein-traced hands, and as she stared at her daughter the expression on her own face was changing yet again. Her lips parted and her brows moved into enquiring points and she became still. Her expression rigidly fixed now, she gaped at Rosie, until, her eyes springing wide, there came over her face a look that could have been taken for terror, that is if the emotion of fear could have been associated with Hannah Massey. 'It's just struck me,' she said in an awesome whisper. 'You wouldn't . . . wouldn't be in any sort of trouble? Name of God! You comin' home on the hop like this, it's just come to me . . .'

'No, Ma, no. . . .'

53

'You're not goin' to have a bairn or anything?'

'I'm not going to have a bairn, Ma.' Rosie's words were cold but without any touch of indignation in them, and Hannah, breathing deeply, bowed her head for a moment before saying, 'I'm sorry, lass, I should've known not to say such a thing to you. You'd be the last creature on God's earth. . . .' She put out her hand. 'Oh, don't turn away from me, lass, I didn't mean it. But there's so many of them at it these days, the town's peppered with them. And some of them still at school. Aye, it's unbelievable but they're at it afore they leave school. Two cases in the papers last week. I said why don't they do the thing properly and have rooms set up for them in their playtime.'

'Oh, Ma!' Rosie sounded shocked; and Hannah put out her hand and pulled her around to face her, and with head lowered she said, 'I'm a rough, coarse-mouthed old woman and I beg your pardon for besmirkin' you with me thoughts.'

The humility was too much. It brought Rosie's hands to her face to press her tears back, and her voice sounded like a whimper as it came from between her fingers, saying, 'Don't, Ma. Oh, don't, Ma.'

'Aw, don't cry, lass.' She was enfolding Rosie now, pressing her between her wide breasts, stroking her hair. 'I can humble meself to you. I couldn't do it to any one of them, but I can to you, the last of God's gifts to me.'

Rosie felt her flesh shrinking away from her mother's. How would she be able to bear it? The circumstances of the last few days had made her obsessed with a longing for home and now she was here there was the

54

old fear rising in her, and the fear was of her mother. This woman who loved her; this strong irrational, masterful and childish woman.

Hannah said, 'Aw, but you're shivering, and me keepin' you in this cruel cold room jabbering.'

'Have you got a hankie, Ma?'

Hannah groped in her jumper, saying, 'No, I haven't one on me but go up to me drawer, you'll find plenty there. . . . But wait.' She put her hand out tentatively now. 'I'm not keepin' on, don't think that, me dear, but it's just come to me you hadn't your big bag with you, you hadn't any handbag. . . . Look, Rosie, there's something not quite right.' She bent her head forward. 'Tell me.'

Rosie took one long deep gulp of air. 'Can we leave it till the morning, Ma?'

'Then there is something?'

'Well . . . yes. But I'll tell you in the morning. All right?'

For a brief second Hannah's face wore a dead expression, then she smiled and said, 'All right, it'll keep; we'll have a long crack in the mornin' when we have the house to ourselves. Go up now and get what you want out of me drawers'.

Rosie went slowly up to her mother's room. Once inside, she stood with her back to the door and looked about her, but without seeing anything.

The room held an ancient brass bed with a deep box spring on it that cried out in protest at the modern biscuit-coloured bedroom suite. But the bed was one thing Hannah would never change. The reason for her clinging to the brass bed was usually gone fully into after a visit to the club, then Hannah, a few double whiskies down her, would inform her family yet again, and almost word for word, the reason why she meant to die in the brass bed. Rosie's skin had never failed to flush on these occasions, but the men grinned or laughed or, when bottled up themselves, went one better than their mother. Anyway it was all like 'God bless you' to them, for hadn't they been brought up to the sound of slaps and laughter, and groans and grunts coming from their parents' room? And hadn't some of them slept on a shake-down for years at the foot of their parents' bed? What was there to hide? Silently they agreed with their mother; if God hadn't wanted it done he wouldn't have provided the implements.

The stark vatality of her mother, almost like male virility, pervaded the atmosphere of the room, and Rosie found her flesh shrinking again, as it had at one time been wont to do from things . . . not nice. As she crossed the room to the dressing-table she glanced at the little altar perched on a wall bracket in a corner to the right of the bed. There were two half-burnt candles on it. When the thought came to her that her mother was putting in overtime on the Brampton Hill project, she chided herself for her caustic comment. Her mother meant well; she always meant well.

Out on the landing, Karen was knocking on the bathroom door, calling, 'Granda, hurry up, will you! I want to get in.' Karen glanced at her as she passed. It was a calculating glance, raking her from head to foot, but she didn't speak.

Downstairs, as Rosie entered the living-room from the hall there came into the room from the far door leading out of the kitchen a man carrying a plate in his hand. When he looked at her with his mouth half-open before exclaiming in amazement, 'Why, Rosie!' she knew that her mother hadn't loudly acclaimed her presence to Hughie, Hughie being of no account.

The man put the plate, which held a portion of fish pie and peas which didn't look hot, on to the table without taking his eyes from her, and again he said, 'Why, Rosie.' Then, 'When did you come?'

'Oh, just an hour or so ago, Hughie.'

Still looking at her, he went to the corner near the fireplace and picking up a chair he brought it to the table and sat down; then lowering his glance towards his plate he said, 'Nobody told me you were coming.'

'They didn't know, Hughie; I made up my mind all of a sudden. They all got a gliff when I walked in.'

'Oh, I bet they did.' He was smiling up into her face.

She went to sit down and face him across the corner of the table, but hesitated, while he, looking at his plate again, took a mouthful of the fish pie before saying, 'Your ma's just gone along to the MacFarlanes. I saw her as I was coming in.' Still eating, he added, 'How are you keeping?'

'Oh, all right, Hughie.' But as she answered him her mind was on her mother running to tell Jessie MacFarlane she was home. That was cruel really.

Hughie lifted his eyes to her where she sat opposite to him now. They were dark brown and round and quiet looking, and seemed at variance with his long, thin, mobile face. He looked at her for a moment before beginning to eat again, but he made no remark whatever on her appearance.

She said to him now, 'And how are you getting on, Hughie?'

'Oh . . .' He smiled, a self-derisive smile. 'Oh, you know me.'

She looked at him softly, kindly. Yes, she knew him. She had for years thought this man was her brother, for there never had been a time when she hadn't seen Hughie in the house. She was seven when her mother said to her, 'He's no brother of yours, he's a waif.' And her father had put in quickly, 'No. Now, Hannah, he's no waif. If the lad gets on your nerves so much let him clear out. He's big enough to stand on his own feet. . . . Nineteen . . . he's a man.' Nor had there been a time when she didn't realise that her mother disliked Hughie, even hated him. Nevertheless, she also knew that twice, when he was just turned fifteen and had tried to run away, she'd had him brought back. Once he had stowed away on a ship. She had never been able to understand her mother's attitude towards Hughie. That day her father had told her Hughie's story.

Hughie was twelve in nineteen-forty when his mother was killed in an air raid; his father had died a year earlier. His mother and Broderick Massey had been half-cousins. Broderick had said, 'We must have the lad.' And Hannah had said, 'Of course. What's one more or less. And the child with no-one in the world.' This wasn't strictly true because Hughie had an elder sister whom he could only remember faintly. She had gone to America as a private nurse before the war. So Hughie had been taken into the Massey household, and his shy nature had blossomed in the warm, rough atmosphere, until he was fourteen . . . well just coming up fifteen, when Broderick remembered

58

that Hannah had turned on the boy. Why, he couldn't get out of her. But from that time he could do no right. Yet when he had run away she had gone to great lengths to get him back. Aw, Broderick had said to Rosie, there was no understanding her mother's heart. It was so big a man would need a couple of lifetimes to get into its workings.

Rosie had always liked Hughie, perhaps because he was so diffefrent from the other men in the family. Yet she liked her brothers too. But Hughie was different, thoughtful. She felt he was clever in a way. Perhaps this was the reason her mother didn't like him. But no, the reason went farther back, before Hughie could have proved his cleverness in one way or another. The lads took Hughie for granted; he was part of the fittings of their home. They chaffed him about the women he had never had, and Miss Springer who lived down the road and who had had her eye on him since they first came to live here. One year he had received a Valentine, and they all declared it was from Miss Springer. But he had never passed more than the time of day with the trim but not unattractive woman who worked in the drapery department of Bailey's store. To Rosie, Hughie was . . . comfortable. He had no male virility oozing out of him, sparking off disturbances. He was a sort of cushion one could lean against, if one dared; but her mother had always checked any friendly contact between Hughie and herself. If she had come across them talking, the subject being nothing more than the weather, she would divert them into separate ways, and to Rosie herself she would speak sharply but with no real reprimand behind it but her voice, when she spoke to Hughie, thrust him

59

back into his place, and his place was a wooden chair in a recess near the door, away from the warmth of the fire. This, when Rosie thought about it, seemed significant of her mother's whole attitude towards Hughie, pushing him away, always pushing him away yet never letting him go beyond the wall, so to speak.

'It's nice to see you back, Rosie,' he was saying.

'Thanks, Hughie. It's nice to be back . . . for a time.' She dared say that to him.

He did not, as the others had done, exclaim about her white, peaked look; but after swallowing the last mouthful from his plate he straightened his shoulders against the back of the chair and repeated her words thoughfully: 'Yes, for a time.' Then glancing round the room and towards the two doors, the one leading into the kitchen, the other into the hall, he brought his head forward towards her and said under his breath, 'I might be making a move soon meself, Rosie.'

'Really Hughie?'

He nodded slowly. 'I haven't told any of them; that is except Dennis. He knows. But it's likely I'll be on me way soon.' He nodded again.

'But where to, Hughie?' She was leaning toward him now, interested, even slightly excited for him.

Again he looked from door to door, then said, 'Another time. I'll tell you all about it another time, only keep it to yourself, will you?'

She nodded back rather sadly now. Perhaps it was only wishful thinking on his part. From time to time over the years she could remember him saying, 'One day I'll make a break, I'll be away, you'll see, you'll see.' When she came to think of it now they were like the words of a prisoner threatening to make a run for it. There were lots of things about Hughie she couldn't understand. Jimmy, who was nearest to Hughie in age, being only three years younger, always said Hughie was the type of fellow you couldn't get to the bottom of, close, tight-mouthed about things. And working in a cobbler's shop by himself for years hadn't tended to open him out.

She had at one time asked her mother, 'Did Hughie want to be a cobbler, Ma?' And Hannah had replied, 'He's damn lucky to have a job at all; he's fallen on his feet. If he's got any gumption in him he'll make a business of it.'

This was at the time when her father, who had tried to scrape a living for years as a cobbler, was turning his back on it to go into a factory. But the cobbling business was still to be kept going, and by Hughie, whom Broderick had trained from a boy.

The cobbler's shop was an eight by ten foot room with a small cubby hole leading off the back. It was placed at the end of twenty similar workshops, all peopled by men striving to make a go of it on their own. When Hughie had worked with Broderick, part of his job had been to collect the boots and shoes for mending, and later to return them. Another part of his job was to solicit orders; but Hughie was no salesman, so when Broderick got the chance of a nine pounds a week job in the factory he jumped at it. And so Hughie was left . . . with the business. Rosie remembered saying to him at the time, 'Wouldn't you like to go into the factory, Hughie, and earn big money?' and he had smiled at her and said, 'I would sooner be on me own, Rosie.'

From the day Hughie had taken over the little shop her mother had forbidden her to go near it.

With the sound of the back door opening Rosie got to her feet and moved from the table, and she was sitting near the fire when her mother entered the room.

Hannah came in blowing her lips out, saying, 'Whew! It's enough to cut the nose off you out there. I've just been along to Jessie's.' She smiled towards Rosie but said no word to Hughie, and he, rising from his chair, gathered up the dirty dishes from the table and went towards the kitchen. But as he passed from the room he turned his head over his shoulder and, looking towards Hannah, said, 'Can I speak to you a moment?'

'Speak to me?' She didn't even bother to look at him. 'Well, I'm here, amn't I? Spit it out. There's nobody in the house but Broderick and Karen upstairs, and Rosie here, and she's me daughter.' She smiled at Rosie as if she had said something extremely witty, and on this Hughie turned about and went into the kitchen.

Hannah bending towards Rosie whispered low, 'There's a sod if ever there was one; deep as a drawn well, he is. Do you know what I learnt the day?' She pressed her lips together, pulling her mouth into a tight line. 'Him and our Dennis are as thick as thieves. He's been over to their place.' She nodded quickly. 'And it's not the first time he's been there. Oh, I could spit in his eye. And our Dennis. Wait till I see him. Five weeks it is since he darkened this door.'

'It's the weather likely, the roads are —'

'Don't you start makin' excuses for him. If you took a tape measure from door to door it would be three miles. But I know who I've got to blame for it. Oh, begod!

62

Yes. Oh, we're not up to the standard of his lady wife. But wait, just you wait; I'll show them or die in the attempt.'

'I think you should know something.' Hughie was speaking from the doorway. He never addressed Hannah by her name or with the prefix of aunt, which would have been natural. He had for the first three years of his sojourn in the house, and at her own request, called her Mam, but this endearing term had come to an abrupt end.

'Well, what should I know?' She was standing facing him, aggressiveness emanating from her.

Hughie, looking straight back at her, said quietly, 'Teefields are putting on a search for stolen parts.'

The shiver that passed over her body seemed to sweep the aggressiveness from it and leave her without support for a moment. Her mouth closed from its gape, then opened again, and in a much mollified tone she asked, 'Where did you hear that?'

'Dave Hewitt went out of his way to call in at the shop.'

'Hewitt? Then the polis is on to it. Name of God!' She jerked her head round and looked at Rosie, who was standing now; then turning back to Hughie, she asked, aggressiveness back in every inch of her, 'You're not just putting the wind up me, are you?'

'Why should I take the trouble to do that?'

It was not an answer Hannah expected from him. The quality of his voice, which touched on indifference, brought her eyes narrowing, and she said, 'Why should Hewitt go out of his way to help me?'

'I don't think that was his intention; but he was a

friend of mine, and still is in a way, and he knew that I wouldn't want Barny to be caught red-handed.'

Rosie was staring at Hughie; she had never heard him speak so boldly to her mother before. It was as if he didn't care a damn for her mother's reactions any more, as if he was freed from something. That his attitude was also puzzling her mother was very evident. She hoped it wouldn't arouse her anger against him still further.

But Hannah had something more serious on her mind at the moment than to dwell on Hughie's attitude. She said rapidly, her words running together, 'How've they got on to Barny? He's not the only one; every man jack of them's at it.'

'They're on to a number. As far as I understand they're going to make a house search.'

'They could come here, you think?'

Hughie didn't answer, he just stared at her. And she put her hand over her mouth as she exclaimed, 'God in Heaven!' Then she asked, 'When?'

'I don't know for sure. It could be tonight or tomorrow morning, I don't know.'

'Jesus, Mary and Joseph!' Again her body shivered; but now with strength and purpose, and flashing her eyes to Rosie, she said, 'Go and get your da down.' It was as if her daughter had never left the cover of her domination. Then turning to Hughie she ordered, 'Get down to the club and get Barny back here as fast as his legs'll carry him.'

As Rosie went from the room she saw Hughie still standing in the doorway. He hadn't moved, and her mother was staring at him. Then Hannah's voice came to her, still loud but in the form of a request, saying, 'Well, will you go for me?'

Rosie heard the back door bang before she reached the bathroom, and there she called, 'Come quickly, Da, me ma wants you.'

'She can just wait.'

'No, Da, there's trouble; come quickly.'

As she ran downstairs again Broderick was on her heels, drying himself and exclaiming loudly. And when he entered the kitchen he demanded to know what was afoot, but Hannah silenced him with 'Less talk and more action, that's what we want in the next hour or so. The polis is on to Barny and the wireless bits.'

'Good God! . . . Who told you this?'

'Hughie; he got it from Dave Hewitt.'

Broderick looked frantically around the kitchen, as if searching for hiding places; then turning to Hannah, he cried, 'But there's no place where we can stick that stuff, woman. We can't bury it in the garden, the ground's like flint underneath the slush.'

'I wasn't thinking of the garden. Only a numbskull would think of the garden. We'll have it upstairs in the box mattress.'

'The box mattress! Oh, aye, begod. Aye, yes.' Broderick nodded his head. 'That's the place for it. But will it stand it? Those bits are a sight heavier than tea and sugar and clothes and the like.'

'We'll have to take that chance. But don't stand here wasting breath, let's get down to the shed and get as much loose stuff up as we can. An' we've got to do it with as little nuration as possible or else Nebby Watson'll have her nose hanging over the wall sniffing

65

like a mangy retriever. And Alice Parkman is not above lifting the blind on the other side. So I'm telling you.'

The shed at the bottom of the garden was fitted up as a workshop. When her mother switched the light on Rosie stood gazing above her at the pieces of electrical equipment and half-finished wireless and televison sets that took up every inch of the bench that ran the length of the shed, and overflowed on to the shelves beneath and those above it. Barny had started at Teefields factory before she had left home, and she hadn't been able to close her eyes to the fact that the stock in the shed had rapidly mounted, or that Barny made quite a bit on the side making wireless sets. But if it had troubled her, she had thought along the lines of her Catholic training – well, what Barny did was between him and God. It was a nice easy way to prevent herself from thinking of Barny as a hypocrite, one who wouldn't miss Mass on a Sunday, nor his duties once a month.

'Here now!' Her mother thrust a box of valves into her arms, hissing, 'Get up with them. Be careful how you go, and don't spill them. Leave them on the bedroom floor; we'll attend to the bed when we come up.'

They had made some inroad in the transportation when Barny came pelting into the house. He looked not only worried, he looked frightened, very frightened. 'This is a to-do, isn't it?' His voice was hoarse. 'I'm for it if they find this lot.'

Hannah had met him in the hall, her arms full. 'Less crack,' she said, 'and get going. Take that big set down there to pieces, and do it quicker than you've ever worked in your life afore. Go on now.'

As he went to run from the hall she shouted, 'Where's Hughie?'

'He's gone back to the shop.'

'He would, the sod, knowing how we're fixed for an extra pair of hands. Oh, I'll see me day with that one. Yes, by God, I will.'

She was mounting the stairs when Barny, dashing back into the hall, cried at her under his breath, 'Don't be so bloody vindictive, Ma; you're always at him. But the night you should go down on your knees and thank God for him givin' us the tip, for if he wasn't a pal of Dave Hewitt's we'd have known nowt until they were on top of us.'

'An' they likely could be that at any minute, and you standin' there defending him. Get going, you young fool!'

In an hour the shed was clear except for a few tools and some garden implements, but Hannah's bedroom looked, as she put it herself, like Paddy's market. The mattress from the bed was standing up against the wall with the top of the box spring leaning against it. The box resting on its iron support should have been full of springs, but these had been disposed of many years ago; in nineteen-forty to be exact when Hannah went into the black market. Now the bottom of the box was covered with wireless parts, on top of which were spread blankets, and into the hollows and dales of the blankets went further pieces, until the floor was clean of every last piece that had been brought up from the shed. Then the lid was screwed on again. The lid had attached to it an overlapping padded cover, and it would have taken a very clever detective to realise it was detachable from the box itself. On top of this the two men lifted the mattress, and then, Hannah, at one side, and Rosie, at the other, made the bed up.

'There, let them find that if they can. . . . Now away downstairs, the both of you.' She looked towards her husband and son. 'And get yourselves to the club, for if they should come on the hop, it's better they find you spending the evening normally.' She nodded at Broderick.

'Spendin' the evening normally!' Barny said. 'I've got the jitters. But if I'd had any bloody sense I'd have known somethin' was going to happen, for every man jack in our shop's been at it lately; all except creeping Jesus.'

'You mean Harry Boxley?'

Barny nodded at his father.

'It wouldn't be him who's given the show away?' said Broderick.

'No, no; Harry wouldn't do that. Come and give you a sermon on the quiet about the evil of covetin' thy neighbour's goods. . . . Neighbour's goods, be-buggered! An' that firm makin' millions a year profit. Keeping old Lord Cote sitting pretty in his marble-floored mansion on the Riviera. Even the bloody manager's got a yacht. . . . Thy neighbour's goods!'

They were in the living room again when Hannah said, 'Where's Karen in all this? She must have known we could do with help. . . . Where is she?'

'Aw, she went out a few minutes ago; I saw her on her way downstairs,' said Broderick.

'And never a word.' Hannah bristled. 'She'll have the back of me hand across her lug one of these days, will that madam. Well now, get yourselves off' – she waved at the men – 'an' I'll deal with anybody should they come. But I pray to God –' her voice dropped now, 'aye, I do sincerely pray to God we'll have no-one comin' to search the house, because it'll be down the length of the street afore they are over the step. . . . Go on, get yourselves off.'

When the men had gone, Hannah turned to where Rosie was sitting staring into the fire, and going slowly towards her, she said apologetically, 'Aw, lass, I wouldn't have had your first night home spoiled for the world, but it was an emergency; it had to be done; you could see for yourself.'

'It's all right, Ma.' Rosie's voice was reassuring. 'It's all right, don't worry. I only hope Barny doesn't get the sack.'

'The sack! Why should he get the sack?' Hannah was bristling again. 'He'll get no sack. They'll find nothing here, not so much as a nut.'

Rosie, looking back at her mother, did not answer. She had worked for eighteen months in the London office of a Midland firm. From that distance men were just numbers. When an order came to cut down, numbers one, two and three were the same as four, five and six to an executive who had never seen the man behind the number. She remembered, too, that their firm – she still thought of it as their firm – stood to lose twenty thousand pounds a year through pilfering. They made allowance for that sum, yet every now and again they would clamp down on the general practice, as Teefields were doing, and there would be dismissals, sometimes followed by lightning strikes. . . . 'Thou shalt not covet thy neighbour's goods.'

69

Hannah, now pulling a big leather chair towards Rosie's, seated herself in it before leaning forward and saying, 'There now, we're settled. Let's forget all that's happened. Isn't this nice, just you and me and the house to ourselves?' She kicked off her slippers and held out the soles of her feet towards the blazing fire. 'You know, when I got up this mornin' I had the feeling it was going to be a good day. I always go by me feelin's first thing in the mornin' an' I said to meself, "Hannah, you're going' to get a surprise the day," and what better surprise in the world than seeing you, lass.' She stretched out her hand and squeezed Rosie's knee; then leaning back, she said in a casual tone, 'We mightn't get another opportunity like this to have a crack, the morrow mornin' Betty'll be in with the bairns; she always drops in on a Saturda' mornin' as you know. So when we've got the chance, let's have our chin-wag now, eh?' She hunched her thick shoulders up around her neck in a questioning attitude.

Rosie turned from her mother's waiting glance and looked towards the fire. A heat came surging up through her body and showed in moisture on her upper lip. She dabbed it with her mother's handkerchief and said, 'Aw, well.' Then went on, 'There's no much to tell, not really. Well, you see, I had words with a girl in the office. It . . . it was about promotion, but she had been there longer than me. And anyway things got unpleasant and I gave me notice in.'

'When? When was this? You never said a word in your letters.'

'Oh . . . oh about three months ago. I – I didn't ask for a reference; because I had had words I didn't like to

70

go back, sort of climb down, you know. And it's difficult to get set on anywhere, at least in a good job, if you haven't a reference.'

'Was that why you haven't written for weeks? I was worried sick at times. An' gettin' your da to write is as hard as gettin' him up in the mornin's. . . . Was that why you moved to the new address?'

'Yes . . . yes, Ma.' Rosie was looking into the fire as she spoke. 'I couldn't keep up the rent of the flat and so I went into rooms . . . with a girl I knew. We . . . we shared everything; she was to pay the landlady. Then about three weeks ago she went off without a word and I found she owed a lot of back rent and the landlady said I was responsible for it. Well . . . well I had the flu as I told you and I ran out of money altogether, all I had saved, and the landlady said she was entitled to keep my things until I could pay. And so' – Rosie turned towards her mother but didn't look at her – 'there . . . there was nothing for it but to come home.'

'Aw, lass.' Hannah was gripping her hands now. 'The heartless bitch of a woman, she should be spiflicated. All your beautiful clothes and your cases. Your fine dressing-case an' all, with all the bottles and things in, she's kept the lot?' Her voice seemed to be pushing up her arched eyebrows and raising her thick grey hair from her scalp.

'Yes. Yes, Ma.'

'Well, the morrow mornin' you'll send what you owe her and she'll send those things on or else me name's not Hannah Massey.'

'No, no, Ma; I don't think I'll do that. I'd rather buy new clothes and cases than write to her. I . . . I don't

71

want anything more to do with her, or London. I just want to forget everything. I . . . I'll get a job and soon stock up again.'

'Well, I for one wouldn't let her get off with —'

'Oh, Ma, just leave it. . . . Please. I'm tired of it all, London and everything.'

'Aw, all right, all right, lass, have it your own way. As long as you're home that's all that matters to me. But I'll say I wish her luck with your things; I hope she falls down an' breaks her blasted neck, I do so. What will she do with them, do you think?' She peered at Rosie through narrowed lids.

'Oh . . . oh, I think. . . . Well, she's my build, perhaps she'll wear them. It . . . it doesn't matter.'

'No, no, it doesn't matter.' Hannah was shaking Rosie's hands firmly between her own, each movement being accompanied by a word. 'But listen to me. Don't let on about a thing you've told me to any of them. Do you hear me? An' tomorrow we'll work somethin' out. You said your stuff was coming on. Well, it'll have to come on. We'll go into Newcastle and get you rigged out, two or three rig-outs for that matter.' She winked. 'An' some cases, one exactly like the other I bought you. And when we get off the train we'll put them in a station taxi and say we've collected them on our way. How's that for strategy?'

Rosie smiled faintly. 'It's marvellous, Ma.'

'Oh, I'm a good liar.'

As Hannah shook her head proudly at herself, Rosie thought sadly, But not such a good one as your daughter.

Saturday

Rosie was sound asleep when her mother brought her breakfast up to her room. 'That's the ticket,' Hannah said. 'The rest will do you the world of good.'

'Oh, what time is it, Ma?' asked Rosie.

'Well, turned nine. You've slept the clock round, me girl.'

Rosie hadn't slept the clock round. It had been five in the morning when she had finally fallen into troubled sleep.

Hannah sat with her, demanding that she ate every scrap of food on the tray, and before she rose to take the tray away she nudged her, saying, conspiratorially, 'Don't forget we're goin' out this afternoon, hail, snow or blow.'

'I'll pay you back, Ma.'

'Who's talkin' of payin' back? Aw, lass, I get paid back with interest every time I look at you.' She lifted the rumpled mass of gleaming hair between her fingers and felt it. 'Like spun bronze, it is,' she said. 'I've never seen the like.'

The shiver went through Rosie's body again. Such admiration was fear-filling, terrifying.

'Look,' said Hannah now, excitedly. 'Get into your things an' come down to me room when we've got the house empty, for it won't be that for long, an' I'll show you somethin'.' She paused; then bending over the tray and bringing her face down to Rosie, she said, 'Your mother's no fool.'

As Rosie looked up silently into her face, Hannah winked broadly. Then walking sideways towards the door, the tray balanced on one hand, she said, 'Come on down with you now, and look slick. Get into anythin'.' She paused, then added, 'Put on your new suit; the other things are not you, not you at all, at all.'

Slowly Rosie got from the bed and put on the new suit. All her movements were slow and laboured. She felt very tired, not only from the lack of sleep but from the reaction of the whole of yesterday. She went down the stairs, and as she was going into the bathroom her mother opened the bedroom door and called, 'Let that wait a minute, come on in here.' And when she entered the room Hannah locked the door behind her, and pointing to the bed, said, 'Sit yourself down there.' Then she went to a short chest of three drawers that stood in a recess.

The chest did not match the modern suite. The edges of the drawers were all scarred, and the bottom and deepest drawer and the bulbous legs showed the imprint of hard toecaps. It was not a chest at all but an original Charles the Second walnut desk with flat top which Hannah had picked up forty years ago for two pounds ten. The sum then was a small fortune and she thought she had been done; she was unaware of its present-day value, but the chest held something even more valuable than itself. After pushing her hand down inside her jumper she brought out a small key and, unlocking the bottom drawer, she lifted it right out of its socket and

74

carried it to the bed. Dropping it down next to Rosie she sat at the other side of it and pointed at its contents.

Rosie's wide lids hid her expression as she looked along the lines of neatly rolled bundles of notes. Line after line of them, some two deep, covering the bottom of the drawer. Then her lips falling apart, she lifted her eyes to her mother, and Hannah, whose every feature was expressing triumph, said softly, 'Can you believe your eyes?'

'But, Ma, where. . . . Whose is it?'

'Whose is it!' Hannah pulled her chin inwards, making a treble row of flesh down her neck. 'Whose is it, do you ask? Why, it's mine of course. An' don't look like that, lass; I haven't stolen it. Oh, begod!' She put her hand up to her cheek. 'Did you think . . . did you think I'd pinched the stuff? Now, where would I be findin' a place to pinch pound notes except in a bank? An' I wouldn't be up to that.' She laughed. 'An' I can assure you, not one of me children have soiled their hands at thievin' either.'

There flashed across Rosie's mind the picture of them emptying the shed last night and what lay beneath where they sat at this moment, but she let the picture slide away.

'How much do you think is there?' Hannah dug her index finger downwards.

'I haven't any idea.'

'Go on, give a guess.'

Rosie didn't answer, 'I really don't know — tell me,' because she knew her mother wouldn't know either, at least not exactly, for this woman could count up to ten and then add three to it because she'd had thirteen children. At a stretch she could put ten and ten together and make it twenty, because there were twenty shillings in a pound note, but that was as far, Rosie knew, as her mother could go, because her mother could neither read nor write. But this lack was never referred to in the house. It was like a disfigurement that was ignored, but more out of fear than pity, for her mother would have slain anyone who made reference to her deficiency. Hannah could discuss the news of the day as if she had read the paper from end to end, when all she had done was listen to the wireless. The wireless was not only her tutor, it was her face-saver.

Rosie picked up a roll of notes and, taking off the wire band, she counted twenty pounds.

'Are they all the same?' she asked quietly.

'They are all the same,' answered Hannah just as quietly.

Rapidly Rosie began to count. She liftged one layer after another, and after some time she looked up at her mother and said in a whisper, 'Roughly about two thousand eight hundred, I should say.'

'Two thousand eight hundred!' Hannah repeated. 'Well now, what do you think of that?'

'But, Ma, how have you done it?'

'Management, lass, management. I'm no fool you know, as I said.'

Rosie looked in amazement at the big smiling woman sitting at the other side of the drawer as she went on, 'Well now, for the last five years they've hardly lost a day, except Shane in the winter on the buildings, and big money they've been makin'. Jimmy could take forty pounds a week at times in the bad weather, making the bridge. Hell the work was, up to his eyes in water, but the money made up for it. And Arthur still makes a steady twenty-five when he's leading from the quarries. Shane's never made much, never more than eighteen, but Barny could make his twenty with overtime. Your da . . . well, it's been twenty sometimes, but mostly sixteen. Then there's Karen and the other one, but Karen's two pounds a week hardly keeps her in the fancy puddings she likes. As for the other —' she didn't say Hughie, 'four pounds is all I've ever got off him, never more.'

At the bitter note in her mother's voice, Rosie felt compelled to say, 'Well, I don't suppose he makes much more than that some weeks. There's nothing much in the cobbling, is there?'

'There's plenty in the cobbling if he would go out an' look for it — people still have their boots mended — but no, sittin' in the back shop readin', that's how he spends his time. His room upstairs is full of nothing else but books. . . . That's where his money goes, second-hand book shops. An' what good have they done him I ask you, for he's nothing but a scug? Aw' — she shook her head violently — 'don't let's talk about him. . . . Now, as I was sayin', about the money here.' She drew her fingers gently over the rolls. 'You wanted to know how I've managed it. Well, when they all got steadily going I said to them, we'll divide it into three, I said, each of your pay packets into three. One part will be for your own pocket, another part will be for your board and your workin' clothes, and boots et cetera, and with the other part I'll buy your best suits and things and put a bit by for a rainy day. An' all said OK, Ma, it was all right by them. All except Arthur. He wasn't so keen, for even then he had his eye on that piece. But I put me foot down. You'll be like the others or not at all, I said. An' there's Jimmy. There's hardly a week goes by even now when he hasn't ten pounds on a Friday night in his pocket, but never a penny he has by the Monday mornin'. If he had twenty it would be the same with him, the big softy. I said to him he should look out for a rainy day. And you know what he said?' She leant across the drawer towards Rosie. 'I'll leave you to cope with the weather, Ma. That's what he said.'

'Do they know about this?' Rosie pointed to the money.

'Begod! No. Not even Broderick knows the amount I've got; nor is he going to. That's me drawer, Broderick, I've said, an' it's the only personal thing I have in this house. I look to you to honour it. An' don't go searchin' for the key. An' I know he never has, an' it's been locked all this many a year. When it only held a few shillings it was locked.'

'But, Ma.' Rosie shook her head slowly. 'What if someone was to break in, if someone got to know?'

'Who's to know? How could anyone outside know when those inside don't? Oh, they chip me about me stockin' leg, an' they know I've got a few pounds put by because they know who to come to when they're up against it; an' they've only got to say they want a suit and it's on their back. But I don't forget to tell them how much I spend on them; I rub it in' – she bounced her head – 'so's they won't think I'm makin' a pile out of them.'

Rosie lowered her head. You had to laugh at her ma,

78

you had to laugh or go for her and say, 'Well, that's what you're doing, isn't it, Ma, making a pile out of them?' But no-one could say that to her ma; her ma was a law unto herself, her ma had her own type of reasoning.

'Begod, listen!' Hannah had jumped up from the bed, her hand held aloft. 'Here they are already, Betty and the bairns.'

As the shouts of 'Gran! Gran!' came from down below, Hannah whipped up the drawer and, shuffling with it to the chest, put it back into place again and locked it. Then pulling the front of her jumper wide, she inserted her hand in, saying the while to Rosie, 'I have a bag pinned on me vest.' She patted her breast. 'There's no-one going to go rummagin' in there.' She laughed as she pushed Rosie in front of her on to the landing.

The three children were grouped around the foot of the stairs looking upwards with eager faces, and Hannah cried at them, 'Hello! Catherine, me bairn. And you, Theresa. Aw, an' there's me big man.' She came down the last stairs with hands extended as if in benediction and laid them on the four-year-old curly-headed boy, saying, 'An' you've still got them?' She lifted one of the curls with her finger. 'I thought you said you were goin' to have them off?'

There came a chorus of, 'He was, Gran. He is, Gran.' And from the little boy himself. ''Safternoon, Gran; I am. 'Safternoon.'

'Aw, a shame on to God it is to cut those beautiful ringlets.' Then looking from one to the other of the children she said, 'Don't you see who's here? It's your Aunt Rosie. Say hello to your Aunt Rosie.'

The children looked to where Rosie was standing on

79

the stair above her mother and chorused, obediently, 'Hello, Auntie Rosie.'

They had heard a lot about their Auntie Rosie whom they very rarely saw, their clever, beautiful Auntie Rosie who was in London, living among the swells. They were shy of her. She silenced their tongues and they turned as one and, scuffling, went back into the kitchen and to their mother, who was emptying a basket on to the table.

'Hello, there, Betty.' Hannah greeted her daughter-in-law, and the plump, matronly girl turned her head over her shoulder saying, 'Hello, Ma.' Then catching sight of Rosie, she turned fully round, crying, 'Rosie, you're home? When did you come?' She was smiling, broadly, kindly.

'Last night, Betty.'

Before Rosie could go on Hannah put in loudly, 'It's the flu she's had; she's as white as lint. Did you ever see her lookin' like this? Oh, I'm goin' to try and persuade her to get a job nearer home so I can look after her and fatten her up. She hasn't a pick on her.'

The two girls smiled at each other.

Rosie liked John's wife; she always had. Betty was an uncomplicated girl. From the first she had fallen like a cat on its feet into the ways of the family; and this was demonstrated in the next moment when she pointed to a large parcel she had taken from her extra large shopping bag. 'You'll be able to use that,' she said.

'What is it?' Hannah quickly undid the brown paper, then some greaseproof paper, and exposed to her glistening eyes a quarter of an eighty pound Australian cheddar cheese, and she breathed deeply as she said, 'Yes, indeed, indeed.'

'We've got a big lump an' all, Gran.' It was six-year-old Theresa speaking, as she gazed up at Hannah.

'Have you, me child?'

'Yes. Me da found it in the grab.'

'He did, did he?' Hannah was bending over the child now, looking down into her face.

'Yes. When me da pulled up the dredger there was the cheese in a wooden box, and they opened it and they shared it out; me da had half and Mr Rowland had half.'

'He did, did he? Well, that was kind of your da to share it out,' said Hannah. The child nodded and smiled before adding, 'He found some butter in the dredger last week.'

Hannah raised her eyes to Betty, but Betty was busy repacking her bag. Her face wore a deadpan expression and she said without looking up, 'They've been warned not to tell anybody outside what their da finds in the dredger. They know they would get him wrong if they did. But as their da told them, if he didn't bring it home it would only be thrown into another part of the river again where they are blocking it up.'

'That's right, that's right.' Hannah nodded now from one child to the other. Then looking at Rosie, she asked, 'Isn't it, Rosie? Isn't that right?' And Rosie nodded, and after a moment said softly, 'Yes, yes, that's right.'

'Take them into the kitchen, Catherine,' said Hannah now, 'and have two bullets each out of the tin. No more, mind, just two apiece.' She thrust her finger at each of them, and they ran from her, laughing, into the kitchen. And now she turned to her daughter-in-law and pushed her with the flat of the hand. 'Cheese out of the dredger! That's a good-un. And they could come out of the river

81

bottom at that; who's to say they couldn't? With all the boats that's sunk outside the piers, the stuff's bound to float back.' She pushed her again, and Betty, chuckling deeply, said, 'Well, you have to tell them something; it's impossible to keep the stuff out of their sight.' She buttoned her coat now. 'I'll have to be goin'. And John'll not be in the day, he says, but he'll look in the morrow mornin' after Mass.'

'Won't you stay for a cup of tea and have a crack with Rosie here?'

'I can't, Ma. . . . You see' – she glanced towards the kitchen door, then muttered under her breath, 'I've got to be at Bill's stall in the market by half past ten; he's to let me know then about a bit of bacon, an' if it's all right John'll pick it up this afternoon in the car.'

'Aw, I see, lass, I understand, I understand.' Hannah flapped her hand. 'And how's the car goin'? The lads have got it into their heads that they're goin' to club together and get one, but I have different ideas; I'll tell you about it later. If you'd had a minute we could have gone into it; perhaps the morrow. But how's the car goin'?'

'Oh, he's always taking it to bits, it's always wanting somethin' spending on it; but as he says what can you expect for forty pounds. He's got his eye on another one. A hundred and twenty they want, but it's in good condition.'

'You'll get it, you'll get it, me girl.' Hannah patted Betty's back affectionately; then turning her head over her shoulder, called, 'Come away, you lot, out of that, your mother's goin'.'

As the children came running into the room again

Betty, looking at Rosie, said, 'We'll be seeing more of you then, Rosie?'

'Yes, I suppose so, Betty.'

'That'll be nice. John'll be pleased to know you're back. Come round and see us, eh? What about the morrow?'

'I'll pop in sometime. I've still a bit of a cold on me, I don't want to go out much yet.'

'No, and you're wise. Did you ever know weather like this? I'm sick of the sight of snow. Come on.' She gathered the children round her, then pushed them out into the hall amid cries of, 'Goodbye, Gran.' 'Bye, Auntie Rosie.' 'Bye, Gran.'

As Betty passed her to go down the steps, Hannah pushed a ten-shilling note into her hand, saying, 'Get your hair done this afternoon, an' all.'

'No, Ma. No, Ma.' Betty made great play of pushing the note back into Hannah's hand, but was eventually persuaded to take it. Then she smiled her thanks. 'There was no need for that,' she said.

Hannah came bustling back into the living-room now, talking all the time. She was in fine fettle. She bustled the cheese off the table and into the kitchen, shouting her conversation back to Rosie, where she stood looking down into the fire.

The whole world was a fiddle . . . life was a fiddle. There was nothing honest or decent or good in it. Life was putrid. Rosie found her teeth clamping down tightly into her lower lip, and even when it became painful she went on biting. There was badness of the body and badness of the mind, and she didn't know which was worse. . . . Oh, yes, she did. Oh, yes, she did. She was shaking her head slowly at herself when the front-door bell rang, and as she turned she saw her mother come to the kitchen door holding the palm of her hand to her brow, the fingers extended wide.

'There's nobody comes to the front door on a Saturday mornin', not at this time.' Hannah hurriedly crossed the room, slanting her eyes towards Rosie. 'Now if it's them, act natural like.' She glanced swiftly about her; then putting her shoulders back, she made her way to the hall, but stopped again at the sitting-room door and, turning swiftly to Rosie, said with a nervous smile, 'Better still, go up to your room. The look on your face would give God himself away.'

When the bell rang again, Hannah went forward, crying, 'All right, all right, I'm on me way.'

Since the stampede last night in getting the shed cleared there had been no more mention of the matter. When the men had come in around eleven, merry and full of talk, her mother hadn't checked them with, 'Whist now! We've got something on our plates.' She had made no mention of the transfer of the stuff nor the fact that the house might be searched, and she had warned Barny to keep his mouth shut. Rosie knew that her mother was living up to the slogan: Sufficient unto the day is the evil thereof. She had always applied this to the ways of the house, and they had been happier for it; but now, apparently, the evil had come upon them.

She was making her way towards the door when her mother's voice from the hall checked her, crying, 'Oh, begod! It's you, Father, and on a Saturda' mornin'. Come in, come in; you look froze to the bone. . . . And what have you there?'

Rosie moved back swiftly towards the fire and stood with her hand pressed across the lower part of her face. Had she been given the choice she would have preferred the men to come and search the house rather than to be brought face to face with Father Lafflin. He was kind and jolly was Father Lafflin, but he had eyes that could see through you.

The priest preceded Hannah into the room, saying, 'It's my wireless I've brought along. I want Barny to have a look at it.' At this point he stopped, and looking towards Rosie, he exclaimed, 'Why! Rosie! And they never told me you were back.' He turned his face towards Hannah. 'You never told me the child was back, Hannah.'

'You've never given me a chance, Father.' Hannah's voice was sharp and her eyes were riveted on the wireless set the priest was holding before him. She was looking at it as if at any minute it might explode, and it might too. The wireless could bring disaster on her house. She grabbed it from his arms, saying, 'What had you to bring it round for, Father?'

'What? What were you saying? Oh.' He dusted the front of his coat down. 'Well, Barny made it and I've asked him two or three times to pop in and have a look at it, but he never has a minute, and I thought to meself, well, I'll take it round, and why shouldn't I? The boy makes me a wireless and I expect him to service it, and to come out of his way to do it. And so I brought it round knowing he'd see to it. But let us forget about the wireless. How are you getting on Rosie?'

'Oh, all right, Father.'

'You don't look all right, child.' He moved slowly

85

towards her. 'You look . . . well –' he paused, 'sort of drained. That's London for you, I suppose. That air's no good for man or beast up there.'

'I've had the flu, Father.'

'Aw . . . aw, that's it, is it? Now that's the thing for pulling you down. I think all the fat women in the land should be injected with flu, it would save all their dieting.' He threw his head back and let out a high laugh. But it didn't reach its full height before it was checked by Hannah saying flatly, 'Father, I'm sorry to ask you so pointedly, but this is no time for gildin' the lily so to speak, but would you mind takin' your wireless back, an' I'll have Barny come down and see to it this very afternoon.'

The priest turned slowly and looked at Hannah. He looked at her for a moment before saying, 'Don't be obtuse, Hannah, what is it? Have I done wrong in bringing the wireless? Is he up to his eyes in work? . . . But I'm in no real hurry for it, although it's handy.'

Hannah bowed her head and put her hands on the side of the table for support; her silence brought the priest's eyes narrowing towards her. He looked hard at her, then at the wireless; then flicked his glance to Rosie before turning to Hannah again and saying flatly, 'What's wrong with the wireless, Hannah?'

Hannah lifted her head and looked at the priest. She had to take a chance. There mightn't be anything wrong with the wireless, there mightn't be a part of it that could be recognised as the firm's, but she couldn't tell if this was so or not, only Barny could do that . . . or them, if they came and searched the house. If she kept her mouth shut the priest would walk out of the door and leave it, and where could she hide a big thing like that? She could burn the case. Aye, she could do that. But what could she do with the innards? Even if she could take it to bits, and she couldn't, there mightn't be time to get it into the box mattress. She couldn't risk it. She looked straight into the priest's eyes and said, 'Barny gets pieces on the cheap now and again; that's how he makes them up.' She stumbled awhile. 'But . . . but the factory's got a bee in its bonnet. It's after some of them that have been helpin' themsleves too freely, not being able to restrain themselves to a bit here and there, and so, from what I understand, they're goin' to do the rounds like. . . .'

The priest looked from Hannah to the wireless. He looked at it for a long while before saying, 'All that stuff in Barny's workshop? He told me he bought it from bankrupt stock. In the name of God, Hannah' – he turned on her, his voice angry now – 'you shouldn't have done this to me. You've got me involved in more ways than one, but enough at the moment is that I'm a receiver of stolen goods! Innocent or not, I'm a receiver of stolen goods. You shouldn't have involved me, Hannah.'

Hannah's head was up, her lower lip thrust out. For the moment she forgot she was addressing the priest. She forgot . . . the cloth. Before her she saw only an ungrateful old man, and she cried at him, 'You were involved enough during the war, Father, God's truth you were. Did I ever see you short of socks or shirts? Or sugar or tea? An' throw your mind back, throw it back to the side of bacon, Father, a whole side, just to mention a few things. Involved, you say? What's black now was black then.'

'The circumstances were different, Hannah, we were in a war. They were different.'

'No, begod, Father, not as I see it.'

'I'm not going to argue with you, Hannah. This present situation goes deeper than you have the insight to realise. I know now where some of the firm's stolen goods are. Don't you see, woman? You shouldn't have done this to me.'

As he walked towards the door, not even saying goodbye to Rosie, Hannah's voice checked him with, 'What about this, Father?' She pointed to the wireless.

'What about it?' He was looking at her over his shoulder.

'You're taking it with you?'

'I don't want it any longer.'

'Look, Father.' Hannah hurried towards him, her hands extended outwards. 'In the name of God, get it out of here. Take it away with you. If Barny was here I wouldn't ask you, but as it is, the very sight of it might put the kibosh on him if they were to come around.'

The old priest drew in a breath that pushed his black coat sharply outwards. Then turning back into the room he grabbed up the wireless and made for the hall, Hannah after him. As she opened the door for him he said, 'Get yourself to confession tonight, Hannah, and make a clean sweep, be finished with it for good and all.'

'I will, Father, I will that.' Hannah's voice now held a soft, conciliatory note, and she ended as if he was leaving after one of his usual friendly and laughter-filled visits. 'Goodbye, Father. Mind how you go. Goodbye.'

In the living-room once more she went straight for a

chair and sat down, and, lifting up her apron, she wiped the sweat from around her face.

As Rosie moved from the fireplace towards the hall door, Hannah asked, 'Where are you going?'

'Just upstairs.'

Hannah made no reply to this, nor did she try to stop her by going into a tirade about the priest.

As Rosie went up the last flight of stairs to her room she was shaking her head. She wouldn't be able to stand this for long. It was the same thing over and over again. But her mother was right about one thing, what was black now was black in the war. Somehow it seemed to her that the priest had lost points in the game of morality.

Hannah was her usual self when the men came in at dinner time. To Barny's query 'Everything all right, Ma?' she answered, 'Right as rain.' She did not tell him about the priest's visit; she would wait until she got him on the quiet. Then she would warn him what to expect from Father Lafflin.

After the meal she said to Broderick, 'Will you see to the dishes for me? Rosie here and me are going out on a jaunt, just to have a look round the shops; I've never been in Newcastle for weeks. I want vests for Jimmy and some shirts for Shane. That fellow must rasp his collars with a razor blade, he goes through them so quickly.'

'Get yersels away.' Broderick smiled at his daughter. 'But I'd have thought you'd have been better in than out the day, the weather the way it is.'

'Aw, she wants to pick her things up from the station,' said Hannah. 'An' we'll come back by taxi. We'll do the thing in style, won't we, Rosie girl?' Hannah put out her hand to Rosie's shoulder and, pushing it gently, said, 'Go on up now and get ready; I'll be with you in two shakes.'

As Rosie passed her father, Broderick pulled her to a halt, saying, 'You're quiet this time, lass. There's hardly a peep out of you.'

She smiled at him, and in an attempt at jocularity she said, 'I talk when I can, Da, but it's difficult to get a word in.'

There was loud laughter at this, and Shane said from across the table, 'There's a dance at the club the night. Why don't you come along and have a fling; they do some old time ones an' all? There's high jinks on a Saturday night, and variety they have . . . the lot, just like on Fridays.'

'I'll see, Shane. Thanks.' She nodded at him.

On the first landing she met Karen dressed ready for out doors, and as she went to pass her Karen stopped dead in front of her, and looking up into her face, said pointedly, 'What brought you back anyway?'

'I . . . I told you I had the flu.'

'The flu! You can't hoodwink me, I'm not a fool.'

Somewhere in the back of Rosie's mind she was saying, She's right. Like me ma, she's no fool. But aloud she said, 'You surprise me.' The cheap quip was her only counter to the forthright attack.

The colour deepened in Karen's cheeks. Her small, full mouth pursed itself further. 'You think you're clever, don't you? Smart . . . the London lady . . . well, you don't impress me. You're in trouble, aren't you?'

No muscle of Rosie's face moved, her whole body

was still. She had the desire, and not for the first time, to lift her hand and slap the small, pert face of her niece. Her voice betrayed her anger as she said below her breath, 'You would like to think that I've come home to have a baby, wouldn't you? Well I'm sorry to disappoint you. That's the only trouble you can think of, isn't it, being landed with a baby? You would have loved it to happen in my case . . . oh, I know. But just you be careful that your wishful thinking doesn't come home to roost.'

'Well' – Karen took a step to the side as she spoke – 'I might be wrong on one count, but I'm not altogether, I know that. And I'll tell you another thing: if you've got the idea into your head to stay home, I'm going.'

'Good, you'd better look out for digs then, hadn't you?' Rosie turned from the small, bitter face and was aware, as she crossed the landing, that Karen was still standing staring at her, and she knew that her jaws would be working, viciously.

In her room she stood looking out through the small attic window at the white-coated roofs opposite. She had her arms crossed tightly about her, her hands pressed against her ribs as if giving herself support, and she stood like this until she heard her mother's voice calling from below, 'Are you ready, Rosie? Rosie! Do you hear me? Are you ready?' She did not swing round and grab up her things, but slowly she got into her coat and pulled on her hat, and when her mother's voice came to her again, calling, 'Are you up there, lass?' she clenched her hands tightly before calling back, 'I'm coming, I'm coming, Ma.'

PART TWO

HUGHIE

Sunday

Hughie was sitting in the back of the cobbler's shop. He was sitting in his shirt sleeves and wearing a pullover, and he looked at home, as he never did in Hannah's house. The little room had no window, and no light but that which came in from the shop through the half-glazed door. But it was extremely bright now, being lit by an electric bulb beneath a pink plastic shade, and the light was reflected from the rough mauve-painted walls. Along one wall was a narrow desk-cum-cupboard, above which were shelves holding books. One step from the desk and against the opposite wall stood two chairs – a straight-backed one and an old extending bed-chair. At the far end of the room was a shallow sink, with a table at its side holding a small grill, on which stood a kettle, now coming up to the boil. To the side of the sink a curtain hung from a rod, which was used to cut off the kitchen section of the tiny compartment. On the floor below the sink was a rough mat, and a piece of carpet ran the length of the room to the far wall, where stood an oil heater. The tiny room gave off an air of compact snugness, and had been Hughie Geary's real home for so long that now, when he was about to leave it, it tugged at him, saying, Don't go yet, there's plenty of time.

But there wasn't plenty of time. There wasn't all that time left, for he was thirty-five. Already there was grey in his hair; already the dreams of travelling that had haunted him for years were fading; at least they had been until a couple of months ago when they had been pleasantly startled into life.

Before him now on the desk lay numbers of travel brochures; there were dozens of them dating back for years. They had been part of his recreation; he knew every route on every map of every folder. He could have told you, without referring to the appropriate brochure, the route to Baghdad as easily as another man could have pointed out the route to the Lake District, yet never in his life had he been more than a hundred miles from Fellburn, never in his life had he had a holiday. But then there was nothing so strange about that. As Hannah had said to him on several occasions, 'Broderick and me have never slept away from home for a night,' so if Hannah Massey didn't need a holiday, why should he?

He lifted his head and looked at the blank wall before him. How much could you hate someone and still live with them? How deep could the hate go before you wanted to kill the object of it? At times he thought he could measure his hate for Hannah; it was so many inches long, and so many inches thick, and it was wedged tight within him. But at other times he knew his thin body could not be measured from his chest to his backbone, for it was stretched wide with hate, hate for the woman who had dominated him since he was twelve years old; who had for a period from the age of fifteen put the fear of God in him, and who had stripped him of his manhood as certainly as if she had performed an operation on him. And she had performed an operation on him, on his mind. But this time next week he would be away, and from the time he left the house he would never look on her again. And yet he knew that he would never forget her, for her personality was imprinted on him as indelibly as the stamp of a concentration camp. But there was one bit of enjoyment he was going to give himself before they parted; he was going to keep his eyes tight on her face when he told her about the money; he was going to draw into himself and hold, like some precious gift, her fury when she realized she had thrown away, not only the fatted calf, but the golden calf.

As the kettle began to whistle the shop door shook and the bell rang, and rising hastily, he pulled the kettle aside, pushed all the travel folders into a drawer, and went out through the shop and opened the door.

'Did I hear the kettle boiling?'

'Oh, hello, Dennis. Aye, you did.'

Dennis hurried around the counter, 'Lord, it's cold . . . ugh!' He took off his coat as he entered the room, then went towards the stove and held his hands above it as Hughie mashed the tea. And for a moment there was a silence between them, the silence of two men who were past the need to fill every minute with sound.

'It won't be a tick, I'll let it draw. Sit yourself down.'

Hughie was speaking to Dennis's back now. It was a thin back, narrow shoulders topped by a longish head with dark hair, close cut, almost black as were his eyes. There was no look of Hannah about Dennis, and very little of Broderick. They said he took after Broderick's father. His face wore a keen, sharp look, and when he turned it towards Hughie the expression was tight and the eyes hard. 'I suppose you've heard the latest?' he said.

'A bit of it.'

'My God!' Dennis shook his head as he sat down. 'What will she think of next? Brampton Hill, number eight of all places! But there's one thing about it; this time the lads are making a stand.'

'Their lines will break.'

'Yes, Hughie, as you say, their lines will break; as they've done before. The woman's mad. . . . Brampton Hill with our lot. Can you imagine it? But she's determined as I've never seen her before. The house was like hell let loose this morning. Did you know she broke the news to them last night after she came back from the club?'

'Yes, I heard the racket from up in my room.'

'Huh! She must have been well fortified and thought the time was ripe. I was flabbergasted when I went in. I was expecting to get it in the neck straight-away for not calling in and for what I had to tell her, but that came later. You know, the atmosphere on a Sunday in the house has generally made me laugh, because it's always so full of restrained holy bustle; this one getting ready for this Mass, the other coming back from Communion, and the virtue of having gone to the seven o'clock Mass oozing out of her like sweat. But not this morning. It was like going into a house where a bomb had exploded, and the worst thing they could have done they did, I mean the lads, they appealed to me. What did I think of it? You can imagine how she took that.'

Hughie jerked his chin as he poured out the tea. 'I can imagine it. But how did she take your news?'

'How did she take it?' Dennis took the cup from Hughie's hand and, lifting the spoon, tapped it against

98

the saucer. It was a nervous movement. 'You know, sometimes I want to laugh in her face, a debunking laugh, or laugh at her . . . but never with her. At times I forget she's my mother and want to slap her mouth for her. I could have done it this morning quite easily. It was during one of the lulls when the lads were coming up for more breath that I told her. We were in the kitchen alone at the time. I broke it gently, saying, 'I've got a bit of news for you, Ma.'

' "Aye?" she said; she didn't even turn from the sink. "Florence is going to have a baby," I said. I was grinning self-consciously as I said it, I couldn't help it. You know Hughie, the way she turned around and looked at me was an insult in itself. And you know what she said?'

'I could give a good guess.'

'She kept wiping up as she turned round, and there was that tight, bitter smile on her face. "Well," she said, "you should feel much better now that you've proved yourself; in fact, you should both feel different and more normal like. It's a great stigma for a woman to bear, not to be able to have a child. She's for ever at a loss to know if the man's no use or it's herself" . . . She's my mother, Hughie, and she said that. And then she finished, "I only hope her body's as strong as her mind and she's delivered safe. Brains are not important to a woman in childbirth, she'll likely deliver hard". . . . I had to come out, Hughie; I just had to come out.'

'Don't you worry, Dennis. Both you and Florence are in a position to laugh at her.'

Dennis took a long drink from his cup, and he stared at the oil-stove for some moments before replying, 'Yes,

99

I suppose we are, but you know we just can't . . . you can't laugh her off for she gets into your skin, pricking you all over like squirrel fleas . . . I don't know how you stand it day in, day out . . . I don't. Florence was saying the other night that she could understand the lads putting up with her because they were nearly all as dim as doornails. As long as they are fed and clothed and have their pocket money, that's all that matters. Like her, she said, they think God will provide, only unlike her they don't help Him with the job. And why should they when they've got Ma? But she said, she just couldn't begin to understand how you've put up with it all these years.'

Hughie smiled now, a quiet, thoughtful smile, and he looked through the glass door into the shop to a shelf where rested a row of cobbled boots and shoes as he replied softly, 'I've asked meself that many times, and given meself the answer, too. And it's very simple, I haven't much gumption.' He cast a smile towards Dennis.

'Nonsense!' Dennis gave a disbelieving jerk to his head. 'But really, why didn't you just walk out?'

'I did. You know I did, twice, and she had me brought back.'

'But that was when you were a lad. I've bever brought this up before, it seemed too pertinent. But what really kept you? I can't believe it's just what happened years ago and the hold she had over you. As I see it, there was nothing to stop you just walking out, any day of any year as far back as I can remember . . . just walking out.'

Again Hughie looked through the door to the line of

100

shoes, and his expression took on a sadness that buried itself deep in his brown eyes. 'You belong to a family, Dennis, and anybody who has a family can't really understand what it's like not to be a member of one. When I first came into the house I felt I was one of you lads, because she was kind, but there were still times when, in a temper, she would say, "As for you, I've got enough to put up with from this horde, you'll go into a home." She'd forget it the next minute, but not me. I was terrified of this thing called . . . a home. I was terrified of not being a member of a family. And you know, on the two occasions she had me brought back I was glad. Moreover, your da was good to me when we worked together here. We could laugh and be easy, and he would make excuses for her, mostly first thing in the morning, saying, "Don't mind, Hannah; all she says is just like God bless you. She's a great woman, a great woman." I often wondered what he would think about me if she had told him the truth, as she threatened so often to do.'

'Just the same as he does now. But the fact that he didn't know, that she kept mum about it all these years, makes her more formidible still, don't you think?'

'Yes, I suppose so. The reason she gave me for not telling him was that he would kill me, in fact they would all kill me if they knew. And then I felt I owed her something after what happened. And as the years went on it wasn't too bad. I had the shop on my own, and this.' He spread his hands out to indicate the little room. 'I had my books; and then the last few years I've had' – he leant his head forward and his voice dropped as he ended – 'you and Florence. That's meant a lot to me,

101

more than you'll ever guess, Dennis. And the pastime you opened up for me.'

'Oh, that was Florence's doing, not mine. She saw immediately that you were a natural writer and would make an essayist.'

'Huh! A natural . . . an essayist who couldn't spell more than a four-letter word.'

'You can spell better than me, it was never my strong point either.' They laughed at each other now. Then again there was silence between them, until Dennis exclaimed, 'Oh, by the way, what I meant to say when I first came in was, what do you think about our Rosie coming home?'

'Oh . . . Rosie.' Hughie got up, took Dennis's cup and went to the stove to refill it, saying, 'Well, I don't really know. What's your opinion?'

Dennis shook his head. 'Well, since you put it like that I feel there's something not quite right. She says she's had the flu. That could account for her being thin and white, but . . . well, I might be imagining it, but she looks sort of scared to me.'

'She's in trouble, Dennis.'

'God, no!'

'Oh, I don't think it's that.' Hughie raised his eyebrows as he handed Dennis the filled cup. 'Yet I don't know. But I just don't want to think it's that, not with her. But there's something. You put your finger on it when you said she looked scared. The others though don't seem to have noticed anything.'

'They wouldn't.' Dennis jerked his chin upwards. 'But if she's in trouble it'll drive the old girl barmy. That would be the end of it, because she's the apple of her eye, as you know. It's a wonder she isn't a completely spoiled brat, yet she isn't. . . . I've always had a soft spot for Rosie.'

'Me too.' Hughie again went to the sink, filled the kettle and set it on the stove, but did not light the gas. And Dennis, looking towards him, was about to say something further but withheld it. Then he bit on his lower lip as if to suppress the question, after which he drained the last of his tea at a gulp and stood up, saying, 'I'd better be making a move or I'll be late for dinner. You'll be along this afternoon?'

'Yes. Yes, Dennis, I'll be along this afternoon.'

They went through the shop in single file, and when they were near the door Dennis turned towards Hughie and said quietly, 'We're going to miss you, you know.'

'It won't all be on one side, Dennis. I'll never forget the pair of you.'

'Will you ever come back this way, do you think?'

'I doubt it; not the way I'm feeling now; but you never know. There's one thing I'm certain of. Wherever I come to rest there'll be room for you and Florence and' – his face spread into a grin – 'the bairns.'

Dennis put out his fist and punched him in the chest, then opened the door, saying, 'So long. See you later.'

'Yes, Dennis. So long.'

Back in the room again, Hughie sat down before the narrow desk. There was half an hour before he need go back to the house. He reached up and took down some sheets of paper from the shelf where the books were, and after thinking for a moment, he began to write from where earlier he had left off. But he had only written a few lines when he stopped, and staring down at his thin,

103

scribbly writing, he thought to himself, an essayist. It was a wonderful word, essayist, and Florence didn't say things for the sake of saying them. He had started scribbling years ago, but hadn't dared show his efforts to anyone, until by chance Dennis had picked up something from the desk here. That's how it had started; and with it his friendship with them both. Dennis had said, 'You're a deep one; I never even thought you thought – I forgot you weren't one of us.' They had both laughed. Now, if he wanted, he could spend all his days just writing. Going carefully, he had enough money to keep him for the remainder of his life; and who knew? He might one day see himself in print. That would be worth all the money in the world. And he was going to see the world, the whole world. From his house on wheels he was going to see the world.

At this point, the shop bell ringing once more surprised him, and when he opened the door there stood Dennis again, but now with Rosie by his side.

'I brought her back to go along home with you. She'll explain.' Dennis pressed Rosie over the threshold. 'I must be off. Look' – he pulled at Rosie's arm – 'what about coming over to our place this afternoon with Hughie, eh? Florence would love to see you.'

'Thanks, Dennis, but Betty has already asked me. But I'd rather come over to you. I'll . . . I'll see if I can manage it,' she smiled at him.

'You do, you do. So long.'

'So long, Dennis. . . . Thanks.'

As Dennis turned away Rosie took a step into the shop and stood waiting, and Hughie, closing the door, said, 'Go on into the back room, Rosie, it's warm there.'

She kept her head slightly down as she went round the counter and into the back shop, but once inside an exclamation came from her, and she turned to him spontaneously, saying, 'By! You've got this cosy, Hughie.' She looked about her now. 'It's something different from when I saw it last.'

'Home from home.' He smiled shyly at her. 'Sit down. I'll make you a cup of tea.'

'No . . . no, don't, Hughie, I don't want anything. Thanks all the same.'

'It would warm you up. It won't take a minute.'

She was looking up at him, and he down at her, and their exchanged glances embarrassed them both. She said quickly, 'All right, all right, I'll have one,' and he turned just as quickly and went to the stove and lit the gas.

The striking of the match was like a whip's crack in the silence. It was a different silence from that which he had shared with Dennis. Aware of the strained atmosphere too, Rosie moved on the chair and turned sideways and leant her elbow on the desk and her eyes dropped to the paper lying there.

Having been trained to read quickly she took in the first paragraph of the writing almost at a glance. It read: 'March 12, looked at programme "The Cosmologist". Speakers were: Professor Fred Hoyle, Professor Sir Bernard Lovell and Professor Hermann Bondi, and Doctor Margaret and Geoffrey Burbidge. This programme interested me so much it set my mind moving, and I thought of the following when I was on the point of sleep and made myself put it down, just as I thought of it. Must extend it.'

Then followed the words: 'The word conscious is the only means we have of explaining our ability to be aware of our surroundings. Yet how do we know that unconsciousness, which now we understand as a state of unawareness, might not, when deprived of this body, be a higher form of mind which will produce another body, which will in turn take up life on a planet suited to maintain it for a span of time in accordance with the properties of that planet, where it will go through the same process – namely, what we now term unconsciousness will be a form of consciousness. This consciousness will eventually merge again into the universe as unconsciousness . . . ad infinitum.

'Unconsciousness, or the subconscious mind, could be the reality. All the universe could be alive to deeper and deeper forms of unconsciousness. The whole universe could be made up of these levels of unconsciousness, and death could be a mere merging into the universe by way of this unconsciousness.'

'It won't be a minute before it boils.'

'Oh . . . oh, I'm sorry, Hughie. I . . . I didn't mean to read it.'

'Oh, that's all right.' He smiled widely. 'It's just some of my scribbling . . . Passes the time, you know.' He sat down opposite to her; their knees were almost touching.

'I . . . I stopped you writing,' she said, 'barging in. It reads very clever. I didn't understand it.'

'There's two of us.'

They laughed together.

'But I stopped you, and . . .'

'That you didn't,' he put in quickly. 'I was on the point of going home. It's on dinner time, isn't it?'

She lowered her eyes, then said, 'I was just passing Waldorf Street when I saw Ronnie in the distance; he was going up the school cut. He stopped when he saw me, but I knew what he would do; he would come out in Baldwin Road and meet me full on. I was standing like a stook not knowing whether to go on, or to go back into the town and to take the bus to the top of our road, when Dennis came down the hill.'

'He's married now, it'll be all right.' Hughie's voice was low.

And hers was just above a whisper as she answered, 'It wouldn't, Hughie, it wouldn't.'

'Well, I suppose you know best.' He cleared his throat, then smoothed his hair back.

Rosie looked at her hands encased in the fur-lined gloves that her mother had bought her yesterday, and she began to pick at the fingers as she said, 'I half told my mother that I would stay home and get a job near, but I don't think I can now.'

He did not speak for a moment, but kept his eyes intently on her averted face before he said, 'His wife's going to have a baby, I don't think he would –'

'Oh, it isn't only him, Hughie, it's everything. . . . You change when you go away, you know, and in a way it's a good thing you do.'

'I wouldn't know about that.'

His tone held regret, and she lifted her eyes to his and said quickly, 'Oh, you don't need to change, Hughie.' She shook her head at him, a gentle smile playing round her lips.

'Huh!' His body moved in self-derision.

'Well, you don't, you've always been sensible. I mean

107

you've thought for yourself, an' you've got more brains than all of us put together.' She glanced towards the paper on the table which had read like double Dutch to her.

He leant towards her now. 'If I'd thought for meself, Rosie, do you think I'd still he here?' Both his look and tone were enquiring.

As she looked back at him, she had the urge to ask him questions, but found herself overcome by a sudden feeling of shyness. What she did say was, 'You said you were leaving. What's made you change your mind, Hughie?'

He looked at her a full minute before speaking. 'I've come into money, Rosie,' he said.

'Into money, Hughie? The pools?'

'No, not the pools. . . . I don't know whether you remember or not, but I had a sister; I can hardly remember her meself.'

'I seem to have heard something about her.'

'Well, she went to America just before the war as nurse-companion to an old lady. She was about twelve years older than me. And she wasn't really a nurse, not a trained nurse, and I never heard of her until two years ago, and in a really odd way. You see she wrote to the Vicar of All Souls, you know, the big Protestant church behind the market, and she asked him did he know of Hugh Geary who had been evacuated to Fellburn during the war. Now you know me, Rosie. I never put me foot inside a church, either Catholic, Protestant, or Methodist, and it's ten to one any other minister but this Mr Pattenden would never have heard of me but for the strange coincidence that he's always brought his boots here to be mended. He always did in your da's time and he still does, and he came to me with this letter. He was as happy about it as if it was affecting himself. And that's how it all started. I wrote to her and she wrote back, a long letter, telling me all that had happened to her. It wasn't much when you summed it up. She had looked after the old lady all these years, and a few months previous to her trying to find me the old lady had died and had left her a good slice of her money. She asked me if there was any chance of me coming to America, and I wrote back and said no, I was settled comfortably here. I didn't want her to think that I was on the cadge – but I told her that if ever she thought of coming to England I would be overjoyed to see her. Well, it turned out that she wasn't very well herself, apparently and wasn't up to travelling; then just before Christmas she died.' From his seat he looked out through the glass door again towards the row of shoes, before he said, as if to himself, 'She must have been bad when she tried to contact me. She likely knew she was going then and she wanted to be in touch with someone belonging to her. I know the feeling. But, you know, I'd rather have seen her than had the money.'

After a pause Rosie said, 'I'm sorry you didn't meet her, Hughie, but I'm glad for you, oh, I am. I would sooner it had happened to you than to anyone else I know of.'

'Why me?' He turned his head and looked at her intently. And she dropped her eyes from his and said, 'Oh, I don't know. Perhaps just because I was brought up with you, and . . . and I never thought you got . . . well, a square deal. And you took everything so quietly, not bashing, or yelling, or swearing as the others would have done, if . . . if me ma had treated them as she did you.'

Following another silence, during which she kept her eyes cast downwards, she asked, 'And me ma knows nothing about it?'

'Not a thing. If Nancy, that was me sister, had written to the priest he would naturally have gone to the house.'

She looked up at him. 'She's going to get a glif.'

'Yes, Rosie, she's going to get a glif.'

'When are you going?'

'As soon as they've altered the caravan.'

'You've got a caravan?'

'Yes, I bought it second hand. A Land-Rover and a caravan. I got it as a bargain an' all. The funny thing is, if I hadn't had enough cash I would never have got the chance of it at the price; I would have been asked to pay through the teeth. It's the irony of life, isn't it?'

'Yes, yes. But why are you having it altered? Is it in a bad way?'

'No, it's in fine condition, but they used it mostly for sleeping. There were five in the family and it's all bunks. I'm having a sink unit put in, and a cooker.' His face looked alight now. 'And a kind of desk-cum-drawers, and a wardrobe. It'll be like a house on wheels. I've taken the design from one I saw in a weekly, and old Jim Cullen, next door, is doing it.' He nodded his head. 'You wouldn't remember him, I don't suppose, but he's a wizard with wood. In fact he makes antiques, you know, copies, when he has orders for them. But things have slumped in his line this past few years, it's with Brampton Hill going down and all that, and so I've given

110

him the job. And I know I won't even have to bother and look at it until he's finished. He's that kind of a worker. The only thing is, he won't be hurried too much, he's a craftsman. If he keeps at it, it should be ready a week come Monday or Tuesday, and the minute it is I'm on the road.'

'Can you drive a car, Hughie?' Her eyebrows were slightly raised.

'Oh, aye. And I've got Dennis to thank for that an' all. I've got Dennis to thank for a lot of things. And Florence, too. When they had the car a few years ago he would insist on teaching me to drive; and then when I could he said, "You go and pass your test." "What for?" I asked. "You never know," he said, "you never know." And you don't, do you Rosie?'

She shook her head.

'But now they've sold the car because they've been trying to raise the money for a deposit to put down on a house. But what they don't know as yet' – he leant forward towards her, his elbow resting on his knee – 'they're going to have a house bought for them.' He nodded slowly. 'A three-thousand pound one. But I can't do it until I'm on the road, because Dennis wouldn't hear of it. But when I'm away and he can't get in touch with me . . . well, he can't do anything about it, can he?'

His plain face looked almost handsome, illuminated as it was with the joy of being able to give. And the look did something to Rosie that nothing else had been able to do for days. It penetrated the terror that was still encased in her body, the terror that had gone beyond fear. On Friday night she had thought when once she was alone in bed she would cry and cry and ease herself,

111

but she had lain dry-eyed, staring through the terror into the blackness of the night; blackness that was disturbed only by the sounds below her; grunts, faint sighs, snores, splutters and coughs; and these had made the terror more real. All those men down there . . . MEN . . . MEN . . . MEN.

'Rosie. Aw, Rosie, what is it?' Hughie was on his feet. 'Don't cry. Aw, don't cry like that.' His hand hesitated as it went out to her shoulder; then it rested gently on it, and at his touch something cracked in her throat and she gulped and gasped and held her face in her hands, while the tears ran through her fingers.

'There, there.' He was kneeling by her side now, his hand still on her shoulder, and when, like a child, she turned her head into his neck, he stared at the wall opposite, and it looked as if he too was fixed with emotion, for his other arm hung by his side like a false limb.

Perhaps she felt the stiffness of his body, the unresponsiveness of his hand, for, pulling herself upright, she turned her face from him, gasping and spluttering as she said, 'I . . . I'm sorry, I'm sorry, Hughie.'

He was on the chair opposite to her again. 'What's to be sorry about? A cry will do you good.' His voice sounded flat.

She groped at her handbag, and taking out a handkerchief, dried her face; and again she said, 'I'm sorry.'

He did not make any remark for a moment, but when he did his words weren't put as a question but as a direct statement.

'You're in trouble, Rosie, aren't you?' he said.

There was no denial from her, only a downward movement of her head.

'Can you tell me?'

Now her head shook slowly from side to side.

'Well, you should tell somebody, it would ease it. Why don't you go to Dennis?'

Again she shook her head. Then raising it, she gulped for breath a number of times before looking at him and saying, 'If . . . if I could tell any . . . anybody, it would be you, but I can't.'

'You're frightened about something, aren't you?'

'Not any more,' she said.

'Isn't it anything you could tell your . . . your mother?'

She made a sound that was something between a groan and a whimper. 'My mother . . . ? I'd sooner jump in the river, Hughie. My mother? I'd sooner die than she knew. She'd want to kill me in any case. You know it's frightening when somebody lays so much stock on you as she does on me. You can't live up to it. But she'd never understand that. She frightens me with her feeling, she's so . . . so . . .' She searched for a word, moving her head the while, and he put in, 'Irrational?'

'Yes, that's it, that's the word . . . irrational. And in everything, in everything. I thought of them going to Mass this morning after the business of Friday night and yesterday morning.'

'What happened yesterday morning?'

She snifled. 'You didn't hear . . . ? The priest came with a wireless to be mended.'

Hughie's face slowly stretched. 'The one Barny made for him?'

'Yes. He came bounding in, all chatter like he always

113

does. When she opened the door to him she really thought it was them coming to search, you know.'

Hughie bit on his lip, trying to suppress a smile, as he asked, 'And what happened?'

'He went for her because he said she had involved him. Then she threw in his face about keeping him supplied with bacon and butter and shirts and things during the war. . . .'

At this Hughie put his hand over his mouth, bowed his head and began to laugh. It was a silent laugh at first, evident only in the shaking of his body; then unable to control it any longer he gave vent to it, and as Rosie watched him her face trembled into a smile, then stretched, and the next moment she, too, was laughing, but with more than a touch of hysteria.

How they came to grasp each other's hands neither of them knew, but as their laughter subsided their hands were joined breast high between them and their heads were almost touching.

It was Hughie who sobered first. He released her hands, and, getting up, reached out and picked up a towel from a rail to the side of the desk and rubbed his face vigorously with it.

Rosie had a bout of the hiccoughs now, and between them she said, 'Oh, Hughie, hic . . . I . . . never thought I would . . . hic . . . laugh in me life again. Oh thanks, Hughie, thanks; you've done me the world of good.'

'Well, if you didn't see the funny side of some things you would commit murder. It isn't often I get a real laugh. No, it isn't often.'

And that's true, she thought. She hadn't, as far as she could remember, heard him laugh heartily before. His

114

laughter had always been controlled, just a shaking of the body.

She rose to her feet, saying, 'Can I wash me face, Hughie, it'll be a mess?'

'Of course.' He pointed to the sink.

As she washed her face and took a lipstick out of her new bag and made up her lips, he got into his coat, and put on a scarf, and picked up his hat and stood waiting for her, all without looking at her. It was as if he was embarrassed now by her personal acts.

As he locked the shop door behind them, Rosie said, 'What are you going to do with it? I mean the shop, goodwill, and stock and that?'

'Oh,' he said, 'I'm passing it on to a fellow called Lance Briggs. He's handicapped in the legs and works in Tullets factory. He's delighted about it. He's a shy bloke . . . not unlike meself' – he laughed – 'and having a quiet place of his own will make all the difference to him. He'll do all right an' all because he was apprenticed to the boot mending until he was twenty. I'm glad he's having it.' He looked at his watch and said, 'We'll have to put a move on, we're late as it is.'

Once, when she almost slipped on the frosted pavement, he put out his hand to steady her, but before he touched her she had righted herself.

After this they covered most of the distance home without speaking. The intimacy that the room behind the shop had created with its snug smallness was gone, and they walked apart, intent on picking their way over the humped frozen snow that covered the pavements.

It was as they rounded the corner of the school that they came face to face with Ronnie MacFarlane.

115

MacFarlane was a tall man, six foot two and broad with it. He was handsome in a rough-hewn way, with strong Celtic features, large blue eyes and a full-lipped mouth above a heavy jaw. He stood one foot on the kerb and one in the gutter, his right shoulder in line with that of Rosie's. His skin looked ruddy and warm as if he was blushing. 'Hello, Rosie,' he said.

She paused only for a second before answering, 'Hello, Ronnie.'

'Hello,' put in Hughie. This brought Ronnie's eyes flicking reluctantly from Rosie as he answered, 'Hello there, Hughie.'

'Awful weather.' He was looking at Rosie again.

'Yes.' She nodded her head.

'Are you home for long?'

'No, no, not long.'

'I'll be seeing you then?'

'Yes,' she hesitated. 'Be seeing you.' As she moved sideways to pass him, he stepped back into the gutter and watched her.

'So long, Rosie.' Her name came soft to his mouth.

'So long, Ronnie,' she answered.

'So long,' said Hughie. And for reply Ronnie nodded to him, but his eyes were still on Rosie.

She didn't speak until they had turned the next corner, and the trembling of her body came over in her voice. 'He . . . : he must have been hanging about. You see, it's as I said, I won't be able to stay; not in the town anyway.'

'Don't worry.' Hughie was walking close to her now. 'He can't do anything. Perhaps he just wanted to have a word with you.'

116

'A word? Huh! I know what he wants.' She put her fingers to her lips. 'I'm sorry, Hughie.'

'Why be sorry for saying what you think, and the truth.'

'It sounds so awful, but . . .' She turned and looked squarely at him. 'You know something, Hughie? There's worse than Ronnie.'

'Yes, I believe that, and by a long chalk; but I'm sorry you've found it out.'

She was looking ahead as she said, 'So am I.'

Again there was silence between them. Yet now it wasn't so strained. But the same thought was in both their minds as they neared the house. Should they go in together?

Rosie knew she should say, 'You'd better go round the back way, Hughie.' But she couldn't. It would be an insult to say that to him. She would rather brave her mother's wrath than hurt him. She said, 'We'll go in the front way, it's nearer.'

He made no protest, but stood with her on the step as she rang the bell.

The door was opened by Hannah herself, and as soon as she saw them together her face darkened. But it was to Rosie she addressed herself, saying, 'Where've you been in all this, the dinner's been on the table this last twenty minutes? The Mass was over at twelve and it's now nearly half-past one. Where've you been?'

As short a time ago as yesterday Rosie wouldn't even have thought of making a reply like 'Do I have to account for every minute to you?' but now she almost voiced it, yet as she took off her coat and hat and hung them on a peg of the hall-stand without answering, she

117

reminded herself of how kind her mother had been to her, and that she owed her for every stitch of clothing she was now wearing.

'You heard what I said.' Hannah was close behind her.

'I . . . I went for a walk, Ma.'

'You went for a . . . !' Hannah glanced to where Hughie at the far end of the hall was disappearing into the kitchen, there to hang up his coat and hat on the back door, the place allotted to him, and coming close to Rosie now, she hissed, 'Don't tell me you've been walkin' with him!'

Rosie shook her head; then turning and facing her mother, she said, 'I went down by the river.'

'In this weather?' Hannah brought her brows together. 'An' answer me, was he along of you?'

'I met him in the street, Ma.' Rosie closed her eyes for a moment. She only hoped that Hughie was listening and had not gone straight through the kitchen and into the living-room so he would know what to say if he was questioned.

Hannah, after giving her one long look, said, 'Well, come an' have your dinner, what's left of it.'

The men had nearly finished their meal when Rosie sat down at the table, and their greeting of her was not boisterous, as it had been on her arrival, for they were still shuddering from the impact of their mother's new venture, which the Sunday beer hadn't been able to show up in a more favourable light.

When Hannah put the dinner plate in front of her with the remark, 'It's kizzened up to cork, so it is,' her father put in placatingly. 'Aw, she'll get it down, won't you, lass? This weather would make a mare eat its foal.' She smiled at him. She liked her da. Her da always wanted peace. Somehow he was like Hughie, or Hughie was like him. As she glanced at Hughie sitting now at the farther end of the table, his head bowed, she thought that, although they did not look alike, they were like enough in nature to be father and son, more so than the other four men at the table.

Karen, too, was at the table, seated next to her grandfather. She hadn't spoken to Rosie, she hadn't even looked at her, that is until Shane asked, 'Did you come out early from eleven o'clock? I hung about waitin' for you, but I didn't see you?'

'What?' Rosie fluffed the question as one taken off her guard, then said, 'Oh, yes . . . I came out early. I was at the back. It was stuffy. I came out just before the end.' It was now that Karen looked at her and spoke. She said, 'I was at the back an' all; I didn't see you. And it wasn't stuffy; the heating had gone wrong, it was freezing.'

The men all looked from Karen to Rosie, and for the first time she had come home they saw colour in her face. She was red to the ears.

'You weren't there, were you?'

Rosie thrust the chair back as she rose hastily to her feet, and looking down at Karen, she said, 'No, I wasn't there, Miss Mischief-maker. Now are you satisfied?'

'You didn't go to Mass? Then why did you say you did?' Hannah was standing with her arms held stiffly some distance from her sides. It was an attitude of surprise, which made her look ludicrously like a cowboy waiting to draw.

119

Rosie turned to her mother, and the restraint sounded in her tone as she answered, 'Because I thought it would save being asked a number of questions. I am tired of being peppered with questions.'

'Who in the name of God is peppering you with questions? What has come over you, girl? What I want now is just a straightforward answer to a straightforward question. Why didn't you go to Mass?'

'I can't give you a straightforward answer, Ma, it would be too involved.' There was that word again, involved. It would seem that everything was involved with something else; you couldn't speak or move unless you involved someone.

'Involved?'

'Oh, be quiet. Be quiet.' Broderick thrust out his hand and pulled at Hannah's skirt. 'Leave the lass be. She didn't want to go to Mass and that's that.'

Hannah tore her skirt from her husband's grasp and, turning on him, she cried, 'There's no child of mine goin' to miss Mass unless I know the reason why.'

'I think I'll go to bed,' said Jimmy, rising to his feet. 'Where's the papers?'

'And me along o' you,' put in Shane.

As their chairs scraped back from the table Hannah swept her glance over her entire family, and cried at them, 'What's this house comin' to anyway, that me wishes are flaunted by every damn member of it? I work me brain, body and guts out from Monday mornin' till Sunday night tryin' to further the lot of you, and what's me thanks? Hair raised because I want to move you to decent quarters, and now lies thrust at me when I ask an ordinary question.' She flicked her eyes reproachfully

120

at Rosie, and, her voice dropping suddenly to almost a pathetic whimper, she ended, 'I didn't deserve it, lass, I didn't deserve it.'

Rosie, putting her hand tightly across her mouth, lowered her head and hurried from the room, and Hannah stood looking towards the open door for a moment before her voice, no longer holding the pathetic note, bawled at them, 'There's something radically wrong in this house. Radically wrong, I say.'

'There always is when she's home.' Karen's thin voice had hardly finished this statement when Hannah was upon her. With one hand gripping her shoulder, she pulled her from the chair as if she was an empty paper bag, and swinging her round she brought her other hand with a ringing slap across the girl's face.

'Here! Here!'

'My God, Ma!'

'Let up, Ma. Hell! What's come over you?'

'There was no call for that.'

All except Broderick and Hughie, one after the other, the men reproached her, but Broderick looked at his wife, a look that brought her to her senses quicker than all reasonable talk could have done. He drew Karen towards him and, putting his arms about her stiff body, said, 'There, there, your grannie didn't mean it.' He had no need to say, 'Don't cry,' because Karen wasn't crying.

Hannah now, looking from her husband into the accusing faces of her sons, swept her eyes over them as if they were of no account, and her gaze came to rest on Hughie, where seemingly unperturbed he was still eating, and as she moved up the table towards him, pushing Shane aside from her path, she addressed his

121

bent head, crying, 'And you! Why don't you do somethin'? Why don't you protest in some way and tell me what a wicked woman I am an' to keep me hands to meself? No, no, you couldn't could you, you gutless sod, you!'

Slowly Hughie rose to his feet. His face very white and strained, he looked at Hannah. All the eyes in the room were upon him, and the men without exception were wondering how he would react to this last insult. He had stood something, had Hughie. Then all of them saw his reaction. It was silent yet yelled aloud. They saw his lip moving upwards leaving his teeth bare; it was as if he were looking upon something repulsive.

No-one moved as he turned from her and walked out of the room, but he was hardly through the door when she lifted up the plate which still held most of his pudding and hurled it after him. It went right through the open door and hit the far wall of the hall. The impact was the only sound in the house before Hannah rent the place with her screaming.

Monday

On Monday morning, the house to themselves again, Hannah, standing before Rosie, said 'I'm sorry,' and the humility in her voice was real, at least momentarily, she believed, but there was something almost obscene about it, something that caused the stomach to tense, the lids to droop, the head to bow. She couldn't look at her, but she said, 'It's all right. It's all right.' Then quickly she added, 'I'm going to Newcastle to see about a job, there's an agency there. And . . . and I'll pay you back when . . .'

'Aw, don't say that, don't keep on about the money, lass, it'll only make me think you're still mad at me. I don't want no payin' back; you know I'd give you the shirt off me back. All I want you to do is to do well for yourself and not take up with riff-raff, not even to walk the length of the street with them. You look a lady, you are a lady, all I live for is to see you in your right settin' and actin' like one.'

'Oh, Ma, be quiet.'

'I needn't be quiet on this point, lass.' Hannah's voice was moderate. 'I can talk as long as I like this way because it's true, and it's from me heart. All I live for is to see you marry well, with a position you can be proud of. It . . . it was that lass' – she put her fingers out tentatively towards Rosie's hand – 'it was that that

123

made me go off me head yesterday, thinking of you walkin' in the same step along of him.'

'Hughie?' Rosie thrust her head up and to the side as she asked the question.

'Aye . . . Hughie.'

'But, Ma, I was brought up with Hughie; what have you against him?'

'Aw, you'll know some day, I suppose. But in the meantime it angers me to see you drawin' in the same air. Keep away from him, that's all I ask you.'

'But what has he done, Ma, that you should go on at him like this? I've never known Hughie say a wrong word, I've never heard him even swear.'

'You don't have to swear, me lass, to be bad.'

'But Hughie's not bad, Ma.'

Because of the defence in Rosie's voice Hannah was unable to control her natural aggressiveness, and she cried now, 'You know nothing about it. And another thing, don't keep defending him or I can't be responsible for me tongue. Aw, lass' – her voice dropped – 'all I want is your well-being and to be proud of you. Is it too much to ask?'

Rosie shook her head helplessly; then turning away said, 'I'll be going, Ma. I'll get lunch in the town.'

'All right, lass, all right.' Hannah patted her arm affectionately. 'I'll have something tasty made for you when you come back. About what time will you be in?'

'Oh . . . I don't know. If there's anything on the books I'll go after it.'

'Now don't take the first thing they offer you, mind. With your qualifications you can pick and choose, you can that.'

124

'Jobs are not so easy to get here, Ma.'

'They are for somebody like you.' Her mother smiled fondly at her, so fondly it was unbearable.

As she left the house, with Hannah bidding her a loud farewell from the top step, the third door to the right of them opened and a woman came out. She was wearing a cheap fur coat and a blue felt hat, and Hannah hailed her with, 'Oh, there you are, Jessie. You haven't seen Rosie here since she was back. Are you away down the town? So's she. You can go together. Where are you off to?'

The woman paused on her step, and looking over the railings, she answered Hannah in a voice prim and tight-sounding by saying simply, 'Hello there, Rosie.'

'Hello, Aunt Jessie.'

'Where you off to?' Hannah called again. And Jessie MacFarlane replied in a tone edged now with superiority, 'The ladies of the bazaar committee are having a coffee morning.'

Hannah's natural retort to this should have been, 'Are they, begod! There'll be some throats cut there this mornin',' but what she said was, 'Oh, that's nice, that's nice. Enjoy yourself.' And now she turned her attention to Rosie again, saying, 'Away you go now, Rosie, an' have a grand day, an' have another look at that fur stole. You know. . . .' She pointed her fingers down the steps at Rosie's back. 'The one you were admiring on Saturday. Go in and try it on.'

Rosie did not bother to ask her mother 'What stole?' but she went down the street towards the plump-faced woman, who was waiting for her, and said, 'Isn't it cold, Aunt Jessie?'

'Yes, it is,' said Jessie MacFarlane. And with this they walked down the street side by side.

At the corner Jessie MacFarlane said in a tone she attempted to make light, 'And how long are you here for this time, Rosie?'

'Oh, I don't know, Aunt Jessie,' said Rosie; 'I may get a post nearer home.' As she said this she felt the woman pause in her walk, but she didn't look towards her and she added kindly, 'But not too near; Fellburn seems to get smaller every time I see it.'

'Yes, yes, we're rather a backwater.' It was a statement without bitterness.

Again they walked on in silence, until Jessie MacFarlane could contain herself no longer and she began to talk rapidly under her breath. 'Ronnie's settled,' she said. 'He's got a good wife, she's not my choice, but she's a good girl and she's going to have a child. Things are going smoothly. I . . . I would sooner have had you than anybody, Rosie, and I think you know it, but you saw it otherwise. My Ronnie was a man when he was going with you and he's still a man, although now when he's got responsibility he'll be different. Yet men are men, you know what I mean?' She was staring ahead, her lips scarcely moving as she spoke. 'What I'm trying to say, Rosie, is you . . . you'll not get in his way?'

When Rosie answered she, too, looked ahead. 'I can promise you, Aunt Jessie,' she said quietly, 'I'll not get in his way.'

'Thank you, lass.' The voice was no longer prim, it was ordinary and thick with the North Country inflection. 'When your mother rushed in on Friday night full of the

126

news that you had come home it was as if she was
pushing a knife in me, and she took the same pleasure
in it. Your mother's a queer woman, Rosie. I've said it
to her face, so I'm sayin' nothing behind her back. You
were hardly indoors but she had to come and tell me. It
was the same when you came home last year. And after
knowing all the trouble that there was, and the lads
fighting like maniacs in the lane after they had all been
brought up together. Ronnie could hold his own with
any two of them, but with the four of them it's a wonder
they didn't murder him.'

Rosie could have said at this stage, 'It's a wonder he
didn't murder me,' but her Aunt Jessie, like all mothers,
wouldn't think along those lines. Again she said, 'You
needn't worry; if I get a job anywhere near, I won't live
in the town, I'll live well away. . . .' She turned quickly
and looked at the older woman. 'But don't tell that last
bit to me mother, she . . . she thinks I'll be living at
home?'

Jessie MacFarlane stopped; a thin smile spread over
her features and she nodded at Rosie. 'Never fear, I
won't. I've got to leave you here,' she said, 'the café's
just down the road. You were always a good lass, Rosie.
I wish things could have been different.'

'Me too, Aunt Jessie.'

'Goodbye, Rosie.'

'Goodbye, Aunt Jessie.'

The world seemed full of worried and troubled people.
She wasn't the only one with things to hide. Her Aunt
Jessie had always hidden the fact that there was something raw and ravenous about Ronnie. She had hidden
the fact that he had attacked a girl when he was fifteen,

127

in much the same way as he had attacked her, in a blind fit of lust.

It had started to snow again when she reached the main road, and as she stood waiting for the bus she could see, between two rows of houses, the rising fells, snow spread, clean, beautiful, untouched by the slag heaps that decorated both sides of the town, where at one end stood the Phoenix pit and at the other the Venus pit. She hadn't been on the fells for years, not since that Sunday when the two men had pulled Ronnie from her and he had fallen on to the grass, crumpled and sobbing like a whipped child, while she had crawled and stumbled like some terrified animal up the dell, and then had run until she came to the first house, where the woman who had been working in the garden caught hold of her and took her indoors and covered her with a coat. And she and her husband had taken her home in their car.

Then Ronnie, driven by his love for her, that was a thing apart from his desires, had come to say he was sorry and the lads had attacked him like a pack of wolves. It had happened in the back garden. If Ronnie had not been of the size and stamina he was, and if her father had not intervened with a pick shaft in his hand, there would have been murder done that day.

Her mother had really been glad that it was finished between her and Ronnie, for, as she had said comfortingly, she was worth something better than a miner. That was until she had heard she was leaving home, and then she would have given her sanction to the dustman to come courting her daughter, if it meant keeping her within sight and sound. . . .

When she reached the agent's in Newcastle it was to

128

find that there were a number of typists required but all for junior positions, and these at a wage rate that made her raise her brows. Did she want to try for them? asked the clerk.

No, she said, she would wait. She had two years London experience working in a big office. Her shorthand speed was one hundred and twenty words a minute and her typing speed eighty words a minute, and she had been used to working with an electric typewriter.

The clerk's nostrils had dilated as he said, 'Well, we've got electric typewriters here an' all. We're not still in the Dark Ages, you know.'

She had apologised and said she hadn't meant anything, but the facts were she had started in London at nine pounds a week and had risen to twelve, and she had been next to the head in her department. She thought there was no need to explain that the staff in her particular department numbered four.

'Well,' said the clerk, 'there might be something in your line in the new factory they're building yon side of Jesmond. It's a way out from the centre of town though.'

'I'll try it,' she said.

It took her half an hour to get to the factory and another fifteen minutes walking around frozen humps of brick and machinery before she found an office with someone in it. The man was busy and abrupt. He said they were interviewing people for the clerical staff on Wednesday afternoon. She could come back if she liked. She thanked him and returned to the town, outwardly freezing with the cold, and inwardly feeling so lost, so alone, that she could have leant her head against the wall and cried.

Since yesterday morning when she had broken down in front of Hughie, the tears had never been far from her eyes. She seemed to be crying inside all the time now and wanting to give vent to it. Her body and mind felt sore, so sore that she recoiled from human contact. A man sat down beside her in the bus, and her body shrank inside her clothes and she was fearful that it would be evident and the man would look at her and say scornfully, 'You needn't move away, Miss, I'm not lousy.' He would have said something like this because he was wearing greasy working clothes; a mac that had once been fawn and was now black, a cap that had lost its shape under grease and dirt. Nevertheless, it was an enviable uniform, one that signified he was at work in some yard.

When she reached the city she was too late for lunch, so she went into a café and had a cup of tea and a sandwich. Afterwards she walked round the stores until the light faded. She had no desire to hurry home, at least not before the men came in; she didn't want to be alone with her mother again. . . .

It was half past five when she entered the house, and the brightness and the smell of fresh baking brought its own comfort. Hannah greeted her with, 'By lass, I thought you were never comin'. Everything all right?'

'Yes, Ma.'

Hannah was placing plates, piled high with bread, on the table. Her father, Arthur and Shane were already in the room, and it was Shane who said, 'Any luck, Rosie?'

'No, Shane; but there may be on Wednesday. They're taking on clerical staff at the new factory.'

'Come and get yourself warm.' Her father held out a crooked arm towards her, and when she went to him he pulled her into its circle and squeezed her waist. 'By, you're cold, you're froze. Just feel your hands.' He took her hands in his and chafed them together, rubbing warmth into them.

'I've made your favourite,' Hannah called over her shoulder as she went towards the kitchen, 'apple puddin'. Did you have a nice lunch?'

'Not bad, Ma.'

'Aw, you can't get a decent bite in them cafés and places. I've done you some plaice cooked in butter, t'would melt in your mouth.'

'Begod!' Broderick bounced his head at Rosie in mock anger. 'Plaice done in butter, t'would melt in your mouth, and apple pudding, at tea time at that. She never puts herself out like that for us, does she?' He appealed to his sons, and they grinned at her and Arthur said, 'Bread and scrape, that's us.'

It would seem that they had all regained their good humour, that there was no issue about Brampton Hill, and that the incident at Sunday dinner had never happened.

'Lucky if we get the bread sometimes from the old faggot.' Shane spoke loudly so that his mother should hear, and he pulled his head into his shoulders and slanted his eyes towards the kitchen like a child, waiting for a clout.

'I can hear you in there; I've got me ears cocked to your slanderin'.'

Rosie looked at her father, and he smiled warmly back, and leaning his face in an endearing gesture against hers, he whispered the familiar phrase, 'She's over the moon, over the moon to have you back to do for.'

'Now if Jimmy and Barny will put their noses in the door, we're all set.' Hannah came marching into the kitchen carrying a great soup dish of stew, and as she placed it on the table the sound of the back door opening made her turn her head, and she cried, 'Is that you?'

Barny's voice answered her, saying, 'Aye.'

'It's Barny,' she said. 'Jimmy won't be far behind. Come on!' she called. 'The tea's ready.'

Hannah was dishing out the stew when Barny came into the room, and it was the way Arthur's face screwed up as he looked at his brother that made her turn towards her youngest son. In a glance, she took in trouble. She placed the ladle in the dish and, facing him, said, 'What's up?'

He passed her without speaking, and he passed Broderick, with his arm still round Rosie's waist, and he went to the fire and held his hands out to the blaze before saying, 'I've got the push, a week's notice.'

The whole room was alerted, and there were exclamations from them all, except Rosie, but Hannah's was the most strident. Questioning and commanding at the same time, she cried, 'Turn yourself about and tell us what's happened. They didn't come here. Did they find anythin' on you?'

'No.' Barny was looking at her.

'What then?'

'Somebody must have croaked.'

'So that's it!' Her jaws pressed themselves through her thick skin, and as she nodded her head Broderick asked Barny, 'Do you know who?'

'It's one of five. Well, you could say four. Creeping Jesus wouldn't split. But he's been kept on with the other four.'

'Twenty-five of you got it then?' It was Arthur asking the question, and Barny nodded. 'Aye, the whole shop's closed. They've been talkin' about reorganizing for months now, and they've taken this opportunity to do it.'

'You can't be sure, man,' said Broderick. 'They might be re-forming the shops at that.'

'Aw, hell, Da.' Barny shook his head impatiently. 'Every man-jack that got his cards was in on it.'

'Did they find anythin' out?' asked Hannah.

'They searched two places. Old Riley's, him whose son-in-law has the wireless store in the market.'

'Did they find anythin'?'

'Plenty, but nothing that Riley couldn't prove he had bought as seconds.'

'How was that? You made up and sold him sets yourself,' said Hannah.

'Aye, but all that stuff is packed away in a little warehouse he's got down near the docks.'

'It's as well for him.' Broderick nodded slowly.

'Well, it hasn't saved him or any of us,' said Barny bitterly.

'What are the others doin' about it?' asked Hannah now. 'Aren't they standin' by you?'

'Huh! Don't make me laugh. The other shops have all become so bloody virtuous of a sudden they make

133

you want to retch. Two years ago, even a year this time, an' they would have been out to the last man if one of us had got our cards, but now,' he pulled his chin into his neck and finished scornfully, 'They're so bloody scared of losin' their jobs, it's who can suck up the hardest and fastest.'

'What about Fred Ward? He's your shop steward, isn't he?' asked Shane, and for answer Barny turned round and spat into the heart of the fire. 'That's for him,' he said, 'him and his parables, I'll push one down his bloody throat the first chance I get. "You weren't content with tiddlers," he said, "but must try to ram carp into your jam jars." I'd like to carp him, begod! I would.'

'Is that all you got out of him?' Hannah's voice was bitter.

'That's all.'

'Well.' Broderick had loosened his hold on Rosie, and now he looked down at the hearth-rug and swung his head from side to side before saying, 'You couldn't expect the chap to do much more about it, could you now?' Then lifting his eyes to his son, he asked, 'And what did Mr Nicholas say?'

Barny looked away from his father before he answered, 'He said nowt to me, but he told Harry Brown that if the boss hadn't been a fair-minded chap who didn't like trouble we'd have been up in court, every damned one of us.'

'So they were on to it really?' said Arthur.

'What do you think?' Barny replied bitterly. Then squaring his shoulders he added, 'Aw, to hell! It might be the best thing that's happened to me. I've had an idea

134

in me head for some time, and now I'll likely do somethin' about it.'

'What is it?' said Hannah. Then turning to the table again she picked up the ladle, saying, 'You can talk while you eat, there's good food being wasted. Come, sit up all of you.'

When they were all served and Hannah herself had sat down, she looked at Barny and asked, 'Well, now, what's this idea of yours? Spit it out. Unlike me family, I welcome new ideas.'

Barny did not pick up this last remark but said simply, 'It's Leonard's shop, you know round in Brookland Street, just off the market.'

'The electric shop you mean?' said Arthur.

'Aye.' Barny nodded. 'Well, he died about three months ago, and since then his wife's been trying to sell. It would have gone like hot cakes a few years ago but now things are tight. And there's another thing, most people who take on places like that know damn all about the inside of the things they sell, but me being able to make most of me own stuff, well I've always felt if I had the chance I would make a go of it. I know I would.' He turned and looked at Hannah, and Hannah looked at him for a moment before dropping her eyes to her plate and beginning to eat.

'You don't think much of it, Ma?' Barny's voice was nervous, quiet.

'Well, I know nowt about it yet, do I? But a shop. Aw, shops are tricky businesses.'

'But people make good livin's out of them. Look at them in the main thoroughfares with their fifteen hundred pound cars changed every year, and their trips abroad.

Look at the Parnells that started just after the war with that little furniture shop; they're rolling in it now; they've got a chain of over twenty of them.'

'We're far past the war, boy.' Hannah went on eating steadily.

'I think it's an idea.' Broderick wagged his fork towards Barny. 'I do indeed. There's no-one cleverer than you with the innards of wirelesses and televisions.'

Barny smiled at his father. 'It's only a small place, but it's got a good stock. I've been in once or twice lately, just looking round.'

'How much do they want for it?' asked Arthur.

'Well, the shop's on lease.' Barny swallowed. 'The rent's four pounds a week and rates.' Again he swallowed.

'But what will she want for the stock?' said Shane.

'Five hundred pounds.' It was a bald statement.

'Five hundred pounds!' The sound seemed to shoot from the top of Hannah's grey hair.

'It's not a lot really, not to get a start.' Barny's voice was low and his tone slightly on the defensive. 'Anyway, I could raise a bit, I dare say, if it's necessary. How much have I got put by, Ma?'

'How much have you got put by!' Hannah screwed up her eyes at him as if she didn't quite take in the question.

'Aye.' His tone was sharp now. 'How much have you saved for me?'

'Oh that . . . that. Well now, I can't tell you off-hand, I don't reckon it up every day, but I should say on the spur of the moment something between fifty and seventy-five pounds.'

'WHAT!' Barny pushed his chair back from the table and the sound on the linoleum was like a stone rasping glass, and it affected them all. Except perhaps Barny himself, for he was being affected in another way. 'Aw, come off it, Ma. You pulling me leg or summat? I've been in steady work for over three years now and never earned less than fifteen a week, and a damn sight more most of the time.'

'Now look here, look here, me lad.' Hannah, too, had risen from the table, the knife in her hand, and she wagged it at him. 'What was the arrangement, tell me that? Divided in three, we all said. One part for your keep and your working clothes, another for your pocket, and t'other to put by and to buy your good things out of.'

'I know all about that, Ma. But what working clothes have you bought me, I ask you that?'

'Two pairs of dungarees you've had, and the oilskin overalls for your motor-bike.'

'Aw, my God, that's over two years ago, Ma.'

'And then out of your savings as you call them, you've had two suits, fifteen pounds a piece they were, two pairs of shoes to go with them not counting a number of shirts and other odds and ends.'

'All right, all right, Ma.' He was holding himself in check now. 'Say I've had fifty pounds worth of clothes . . .'

'Fifty pounds! Begod, you're a cheap jack. Make it a hundred and you'll be nearer the mark.'

Barny closed his eyes and thumped his forehead with his fist, and still with his eyes closed and his fist to his head, he said, 'All right, say a hundred pounds. Take a hundred pounds off two hundred and fifty and that leaves a hundred and fifty. And that's for only one year. You've been saving for me for three years; I reckoned on four hundred pounds up there.' He thumbed the ceiling. 'Or nearer five.'

'God Almighty and his Holy Mother!' Hannah collapsed with a thud on to the chair. 'Four hundred pounds . . . nearly five!' She appealed from one face to another of her family, but when she looked at Rosie, her daughter had her face turned away. And now with her arms across the table, her hands out-stretched, supplicating, towards them, she asked, 'Who's paid for the fine new furniture we've got, and the carpets that are in every nook and cranny of this house bar this room? And who's paid for the new bedding?'

Barny shouted back at her, 'I know, I know all that, but we've all had to fork out towards them. It wouldn't all come out of mine, would it? . . . Now look here, Ma.' His voice dropped. 'I should have a few hundred up there.'

Rosie, being unable to stand any more, picked up her plate from the table and went into the kitchen, there to see Hughie standing by the stove. It was evident from the look on his face that he had heard a good deal of what had happened in the living-room, also that in the hubbub his entry had gone unnoticed.

As Rosie put her plate on the table she whispered, 'Oh, Hughie!' and the words were laden with shame. At this moment she was not only ashamed of her mother, she felt she disliked her, even hated her. Nearly three thousand pounds in that drawer upstairs, and denying Barny his bit of savings. Surely she couldn't think the

138

lads were so stupid. But apparently she did. She had just to yell and shout and point to what she had bought and she could convince them of where the money had gone.

'Don't let it trouble you,' Hughie was whispering back at her now.

'But, Hughie, she's got it.' She did not feel that she was giving her mother away to him by saying this.

'I know, I know.' One eyebrow moved up. It seemed to tell her that he knew as much as she did.

As Hannah's voice reached a blaring peak, he pushed Rosie gently from the table, saying, 'Go on in, go on.' And she turned quickly from him and did as he bade her. She knew he didn't want her mother to come in and see them together. As she entered the living-room Hannah was again appealing to the family as a whole, crying at them, 'I want the few pounds saved to get us out of this. We can't move up the Hill on goodwill.'

'Who the hell wants to move up the Hill?' Barny was squarely confronting his mother now. 'Here's one who doesn't. I've told you afore I don't want to leave here, and I'm not going to; we've made enough moves up the ladder I think to satisfy you.'

When he stopped speaking there was a quivering, uneasy silence in the room. And then Hannah, her voice now quiet but intense, said, 'Of all the ungrateful sods in this world, I've bred a bunch of them. For years I've slaved the living daylights out of meself, and what for? What for, I ask you? To make you respected, looked up to.' The tone was rising, and as Rosie passed from the room through the hall on her way upstairs the crash of

139

her mother's fist on the table and the sound of the jangling dishes caused her to start and shrink as if from a blow.

Up in her room, she looked at the evidence of her mother's generosity. The two new cases, the two dresses, the shoes and stockings and underwear, not to mention the coat she had worn today. She had spent forty-seven pounds as if they were pennies, and joyed in doing it. Yet there she was downstairs denying Barny his savings, and all because she was determined to have her way and buy the flat on Brampton Hill. There wasn't a doubt in Rosie's mind but that Barny would make a go of a wireless and television shop if he got the chance. But what prestige would there be in such a shop in a back street for her mother? There would be nothing to show off or brag about in that.

There was an easy chair in the room that hadn't been there when she left this morning. Her mother must have humped it up at least two flights of stairs. She sat on the side of her bed and looked at it; evidence of a reasoning she knew now that had sent her eldest brother, Patrick, to Australia, and Colin to Canada, that had made Michael leave a good job here for one in Cornwall at half the wage. The same reasoning that had frustrated Dennis for years and made him bitter, the reasoning that had scorned his intelligence. The reasoning that pointed the finger of sin at Arthur's association with a married woman and which had intimidated him so much that he was really afraid to do what he desired, and go and live with her. The reasoning that was now determined to deprive Barny of making a living in the way he wanted to. The reasoning had not yet touched Shane or Jimmy

140

simply because, as yet, they had made no protest against her. The reasoning that made fiddling almost a virtue every day in the week except Sunday.

Then there was Hughie and Karen. Her mother's reasoning, Rosie thought, had made very little, or no impact, on Karen, for Karen had in her a great deal of Hannah herself. Added to this, she had a sharp intelligence. This advantage had, it was supposed, been inherited from Karen's father, a mysterious figure, who was never mentioned, and who had been known only to Moira.

And Hughie? The one person in the house who had always borne the weight of her mother's spleen, derision and unreasonable reasoning. And in his case one had to ask, Why? Why?

Now and again over the years she had wondered, but just vaguely, about Hughie. Why, for instance, did he stand her mother? Why did he always take a back seat? Why did he scarcely open his mouth in the house? To a stranger in the house he must have appeared like a numbskull. But Hughie was no numbskull. She had always known it, and that had been made evident in the back shop yesterday morning. Look at that piece of writing. Who would think Hughie could work things out like that? Certainly no-one in this house.

What, she thought now, would be her mother's reaction when she learned he had come into money? She could almost feel the bitterness and rage that the irony of the situation would arouse in her at a time when she needed money, real money, to further the ambition of her life, when the last person in the world she could have relied on to further that ambition was now . . . rolling

141

in it. . . . Well, if not rolling in it, he must have come into enough to set him on his feet.

Rosie rubbed her hand up and down her cheek. She only hoped she wasn't in the house when he told her mother. For no matter how she felt about her she wouldn't be able to bear watching her reaping what she had sown.

Tuesday

But Rosie was in the house when, later on Tuesday, Hughie told her mother.

In the lull that followed the exodus of the men to work Hannah was busying herself with the washing-up and tidying of the rooms. When Rosie came downstairs Hannah just bade her good-morning and asked how she had slept. Her manner, tellingly quiet, forbade any questioning at this point, so nothing concerning last night's row or the bottom drawer of the chest was mentioned until sometime later in the morning, when, dressed for outdoors, Rosie went to her and said, 'I'm going into Newcastle, Ma, to have a look round.'

'You're going out in this?' Hannah was in the kitchen hacking at a large shin of beef, and wiping the blood from her hands, she added, 'It's snowing again, lass. I thought you said Wednesday.'

'Oh, there are plenty of other places to try.'

As Rosie went towards the back door Hannah said appealingly, 'Aw, come out the front, come out the front, lass.' As if it made just that difference which way her daughter went out, she led the way into the hall; then, with her hand on the front-door latch, she turned to her and said quietly, 'There's no hurry, you know, lass; there's no hurry. In fact, I don't see why you want to take a job outside at all. You could give me a hand in

143

the house, and we would come to an arrangement.' She nodded knowingly. 'There I am, paying that Mrs Pratt a pound every Friday to do down, and begod, there's never a time I haven't to go behind her after she's gone.'

'Thanks, Ma, but I . . . I couldn't . . . Anyway, I couldn't stay in the house all day. You see, I've been used to going out, and I want to earn my own living.'

Hannah, her face unsmiling now, but her expression disarmingly soft, said, 'You're not holding it against me about last night, are you? You see, I know Barny. Lass, if I'd given him the lot it would've be blued one way or another within a few months. . . . Aw, I know me lads; they haven't got the sense they were born with, not one of them, where money's concerned anywhere. . . . And women. Although I've got nothing to say against Betty.' The inference was against Dennis's wife, and the mercurial change that came over Hannah's face for an instant expressed this fully.

'But, Ma.' Rosie looked straight at Hannah. 'As Barny said, his share must go into a few hun –'

'Now look here!' Hannah was flapping her fingers within a few inches of Rosie's face. The action was annoying in itself, and Rosie moved her head to one side away from their contact as her mother exclaimed again, 'Now look, lass, leave this to me, I know how to deal with me family. Barny won't go short, you needn't worry about that, but he's not going to throw money down the drain. He may be out of work for weeks – he has been afore and I've never thrown it up at him.'

As Rosie turned away she thought, No, but you took every penny of his dole.

144

Opening the door, Hannah said under her breath, 'You understand me, lass, now don't you?'

Rosie nodded, saying, 'Bye-bye, Ma.'

'Bye-bye, lass. . . . But look' – she blinked at the falling snow – 'you can hardly see your hand afore you, you shouldn't be going out in this.'

'I like the snow. I'll be back by tea. Bye-bye.'

'Bye-bye, lass. Bye-bye.'

You understand me, lass, her mother had said. She had thought that the experience she had endured these last few months had stretched her mind so that she could now understand all the intricacies of human behaviour. Badness, she had discovered, was relative. Everything was relative to something else. She understood that now. But even so she couldn't understand her mother. Her mother was too subtle. Yet some would say she was simple because she was ignorant – but her mother wasn't simple.

As Rosie said, she liked snow, but not to wander about in it all day, and not wanting to return home before the others were in, she spent the time during the afternoon in going to see a film. So it was just on six o'clock when she alighted from the bus in the market place. There were a number of men waiting to get on the bus. They weren't queueing orderly but standing in a bunch, and as she made her way through them a hand came out and caught her arm; not roughly, yet the action almost made her scream. In the driving snow and dim light she did not recognise Ronnie for a moment, and when she did she dragged on her breath, filling her lungs with short gulps of air . . . and also with relief, for she had thought . . . she had thought . . .

145

'I'm sorry, Rosie, I . . . I didn't mean to startle you but you didn't see me.'

'It's all right,' she said. And then turning her head towards the bus, she pointed: 'It's going, you'll miss it.'

'It doesn't matter. I'd rather have a word with you.'

She stood silent, waiting, while he looked at her, an undying hunger and ever-present remorse in his look. 'Don't be frightened of me, Rosie,' he said.

'I'm not frightened.' Her voice was soft, reassuring; and she meant what she said, for she wasn't afraid any more of Ronnie. At one time she had thought he was bad, but now she knew there was badness and badness, and if she had been forced to choose between the types of badness she knew she would take Ronnie's kind gratefully. Yet when he went to touch her, her whole body recoiled from him, and he stood, his hand half-outstretched, stiff, as was his voice when he said, 'You're not frightened of me but you're wary. That's it, isn't it? I'm not safe, can't be trusted.'

'Oh, Ronnie.'

'Oh, I don't blame you. But Rosie –' He moved, almost imperceivably, nearer to her. 'I've got to tell you. I . . . I can't get you out of me mind. I can't for one minute. I thought getting married an' that. . . . But it was no use. I'm in a hell of a mess inside, Rosie . . . Rosie, I've got to see you.'

'No, no.' Her voice was harsh, even grating. 'You're married and that's that.' She stepped aside from him. 'I said no, Ronnie, and I don't want any more trouble.'

'Just to see you now and again to have a word . . . ?'

'I said no.' She was some feet from him now. 'I'll be

146

leaving the town shortly, anyway, and I won't be coming back.'

As she watched his head slowly move downwards she darted away and ran across the open market square to where a bus was standing that would take her to the top of their street. She was trembling as she sat down. She was still trembling when the conductor came for her fare. 'Enough to kill a horse, this,' he said. 'It's no wonder there's nobody out. You look froze.'

She said she was. She wished he would leave her and go down the bus; men could always find excuses to talk.

When she entered the house her mother's voice did not greet her tonight, but she heard it coming from the living-room, saying, 'I don't believe a word of it.' She took off her wet things and hung them on the rack behind the kitchen door, and she was stroking her damp hair from her forehead when she entered the living-room.

Only her father addressed her immediately. 'Some night, isn't it, lass? Are you froze? Come to the fire.'

As she made her way to the fire her mother turned from the four men at the table, saying, 'Have you heard anything about this?'

'About what?' asked Rosie.

'About him, Hughie, buying a car and a caravan? Shane here's just come in and told us that he's bought a car and a caravan . . . Hughie. Did you ever hear the like of it?'

'I tell you, Ma,' said Shane, 'it's a fact.' He looked around his brothers now. 'It was as I said, up came Robbie Gallagher and he said, "Your brother" – he thought Hughie was me brother – he said, "Your brother's done well for himself with our Paul's car and

147

caravan." And like I said, I told him he'd made a mistake, and he said, "Your brother keeps a cobbler's shop, doesn't he? And his name is Hughie, isn't it?" "Aye," I said. "Well," he said, "he's bought our Paul's Land-Rover and caravan for five hundred quid. He bought them just two years ago but there was still some to pay off. Your brother saw to that and gave him five hundred for the two. But he's still got a bargain." '

Hannah was looking from one to the other but she wasn't seeing them, 'The swine's been cocky this past few weeks.' She looked at her husband now and asked, 'Does he do the pools?'

'How should I know, woman? I've never been with him this last ten years.'

'Well, does he?' She turned to her sons, and one after the other they shook their heads.

'Not that I know,' said Jimmy. 'I asked him to go in the club syndicate, but he said he hadn't the cash.'

'Five hundred pounds! FIVE HUNDRED POUNDS!' Hannah was blinking. 'And anybody who spends five hundred pounds on a car an' caravan has more than five hundred pounds. It would be just like him to have a win and keep it to himself. . . . But what would he be wanting a car and a caravan for?' She was now addressing Shane.

'Search me, unless he's goin' touring. Aye, likely that's what he's going to do. When I come to think about it, he used to be always sending away for travel catalogues. You remember?' He jerked his head at Jimmy.

Jimmy said, 'Aye. Aye, come to think of it, the back shop used to be full of 'em.'

'Well, if he's had a win,' said Broderick, knocking

148

the dottle from his pipe against the bars of the fire, 'good luck to him. Aye, I say good luck to him. I only hope it will be my turn next. And if it is' – he straightened up and thrust out his hand towards Rosie's chin – 'I'll take me daughter to Paris and we'll do the sights. Begod! We would, wouldn't we, Rosie?'

'Stop talkin' sheelagin, Broderick, for Christ's sake! . . . Now what I'd like to know is where that 'un's got the cash from. And how much. Because . . .'

'Because what?' Broderick was looking at Hannah steadily.

'Never you mind. I'll keep it to meself until I see which way the wind's blowing. In the meantime, sit you all down and get your teas; it will be as cold as clarts in a minute if it isn't already. Oh, lass' – she forced a stiff smile on her face – 'I've left yours in the oven. Would you be goin' gettin' it?'

Rosie went into the kitchen, and as she opened the oven door the back door opened and Hughie entered. With a swift glance towards the other door she went towards him and muttered hastily under her breath, 'They know, Hughie, about the money. Shane heard about the caravan and car.'

Hughie had his cap in his hand and he turned and hung it on the hook on the door next to her coat before looking at her again. His smile was quiet; his whole attitude seemed serene to her, while she herself was feeling strung up and nervous; first from her encounter with Ronnie, and then from the feeling her mother's attitude towards Hughie aroused in her. She went hastily back to the oven and was taking out the plate when again the back door opened, with a thrust this time, which

149

almost knocked Hughie off his feet, and Karen exclaimed as she came in, 'Well, you don't expect me to see through it, do you?' He straightened the sleeve of the coat he was hanging on the door as he said, 'No, I don't.'

Karen was pulling her outdoor things off now, and, looking at Rosie's retreating back, she said, 'It's not a night to linger on the doorstep; it's all right for some people who can stay put all day.'

Rosie hesitated; then glancing quickly over her shoulder said, 'I've just come in.'

'Poor soul! Have you had to battle against the elements an' all? It isn't fair, is it?'

As Rosie went on into the living-room without retorting to this, Karen turned to Hughie staring at her from across the table in a peculiar way, and she asked, 'What you looking at me like that for? I don't happen to be a man so I'm not in love with her. Men are fools . . . formless idiots.' She flounced her body around, but turned it back as swiftly again, saying, 'As for you, you haven't got the gumption you were born with.'

'No, I haven't, have I?'

The admission was disconcerting, and all Karen could say to it was, 'Oh, my God.'

When she entered the living-room, Hannah spoke to her across the room, saying, 'Who is that out there?'

'Hughie, of course. Who else would it be, you're all here?' The sharp, round eyes swept the table, and the voice with which she had answered her grandmother bore no resentment for the blow she had received yesterday. She did not blame Hannah for that. She knew who was to blame.

150

Hannah knew it was Hughie in the kitchen. She had asked a voiceless question of Rosie when she had come back into the room – she had done it with the jerk of her head – and Rosie had answered with a single nod, her eyes downcast.

And when Hughie came in, he came in as he always did, quietly, his whole manner unassuming, not looking towards the table, not looking at anything really.

They were all seated except Hannah. She stood to the side of her chair and she stopped him when he was opposite the fireplace – he was going, as he always did, to bring his chair from the corner to the table. She stopped him by saying, 'Well!'

'Well what?' He was looking straight back at her.

'What's this I'm hearing?'

'I wouldn't know. You don't often tell me any news.'

'Have you or have you not bought a car and a caravan?'

Rosie was looking at Hughie now. She had an odd feeling inside of her, a racing, excited, odd feeling. Whereas yesterday she felt that she wouldn't be able to bear seeing her mother vanquished, now she knew that if Hughie were to come out on top her mother would have to be brought low, and, she wished, oh, she even prayed, that he would show her, show them all what he was really made of, and he could only do that by talking. Oh, if he would only talk as he had talked in the back room of the shop. . . . Talk as he wrote.

And he did. 'Yes, I've bought a caravan and a car.' Hughie looked from Hannah around the staring faces at the table. Jimmy's, Arthur's, Shane's, Barny's, Broderick's, and lastly Karen's. He looked longer at

151

Karen than at the rest; he did not look at Rosie. And then he was staring at Hannah once more.

'Where did you get the money?'

'I came into it.'

'You – came – into it?'

'That's what I said.'

'Was it a win or something, Hughie?' Broderick's good-tempered tone tried to bring a lightness into the proceedings.

'No, it wasn't a win, Broderick.' Hughie was smiling gently down on the elderly man, who alone in this house had ever gone out of his way to show him a kindness. 'It was a legacy, Broderick.'

'A legacy!' Hannah had grabbed at the lead again. Her eyes screwed up, her brows beetling, her chin pulled in to the deep flesh of her neck, she repeated, 'A legacy! Who, in the name of God, have you got to leave you a legacy, I ask you that?'

'I happen to have had a sister. Perhaps you've forgotten about her.'

'Your sister! But she was no better than . . .' Hannah prevented herself from adding, 'meself'; instead she turned it into 'the rest of us. She went to America as a servant if I remember rightly.'

'She went as a nurse-companion if you remember rightly,' corrected Hughie. 'And she was left some money. But unfortunately she didn't live long enough to enjoy it, and before she died she remembered me.'

Hannah, her eyes still on Hughie, groped at the back of her chair. She wanted very much to sit down but she remained standing.

'When did this happen, Hughie?' It was Arthur on his feet now, coming round the table.

'Oh, some weeks ago, around Christmas time. It takes a while for these things to get settled.'

'By! You're a deep 'un.' Shane, too, had risen to his feet. 'An' keepin' this to yourself all the time,' he said.

'How much did she leave you?' It was the first time Barny had spoken.

'A bit over twenty thousand. Round about twenty-four I should say when everything's settled up.' His tone was quiet but self-assured. He spoke of twenty-four thousand as if he was quite used to thinking in thousands.

For a full minute no-one in the room moved or spoke a word. Each of them was digesting this news, and most of them were wondering what was in it for them, if anything. Strangely it was the two girls who were the exceptions. Karen knew she would get nothing out of Hughie's legacy, for there had always been a mutual dislike between them. She had become aware of it as a small child and reciprocated the feeling in full, but, thinking along the lines of her grandmother, she was saying to herself, God, it would be someone like him who would come into money, a mutt who won't know how to enjoy it.

If Rosie was thinking of the money, it was to the effect that it had put power and courage into Hughie. It had also endowed him with a dignity. His back was straighter, his look even bold, he was no longer afraid of her mother, that's if he had ever been afraid of her. But he must have been, because for some reason or other he had always knuckled down to her.

Rosie saw that her mother was utterly flabbergasted,

153

but she also saw that she was determined not to show it.

Sitting herself slowly down, Hannah again took charge of the situation. She jerked her head up towards Hughie and said, 'Well, sit down, and tell us what you're going to do.'

Hughie sat down, after going and picking up his chair and bringing it to the table. No-one had said, 'Stay where you are, I'll get it for you.' As much as they would have liked to they hadn't the face to do that, it would look too much like sucking up.

Hughie sat down opposite to Jimmy and Karen. Jimmy's expression was eager, bright. He looked as if he wanted to say something but was withholding it with difficulty. Karen still looked surly. She had the intelligence to know when it was fruitless to beat a dead horse. Shane and Arthur had sat down again, and now they were all around the table like a family. Again Hannah said, 'Well?'

Hughie moved his knife and fork to one side and surveyed them for a moment before looking along the table towards Hannah. 'You want to know what I'm going to do, is that it?' He stared at her while waiting some response from her; but receiving none, he went on, 'As soon as the caravan's ready – I'm having it all rebuilt inside. Jim Cullen's doing it for me.' He turned his head now and addressed himself to Broderick. 'He's a good craftsman, as you know.'

'Oh, you'll get a good job out of old Jim,' said Broderick, nodding his head quickly. 'He's a grand fellow when dealing with wood; you'll get a good job out of him.'

154

'I know that, Broderick.' Hughie turned his gaze slowly back to Hannah again and unhurriedly went on, 'Well, when it's ready, and it should be towards Monday of next week, I'm starting on my travels; that's if the weather allows. Anyway, I'm going to make for the Continent and just jog along where the fancy takes me. . . . That's all.'

They had all been looking at him; now they were all looking at Hannah, their eyes brought to her by the sound of her strong short teeth grinding over each other. They watched the invective rise in her and fill her mouth, and they watched her check it and select words which had to be pressed through her lips to ask him, 'How much are you going to leave behind you?'

'How much? Nothing, not a penny.'

'Ma. . . . Ma, go easy, go easy; give the fellow a chance.' Barny had put his hand across the table towards Hughie, and he brought Hughie's attention away from his mother, saying quickly, 'I'm not asking you for anything, Hughie, but I could do with a loan. Is there any chance? I want to start a shop.'

Hughie's eyes held a kindly expression as they looked back at Barny, but he shook his head twice before he spoke. 'No, Barny, not a chance. But you could still start your shop. Your mother has around four hundred and seventy-five pounds of yours upstairs.'

Barny's hand lifted from the table; his face jerked towards his mother as she jumped to her feet. Then he looked again at Hughie; and Hughie finished evenly, 'I've had nothing much to do these last few years when I was in the house but count up. About four hundred and seventy-five I should say, Barny, would be your share.'

155

'You dirty sod!' Hannah picked up a knife from the table, and as her arm swung up Jimmy gripped it, crying, 'Here! Steady on. Steady on, Ma.'

'Put the knife down, woman!' Broderick was standing before her. 'Have you gone out of your senses?'

'I'll kill him! I'll kill him! The ungrateful sod that he is. And what money he's got belongs here, for haven't I looked after his offspring for years? He owes me a share of that money, he killed me daughter.'

'Stop it, woman! An' don't talk wild. Stop it! Do you hear me?'

With a jerk of her elbow, Hannah thrust Broderick aside, and because Jimmy was still holding one arm she leant crookedly over the table towards Hughie, crying. 'Do you want me to tell 'em? They'll murder you.'

'Yes, tell them.' Hughie slowly rose from the table; his face had lost it taunting expression. 'You tell them your side of the story and I'll tell them mine, and let them judge. If I hadn't been such a blasted fool that's what I'd have done years ago, and you would have had one less to suck dry then. Go on, tell them. Or will I do it without the hysterics?'

'You rat, you! You bloody mealy-mouthed rat, you!' There was froth gathering at the corner of Hannah's mouth. She turned her furious face now towards Broderick, then flashed her eyes towards her sons, and with her free arm she pointed dramatically at Hughie and cried, 'he raped me daughter, Moira, and she died with his child . . . her there!' She was pointing at Karen.

Again a silence came upon the room, and it would have been broken long before it was if the contortion of features had made any sound, for the faces of the men were twisting with amazement. They looked from their mother to Hughie, then to Karen, and then back to their mother. And it was Jimmy – big, thoughtless Jimmy – who spoke first. 'But, Ma,' he said, his face a mass of bewilderment, 'Moira was eleven years older than me; she was a woman when Hughie was a lad.'

'There you have spoken my defence, Jimmy.' Hughie motioned his head towards the big, puzzled man. 'I was fourteen, not quite fifteen, when I, as your mother put it, raped her eldest daughter. And into the bargain I was a thin, puny lad, as was pointed out to me practically every day, and was always ailing. Moira was twelve stone if an ounce. She came up into the room one night and ate me alive. Granted there was a raping, but I had very little share in it; yet there were results.' He dropped his eyes now to where Karen was staring at him, her full-lipped mouth agape. 'We've never liked each other, Karen,' he said sadly. 'It's a pity. I suppose it was my fault because I blamed you. I was held like any prisoner because of you, and also because' – he smiled wryly now – 'I hadn't, as you said a few minutes ago, any gumption. But whatever gumption I was born with and retained until I was fourteen, she kicked out of me.' He lifted his eyes again to Hannah; then they flicked to Broderick, where the old man stood, his hand to his brow, exclaiming over and over, 'God Almighty! God Almighty!'

'I'm sorry, Broderick, I'm sorry. I wouldn't have had you hurt for the world.'

Hannah gazed around her family in nothing less than blazing amazement. Their reactions were maddening her still further, and she cried at them, 'Well, what are you goin' to do? Standin' there like stuffed dummies!' She tried to pull herself from Jimmy's hold, but he held her fast and shook his head at her. 'Leave go, will you!' She was lifting her other hand, the fist doubled at him, when Broderick spoke to her, calmly, deadly. 'Enough woman, enough,' he said. 'I think whatever Hughie did he's had to pay for.'

'My God!' The words were deep and guttural, as if they were issuing from the throat of a bass singer. At the moment she was seeing no-one but her husband. 'You would turn against me in this. I've carried the load for years, on me own shoulders I've carried this load and you would –'

'I've said be quiet. For your own good, be quiet!' Broderick now turned to Hughie, and his voice still low, he said, 'We want none of your money, Hughie. . . .'

'I know that, Broderick, at least I know you don't. And I wouldn't see you short, only I know you'd never keep it for yourself.'

'What about her? He owes her something.' Hannah was spitting the words out like grit as she pointed to Karen, and Karen snapped her fascinated gaze from Hughie's face, the man who had become her father, and looked at her grannie. A moment ago she had wanted nothing from Hughie because then she thought she stood no chance, but now things were different, she had a claim on him. And when she looked back at him her expression showed this claim and he read it. And he answered it, but looking again at Hannah. 'Not a farthing, not a brass farthing,' he said. 'I paid you for her keep from the day she was born until she started to work. Many's the time I could only meet me board, but you wanted that two

158

pounds for her or else. . . . Yes' – he nodded towards the staring faces that surrounded him – 'two pounds a week I had to pay. Do you wonder now that she had me brought back twice? My wage was four pounds five.' He glanced at Broderick. 'And as the years went on, many a time you had a job to find that, hadn't you, Broderick? But it all went back into the kitty, two pounds for me keep and two pounds for Karen. . . . And you took it, didn't you, Hannah?' His eyes were on her furious face again. 'And let me go around with hardly a rag on me back; and this too' – he nodded at her – 'whilst these last few years the lads were being decked out like lords. Nor did you spare me when Karen started work either. No, I had to pay for the goodwill of the shop then, if I wanted to keep it on, you said. So you had four pounds a week from me.'

'Then why the hell did you put up with it? It's your own fault and it's no use yarping on now.' It was Arthur speaking, and Hughie turned towards him and nodded at him before he said, 'I'm not yarping, Arthur, I'm opening me mouth for the first time in me life in this house. And why did I put up with it? Well, as I said, I hadn't any guts. Time and time again she threatened to tell you all and set you on to me. And' – his lips went into a twisted smile – 'you were all big lads, the lot of you, and somehow I didn't fancy seeing meself battered to death. But there was another reason, a reason none of you would understand because you had what I wanted, what I needed, a family, somebody belonging to you. . . . Well now, I think everything's been said that need be said, so I'll be leaving you . . . I'll . . . I'll just get me things and then . . .'

159

'Begod! you won't. You won't take a stick out of this house; that's somethin' I can stop you doin'.'

'Oh, very well.' He smiled at her. 'You're welcome to what there is.'

Except for Rosie and Karen, they were all on their feet. Rosie had her hands joined together on the table. The knuckles were showing white and she had her eyes fixed on them.

But now Karen rose from her chair and her movement stopped Hughie from turning about. She was going to speak to him, and he waited, looking at her quietly, even gently, waiting to hear what she had to say. And what she said was, 'I never liked you afore, and I like you less now, and you can keep your money and stick it. I hope it does you some good. You said you had no gumption and you're right, you're gutless. I've often wondered who me father was. But you! You'd be the last man in the world I'd pick for a father. So now you have it.'

'Thank you.' He moved his head as he spoke. 'Over the years I've been glad there was little of me in you, but on the other hand, I was sorry there was so much of your grannie in you.'

On this last shaft, Hughie turned, and amid a moment's silence walked across the room towards the kitchen door, but as he opened it a glass dish, accompanied by the concerted cries of protest from behind him, caught him on the back of the head and sent him flying, covering him at the same time with sliced peaches.

Hannah, with all the power of her big body concentrated in her right hand, had grabbed the thing nearest to her, a heavy glass fruit dish, and she had flung it like

160

a disc, and it had held most of its contents until it reached its object.

Rosie was the first one to reach Hughie. He hadn't fallen but had staggered back against the door. Then her father and Arthur were on either side of him. 'Are you all right, lad?' shouted Broderick above the screaming voice of Hannah and the cries of Jimmy, Shane and Barny, as they restrained her from sending the other articles on the table in the same direction as the glass dish.

Hughie looked dazed. Slowly he flicked a peach from off the lapel of his coat; then pushing his hand out in an assuring gesture towards Broderick, he nodded before going into the kitchen.

'Are you fit enough to go?' Broderick closed the kitchen door behind him as he asked the question.

And Hughie said, 'Yes, I'm all right.'

'Go with him, Arthur,' said Broderick.

Arthur did not speak and Hughie said, 'No. No, thanks, Arthur. I'm all right. I'd rather be on my own. It's nothing.'

'You're bleeding behind the ear, Hughie.' Rosie's voice was full of sympathy.

'Am I?' He still seemed dazed, and when he put his fingers to his neck, then looked at the blood on them, he said, 'Oh, it isn't much.'

She took a tea-towel and wiped the syrup from his jacket, then she held his top coat and he got into it, and as he buttoned it slowly he said, 'Thanks, Rosie, thanks.' And looking at Broderick, he added, 'I'm sorry, Broderick. I shouldn't have done it like this. I'm sorry.'

'I'm sorry too, lad, but it's done. An' you wouldn't

161

have been human not to have hit back. I understand, I understand. But go now, if you're able to.'

Hughie lowered his head, then pulled on his cap and, turning about, went out of the back door.

When he was gone Broderick looked from Arthur to Rosie and said, 'Who'd have believed it? God Almighty, who'd have believed it? Him, Karen's father an' I never knew! All these years livin' with her and I never knew.' He shook his head.

He looked at Rosie now. 'Your mother's a strange woman, lass, a strange woman. She's got power in her that's too big for her body.' Still shaking his head, he turned from her and went towards the room door, and as he opened it the sound of her mother's crying came to Rosie.

Arthur, standing near her, waited until his father had closed the door, then turning to her, he said under his breath, 'This has been an eye-opener for all of us, I'd say. But it's learnt me one thing; she's not going to keep me fastened the same way she did him. You don't blame me, do you?'

Rosie didn't answer his question but whispered back, her voice shaking, 'I think you'd better go after him, he looked dazed, he might collapse in the street, and there'll be few people about tonight.'

Arthur shook his head. 'He won't take it that way, not kindly, he'll think I'm sucking up, an' I don't want any of his bloody money. Not that I don't think he's a mean swine to go off like that. He could have given us all a night at the club to show there was no ill-feeling, that wouldn't have hurt him. No, I'm not goin' after him.' On this, he too went into the living-room, leaving Rosie

162

alone in the kitchen. For a moment or two she stood
nipping rapidly at the ends of her fingers, then she pulled
her coat off the peg and got quickly into it, and wrapping
one of the men's mufflers round her head, she opened
the back door quietly and ran, slithering, down the
garden path and into the back lane, then along its length
and round the corner and into the street. The knowledge
that Hughie would likely make for the shop took her in
that direction, and she came upon him walking like
someone slightly drunk as he crossed the road towards
the school.

Gasping for breath from running and the cold snow-
filled air, she caught at his arm, saying, 'Hughie, Hughie,
are you all right?'

He stopped for a moment in the middle of the road.
Then as the headlights of a car approached he moved
forward to the opposite pavement, and there he stopped
again, peering at her through the dim light. 'You
shouldn't have come out a night like this,' he said. 'Go
on back, I'm all right.'

'You're neck's all blood.'

'I'll . . . I'll soon see to that . . . there'll only be trouble
for you. I've caused enough the night.'

'Are you going to the shop?' she said.

'Yes.'

'Why don't you go to Dennis's. Florence will see to
you; you're all shaken up.'

'I'll be all right when I get to the shop. Go on now.
. . . ' He went to push her away but his hand didn't touch
her, it groped at the air as he swayed; and she caught
at his arm and steadied him, then said firmly, 'Come
on.'

163

'No, no, Rosie.' He still protested weakly, until she moved him forward. Then he became quiet and they spoke no more during the journey, except once as they were going up the hill towards the shop, when he said to her, 'Can you stop a moment, Rosie, I'm out of breath?'

When they reached the shop he gave her the key and she opened the door; in the back room he dropped down into a chair and, putting his head on his folded arms on the desk, muttered, 'There's some whisky in the cupboard beneath here, Rosie.'

She had to move his legs before she could get at the bottle. She poured him out a good measure, but had to hold the cup while he drank it. Then she lit the oil stove and put the kettle on the gas-ring; and when she turned to him again he was attempting to lift the seat of the chair.

'The foot comes out and makes a sort of bed,' he said; 'I'd feel better if I could lie back.'

'Let me do it.' When she had fixed the chair and he was lying on it he smiled at her faintly and said, 'That's better. It'll pass in a minute, I just feel dizzy.'

As she stood looking down into his grey face she murmured, 'She could have killed you.'

'I'll take a lot of killing.' Again he smiled, but kept his eyes closed.

When the water was hot she bathed his neck. The cut was just behind his ear and about half an inch long.

'You should have a doctor, Hughie it's quite open.'

'Just put a bit of sticking plaster on, there's some in that drawer.' He pointed.

When she had done so, he said, 'Thanks . . . thanks,

Rosie. . . . I'm all right now; you'd better get home.
She'll only go for you if she –'

'I don't care.' She had her back to him now, speaking
from the sink. 'I don't care what she says. . . . I'm getting
out as quick as possible. I'll know tomorrow if I'm to
have this job and then I'll get myself a room. I couldn't
stay there, not after tonight I couldn't.'

'Rosie.'

When she came to his side, he had his eyes closed
again, but his face was turned up to her as he said, 'I
can think what I like and say what I like about her
because she's not my mother, but she's yours and she's
been good to you; she . . . she thinks the sun shines out
of you.'

'I know, I know.' She turned quickly about and
walked the short distance to the oil stove and back before
she continued, 'That's what nearly drives me mad. She
steals from the others . . . because that's what it amounts
to, and then gives it to me with both hands. It frightens
me. It always has, but more so since I came back this
time. I've got to get away from her. I was in a hole . . .
I was near my wits' end or I wouldn't have come back
this time, but now I know I must get away and stay
away.'

'Yes, I know, I know, you've got to get away or she'll
eat you alive. People like her can. All their emotions
have power, their hate equally as much as their love.
Were you . . . were you shocked at what you learned
the night, Rosie?'

'Shocked?' She gave a 'Huh!' of a laugh, as she
looked down at him. 'Shocked at that? No, Hughie.
Surprised, yes, because she's not like you; Karen, I

165

mean, not any part of her. We've never got on as you know, and if there'd been anything of you in her we would have.' She smiled weakly at him; then bit on her lip before she ended, 'She must have put you through the mill all these years . . . me mother.'

'It was my own fault entirely. I should have up and gone. When I got older I mean, but in the beginning she scared me to death, she seemed to melt the spine in me. I suppose before I die I'll forgive her many things, all, I think, with the exception of one.' He opened his eyes with an effort and said, 'She made me afraid of women, Rosie.'

'Aw, Hughie.' She was gazing down at him with pity and compassion in her face and her voice fell on him softly as she said, 'There plenty of time. What are you, thirty-five? You'll meet some nice woman, and she'll be lucky, very lucky. I could tell her that. Because you know' – she shook her head at him – 'you're quite attractive. Oh, you don't need looks to be attractive, you've got something in your make-up. And then . . . then you're kind, Hughie, besides.'

He opened his eyes wide now as he stared into her face, then his lids drooping once more, he said, 'You're a great comfort, Rosie.' He remained quiet after this for a few minutes, and when he next spoke his voice was a faint whisper. 'Rosie,' he said, 'I feel I'm going to pass out,' and before she could touch him he had fainted.

Two hours later Hughie was comfortably at rest on the studio couch in Dennis's sitting-room. The doctor had been and proclaimed that he had slight concussion, nothing serious, nothing that a couple of days' rest wouldn't cure. He had given him some tablets that made him drowsy, so he did not notice Rosie's departure.

She stood in the little cramped kitchen of the flat, opposite to Florence and Dennis. They were waiting for the sound of the taxi, and looking at his watch, Dennis said, 'He's late, but he'll come. If he got here once he'll come again.' He smiled at Rosie. 'It's a good job you made the arrangements without asking him' – and he nodded towards the main room – 'else he would have slept there all night and you never know what the result might have been.'

'He scared me. I thought he was dead . . . I thought all kinds of things.'

'It isn't her fault that he isn't dead, is it? By!' – Dennis moved his head from shoulder to shoulder – 'that woman will do something one of these days that'll put paid to her. I know it, I've always felt it.'

'What will you say when you get back, Rosie?' Florence spoke in a clear, precise way.

'If she asks I'll tell her.'

'You can be sure she'll ask all right.'

'Yes, she'll ask all right.'

'Do you want me to come back with you?' Dennis was bending towards her, but Rosie shook her head. 'No. After tonight I'll tell her what I think . . . I mean if she goes too far. But I want to get away without any trouble.'

'I wish we had another room,' said Florence.

'Thanks, Florence, but . . . well, you know what would happen if I were to come here.'

'We won't go into it,' said Dennis, pursing his mouth and looking down at his lips. 'We just won't go into that.'

'There's the car now,' said Florence. And as she opened the door she turned to Rosie and added, 'Come over tomorrow, you'll want to see how Hughie is anyway.'

'I'll try, but if I don't come you'll understand.'

'Goodbye, Rosie.'

'Goodbye, Florence.'

Before Dennis closed the taxi door on her he said under his breath, 'I would have given a month's pay to have heard Hughie drop his bombshell.'

'It was worth hearing.'

'I bet it was. Goodbye, Rosie. Keep your pecker up.'

But the taxi hadn't been moving for a matter of seconds before she thought, 'It's unnatural, we're both glorying in her humiliation. In Dennis's case it's understandable, but not in mine. I was glad to have her to come home to last Friday. Yet I can't help feeling against her, I can't.'

She got out of the taxi at the top end of the street and went down the back lane and up the garden and let herself quietly into the kitchen, but quiet as she was Broderick came hurrying out of the living-room before she had her coat off. 'Where've you been?' he said.

'I went after Hughie. And it's as well I did, he passed out. He had to have a doctor, he's got concussion.'

Her father moved nearer to her. 'Bad?' he asked anxiously.

The self-condemnation that she had felt in the taxi had vanished on entering the house and the nearer proximity to her mother. She wished at the moment that the news of Hughie was such as would worry her mother – that is if she was capable of feeling remorse for

168

anything she did – and she had the desire to pile it on, but she could not distress her father. 'He just needs a few days' rest, the doctor says. But it could have been serious. He had to stitch it.'

'Where is he now?'

'At Dennis's.'

'Oh, dear God, that'll cause more trouble.' He turned his head towards the living-room, adding in a low voice, 'Your ma's gone up to bed.'

Rosie drew in a long breath. The words were like a reprieve, and her relief was not lost on Broderick. His voice muttering now, he said, 'In the mornin', when she's more herself, she'll want to talk. Be kind to her, gentle, for she's suffered a bad blow this night. No matter how things look to you or anybody else she's suffered a bad blow.'

There were many replies that Rosie could have given to this, such as: She's asked for it. She's treated him like a dog for years. The blow she's suffering from is the awful truth that the despised Hughie could have lifted her wholesale into number eight Brampton Hill. But she said none of these things for she did not want to hurt him.

'Will I make you a hot drink?' he said.

'No, Da, thanks; I had something at Dennis's. I'll go to bed now if you don't mind.'

'Away with you then, lass, and get a good night's rest. The morrow, things'll look different. It's a new day, the morrow. . . . Forget and forgive. And what you never had, you never miss. That's what I say.'

Her father's philosophy held no comfort; he was just using platitudes that had been stuffed into his ears from

169

birth, and which he selected to fit certain situations. He didn't believe in anything he said, but he had to say something.

Rosie went quietly up the stairs, but as she crossed the landing her eyes were drawn to her mother's bedroom door. It was half open and Hannah's voice came clearly to her. It was as if she was talking to herself, but Rosie knew that her mother never wasted words on herself. She was saying, 'Them that aren't with me are against me. You can cut your heart out and serve it on a plate and still some folks wouldn't be satisfied.' There were more words in the same vein but fainter now, and the reproaches followed her up to the attic. Even when she closed the door and she could no longer hear her mother's voice, Hannah's power weighed on her, seeming to press her shoulders forward, making her want to double her body up.

There was no bottle in her bed tonight, nor the oil stove warming the room. As she stood shivering inside and out, she said to herself, 'You've got to get away; you mustn't wait till next week, for if she goes too far with you, you might even tell her the truth, and then what will happen? If she thinks what Hughie's done is bad, then what you've done will bring her to murder.'

Wednesday

In the morning Rosie escaped from the house early, leaving Hannah surly and beetle-browed. Not a single word had passed between them. Hannah needed time to come round after the shock of last night, on top of which there was the open defection of her daughter.

Rosie had no idea what she was going to do with herself until the afternoon when she would go for interview at the factory, and it was more to occupy her time that she called at another agency in Newcastle and was given the name of a firm of wholesalers who had just phoned in, requesting a shorthand-typist.

Within half an hour she was in an office above a warehouse demonstrating her skill to a fatherly man who smelt of bacon and nutmeg. He seemed very pleased with the letter that she had taken down from his dictation, and then he went on to explain why they needed someone in a hurry. It appeared that his secretary, whose name was Miss Pointer and whose age was forty-five, had run off with the storekeeper, a man with a wife and three grown-up daughters. 'The older they are the dafter they get,' he said to Rosie; and ended, 'The silly old trout!'

In spite of his bald description of his late secretary, Rosie felt she would like working for this man. What was more, she would be working on her own, with no-one to boss her except the boss. When he asked her how soon she could start and she replied, 'Now if you like,' he slapped her on the back, saying, 'You're a lass after me own heart. Get at it. There's three days' work piled up there.' He pointed to the desk. 'I gave her three days to find out her mistake, but apparently it's not long enough, and the work can't wait. Our business depends on letters.'

'You'll want my reference,' said Rosie.

'Aye, I suppose I will,' he said.

'I'll give you the address of the London firm.' As she wrote the address he laughed as he asked, 'Will they give you a good one, do you think?' and she laughed back at him as she replied, 'I've no fear of that.' And she hadn't.

So Rosie started her new job at eleven o'clock on Wednesday morning, and when she left at quarter-past five in the evening her new boss, looking at the pile of letters ready for the post, nodded his head and said, 'You'll do.'

She felt better, not happy or elated, just a little better.

When she arrived home the tea was over and there was no place set for her. Her mother must have cleared away almost before the men were finished, and she imagined she could hear her saying, 'Well, I'm the kind of woman who, if met halfway across the river will carry you over the other half on me shoulders.'

Hannah, bustling about the living-room, neither spoke nor looked at her, but kept her broad back turned towards her all the time.

It was Broderick, whose face wore a troubled look

172

tonight, who tried to put things on a normal footing. 'Well, lass, had a nice day?' he asked her.

Rosie went to the fire and held out her hands. 'In a way, Da,' she said.

'What you been doin' with yourself?'

'Working. I've got a job.' She smiled down at him.

'Begod, you have?' He screwed himself to the edge of his chair.

'Where? In that factory? What doin'?'

Rosie was conscious that her mother had stopped her bustling and had turned towards her as she answered, 'My own kind of work. Shorthand-typist, but not in the factory. It's in a wholesale firm, just a small place. I'm the only one.'

'I'm glad for you.' Her mother's voice, coming soft and controlled from behind her, forced her about. Hannah was smiling at her, the old apologetic look on her face. 'I'll get you some tea, lass,' she said. 'I didn't know.'

When Hannah walked quietly from the room to the kitchen, Broderick put his arm around Rosie's waist and shook his head as he whispered, 'She's been through hell the day. She . . . she had the idea you were along of Hughie. . . . You haven't seen him?'

'I've been wondering how he is all day. It frightened me last night, that concussion business.'

'I'll slip over to Dennis's after tea and find out.' She was whispering, and he whispered back, 'No, no, I wouldn't do that if I was you. Things are quietenin' down; let them simmer, there's a good girl, let them simmer.'

'Tell me about it. Where is it? I mean, where in

173

Newcastle is it?' Hannah was coming into the room, talking now as if there had been no interlude between yesterday morning and tea-time tonight.

And Rosie told her where the warehouse was, what it was like inside and the type of work she was expected to do. And all the while Hannah fussed around the table, handing bread, pouring tea, pushing a tart to her hand; cutting a pie and placing a fish slice under a portion of it ready to be lifted.

Then, 'What's his name?' she asked.

'Bunting,' said Rosie.

'Oh, Bunting. It's a plain name. Is it young or old he is?'

'About sixty I should say, and he's got a slight cast in his eye.'

At this Broderick let out a bellow of a laugh and cried at Hannah, 'Are you satisfied, eh? Are you satisfied?'

'I just wanted to get a picture of him in me mind,' said Hannah, 'that's all.'

'That's all,' said Broderick. 'That's all.' And he laughed again.

When Rosie had finished her tea she sat by the fire for a few minutes before she remarked in an off-hand manner, 'I think I'll go to the pictures, I haven't been for ages.'

Hannah looked sharply at her averted face, and her eyes narrowed for an instant before she exclaimed, 'Why! Those are the very words Arthur said, just afore he went upstairs. He said he thought he'd go to the pictures. I'll call him an' you can go along together.' She was out of the room before Rosie could protest, calling, 'Arthur! Arthur! Are you up there still?' And

174

when Arthur's voice came to her, she called back, 'Rosie's goin' to the pictures an' all; you can go along with her.'

She came back into the room, saying, 'Go an' get yourself ready, go on now, a night out'll do you good.'

As Rosie went out of the room she knew that her father had grown quiet and was looking into the fire, and she knew also that Arthur would be cursing her upstairs. She met him on the landing coming along the little passage from the end room, his face glum, the corners of his mouth drooping, and she said to him aloud, 'I won't be a minute. Well, not more than five,' but she accompanied this with a wagging of her head and a shaking of her finger, and the action drew the lines from his mouth and brought his head nodding at her.

Upstairs she powdered her face and combed her hair and put on an extra jumper beneath her coat. Altogether it didn't take her five minutes, and then she was down in the living-room and her mother was spreading her smile over her and Arthur. It was like a blessing. 'Where you goin'?' she asked them.

'Oh, likely the Plaza, Alec Guinness is on there. He's always good for a laugh. What about it?' He looked at Rosie.

'Suit me. Yes, I'd like that. I like him.'

As she let them out Hannah said, 'I'll likely be in bed when you get back, but enjoy yourselves.'

Yes, yes, they said, they would enjoy themselves.

When they reached the street they walked in an embarrassed silence for some minutes, before Rosie asked, 'You weren't going to the pictures, were you, Arthur?'

'No. Were you?'

'No. I was going to see how Hughie was.'

Arthur didn't say where he was bound for, he didn't have to, but he did say, 'Well, it isn't much out of my way, I'll look in on Hughie with you. But afore we get that far we'd better call at the Plaza and see the times of the pictures. You never know, she might start cross-examinin' us the morrow night. We'll get a good idea from the stills what it's all about.'

They examined the stills at the Plaza, and in the bus ride towards the outskirts of the town Arthur brought laughter to Rosie in giving her his version of the sequence of the story. Later, as they neared Dennis's flat, he suddenly exclaimed, 'Look, Rosie, I won't come in now; if I do I'll likely get stuck. You know what it is when we start talkin' and especially if last night comes up. So I'll go straight on, but I'll come and pick you up, say . . . about ten?'

'All right,' she said. 'About ten.'

'So long then.'

'So long, Arthur.'

Dennis's flat, Rosie had always considered, was bare when compared with her own home, and she never visited it, or her brother and his wife, without a sense of embarrassment. Her mother had at one time made her believe that Dennis was estranged from his family solely because of his wife, who was nothing but an upstart and a nagger. But the opposite was the truth, for on her previous visits, embarrassed as she was, she had sensed an odd something between them that she wasn't able to define. It wasn't until her return home last year that she realised that what had puzzled her between this husband

176

and wife was a sort of friendship. She had never thought of friendship between a married couple. Girls of her acquaintance had married and for the first few months the husband and wife were seen about together, then the pattern changed. The man went back to his nights at the local club, and his Saturday afternoons at the football match, and if they were fortunate enough to possess a car they went out on a Sunday, very often accompanied by one set of parents. But that wasn't Dennis's or Florence's pattern. They had always gone everywhere together, even to the football match. And Dennis didn't belong to any club. Yet they argued, even violently at times. One ordinary word would start a discussion between them which often led to an argument but it nearly always finished with them laughing at each other and saying, 'Well, we'll work this out later.' Before she had first left Fellburn for London, Rosie considered that Dennis and Florence were a funny couple. But now, as she entered their uncluttered sitting-room, she knew that she envied her brother and his wife their way of life, and that she was jealous of Florence, not because she was the wife of her brother, or that she was happy, but because what had happened to herself would never, or could never have happened, to Florence. Florence would have used her mind and it would have guided her heart, whereas the power of her own mind became non-existent where her feelings were concerned.

'Oh, I'm glad you've come, Rosie.' Florence was leading the way into the room. 'Hughie wondered if you would make it.'

'Is he any better?'

'Yes. Here's Rosie, Hughie.'

She went slowly towards him. 'Hello, Hughie.'

'Hello, Rosie.'

'How are you feeling?' She was standing over him, where he lay propped up on the couch.

'I've never felt so good before. This is the life.' He patted the back of the couch. 'Talk about being pampered. I'm going to make something out of this, I'm going to make it last as long as I can.' He nodded up at her, then turned his smile towards Florence.

'Look, take your things off and settle down.' Florence pushed a chair forward towards the couch, and as she did so Hughie said to Rosie, 'How long can you stay?'

'How long?' She glanced quickly back at Florence. 'All the evening if you don't mind. Arthur's picking me up about ten.' She looked back at Hughie; then down at her hands as she admitted, 'We're supposed to be at the pictures guarding one another.'

A ripple of laughter passed between the three of them, then Hughie said, 'Good. Now get yourself away, Florence. There's a do on at the school' – he looked at Rosie, explaining, 'Florence's got the idea in her head that I mustn't be left alone, and I don't want to be.' He smiled over Rosie's shoulder. 'But now you can go in peace, go on.'

'All right, then, I will.' Florence protested no further. 'We'll be back before you go, Rosie.'

Dennis's voice now came from the hall, calling, 'Is that you, Rosie?' The next moment he appeared in the doorway, naked to the waist, rubbing his head with a towel.

'Hello, Dennis.'

'You made it?'

'Yes, I made it.'

'I'm coming with you; Rosie's going to stay until we get back,' said Florence.

'Good.' Dennis flicked the towel towards his wife. Then turning to Rosie again, added, 'This problem of baby-sitting is difficult . . . and if you do well tonight we'll book you for later on.'

'Go on, get yourself ready.' Florence was pushing him into the hall.

When the door closed behind them Hughie looked at Rosie and asked quietly, 'How's things?'

'Oh, very subdued, Hughie.'

'How about last night when you got back? I was worried. . . . At least I was worried today, last night seems very hazy to me now. There's a blank between when I left the kitchen and when I woke up here on the couch. The only thing I seem to remember is that you were with me all the time, and then this morning when my head cleared . . . well, I wondered what happened when you got back.'

'It was all right, she was in bed.'

'And she didn't say anything to you at all?' He seemed surprised.

'Well, just a parable.' She smiled faintly at him. 'The bedroom door was open and it was thrown at me as I passed.'

'Just a parable?' he shook his head as if in disbelief.

Dennis came into the room now, putting on his tie, and looking at Rosie, asked, 'Well, what have you been doing with yourself all day?'

'Working.'

'Working!'

179

'I've got a job.'

'What, already? Where?'

'At a little wholesale place called Bunting's in New-castle. I think I'm going to like it.'

'Well, well, you haven't lost much time. . . . What do you think of that, Hughie?'

Hughie jerked his head to the side but he said nothing.

Florence now came into the room fastening up her dress at the back. 'Do this top button for me, Dennis, will you?' She turned her back to him.

'What do you think? Rosie's got a job already.'

'You have?' Florence screwed her head round.

'In her own line too.'

'Oh, I'm glad. Where is it, Rosie?'

'In Newcastle.'

'Are you going to travel or get digs?'

'I'm going to get a room.'

'Have you told her?' asked Dennis.

'About the job, not about getting a room.'

'Coo!' Dennis closed his eyes. 'I would get yourself built up before you spring that one. . . . Well' – he put his hand on Florence's arm – 'if we want to get there in time we'll have to be off. Be seeing you.' He nodded towards Hughie and Rosie.

As Florence was hustled towards the door she called over her shoulder, 'Make some coffee, Rosie. And there's plenty to eat in the pantry.'

For some minutes after the front door closed they sat without speaking, until the silence made itself felt and Rosie said, 'Do you think you'll be able to go on Monday, Hughie?'

'Oh, aye. Yes, I'll be quite fit by then. I should be all

180

right by Saturday. The doctor said two or three days.'

'Did he . . . the doctor ask how it happened?'

'Yes, an' I told him some bairns threw a snowball with a brick in it.' He laughed weakly.

'Oh, Hughie.'

'Well I couldn't say I was walloped with a dish of peaches, could I?' He was aiming now to make her laugh, but didn't succeed.

She said quietly, 'I'm going to miss you when you're gone. I . . . I seem to have got to know you more these last few days than during all the years we lived together. . . . Funny, isn't it?'

'Aye, it's funny, but it wasn't my fault that we didn't know each other better.' He lay back against the head of the couch and stared towards the low ceiling as he said, 'I once bought you a birthday present. You were sixteen. It was a bunch of anemones. They were all colours and very bonny, and I had them in me hand when she came into the kitchen. She didn't ask who they were for, she knew, an' she took a big gully and sliced the heads off them as clean as a whistle, there in me hands.'

'Oh, Hughie.' She lowered her head.

'Oh, I suppose she was right. I suppose in her way she was right. To her mind I had raped her eldest daughter and she was making sure it wasn't going to happen with her youngest.'

'Oh, don't say that.' She screwed up her face at him. 'It sounds awful . . . you would never have . . .'

'How do you know, Rosie, what I would have done?' They were looking fixedly at each other, and it was some seconds before he went on, 'She had made me almost

181

petrified of girls; but not you, you were easy to talk to; you were the only girl I could talk to, although you always appeared like a child to me, and even from a baby you were extraordinary beautiful . . . and good . . . the goodness shone out of you. I saw you the day you were born, and it was evident then. I had just turned thirteen the day you were born.

She looked for a moment longer at the warm, tender expression on his face. He was looking at her as she had seen people look at the statue of the Virgin Mary in church, almost in rapt contemplation; it was unbearable. She sprang up from the chair and walked towards the gas-fire in the far wall, where his voice came to her, contrite, saying, 'I'm sorry, Rosie, if I've upset you.'

'Hughie' – she paused and cleared her throat – 'I'm . . . I'm not a child any longer, or even a girl. I'm a woman. And . . . and I'm not good.' She had her head back on her shoulders as she spoke, staring at the picture above the gas-fire. It was the only picture in the room and it showed a scene of sea and sky with no dividing line between them.

'It all depends on what you mean, Rosie.' His voice was low and his words slurred as if he were thinking hard, but about something else. 'Nothing you could do in the world would ever make me think of you as bad.'

'No?' She was still looking upwards.

'No, Rosie.'

Her eyes were moving over the picture as if she was searching for the horizon line as she said, 'When I left home, Hughie, I thought I knew all about men, good men and bad men. I was Rosie Massey, brought up among a horde of men and with a mother to whom the

182

word delicacy was unknown. I grew up with the feeling that every conception of hers had been a public affair.'

'Don't, Rosie.'

'Am I shocking you, Hughie?'

'No.' He paused. 'You couldn't shock me, but still I don't like to hear you, above all people, talking like that.'

'Not if I think like that? Have always thought like that?'

'You don't think like that, you're upset inside.'

There followed a stillness, and it was broken by him saying tentatively, 'You said the other night that if you could tell anybody what was troubling you it would be me.'

She turned from the fire and looked towards him; then coming slowly across the room again and sat down by the couch facing him, and crossing her feet she joined her hands around her knees and began to rock herself. Leaning forward he put his hand across hers and stilled the motion. 'Try me,' he said.

She looked into his face, close to hers, now. Hughie was nice, kind. That's what you needed in a man, kindness. But that's what had trapped her, hadn't it . . . kindness? When she shuddered he straightened himself and lifted his hand quickly from hers and as quickly she grasped at it, saying, 'If I tell you and . . . and you think I'm dreadful, don't show it, will you, Hughie? Don't show it, I couldn't bear it.'

He looked at her solemnly, 'I tell you nothing you could do could alter my opinion of you, so go ahead.'

'Hold my hand,' she said; and when he gripped her hand and rested it on his knees she began.

183

It was quarter to eight when with her eyes cast down she had started talking. It was half-past eight when she finished and she hadn't raised her head once. When she ended and slowly and stiffly straightened her neck it was she who spoke again. Her green eyes looking almost black in her white face, she stared at him as she said, 'You're shocked, aren't you? Shocked to the core?'

'No.' His voice sounded husky as if he hadn't used it for a long time, then clearing his throat he repeated, 'No, only . . . well – he wetted his lips – 'hurt to the heart for you. . . . Oh, Rosie!' He looked down at their joined hands.

'You won't tell Dennis or anyone?'

'No.' They remained quiet for some moments. Then letting go her hand, he said, 'Whatever happens you'll have to keep this from . . . from your mother. Don't ever feel there'll be a time when you could confide in her.'

'I know that,' she said. She moved from the couch and began to walk about the room, round and round. Then stopping quite suddenly, she asked, 'Would you like some coffee?'

'Yes . . . yes, I think I would.' He did not look at her as he spoke, and when she reached the kitchen she stood near the table with her two hands cupping her face. It had been a mistake – she shouldn't have told him; she shouldn't have told anyone. It came to her now that Hughie was the last person she should have told. She liked Hughie and she knew he liked her. She wanted him to think well of her. She had imagined that in telling him what had happened to her he would have seen that she wasn't to blame, well not altogether, and the burden of guilt would have been lightened. But somehow he

184

hadn't. He said he wasn't shocked, but he was shocked as much, or even more, than any of the lads would have been if she had told them.

She became overwhelmed by a feeling of emptiness, as if she had lost something she valued. But she had never valued Hughie, not until this moment. How much she valued his good opinion came to her now almost in the form of a revelation. And she whimpered to herself: No, no, not that. Why couldn't I have known before I told him?

Thursday

When her mother opened the back door to let her out the air cut their breath from them and Hannah exclaimed, 'My God! Every place is like glass; all that slush frozen hard. Now mind how you go, lass; it's far too early to make a start to my mind.'

'I can go later tomorrow but the buses mightn't be running to time and I don't want to be late the first morning.'

'No, that's understandable the first mornin', but keep that coat buttoned up.' She put her hand towards the top button of Rosie's coat and went on, 'And mind, go and get a good dinner into you, no sandwiches and tea mind, and I'll have somethin' hot and tasty ready for you the minute you enter the door. About six, you say?'

'Yes, if I can get a bus. But you never can tell.'

'Goodbye now, lass; mind how you go.'

'Goodbye, Ma.' As Rosie stepped carefully on to the icy path Hannah, turning into the room, exclaimed, 'Are you off an' all now, Jimmy? Well you can go some of the way with Rosie, here. See her to the bus or she'll be flat on her back afore she gets to the end of the street.'

'Aye, Ma, aye. So long.'

'So long, boy.'

When they had let themselves out of the garden gate Jimmy took Rosie's arm up the lane, saying, 'It'll be all

186

right when we get on the road, the lorries will've been out with the gravel. You won't want me to come with you to the bus, Rosie, will you?'

'No, of course not.'

'I would but I'm a bit late, an' if you're not on the job afore the whistle they cut your time, crafty bastards.'

'It's all right,' she said. 'I'm going up Tangier Road, anyway; it'll bring me to the bus depot and I'll have more chance of getting a seat from there.'

'Aye, aye, you will.'

Just before they neared Tangier Road Jimmy asked in an assumed off-hand way, 'You and Arthur went to the pictures last night?'

'Yes.'

'No kiddin'?'

'Of course we went; where else do you think we would go?'

'Well' – he laughed – 'I know where Arthur would go if he got the chance, an' I thought he might have given you the slip or somethin'. I can't see him sitting in the pictures all night when he could be with her.'

'Well he did . . . he was.'

Rosie didn't ask herself why it was necessary to lie to Jimmy. Instinctively she knew she didn't trust Jimmy; of all her brothers she trusted him the least, he was too close to her mother.

'Well, I'm turning off here,' she said. 'Goodbye.'

'Goodbye, Rosie, an' mind how you go. An' see you work for your pay.' He laughed as he turned from her.

It was not yet fully light, and as she hurried as fast as she could down Tangier Road, the scurrying figures of the men making their way to the factories, and to

187

buses to take them into Newcastle, and as far away as the docks on the Tyne, all looked like black huddled phantoms. Collars up, cap peaks down, their breath fanning out from scarves, they went their particular ways. Some had travelled the same road at the same time each day since they were lads, and would go on until they retired or died, or, fearful thought, were stood off. But Rosie, although she had not been a part of this scene at this time before, was unconscious of any strangeness, for it was almost the same scene as was enacted at the other end of the day. She had been familiar enough with that.

She did not go straight to the bus terminus, but she cut down a side street, and this brought her to the bottom of the hill where Hughie's shop was. When she reached the shop she passed by with just a glance towards the window and knocked on the door next to it, thinking as she did so that if this was a door to a shop it gave no indication of it because there was no window in the wall to the side of it, just a board hanging there with the faded letters on it, reading, JAMES CULLEN – Furniture Repairer.

After knocking three times on the door and receiving no answer, she looked at the key and the paper she had taken out of her bag. Hughie had asked her last night if she would take the key of the shop and the written notice to Mr Cullen. He, Hughie said, was always in his shop around seven. Rain, hail or snow, he'd be there, whether he had work to do or not, and he would see to any customers who called for their shoes.

Now, after knocking yet once again, she was left wondering what to do. Hughie had added that if for some reason Mr Cullen shouldn't be there, she should put the key at the back of the hopper head on the top of the drain pipe. She would have to give herself a boost up from the step, he had said. And she could push the notice through the letter-box. But that he knew she wouldn't have to do, for there had never been a morning in years that old Jim hadn't been in his shop before him.

Hughie had not asked her to do this service for him until Florence and Dennis had returned, and it had created the impression that everything was normal. But she knew that it wasn't.

But this was the one morning when Mr Cullen wasn't here before Hughie, so she pushed the piece of paper which said, 'Closed for a few days. Please apply next door,' through the letter-box, and standing on the step and putting one foot on the coping of the wall, she gripped the drain pipe and hoisted herself up. She just managed to place the key on the ledge of the hopper where it joined the wall. This done, she made her way carefully down the hill again and to the bus station.

Although her new job, which she found very pleasant and knew she was going to like, kept her on her toes as it were, on this first day there still remained a section of her mind that was not touched by it. All day long, from the moment she had got up, she had not been able to get the thought of Hughie out of her mind. She wished now, oh she wished from the bottom of her heart that she hadn't talked last night. She had felt sure that telling him would ease her, and that he would comfort her. That's what she had thought, he would comfort her, saying, 'It wasn't your fault, Rosie, you're not that kind

189

of girl. You would never have got into that scrape on your own.' She had thought he would tell her the things she tried to tell herself, and coming from him she could believe them, then she would again be able to like herself . . . just a little. But Hughie's reaction had taken the form of silence. Except for an odd word now and again, he had said nothing until Dennis and Florence had returned. It was as if he had again been hit on the head, and this time the blow had knocked him stupid.

Just before she left the office Mr Bunting again expressed his pleasure at her work. 'I see you're going to do fine,' he said. 'And as Joe down below said, it's a change to have something good to look at, for there's no getting away from the fact that although Miss Pointer was good at her job she had the kind of face that put you off, if you know what I mean. Joe always said it was like a battered pluck. He meant no offence, but that's how she appeared to him.' He had hunched his rounded shoulders at her as he ended, 'An' to me an' all.'

As Rosie left the office she smiled ruefully to herself. A face like a battered pluck . . . no offence meant! It was funny. People were funny, the things they said. But Miss Pointer with her face like a battered pluck had run off with a married man. Love was another funny thing. . . . Love! She found her lip curling backwards from the word.

A thaw had set in and the market place was a river of slush when she alighted from the Newcastle bus. As she went to cross the square Shane's voice came from behind her, calling, 'Rosie! Rosie there! . . . Gettin' the bus?' he said as he came up to her.

'Oh, hello, Shane. Yes.'

'Isn't this hellish? It's never going to end. We'll all be in the workhouse if it keeps on; we're not goin' in the morrow.'

'You haven't been working on the building today, have you?'

'No, they've kept us busy inside the last few days, but that's finished. It means the Exchange the morrow. The bloody dole. An' what's that?'

Shane talked about the work on the building, and the uncertainty of it; the rotten gaffer; the way they were throwing the houses up on the estate; the money the speculators were making out of them; the Labour Party; the Bosses; and the scapegoats in the Union until they got off the bus at the top of the road. Shane never needed answers. But as they were making their way down the back lane to the garden gate he said something that did need an answer. 'What really brought you home, Rosie?' he asked.

'Eh?' The question, apropos of nothing he had been talking about, startled her, and he went on, 'Well, I mean to say. Well, we got talkin', the others and me, and we wondered . . . well, if you'd had a row with a fellow up there. . . . Had you a fellow?'

'No, no, I hadn't a fellow.'

'All right, Rosie, all right, don't snap me head off.'

They were going up the garden path now between the mounds of snow and he put his hand out and touched her shoulder, saying, 'Don't be ratty, Rosie; I don't want to know anything; it was just . . .'

She hurried from him, and opened the kitchen door, and the warmth flooded at her. And so did her mother's voice, crying, 'Three lots today there's been. Two lads

191

at dinner time sayin' they wanted their boots. Where would they find them, they wanted to know. An' . . . an' I told them to to to hell and he'd likely be there.'

Shane, looking at Rosie, pushed his brows up and wagged his forefinger under his nose. He was about to lean forward to whisper something when Hannah heralded her approach to the kitchen and came in, saying, 'Oh, there you are. Did you meet up? You go out with one and you come home with another.' Hannah was nodding at Rosie, her face one large beam. 'Well it's been a day and a half, hasn't it? Come here and let me have your coat. Oh, look at you! you are clarts up to the eyes. I'll let it dry and then give it a sponge down. Away into the room and get warm. Your da's just in. I've been baking, that Swedish cake with the apples that you liked, and steak and chips it is, afore that, with mushrooms.'

'Pass it along! Pass it along!' Shane went into the kitchen sniffing the air, and Rosie followed him. She hadn't opened her mouth; it wasn't necessary when her mother was in this happy mood. . . .

The meal over, the boys upstairs getting ready for their nightly visit to the club, she sat for a while telling her father about the work at the office and Mr Bunting, while her mother, her ears wide, busied herself about the room. It wasn't until Karen came in that she went upstairs and changed; and when she came down dressed for outdoors once more Hannah exclaimed tersely, 'Where you off to? You're not going out again? I thought you were telling your da you were goin' to look at the telly.'

'Yes I am, but later on. It's Thursday. I'm . . . I'm going to church.'

'Ooh! Aye.' The ooh brought Hannah's chin up and

the bun of hair at the back of her head nodding loosely from its pins. 'Oh, aye, I forgot it was Thursday. That's a good lass. Are you going to confession?'

'Yes, Ma.' Rosie did not look at her mother as she spoke.

'You won't be long then,' said Hannah loudly. 'There's not many that'll turn out the night.'

'No, I don't suppose so. Bye-bye, Da.'

'Bye-bye, lass.'

'Bye-bye, Ma.'

'Bye-bye, lass.' Hannah followed her into the hall. 'If it wasn't so treacherous underfoot I'd come along with you.'

Rosie made no remark to this but went hurriedly through the door that Hannah held ajar, and she walked up the street because that was the way to the church, and she knew her mother would be at the front room window, and the street was well lit.

When she got out of sight around the corner she doubled back down the next road and made her way to the shop.

The long cul-de-sac at the top of the hill was not well lit but she could make out by the light from a distant lamp that there was no notice in the window.

With her foot on the coping and gripping the drain pipe once again, she found the key where she had left it that morning. She opened the shop door and, switching on the light, picked up the folded piece of paper that she had dropped through the letter-box. On the shop counter there was a reel of sticky paper used for sealing the parcels; she tore off a few strips and with them pressed the notice on to the window.

She should now go to Dennis's and tell Hughie that Mr Cullen hadn't been at his shop today. Hadn't she come here to give herself some excuse for going to see Hughie? All day long she had felt she must go and see him tonight. But she wanted an excuse; it wasn't enough to say she had come to see how he was. He had money now, and then Dennis and Florence might think. . . . Well, you never knew what people thought. Relations were the worst. She stood looking about her for a moment sniffing at the dry, musty air. She was uncertain what to do. She had the excuse but she was afraid to use it, afraid, not really of what Florence and Dennis might think but of the silence with which Hughie would greet her, the awful silence that had come between them after she had finished talking last night. And his opinion of her would likely be no better tonight than it had been last night; with time to think it might even have got worse.

She went into the back shop and switched on the light, then putting out the shop light she closed the door to the back room and pulled the blind down over the glass half of it. And as if she had been used to doing it every day she put a match to the oil stove, lit the gas and put the kettle on; then sat down near the stove and waited for the kettle to boil. She didn't really want any tea but she wanted something warm, and she wanted to do something, occupy herself in some way. After she had made the tea she remembered the whisky that Hughie kept in the cupboard underneath the desk, and as she took out the bottle she thought, Hughie won't mind. Then she poured a good measure into the cup of tea. She didn't like whisky, or brandy, or gin. She knew she had no real taste for liquor of any kind, but she needed something; as her hands needed to be busy to check the unrest in her mind so her body needed warmth. The fact that Hughie had offered her no warmth last night was affecting her strangely. She had never imagined she would lay such stock by his good opinion.

After she had drunk the laced tea she pulled the chair nearer the desk, and more because her hands were restless than out of curiosity she opened the drawer. It was filled with neatly stacked sheets of paper, and she sat looking down at them for some time. If she read them she would be prying she thought. Perhaps Hughie wouldn't like her to read what he had written. Well Hughie wasn't there, was he? She moved her head as if asking the question of the desk, and she wanted to pry, to pry into his affairs, into his mind. She lifted a few sheets from one pile and put them on the desk; then closing the drawer, leant over them and began to read. There was no title to the first page, it just began:

'What is more important than education today? What will get you in, what will give you preference is . . . an accent, just an accent. Accent still has the power to give one person an advantage over another, and strangely enough it has nothing to do with intelligence or learning but everything to do with background. So the solution for success would seem to be get yourself born with a background; then automatically you'll have an accent. . . .'

Underneath this piece of writing were the words 'Strip and extend. Could be made amusing.'

Yes, it could at that, she thought. Fancy Hughie being funny.

On the next page, headed 'Return to the soil after imprisonment' were the words:

'I walk on you, my soles tight pressed; I lie on you, and my body wallows in your lushness; I weep my tears of love and see them soak into your groins; my sweat lies on you in glossy globules. In ecstasy I rise and take up the blade and in your rich black blood my soul is reflected. I am one with eternal life.'

After reading this three times, Rosie looked at the wall opposite. Her eyes were narrowed and her mouth hung slack. She couldn't associate the writing with Hughie, not any part of the Hughie she knew. When she had poured out her troubles last night she had been seeing the man who sat in the corner of the kitchen, but the man she had been talking to and who had fallen silent was the man who wrote stuff like this. She didn't know anything about this man.

She brought her eyes down to the papers again and began to read the next page. It had no heading.

'From the bed I rise and fly, my body draped in skin alone. The air, the width of the universe, the length of eternity, is my raiment and enfolds me but does not hide me, and I care not. I pass over nations all peopled with faces of my neighbours, and they look at me and I laugh and cry down to them: "Why be afraid of your body? Look at me, look at me." And they look and I laugh. And on I float, and glide, and soar, and whirl in wind pockets, and I grip a tall spire and dance round it and my feet bounce off the air as off a trampoline, and I shout at the life that I know is within me: "You're there! You're there! This is you . . . jumping, jumping." And my shouting cleaves the clouds as it always does. And

196

then I fall and fall and land in a field full of men, with one woman in the midst, and she is standing up to her waist in filth, and I awake in the blackness and wonder if I'll ever drop into a field of flowers. . . .'

'Oh! Hughie . . . Hughie.' The name came out of her mouth like an expression of pain, and again she said, 'Oh! Hughie, Hughie.' As fantastic as this piece of writing was she could understand it . . . oh yes, she could understand it. Dreaming of a field full of men with a woman in their midst . . . her mother. Dreaming that he was afraid of his body except in the night. . . . And last night she had told him what had happened to her and her body. No wonder he was silent. Gently she pushed the papers aside, and leaning her head on the desk she began to cry.

It wasn't long after this that she returned home, and as she mounted the steps the front door opened to let out Councillor Bishop. Her mother stood behind him, the door in her hand, her face bright, her manner at its best. 'Oh, there you are, me dear,' she greeted her. 'You've met me daughter, Councillor?' She inclined her head towards the plump, bespectacled man.

'Indeed, yes, I've had that honour. But many years ago. How are you?' He held out his hand.

'Very well, thank you.'

He was holding her hand, pumping it up and down as he went on, 'Your mother tells me that you've come home to stay. Now this is good news.' He spoke as if he knew all about her, as if her going or staying was of some importance to him. 'Now you must come round one evening and meet Mrs Bishop. I know she would love to meet you.' Still holding her hand in a grasp which did not allow her to extricate her fingers without tugging them from him, he turned to Hannah and ended, 'When you've moved we'll do an exchange of evenings, eh?'

'That'll be grand, that'll be grand indeed.'

'It's settled then.' Mr Bishop patted the hand within his own before finally releasing it, and as Rosie turned away, her face unsmiling, he said to Hannah, 'We'll be meeting again on Saturday then, Mrs Massey. I'll have all the papers ready. There's nothing to be gained by hanging about in matters like this. It could be snapped up.'

'I'll see that it's snapped up, Mr Bishop, but by the right one.'

Hannah's laugh followed Rosie into the living-room. She took off her coat and hat and, leaving them on the chair, went to the fire and stood waiting.

A few minutes later Hannah entered the room. She did not speak immediately, but engaged in her usual technique, that of preceding anything of importance she had to say with a silence, a telling silence. But on this occasion Rosie did not allow her mother to play her little game; instead, turning to her, she asked, 'You're not really going to take the place, are you, Ma?'

'Not really going to take it!' Hannah's voice was high but quiet; it held a surprised note as if it was unbelievable to her that anyone should imagine that she wasn't going to take number eight Brampton Hill. 'Of course I'm going to take it, child. . . . We're going to take it, an' it'll all be settled on Saturday.'

'But me da . . . and the lads?'

'Your da has always left things of this nature to me.

198

As for the lads, if they don't like it there's the wide world before them and the door is open.'

Rosie gazed at her mother. You really had to admire her effrontery and the game of pretence that she played. . . . There was the wide world for the lads and the door was open! Without the lads she could never hope to make Brampton Hill, and yet she could talk like this with apparent sincerity.

'But if you don't sell this . . . ?'

'This house will be sold, never fear. Mr Bishop put it on his books three weeks ago. He's had several enquiries. He's not in the smallest doubt that it'll go like wild fire once the fine weather comes. He's so sure of it, me dear, that he says he'll take it off me hands himself if it isn't sold.'

Mr Bishop, Rosie thought, was an astute man, a crafty, astute man. A councillor, a speculator and a chairman of a building society. He had, since the day he rented Hannah her first house after Bog's End, taken her measure. For all her cunning, her mother was so naïve in some things. . . . Exchange of visits for instance. She could see Mrs Bishop entertaining her mother. Mrs Bishop who in her young days had graced the Ladies' Circle, who had, as her husband alternately clawed and sucked himself up through the business élite of the town, made the right friendships, the right connections. Her mother and Mrs Bishop exchanging visits! If it wasn't pathetic it would be laughable.

As if Hannah were reading her thoughts she said, 'What you don't seem to understand, lass, is that times are changin'. I'll grant you that at one time it would have been out of place, the very thought of us moving to Brampton Hill, but not now. There's been a levelling, and not afore time. It's the front you put on the day that you're judged by. Half of them in this town are living on an overdraft. Now I know that for truth.' She wagged her finger in Rosie's face. 'It was Mr Bishop himself who told me that. He's opened me eyes about lots of things. "Mrs Massey," he said, "anybody who can put two thousand pounds down in cash for a house the day needn't have any worries for the future." '

'You're putting the two thousand down?'

'I am. But mind you' – she lifted both her hands towards Rosie now – 'this is atween you and me, for the present moment at any rate. Now don't you let on; mind, I'm tellin' you. Anyway, putting the two thousand down will bring the mortgage to practically half; we'll be paying no more than what we're paying off the house at the present moment, it's all been worked out. And when we sell this there'll be three thousand in the bank to set us up with.'

'It's all cut and dried then?'

'It's all cut and dried as you say, lass,' Hannah nodded at her.

'Barry'll be on the dole next week. He won't feel like giving the Hill as his address at the exchange.'

'Now, are you trying to be nasty, lass. What's come over you?' Hannah scrutinised her daughter through narrowed lids. 'Fancy sayin' a think like that, aiming to put a damper on the whole enterprise. It isn't like you; you never used to have a barb to your tongue. And as for Barny not wantin' to give the Hill address to the exchange, there'll be no need, for if I know Barny he'll be in work afore he's out of it.'

200

'I hope so.'

As Rosie turned away and picked up her coat and hat, Hannah said to her, 'I'm the one for speakin' me mind an' I'm goin' to say now that I feel there's something wrong with you. From the minute you stepped in at the door I felt it. You've hardened, lass, all the gentleness has gone out of you. As I remember you, you never contradicted me in your life, nor yet raised your voice in opposition to me, yet you've never stopped battling since you've been home. An' what's cut me to the quick is to know that you took the sod that's gone's part. Him that wronged me. You know, I've the feelin' that if the devil was to appear in the kitchen this minute yes, begod, I've the feelin' that you'd even take his side against me, I have.'

There was so much truth in what her mother said, and so much hurt in the tone in which she said it, that Rosie was forced to turn round before she left the room and say quietly, 'I'm sorry, Ma; it's because I'm not feeling well, I suppose.'

'All right, all right, we'll leave it at that, lass.' Hannah hurried forward. 'Go and get yourself up to bed, it's rest you want. Good feeding and rest. I've put your bottle in and the heater's on, and by the time you're in I'll have somethin' hot up to you.'

She patted Rosie's arm as she pushed her towards the stairs.

What could you say in the face of such tenderness and concern? You could say nothing, but you could do something, you could run . . . run before you reached Brampton Hill.

PART THREE
HANNAH

Friday

It was the events of this day, Friday, which were to point the way to Rosie's future life.

The routine of the day was the same as yesterday, except that during her dinner hour she went looking for a room, and by chance found one only five minutes' walk from the office. It was clean and comfortable and in a respectable neighbourhood. She liked the woman, a widow, who owned the house and made her living by letting. She paid her a small deposit in advance and told her that she would come on Monday next.

During the afternoon she hadn't much time to worry about how she would break the news of her going to her mother, but as she neared home in the evening she became agitated.

When she went into the house she still hadn't decided whether she would tell her mother straightaway or leave it until tomorrow, after she had signed the lease on eight Brampton Hill, for by that time she would be in a much better frame of mind.

But Hannah herself decided, for she greeted her with such heartiness that it would have been impossible to say to her, 'I'm leaving, Ma.'

They were all in except Barny and Karen. Jimmy had come home early because a severe gale had held up the work on the bridge. Arthur, too, was on short time from

205

the quarries because they couldn't get the lorries to move. Shane had apparently returned home first thing this morning after signing on at the labour exchange. Yet in spite of all this, which meant lighter pay packets, Hannah was gaiety itself.

Being Friday, there was naturally fish, and the men had finished a large side-dish full of fried cod and chips.

'I didn't do yours, me dear,' said Hannah, 'I wanted you to have it fresh.' And when she went scurrying into the kitchen, Broderick, pulling at Rosie's hand, drew to his side of the table, saying, 'Sit yourself down and have some tea and this new bread to be getting on with. There's nobody bakes flat cake like your mother. In fact,' he widened his eyes at her, 'I'd like to bet you she's the only woman in this town who still bakes her own bread.'

As Rosie sat down Shane passed her the plate of bread, saying, 'How's it going?' But before she could answer him Arthur put in, 'Don't ask daft questions, man, the boss has asked her to marry him, didn't you know?'

'No!' said Shane, his hand still extended with the plate but looking at his brother now, his whole face portraying an idiotic expression of wonder.

'It's a fact, I'm tellin' you.' Arthur raised his hand. 'As true as God and Hannah Massey's my judge. He asked her this very day; an' he's got a title an' all.'

'No!' Shane's hand was still extended, holding the bread plate, and now he moved it upwards until it was above his head.

'Aye.'

Broderick and Jimmy were laughing now and Rosie was forced to join in.

'Give over, you couple of clowns,' said their father.

'Clowns! He's calling us clowns. Do you hear that, Arthur? Roll your sleeves up, go on, get at him.' Shane dropped the plate on the table.

'No, no, I never raise me hand to little chaps.' At this Arthur put his forearm up as if warding off a blow, and, his eyes laughing, he peered over his fist at his father. And Broderick said, 'Little chap is it? I'll have you turning a somersault and you won't know but 'twas a cuddy that'd kicked you.'

And so the chaff went on; it was almost a repeat of the same time the previous week. When Rosie had longed for home it was this part of it she remembered, the lads pulling each other's legs, and their father's, while her mother bustled about feeding them all. And by their attitudes now Rosie knew that as yet they were unaware of what was going to happen tomorrow. Had they known they were really booked for Brampton Hill the scene in the kitchen tonight would have been quite different.

Hannah, coming to Rosie's side now and putting her arm around her shoulder and her face down to hers, said, 'Look, what about comin' along of us the night to the club an' seein' a bit of life? It's all very nice and refined. Now isn't it?' she appealed to her sons. 'Since this new manager's been in she wouldn't know the place, would she? What about it?' She brought her eyes back to Rosie, adding, 'You can have a bit of a dance, or a quiet drink, just as you like. There's a room been opened just across the passage, select it is. . . .'

'An . . . an' a penny a pint on the beer for the selectness.' Broderick opened his eyes wide and threw his head back as if he had just voiced something extremely funny.

207

'Aye, come along, Rosie,' Shane said over the table. 'It's a long while since we had a dance together.'

'I used to love to see you two dancin' together,' said Hannah, nodding from one to the other. 'You were so smooth it was like running water. What do you say, lass?'

What could she say without appearing churlish or ungrateful. She could say nothing but 'All right, Ma. Yes, I'd like to.' She nodded towards Shane now.

'That's settled then. Good, good. Aw, we'll make a night of it. It's about time we had a bit of jollification. We've all been acting like frozen corpses for long enough . . . Come on now, finish up the lot of you and let's get cleared and away. I'll leave the others' set for them; they can see to themselves for once.'

The next few minutes was all bustle, and as Rosie went to leave the room Shane called after her, 'By the way, what you wearin'? Put on something dandy, I want to show you off . . . that suit you came home with, that'll do.'

Hannah's voice followed Rosie up the stairs, crying at Shane, 'Did you ever! Wantin' to show his sister off! Now I ask you.' There was laughter in her tone, but it died away as she ended, 'And that suit she came back with, I'm not struck on it a bit. It's as plain as a pikestaff, there's nothing to it. . . .'

When, sometime later, Rosie came down the stairs with her coat on they were all gathered in the living-room. Hannah was wearing a heavy blue coat with a high collar, the whole tending to emphasize her largeness. She wore a blue velour hat set straight on top of her grey hair, and although there wasn't any sign of taste

208

in her clothes she looked an imposing figure – regal, one would say. As she pulled on her gloves she turned to Rosie and said, 'Ah, there you are, let's have a look at you. Open your coat.'

'But you've seen it before, Ma.'

'Yes, I know, but I want to see it again.'

When Rosie opened her coat Hannah, looking at her from head to foot as if she were appraising a model, remarked, 'I maintain what I said, it's too dull.'

'You don't know class when you see it. Come, let's away,' said Shane, taking hold of Rosie and pushing her forward.

'And come along all of you, else it will be closin' time afore we get there. We should have had a taxi, anyway,' said Hannah as she went down the front steps.

'Taxi! Listen to her,' called Broderick. 'You'd think she'd come up by way of the landed gentry. Taxis to go to the club!'

Between them Broderick and Jimmy helped Hannah along the slushy street to the bus stop while Shane and Arthur took Rosie by an arm, and, all the way, there was laughing and chaffing. And like this they entered the club.

The Workmen's Centre, or The Club as it was usually called, was the most modern of its kind. The main room was well over fifty feet long with an added L piece half that length. The bar counter took up the curve on the corner of the L; in this way it protruded into the dance section while dominating the main portion of the room which was filled with small tables. Adjacent to the end of the bar was a raised platform on which stood a piano, and as Hannah and her party entered the room there were two men on the platform giving an imitation of famous mimers, as was indicated by their small gingham skirts and bibs.

The Fellburn Club was very proud of its standards of entertainers; hadn't two of their local talent been snatched up by telly? That the two men had only appeared once on television made no odds, they had been . . . snatched up by talent spotters. And so everyone who went on the stage at the club acted as if for an audition.

The room was already packed, and Hannah and Rosie alone found seats in a corner against the wall, while the men stood about them making signs with their hands and heads to acknowledge greetings from the occupants at other tables.

When the turn was finished, amid great applause, the men made their way to the bar counter while Hannah, with restrained conviviality, acknowledged the greetings from those around her. To their 'Hello there, Hannah,' 'How goes it the night, Hannah?' she made suitable replies accompanied by dignified movements of her head; and when a woman from close by rose and came towards her, saying, 'Don't tell me it's Rosie you have here,' Hannah replied, 'Who else, Mary?'

'Why, hello, Rosie!' The woman bent forward 'By! I wouldn't have known you . . . you've grown so.'

Rosie didn't bother to answer that, but smiled her greetings. What the woman really meant to say was, 'I wouldn't have known you, you look so changed.'

'How long are you here for?' the woman asked.

'Oh, for some time.'

'She's home for good, Mary.' Hannah nodded

210

solemnly. 'She's already fallen into a fine job in Newcastle.'

'Ah, there's no place like home, is there? It's always the same; they go off to London but they're glad to come scurrying back to their ma's.' She pushed her hand towards Hannah's.

'Yes, yes, you're right there, Mary.' But Hannah did not enlarge on her friend's remark. Perhaps it was something in Rosie's face that deterred her, a certain tightness.

The men returned with the drinks, a double whisky for Hannah and a glass of Guinness, pints of beer each for themselves and a gin and ginger for Rosie.

As they drank, talked and chaffed, Rosie looked about her. The atmosphere was one of jollity and good fellowship. When the master of ceremonies announced they were going to have community singing, this was acclaimed by loud clapping. And when everybody sang she, too, sang, and she wondered why she was singing. She wondered why she was here at all, for she had never liked the club and she didn't like it now. If she'd only been strong enough to say no; if she'd only had the gumption now she would finish her drink and say to her mother, 'I'm going home.'

But why didn't she like this kind of thing? These were her people. She had been brought up amongst them. In the main they were good solid people, working hard and playing hard, like now, the way that suited them. She had found from experience that you couldn't judge by accents, smooth tongues, or by clothes, yet this noise and bustle from table to lip, depressed her. She remembered Florence once saying to Dennis during

211

one of their . . . queer arguments, 'The working classes need stimulating today more than they ever did, for there's very little natural gaiety left in them. And is it to be wondered at? What in their lives stimulates gaiety? They had to have the gin shops in the last century, and just as badly they need the clubs in this.'

So what was the difference between the working man being stimulated in a working-man's club or other men in a smart restaurant or a night club in London. As Florence had said, natural gaiety was like inborn holiness, it was very rare. At one time people had said that she herself was naturally gay, but she would never be naturally gay again, and she didn't want to be stimulated into being gay. What did she want? Some hole, perhaps, or quiet place into which she could crawl, and stay there until she died. She understood why animals sought solitude when they were wounded, there to die, if not in peace, alone with their agony. Yet if she felt like this why had she come back at all? Certainly her home was no hole in which to hide, more like a market place, or, more appropriate, a stage where all the emotions were up for viewing.

She was brought back to the present by Shane saying, 'That's over. Now we'll have a dance. Come on.' He pulled at her arm.

'But they haven't started yet.' She was reluctant to leave her seat.

'They will in a minute. Let's go to the other side.'

'Go on,' said Hannah, 'an' take the floor.' She was desirous of seeing her daughter being viewed, not as one of the crowd, but as one standing out from the crowd.

And this would be achieved only if they were first on the floor.

And so for the next two hours the entertainment went on; dancing, ballad singers, community singing and comic turns, one following hard on the other. And during this time they were joined by Barny. Also during this time, Hannah had consumed three double whiskies and three glasses of Guinness, and now she was mellow. Her eyes dancing, her lips ever parted, there had flowed from them joke after joke. Most of them against herself as a Catholic, and the Church as a whole. For was it not known that the best Catholics always told jokes against their creed? It was a way of proving that they were thick with God who also had a sense of humour. Above all, it proved that nobody could entertain like Hannah Massey when she got going.

Rosie had just started on her second gin when Jimmy asked her to dance.

She looked up at him, saying, 'But it's a twist they're playing.'

'Well, who says I can't do the twist. Listen to her!' He looked around the group at the table. 'She thinks it's only in London they can do the twist. Come on with you.' He tugged her out of the chair as if she were a child and pulled her through the crowd of tables to the dance floor, where already there were couples wriggling and contorting amid jeers and calls from those seated at the tables.

'Come on, let's make for the far corner and I'll show you who can do the twist.' Jimmy was at an amiable point of fullness and in high fettle, and he went into the dance like a big lumbering cart-horse, and at the sight

213

of his efforts Rosie, in spite of herself, began to laugh. When her body began to shake, she put her arm round her waist and cried, 'Oh, Jimmy! Jimmy, stop it.' But Jimmy, like his mother, knew when he was being amusing and her laughter only encouraged him to redouble his efforts, and not only because of Rosie but because now he was attracting attention from the tables in the far corner of the room.

Rosie was standing with her back to the wall as Jimmy contorted himself before her, and it was as she turned her face sideways that she looked towards the end of the bar counter and to where a woman was standing talking to a man. The woman was wearing a fur coat which was open, showing beneath a tight-fitting yellow wool dress. But it was not the dress that Rosie was looking at, but the woman's face, a long, narrow face with thin, red lips. She was hatless and her hair was dyed a pale mauve and dressed in a youthful style with a fringe which made her appear rather ludicrous.

As quickly as water rushed from a burst pipe the laughter rushed out of Rosie's body. Her mouth fell agape and she closed her eyes, but only for a second. When she opened them again it was to see that the woman, following her companion's gaze, was looking at Jimmy. Rosie remained still, fixed against the wall as if she were nailed there: If she made no movement the woman wouldn't see her and she would be able to get out. Her heart-beats pumping against her ribs vibrated through her head and seemed to cut out the blaring sound of the band. Without moving her eyes, she saw that the woman wasn't amused at Jimmy's antics. She wouldn't be, she wouldn't be. She prayed that Jimmy wouldn't call to her but would be satisfied with his own exhibition. But Jimmy did call to her. He held out his hands and cried, 'Come on, Rosie, girl. Shake a leg.'

As the woman came slowly forward, Rosie kept her eyes fixed on Jimmy.

'Well, hello there. Fancy running into you.'

Rosie turned her head slowly and looked at the face before her, and as she looked she wished she had the power to strike the woman dead; yet it was to this woman she owed the fact that she was in Fellburn at this moment.

'Well, if this isn't a bit of luck. . . . Come on, say something, don't look so surprised.'

The band stopped amid loud applause, and a special kind of applause from the people sitting near for Jimmy, who, puffing and blowing, came towards Rosie now, saying, 'You're a fine partner.' As he finished speaking he stopped and looked at the woman. He looked her up and down before turning to Rosie, saying curtly, 'Come on . . . come on, girl.'

'Aren't you going to introduce us?'

Rosie's chin made a wobbling movement. 'This . . . this is my brother, Jimmy. Miss . . . Miss Lang,' she was stammering.

'Please to meet you.' The woman inclined her head towards Jimmy, and he inclined his, too, but he did not speak.

Definitely Jimmy was puzzled. He might have more brawn than brain but he was no fool where women were concerned, and he was asking himself how in the name of God their Rosie had come to know a Flossie like this one, and an old worn one into the bargain, not one of

215

the smart new types that you couldn't tell from respectable lasses.

'Well, it looks as if I'm on me own. Can I join up? I was with a fellow, but I can't see him about.' She looked around. 'He's scarpered.'

Rosie, half turning away and speaking to Jimmy in an undertone, said, 'Tell me ma I won't be a moment and . . . and bring me bag, will you, Jimmy? . . . I'll be in the saloon.' She lifted her hand in a despairing motion and pointed to the door just to the right of her.

Jimmy made no reply, but he cast another glance at the woman before turning away, and he had gone some distance across the floor when Rosie running after him caught hold of his arm and whispered urgently, 'Don't . . . don't say anything to me ma, will you not?'

'Where's she from?' His face looked dark, no vestige of laughter on it now. 'How in the hell did you get to . . . ?'

'Jimmy . . . Jimmy, go on, I'll try to explain later, but . . . but don't say anything to me ma about her, will you?'

'I'm not a bloody fool altogether.'

He turned away and Rosie went back towards the woman. Passing her without speaking, she walked towards the door, then into the passage, and through another door and into the saloon.

There were only three couples in the room, which made it almost empty, and going to the corner farthest from the door she sat down, and the woman, following after her, took a seat opposite to her. She took a packet of cigarettes from her bag and she lit one before asking in a flat, sulky tone, 'Who's that?'

'I told you. My brother.'

'Huh! Your brother. Honest . . . ? Well, he's some beef, isn't he?'

Rosie looked down at the polished table. She picked up a drip pad and bent it back and forward between her hands, and as she did so the woman leant forward quickly and said under her breath, 'Aw come off it, you don't have to be afraid of me; at least you should know that. 'Cos remember if it wasn't for me you'd likely be getting dressed up . . . or the reverse, for your first night among the dusties this very minute . . . an' I'm not kiddin'.'

Rosie closed her eyes and swallowed, then asked, 'Why are you here, Ada?'

'All right, straight answer to a straight question. I came along to find out what you did with the ring. That's all.'

'The ring?' There was surprise, yet relief, in Rosie's tone.

'Yes, the ring.'

'I . . . I pawned it.'

'I guessed you would, not having anything on you. Well . . .' She drew on her cigarette, then blew out a thin stream of smoke before she said, 'I would like the ticket. That's all, so you needn't look so damned scared, you needn't be afraid of me.'

Slowly Rosie slumped against the back of the seat. 'How . . . how did you know where to find me?'

'Well, you'd told him you lived in Newcastle, but that time I was out with you – the time I tipped you off, remember? – I saw you posting a letter. It had the name Fellburn on it; so . . . well, I took a chance and came down yesterday and my God I can understand you saying

217

you lived in Newcastle, because this is a dump if ever there was one . . . Talk about the last place God made. And the customers! Good God! Customers! They can't make up their minds. Anyway, I found out where you lived this afternoon and I was going to look you up . . . but here we are. Well now, that's my story so what about the ticket, Rosie?'

'I haven't got it.'

'Aw, now, fair's fair. Don't come that line with me. Look, I mean you no harm. I've proved it, haven't I? I risked something when I put you wise, I'm telling you. Now come on, all I want is the ticket. . . . By the way, how much did you get on it?'

'Ten pounds.'

'Christ! What? You telling me the truth?'

'Yes.'

'The bugger only gave you . . . ?'

'That's all I asked.'

'Are you barmy?' The woman screwed her face up at Rosie, 'Well, I suppose you are, that's why I was sorry for you. I could see right away you hadn't any sense, not for this game, you hadn't. But God almighty! Ten pounds! Do you know what that ring's worth . . . ? Five hundred to say the least.'

Rosie's eyes stretched wide and her jaw sagged, and the words came out in awe. 'Five hundred? But why did he give it to me if it was worth all that?'

The woman shook her head slowly. 'Have you asked yourself why he gave you all the grand furniture and clothes, eh? Why a mink stole, eh? Why? Because they were all part of his stock in trade, and that ring was the biggest draw. I've lost count of the times he's had it altered to fit different fingers. It's part of his bank, that ring, and the centre diamond is worth God knows what. Do you know where that stone came from?' She pulled a face in enquiry at Rosie. 'A tiara. The dame that lost that tiara has sleepless nights even now. There's one thing I'll say for you, you had some nerve to go to his pocket and take it.'

'He'd given it to me. When we first met he gave it to me. It was a sort of . . .'

'A wedding ring. Yes, I know. Oh, God almighty! You know, Rosie, you make me want to vomit just to listen to you. Still, I suppose,' she spread out her hands on the table, palms upwards, 'if it wasn't for the innocents he'd be out of work. But it's hard to believe the likes of you are still born in this day and age. But now,' she leant her body halfway across the table, 'about the ticket.'

'I haven't got it, Ada. I'm telling you the truth, I tore it up.'

The woman remained still for a time as she stared into Rosie's face, then slowly moved back until only her hands were resting on the edge of the table. 'No kidding?' she said.

'It's the truth.'

'Well, you didn't think you'd get away with that, did you? What if he had found you? You might have smoothed things over by giving him the ticket.'

'I didn't know the ring was so valuable. Honest . . . honest.' Rosie rubbed her hand across her mouth where the beads of perspiration had gathered, then whispered, 'Did he send somebody down?'

'Yes, he did; he sent Scottie to Newcastle on Saturday

night. He came back on Tuesday saying he'd drawn a blank. It was when I heard this that I thought I'd take a trip meself and see if I'd have any better luck . . . in Fellburn. I had to get out of his way, anyway, because he threatened to put Dolan on to me. He guessed I'd tipped you off in the first place. He's no fool, is Dickie, and I didn't fancy meeting up with Dolan. I saw the last girl Dolan handled. She was out of business for a long, long time, so I said to myself, "Ada, you're due for a trip. You find Rosie and she'll tell you, out of gratitude like, where she pawned the ring". Because I knew, as he did, that was the only way you'd get the money. Lord! If you could have seen him when you didn't come out of that shop. He was watching out of the window all the time. I must say you put on a good show. If you had sauntered on the beat like you did that morning you'd have been made, and him and you would have lived happy ever after. You had got a good ten minutes start before he thought of looking in his pocket. The ring was the last thing he took off you, wasn't it?'

Rosie bowed her head.

The woman laughed, a thin confined laugh. 'Same old pattern,' she said; 'but none of them had the nerve to go to his jacket. You must have done it like lightning, you weren't in the bedroom a couple of seconds.'

'Well, what did you expect me to do?' Rosie glanced fiercely upwards as she asked the question.

'Oh, I just expected you to make a run for it once you got in the street, then go to the Salvation Army or something, anywhere that would get you home. Except the Police Station; I didn't expect you to go there after I warned you.'

'I nearly did.'

'It's as well you didn't, kid, for he would have got you. If he had done time he would still have got you. Dickie's vindictive, I've seen it. An' he's scared of jail. . . .'

'Be quiet!' Rosie was looking towards the door through which were coming Jimmy and Shane, their faces set. She knew what had happened. Jimmy had brought Shane with him to confirm his opinion of the woman their Rosie knew.

Ada, following Rosie's gaze, turned her head slowly towards the approaching men. Her look was lazy, confident. 'Another brother?' she mumbled through her teeth.

'Yes.'

'I don't believe it.' She pulled herself up straight, and looked at Shane as he came to the table, and as Shane stared down at her, she said, 'Rosie's brother?'

'Yes, I'm Rosie's brother.'

The woman laughed. 'Any more at home like you two?' She moved her head in Jimmy's direction, then looked back at Shane.

'Two more,' said Shane; 'and me mother's a nig woman an' all.'

'No kidding?'

'No kidding.'

'I'd like a drink,' she said.

'Come on, Rosie.' Jimmy lifted his head in a beckoning movement to Rosie, but looking pleadingly at him she said, 'I'd like a drink an' all, Jimmy. Would you bring two gins?'

Jimmy hesitated for quite some time, then sucking in

his lips he went to the bar counter at the end of the room for the drinks. Shane remained standing gazing down at the woman, taking in the nipples of her breasts imprinted sharply through the dress, the length of uncovered knee crossing the other and the tightness of the dress where it pulled in under her stomach. He said to her, 'Staying long?'

'It all depends.'

'How did you get in here?' her asked her. 'It's members only.'

'A gentleman friend brought me.' Her eyes narrowed and her face became grim. 'And don't you be so snotty.'

'Shane . . . look, Shane. Go on, please. I'll come along in a minute.'

'I've plenty of time. I'll go when you do.' Shane was now carrying a good few drinks and he looked and sounded stubborn.

When Jimmy came back to the table bringing the two gins and no drink for himself or Shane, Rosie said to him, 'I won't be five minutes, Jimmy, I'll join you in five minutes.'

'I've told her we'll go when she goes, not until.' Shane nodded at Jimmy.

At this Rosie bounced to her feet saying under her breath, 'Look, Shane, leave me alone. I'm not a child. Now get yourself away. And you an' all, Jimmy. You don't want me mother to come in here looking for me, do you?'

At this pointed question the men exchanged quick glances, and Shane said, 'All right, all right, but if you're not back in five minutes, ten at the outside, we'll come for you.' He nodded significantly at her. And Jimmy

222

repeated like a parrot, 'Aye, we'll come for you.' He, too, nodded at her before turning away.'

'Who do they think they are, anyway?' The woman pulled the glass of gin towards her and gulped at it.

'They didn't mean anything,' said Rosie.

'Oh, don't start to consider my feelings or I'll cry.' She knocked the bottom of her glass twice on the table. 'And look, you're not getting rid of me until I know where I can lay my hands on that ring.'

'I can tell you the name of the shop; it was Gomex's.'

The woman's eyes stretched wide, and there came into them a gleam that looked like a smile. 'Gomex's?' she said. 'Well, fancy! How did you know about him?'

'What do you mean? I didn't know anything. I . . . I used to pass the shop coming from the office, that's all. It was quite near the office.'

'Well, for your information you hit on one of the biggest transferers . . . that's a nice term, isn't it, transferer, one of the biggest in the business. I bet he put two and two together and hoped you would die before you got that ring out again.' She paused. 'Did you put your own name and address on it?'

'I put my own name but not my address.'

'What address?'

'Eight Brampton Hill.'

'Rosie Massey, eight Brampton Hill, eh?'

'Yes.'

'Well, things seem to be going my way after all. From what I know of Mr Gomex, he's not partial to our dear Dickie. Here.' She pulled open her bag and pulled out an address book. 'Write along there: I authorise Miss Ada Lang to redeem the ring I pledged under the name

223

of Rosie Massey, of 8 Brampton Hill, on February twenty-second. I have lost the ticket . . . and sign it at the bottom. It mightn't carry any legal weight but it will help to convince him that I know you, and when I tell him the whole story he'll likely see it my way and we can come to some monetary arrangement.' She smiled now with her lips only. 'That's after I point out to him that if he doesn't produce it after twelve months and you fail to turn up there could be some enquiries. . . . Now what about another drink, just for old times' sake, eh?' As she turned her face towards the bar, the room door opened again, and as a man entered she exclaimed, 'Oh, I know this bloke, I was talking to him last night. He could be easy. Ooh-ooh, there,' she called down the room.

Rosie made no protest, but just stared like a fascinated rabbit as Ronnie MacFarlane came walking towards them.

When she had hailed him Ronnie had looked at Ada Lang, but only for a second before his gaze had jumped to Rosie, and he kept his eyes on her until he reached the table; and not until Ada Lang asked, 'You looking for me?' did he blink and turn towards the woman, saying, 'Yes. . . . No . . . no, I wasn't, I was looking for a pal.'

'Well, make up your mind. . . . Anyway, sit down now you're here.' She flicked out a chair with the point of her long shoe, and he looked at it for a moment before he sat down. Then he stared at the table for another moment before, his glance slipping between them, he said, 'You two know each other?'

'Of course we know each other. This is,' the woman

jerked her thumb across the table, 'this is Rosie, Rosie Massey.'

'I know it's Rosie Massey.' Ronnie was staring at the woman now, then slowly turning his head and addressing Rosie's averted face he said in an odd tone, 'Hello there, Rosie.'

Slowly Rosie pulled herself to her feet. She had felt sick before but it was nothing to the feeling she was experiencing now.

'What's your hurry? Sit down.' As Ronnie put out his hand to touch her she curved her body from it as if it was a reptile. At this he laughed, a deep laugh, a man's laugh, yet it sounded like laughter preceding madness.

'Look, sit down . . . sit down. What's your hurry?' The woman was looking up at her. 'Anyway wait till those pieces of beef come for you.' She put out her hand, and Rosie, knocking it aside, snapped, 'You've got what you want, now leave me alone.'

As she walked down the room she was conscious that they were both looking at her and she had the desire to run. She was almost on the point of it when she reached the door, there to be confronted by Jimmy and Shane again. She walked between them and into the passage before turning and facing them.

Jimmy's brows were down, his lower lip was moving as though it were an independent feature from side to side, as it always did when he was beginning to carry a heavy load.

She was surpised at the steadiness in her voice as she said, 'It's a long story, and you wouldn't believe me if I told you.'

'We'll take a chance on that.' It was Shane speaking.

225

'She's a tart. You know that, don't you? And an old one at that.'

'How do you know?' Her voice was snapping now.

'Ah, come off it, Rosie, it's sticking out all over her. An' what's more, she was here last night and tried it on with one or two of the lads.'

'If me mother knew you knew anybody like her she'd go clean up in the lum,' said Jimmy now, 'an' if I catch you with her again I'll clout your lug, as old as you are.'

'Steady on, steady on,' said Shane, pushing his brother with the flat of his hand. 'Those dames are clever; they make friends with people an' not everybody can spot 'em. Come on, come on.' He took hold of Rosie's arm. 'Me mother's been asking for you. An' for God's sake, an' your own,' he nodded solemnly towards her, 'don't let her and that piece meet up.'

'I'm going home.' She pulled her arm from Shane's.

'Oh no, you're not, you're coming back to me ma and we'll all go home together. Come on.' Jimmy's grip was not as gentle as Shane's, and Rosie found herself being hustled through the door into the main room. Someone had just stopped singing and everybody was clapping. When they reached the table Hannah greeted her with a broad, oily smile. 'Where've you been, me dear?' she asked. Her voice was thick and lazy sounding.

'Talking,' said Rosie.

'Talking? Who to? Was it young Graham Benson? He was at me a while ago enquiring after you. "How long is she staying?" he asked. "She's a smasher," he said. He's a nice fellow is young Benson, and doing well.'

'I think I'll go home, Ma, I'm feeling a bit tired.'

226

'Aw, home hell!' Jimmy looked warningly at Rosie. 'We'll all go shortly. Let's have another round first. An' it's your turn, Shane, me boy.' He turned to his brother. 'An' I'll have a double meself this time, I'm sick of beer.'

There was a babble of talk now and it went over Rosie's head. She watched Shane go for the drinks and return with them, and as he placed them on the table someone began to play the piano and a voice broke into song, and soon almost everybody in the room was singing.

It was when the community singing ended that Rosie saw Ada Lang and Ronnie standing by the bar. Ada had one elbow on the counter and was looking at Ronnie, but Ronnie, with his broad back tight against the counter, was looking directly at her.

Hannah had seen him too, and leaning heavily towards Broderick, she whispered thickly, 'Who's that piece with Ronnie MacFarlane over there? I've never seen her here afore. She doesn't fit in . . . cheap she is. What's things comin' to? She can't be a member, I've never seen her here afore,' she repeated. 'He should have his wife with him; aye, he should. She looks loose, that one. . . .'

'I'm going home, Ma.' Rosie was on her feet and she glanced at Jimmy defiantly as she made this statement, and Hannah looking up at her and still smiling said, 'Oh, it's early. What time is it?'

'It's after ten.'

'Aye, it's after ten,' put in Broderick, 'an' not far off shutting-up time.'

'Is it, begod! Well then, just a minute, just a minute.' As Hannah looked back at Rosie she appeared to be the

227

essence of amenity. 'Let me drink this an' I'll come along. Always go when you're feeling happy I say, never overdo a good thing. It's been a grand evenin'. What say you?' She looked round the table but did not wait for their affirmation, and emptying her glass she rose unsteadily to her feet, crying, 'Ups-a-daisy,' and as she staggered slightly she grabbed at Broderick and they both laughed.

'Where's Barny and Arthur?' she asked.

'Over at yon side,' said Shane. 'You get goin' an I'll collect them. You go along with them, Jimmy.' Shane nodded at his brother, and Jimmy said thickly, 'Aye, I'll go along with them.' What his tone implied was that he would go along with Rosie.

And he did go along with her. He preceded his mother and father out of the room, pressing Rosie before him as he waved goodbye to right and left, and swaying and lunging on the crusting slush, he hung on to her until they reached home. Yet he didn't speak a word to her. Although he was talking all the time all his remarks were thrown over his shoulder to his mother and father, who, arm in arm, came slithering and laughing behind them.

Rosie made no protest whatever against Jimmy's possessive hold on her. Outwardly, she appeared docile, but inwardly she was in a turmoil. She must get her things together and get out of the house as soon as possible. It wasn't Jimmy or Shane's questioning she was afraid of as much as Ronnie MacFarlane's. Whereas Jimmy and Shane could not believe that she was more than lightly acquainted with a woman like Ada Lang, Ronnie seemed to have gauged the truth from the moment he saw them together. And Ada's form of

228

introduction had clinched it. When she had left them she hadn't considered whether or not Ada would give her away, and when she had seen Ronnie looking so pointedly at her she had come to the conclusion that Ada hadn't said anything. But the fact remained that Ronnie guessed at what the lads didn't want to believe, and she must get away. When they were all in bed sleeping their drink-drugged sleep, she would bring downstairs just what she could carry, and she would go to Dennis's until the morning, and from there she would go to her new digs in Newcastle.

Flopping into the big chair near the banked-down fire, Hannah shouted at Broderick, 'Oh, take me shoes off, lad, they're killing me.' Then flinging her arms out towards Rosie, she cried, 'Have you had a good night? Have you enjoyed yourself, lass? You still dance like a fairy. I came and watched you once or twice. You didn't know I did but I did. Oh, you were a sight, with the finest pair of legs in the land. I've always had the faculty of enjoying a pair of legs, like a man.' At this she let her head flop back and the laughter gushed from her. And Broderick roared with her, but not Jimmy. Jimmy was looking really surly now. He was sitting by the table, his elbow on it, his head resting on the palm of his hand, his brow puckered and his lip working as if his fuddled mind was trying to puzzle something out.

'Let's have a bite to eat.' Hannah was shouting now as if they were all in another room. 'I'm as hungry as a hunter. Oh God, oh God, I wish it wasn't Friday so I could have a shive of meat. But there's cheese and pickles and cold fish in the pantry. Go on, fetch them

229

out, Broderick; you're steadier on your pins than me, man.'

'That I am, that I am. You can't carry it, girl, that's your trouble,' said Broderick. 'Come on, Rosie. Let's see what we can rake up.' He held out his arms to her.

In the quiet of the kitchen, his arm still about her, Broderick attempted to focus his wavering gaze on his daughter, and he asked gently, 'Are you all right, me girl, are you all right? It's quiet you are.'

'Yes, I'm all right, Da. Yes, come on.' She turned from him. 'Let's get the things.'

As they went back to the living-room with the food on a tray, Broderick waving a jar of pickles in each hand, the others came in the front way. They were headed by Shane, and as soon as Rosie looked at them and found their gaze directed pointedly towards her she knew that she had been under discussion.

But if the lads were not their usual rowdy Friday night selves, it went unnoticed, because Hannah and Broderick kept up an exchange of quips that evoked their own laughter, and all the while Broderick hung on to Rosie, protesting against her wanting to break up the party and go to bed.

It was nearly an hour later, when Jimmy and Shane were making for upstairs, that the front bell rang. It silenced them all for a moment, and Hannah looking about her said, 'Who can it be at this time of night? You did say Karen was in, didn't you, Arthur?'

'Aye, I saw her coming out of the bathroom.'

'See who it is, Jimmy. See who it is.' Hannah made the request while Jimmy was already on his way to the door.

'Perhaps old Watson's bad next door.' Shane jerked his head to the wall.

'Aw, she would have knocked through if that had been the case,' said Hannah.

'Perhaps old Ma Parkman can't get to sleep for us laughin', an' she's come to complain again.'

'Begod! If she has it'll be the last time, for I'll spit in her eye and christen her Paddy. . . . But whist! Whist! What's that?'

When they all became silent a voice came from the hall, crying, 'I want to see her.'

'It's MacFarlane!' All eyes in the room said it, and Hannah looked quickly towards Rosie where she was standing at the end of the table one hand holding her throat. Then as Jimmy's voice came to them, shouting, 'Look, get yourself to hell out of here unless you're askin' for trouble!' They all, with the exception of Rosie, moved towards the hall, and there wasn't a steady gait among them.

Now Ronnie's voice, thick and fuddled, rose above all the exclamations, crying, 'I'll . . . I'll take you on . . . but one at a time, if you're men enough to do one at a time. An' after I've finished with you all I'll see her. But see her I will.'

'Is it mad you are, Ronnie MacFarlane, disturbing a respectable household at this hour of the night?' Hannah was bawling. 'Get yourself home and to your wife. Aye, to your wife who at this minute might be bringin' a soul into the world. It's ashamed of yourself you should be.'

'Ashamed? Me? Huh!'

The huh! was cut short by Shane. 'Are you goin' to

get out,' he cried, 'or do you want your bloody teeth knocked in?'

'Knock me teeth in, will you? Let me tell you, lad, it won't be like last time. I've come prepared.'

There was a pause; and then Broderick's voice, saying, 'Knuckledusters, begod! That's a low trick, Ronnie. Now look, we want no trouble; get yourself away, man.'

'You dirty sod!' It was Hannah again; and quick as lightning Ronnie answered her. 'Dirty sod, am I? You call me a dirty sod, Hannah Massey? With a daughter like you've got, you call me a dirty sod?'

'Shut your bloody mouth and get out!'

As Jimmy's voice came to Rosie she groped blindly at a chair and sat down. And she held her face in her hands as Ronnie cried, 'Come a step nearer an' I'll let you hev it right atween the eyes. You all know, don't you? You all know what she is. That's why you're scared bloody stiff. But perhaps your dear ma doesn't know. No, perhaps she doesn't. You'd be frightened to tell your ma, lads, wouldn't you? But I'll tell her. . . .'

'Get him out!' It was Shane yelling.

'Hold your hand . . . I'm warning you!' The voice was like thunder. 'Mind it! Mind it! Afore this fist splits your face open. No, the lot of you big sods'll not shut me mouth. I wasn't good enough for your Rosie, was I, Hannah Massey? I mustn't touch her. An' begod! I wouldn't now if you paid me, for she's a whore! An' she's been workin' under a whore master for the last three months with that tart in the bl . . .'

As the house vibrated to the screams and shouts and the thuds of blows, Rosie put her hands over her ears,

232

and, dropping her face down to the table, she moved it back and forward in agony. Then her head was brought up to see Karen by the table shouting 'What's the matter? What's it all about?' When she looked at her for a moment before dropping her head again, Karen ran back towards the hall but it was empty now.

Outside Jimmy and Shane and Ronnie were tangled up on the icy road, while Arthur and Barny, trying to separate them, were involved in the blows. And as Hannah, at the bottom of the steps hanging on to Broderick, screamed unintelligibly, light after light appeared in the windows of the houses up and down the street.

The Parkmans and the Watsons were at their open doors, and now Bob MacFarlane came rushing down his steps buttoning up his trousers and shouting, while Jessie followed him, hugging her fur coat over her nightdress.

The light from the Batemans' front door across the road streamed on to the huddle of men. The Batemans had never been on speaking terms with the Masseys, they considered that the whole family was out of its element living in Grosvenor Road, and now Mr Bateman did what he had wanted to do for a long time, he phoned the police.

When the patrol car, which must have been in the vicinity, came whisking down the street and two police-men joined the mêlée, Hannah's loud voice was stilled for a moment and she staggered back against the stone pillar of the gate, exclaiming in a whisper, 'No! No! Jesus, Mary and Joseph.'

Mr MacFarlane was now aiding the police, as was Mr Bateman, and when the combatants were separated it

233

was hard to tell which was Ronnie or Jimmy or Shane. The only difference between them was that one of them lay still on the ground, and Mr MacFarlane, recognising his own, lifted the blood-stained head, shouting, 'Ronnie! Ronnie!'

The policeman now spoke to Mr Bateman, and once again Mr Bateman was pleased to go to his phone.

At this point Jimmy went to tug himself from the policeman's hold. He didn't like policemen. 'Leave go of me!' He felt fighting mad now, and when he found he was still being held he lashed out with his other arm, and the policeman, losing his balance on the slippery road, fell on his back. He wasn't down for more than a second, and when he got to his feet again his companion came to his aid and they advanced on Jimmy. Shane, standing swaying on the kerb, was in a bad way, but not so bad that he was going to let the 'bloody polis' get at their Jimmy.

Once again there was a mêlée in the road, and now Hannah was only restrained by Broderick from joining in, but her voice soared above all the sound, screaming at her brood to give over, to give over. She did not recognize the police van as such until it stopped almost at her feet, and when she did the disgrace cut off her voice and there was nothing left in her but a whimper which said, 'The Black Maria! The Black Maria!' The Black Maria had come for her sons.

The road seemed full of policemen now, and they were bundling her lads into the van. Barny went in protesting, 'I've done nowt, I've done nowt. Me an' Arthur's done nowt.'

He gripped at the side of the van door and, putting

234

his head back on his shoulders, he strained to look at Hannah, where she was being held in his father's arms, and he cried to her, 'Ma! Ma!' before being pushed forward.

They did not put Ronnie MacFarlane into the van, but into an ambulance. His father was allowed to go with him, but his mother stood on the pavement hugging the coat around her shivering body, and as the police van and the ambulance drove away, one after the other, she turned and looked towards Hannah. And Hannah looked back at her, and neither of them spoke.

Broderick, his face wearing an utterly stricken look now, turned Hannah about and led her up the steps and into the hall; and of a sudden Hannah's legs gave way beneath her and she would have fallen to the floor had not Karen pushed the hall chair forward. 'Almighty God! Almighty God!' Hannah moved her head in a slow wide sweep. 'Me sons, every one of them, taken to jail. Me lads.' She looked up at Broderick. 'What's happened to us? What's happened, I ask you, that me sons . . . What's to be done?' She stared at him wildly.

'They . . . they can get bail, I think, sort . . . sort of,' Broderick stammered. 'I . . . I better go and get D . . . Dennis.'

'Dennis? No! No! Begod, no!' The name seemed to rouse her back to normality.

'I'll have to, woman. He's got a head on his shoulders, he'll know what to do better than me or any of us. You'd rather have that than they'd be kept in jail, wouldn't you now?' He bent towards her. 'I'll put on me coat and get a car and I'll be there in a few minutes. Now stay quiet.' He turned to Karen. 'See to your grannie, that's a good

235

girl, see to your grannie.' He did not go into the living-room or mention Rosie's name, but lifting his coat from the hall-stand and not bothering about his muffler or cap, he slunk out of his front door like a thief in the night, and Hannah was left sitting looking at Karen. She looked at her for some minutes before she said, 'Go on up to your bed.'

'No, I'll stay with you. Me grandda . . .'

'I've told you . . . go to bed. I'm all right.'

'But . . .'

'Did you hear me?' It was the old Hannah speaking, and hearing her, Karen saw no need to worry, at least about her grannie's condition. Shrugging her shoulders, she crossed the hall, glancing into the living-room before she mounted the stairs.

Hannah continued to sit on in the cold hall, and as she sat she looked about her. She looked towards the door of her front room, and through the heavy panels she could see every article of the fine furniture that adorned the room. She looked at the bright red-and-green-patterned stair carpet. She looked down at the rug on the hall floor; it had a two-inch fringe on it. She could have got the same rug without the fringe for four pounds less, but she liked the fringe, it gave an air of quality to the rug. And lastly, she turned her eyes towards the open door of the living-room, and she kept them there until she pulled herself to her feet and advanced slowly towards it.

When she entered the room she saw Rosie sitting at the top end of the table, her face as white as a corpse, her eyes staring out of her head; and as she went towards her she saw her rise to her feet and then back towards the wall. And she followed her until she could touch her with her outstretched arm. But she didn't touch her, she just stood looking at her. And then she began to speak, her voice quiet. She said, 'It's true, isn't it? It's true what he said, that you're a whore?'

'No, no.' Rosie moved her head – it was tight back against the wall, her chin up – not in defiance, but in fear.

'He said you were a whore, and you lived with a whore master for three months.'

'I wasn't, I wasn't. I lived with him . . . I didn't know. . . .' Her head was moving in a tormented, desperate fashion.

Hannah made a movement with her hand that said, 'Say no more', and she went on, 'I wondered who you reminded me of when you stepped into the house a week ago this night with your skin-fit skirt and your short waist jumper that pushed out your breasts like balloons. I wondered then. But who, I ask you, but somebody with the mind of the devil would have put the tab on you. An' that piece that Ronnie was talkin' to standin' at the bar, that was her he meant . . . your pal! It was her you were with, wasn't it, when you disappeared during the evening? And then the story you told me the night you came back. There wasn't a word of truth in it, was there?'

'Ma . . . Ma.' Rosie's head was still moving, and now her eyes were closed and the tears raining from beneath her lids. 'I didn't know, I didn't know.'

'You didn't know you were a prostitute?'

'I wasn't, I never was.'

'Did you live with a whore master?'

'I didn't know he was, I didn't know, I swear by our Lady. . . .'

'Quiet! Quiet!' Now Hannah's voice had changed and it came as a deep growl from her throat. 'Don't dare soil her name with your lips. . . . You tell me out of your own mouth that you lived with this man, and for your companions you had pieces like that one the night, an' you tell me you know nothin' about whoring? I wasn't born yesterday, girl, at least not all of me.' She shook her head until her coiled hair became loose and a strand fell down on to her shoulder. 'Only the part that believed in you; you the shining light of me life, me daughter Rosie. I always held me head high when I mentioned me daughter Rosie. They used to laugh behind me back . . . the neighbours. . . . Oh, I knew. I knew. But when they saw you with their own eyes they thought, She's right. She's right. Her Rosie's a lady if ever there was one. An' those that didn't think along those lines I sensed it, and plugged you at them until they did. Until they knew that Hannah Massey's daughter, Rosie, was a somebody. . . . Aye, begod!' Her voice dropped now and her mouth fell agape before she went on, 'A somebody! A London street whore, a strumpet. Can you hear them? Can you hear them laughin', Rosie?' It was a question. 'Answer me, girl.' Her voice was as terrible as her face now. 'Can you hear them laughin'? They're splitting their sides. They're sick with their laughin'. They're spewing with their laughin'. "The higher they climb," they're sayin', "the longer the fall", and begod! Hannah Massey's fallen hard. Her an' her beautiful daughter, Rosie! Can't you hear them? Can't you hear them laughin', Rosie?'

'Oh, Ma. Oh. Ma, stop it, stop it.'

Hannah stepped back, making a wide sweep of her arm as she did so, crying, 'Don't Ma me, I'm no relation to you. From this minute onward I'm no relation to you, do you hear?' Bending her body forward now she said, 'Do you know what you've done to me this night? Do you?' The words were once again coming deep and guttural, but now they were coated with a terrible anger. 'You've destroyed me. If you'd taken a razor and cut me throat it would've been kind, but no. No . . . you had to disgrace me. Me sons are in jail, me four sons are in jail because of you, do you hear? As for me . . . me life's over. The morrow I was goin' to sign the contract that would take me to Brampton Hill . . . and now what have I?' She wagged her head slowly. 'I haven't even got this home, I'm finished.' Again she wagged her head. 'I've put a face on things, all me life I've put a face on things, but I couldn't put put a face on this, I couldn't look the street in the eye after this. Nor the town. I'm crawling in the muck . . . in the muck. From this moment on I'm dead and I'll have you remember it's you that's done it. You'll take it to the grave with you. Oh dear God, when I think.' She dropped her head back and looked at the ceiling now, her big body sagging as she went on, 'Puttin' you afore everythin' and everybody. Worshipping you. . . . Aw God has strange ways. Indeed, indeed. Ye shall not have false gods afore me, He says, an' if ever a woman has been paid out for havin' a false god it's me this night.' She brought her head forward again, and her lips curling widely from her large square chin, she allowed her eyes to range slowly from Rosie's hair over her terrified face

239

and down to her feet, then up again. And her nose pushing upwards from the force of her curling lips, she ground out, 'You smell! You stink! You're not fit to touch. Me own flesh has gone putrid on me.' As she spoke her body drooped forward into a crouch. Her arms lifting, she shuffled a half-step nearer to Rosie, muttering thickly as she did so, 'You're not fit to touch but I'm goin' to touch you, an' for the last time, I'm goin' to give you somethin' you'll remember for destroying me an' me house.'

At this, Rosie, who had been spread-eagled against the wall, brought her arm in front of her face, crying, 'Don't hit me, Ma! Don't hit me.'

For answer, Hannah's fist shot out, and as the blow caught Rosie between the eyes her scream seemed to rend the house. And when again the fist landed full on her mouth and then on her nose, Rosie's screams turned to a moaning whine.

Hannah, her face distorted, her fist ready to strike again, paused as she watched her daughter slide down the wall to the floor. Her thick arms dropping to her side, she stepped back and looked at the huddled, shaking, moaning form, and she cried, 'Get up!' Then again, 'Do you hear me? Get up!'

After a long moment Rosie got up, raising herself like a cowed animal from the floor, and when she was on her feet she covered her face with her hands as she stumbled forward intending to go towards the table to sit down. But Hannah's voice checked her, screaming at her now, 'Get out! Get out! You trollop you!'

Dazed, moaning and swaying, Rosie stood, until Hannah's single finger dug in her back, thrusting her

240

towards the kitchen, through it and out of the back door, which Hannah almost lifted off its hinges, so fierce was the pull with which she opened it. Then not pausing a moment she closed the door with a bang and bolted it. Following this she moved towards the table and stood leaning against it, blinking down at the conglomeration of dirty plates and cutlery on it. Then lifting her head with a jerk she went out of the kitchen, through the sitting-room and up the stairs, pulling herself up by the banister, and into the bathroom, and there, after taking a bottle of tablets from the cupboard and filling a glass with water she went into her own room and put the bottle and glass on a little table near the bed.

Now inserting her hand into the front of her dress and vest she took out the key of the bottom drawer of the chest, and when she had opened the drawer she carried it to the round table in the middle of the room, after which she went to the altar in the corner near the bed and took from the shelf a box of matches. Following this she went back to the table, and, without even pausing to consider, she lit a match and applied it to the end roll of notes in the drawer. When it was well alight she went to the bed and, sitting down, emptied the tablets from the bottle into the glass of water; still without a pause she swilled them round once or twice then gulped at them, choking and spluttering on the half-dissolved mass. And now she did pause; her movements became less controlled. Slowly she drew the pad of her thumb across each corner of her mouth, then she took in a deep breath and sat watching the smoke rising from the drawer for a moment or two, waiting for the flame to come over the top, but when a whirling movement in her head told her she was going to fall forward she lifted one heavy leg after the other on to the bed and lay down and waited. There was no panic in her waiting, only thoughts of the impress her death would make on her family, and on one member in particular until the day she too died.

She was dead before the breath left her body, and she knew this. She knew she had died when Ronnie MacFarlane knocked on the door.

The Aftermath

It was 5 a.m. when Dennis returned home for the second time that morning. Florence had heard the taxi and was standing at the open door. She put out her hand to him but didn't speak. His face looked white and pinched and his eyes wide. She helped him off with his coat, and still she didn't speak. It was Hughie, standing between the kitchen and the room door, who asked, 'How did you find her?'

'She's dead.'

As Dennis came towards him, Hughie turned and walked back into the room, and together they sat down side by side on the studio couch that was still made up as a bed.

'Give me a drink of something?' Dennis looked up at Florence, who was standing in front of him now.

'Coffee?' she asked quietly. 'It's all ready.'

'No.' Dennis shook his head. 'Have you got a drop of whisky left?'

When she brought him the drink he just sipped at it. Then he looked at the carpet as he said, 'I can't take it in. She was so full blooded you would have thought her aggressiveness would have defied death itself.' Then raising his eyes, he looked at Florence, and it was as if he had forgotten Hughie's presence when he spoke to his wife, saying, 'When I looked at her lying there, so

243

quiet, so peaceful, shouting no more, never again to be unreasonable, or irrational, I felt a flood of tears rising in me; and then I thought of what you've always said about death, and it being the plastic surgery that turns a renegade into a saint, and it checked the flood.'

'Oh don't let it, Dennis, don't let it.' She dropped on to her knees before him and took hold of his hand. 'It's all right talking about these things and being clever when they don't affect you, but . . . but she was your mother.'

Dennis had his eyes closed now and his head was moving in small jerks as he said, 'Don't recant, Florence. Please don't recant, because I'm not going to. She killed herself; out of spite she killed herself; just because her idea of respectability had been shattered, she killed herself. Yet all her life she's been her own stumbling block in her efforts to reach her goal, and by her very last act any glory that her family might have bestowed on her will be tarnished in their own minds by what she did. And I don't mean just her taking her life. Do you know how much money she had stacked away?' He looked from Florence to Hughie.

Hughie, inclining his head, said softly, 'I could give a pretty good guess.'

'I never dreamed she had that much. Nearly three thousand.'

'Three thousand!' repeated Florence in awe. 'Where?'

'In the bottom drawer of the old chest in the bedroom. And she set fire to the lot before she took the pills.'

Florence moved back slowly on her heels, and her buttocks slipped to the floor and she rested there staring at Dennis; and he nodded at her, and then to Hughie, saying, 'When I dropped me da off at the door from the taxi after coming from the station, apparently he went straight upstairs to find the place full of smoke and Karen nearly demented. She had smelt the smoke and gone into me mother's room. The drawer, full of notes, was smouldering, some apparently had been alight but had died down, but the whole could have burst into flames at any minute. She didn't know what was in the drawer at first, she just threw water over the lot then tried to wake me mother up. It was then me da came in. He tried to get her on to her feet and make her sick, but she was too far gone. It would have been all right but she'd had a number of chasers in her before she took the tablets. Karen ran out and phoned the hospital, and then . . . well, you know the rest, she came on here for me.'

'Have they let the lads out, knowing this?' asked Hughie.

'No. I haven't been back to the station yet, and I don't know how I'm going to tell them. Anyway, their case won't come up until the first Court. If our Jimmy and Shane hadn't hit the polis they might have stretched a point, but they weren't too easy with them when they got them down there I understand.'

Dennis finished off the whisky; then looking at the glass, said, 'They'll mourn her. Each in his own way they'll mourn her, but on the quiet they'll be thinking she meant to burn every penny of that money . . . their money. Yet being very much her sons they'll remember what she used to say, "Speak nicely about the dead", she used to say, "for where they've gone they've got power and can bring good or bad to you." '

'Rosie will get the blame for this.' Hughie was speaking almost to himself, and Florence answered, saying, 'Yes, from all sides it'll be levelled at her.' She turned her head towards Dennis. 'You didn't hear any more, where she went I mean?'

'No, only Karen heard me mother at her. But I found Karen a bit cagey about what went on. Of course she's upset. She said she heard me mother put her out and bang the door. You know I . . . I just can't take it in about her. If it hadn't been me da who told me . . .' He shook his head. 'Rosie on the streets. . . .'

'No, no!' Hughie's tone brought Dennis's head round, and also Florence's eyes towards him, and he said again, and emphatically, 'No, no! She wasn't on the street, Dennis. I . . . I didn't say anything afore, because . . . well I was shaken about it all coming out and wondering where she had got to in the dark, and on a night like this, but I can tell you now the mess she got into wasn't her fault. She told me about it the other night when she was here, the night you went out.'

'Aye?' Dennis moved slowly round to face Hughie, saying, 'Well, go on. What's her side of it?'

Hughie pursed his lips. 'Well, as she told me it was like this. As you know, for the first year or more she was up there she shared a flat with two other girls at the office. Well, she said it was an expensive place and very nice. Then one of the girls goes back home to Gloucester and the other gets married, and it was impossible for her to keep it on. She then pals up with another girl and shares her flat. But this place is real slummy and dirty. And she doesn't like the girl either, and she's lonely. She was on the point of packing the job up, she said, and coming home, when one Sunday night, coming out of Benediction, she sees a fellow standing on the kerb

246

right opposite the church. She had seen him there two or three times before when she came out of church and had thought naturally that he'd just come out too. Well this night he speaks to her, and that was the beginning. He's very smartly dressed, he speaks well, he's courteous and extremely kind and . . .' Hughie looked down at his hands. 'To use her own words, she went down before him like warmed snow off a roof. Apparently he was quite open about himself. He was married but his divorce was going through. He was in the property business which fluctuated from time to time. Sometimes he was in the money, he said, and sometimes he was broke. At this particular time, apparently, he was in the money. He asked her to go to his flat, but it was six weeks before she finally paid her first visit. It was a beautiful place, she said, furnished with the kind of things you see in expensive magazines. A month later she gives up her job and moves in.' Hughie pulled the knuckle of his first finger, and there was a sharp cracking sound; then he went on, 'He had to be away a lot on business, she said, but when they were together everything was marvellous. The only thing she didn't like was that he had to go to clubs to meet business associates and he always insisted she went with him. She didn't like his business friends, and apparently neither did he, and he apologised for them. All this time he is piling on her furs, jewellery and expensive clothes. Then one night he comes home worried. He's in a bit of a jam, he says, he's got to meet a client who can make or break him. Will she be nice to the man? They meet this client in a private room in a hotel, and after dinner this fellow of hers is called away and she is left alone with this man, who begins to paw

247

her. But . . . but she manages to push him off and get out of the room. She can't find the other fellow and she goes home. When he turns up he's terribly upset for her. Later in the week he tells her that the client has been spiteful and has put him in a real fix, in fact he's broke; at least for a time and won't be able to keep up the expensive apartment. Rosie said it didn't matter a jot when it came to pawning her clothes and furs and all the expensive presents he had given her. But now she was uneasy, yet she really wouldn't face up to why she was uneasy.'

'It's . . . it's fantastic,' put in Florence. 'Like . . . like a novelette. Fancy her being taken in by it . . . Rosie . . . she seems so all there.'

'Be quiet a minute,' said Dennis. 'Go on, Hughie.'

'Well, she tells him she would take up a job again, but he won't hear of it. Then they moved to another flat . . . one of three in an old house, towards the outskirts of London, and it's in sharp contrast to the luxurious place they have left. The fellow gives Rosie to understand that she has the power to put him back on . . . on his business feet if she'll only be nice to the fellows he introduces her to. Even when she knows what these supposedly business associates want she doesn't really connect it with him until she realizes the girl in the flat above and the one in the flat below are call girls; and not until it's brought home to her that they are both known to this fellow does she face the truth. And then she is terrified. The fellow now hardly ever goes out, hardly ever leaves her alone. The only time she goes out alone is when she goes to the shops along the street, and then he doles her out the money for food. She has no

248

clothes, only those she stands up in, and he had bought her these. And by now she is so frightened she does everything without protest. When the other girl upstairs – her name was Ada – hadn't customers she came down and talked to Rosie, and apparently she felt a bit sorry for her. Rosie even heard her telling the man that he was wasting his time and that she, Rosie, hadn't . . . hadn't what it took for the game. Eventually, the fellow seemed to realize this himself but he wasn't going to lose anything on her. Apparently he did a side line in shipping girls abroad, and that's what he intended to do with Rosie. It was this girl Ada who gave her the tip that she was to be moved on that Saturday night.'

'God in Heaven!' Dennis looked at Florence's stretched face. 'Can you believe it?' he asked now, and when she just moved her head, he said to Hughie again, 'I'm sorry, go on.'

'Well, Rosie said when she first met him he had given her a ring, it was an ornate affair and he called it their wedding ring. She thought it was worth about twenty pounds, and he had let her keep it when he took all her other things. As long as we have the ring, he had said, we'll be able to eat. But on the Friday morning, he took it off her hand, seemingly full of regret, and said, "It's the last lap." And then he asked her would she like to go home because he couldn't see himself ever getting on to his feet again. It was then that she used all the resources in her and played his game and said yes, she would like to go home.

' "We'll see about it the night, the sooner the better," he said, and having, he thought, allayed her fears, he had no hesitation in giving her the money to go and get some shopping. Yet she knew that every move she made was watched by him through the man who sold papers on the other side of the street. When she went into the bedroom for her coat she whipped the ring from his pocket. It was the only way she could think of to get the money to come home. It was either that or go to the police, and she couldn't bear the thought of coming into the open about her position in case the news was transferred to the police here, and the thought of . . . of her mother hearing of what had happened terrified her even more than the man. . . . Well, she pawned the ring for ten pounds. That was last Friday.'

They were all silent for some time; then Florence, rising to her feet, murmured, 'It's unbelievable, yet it's happening every day. But you wouldn't think girls would be so gullible now. . . . And . . . and Rosie. I say again, she looked so all-there, so self-assured.'

'What we've got to remember, Florence,' said Hughie, 'is that Rosie didn't fall in love with a pimp, she fell in love with a polished, soft-spoken, kind man. She went to live with him because she was fascinated by him and thought she loved him, and she stayed with him because she really believed he was going downhill and in trouble. The pattern was so simple, it was almost diabolical. And you know what influenced her in the first place?' He looked directly at Dennis. 'She had met him outside a Catholic church. It was a sort of symbol to her.'

'Shades of Hannah Massey,' said Dennis pitifully, as he rose to his feet. Then covering the lower half of his face with his hand, he went out of the room.

Florence gazed after him but did not follow him; she got up from the floor and sat down beside Hughie, and pressing her hands between her knees, she said, 'All our philosophizing and theorizing doesn't mean much when it comes to the push, Hughie, does it? The plastic surgery takes effect whether you like it or not, at least with most of us. I only hope it does with Dennis, I do. I never liked his mother and she always hated me, but then there was no blood between us; but no matter what he says or thinks he still remains part of her, and you can't get away from yourself, can you? That's the one thing no theory can do for you, remove you from yourself. But,' she straightened herself, 'the one I'm worrying about at the present moment is Rosie. Where do you think she got to in the night? She couldn't wander the streets, she would freeze, or the police would pick her up. Do you think she would go into any of the neighbours?'

'No, I don't think so, Florence.' Hughie was staring across the room. 'And she wasn't at the station; I thought this was the likely place.'

'You went to the station?'

'Yes. When I found Dennis and Broderick had left the police station I called on me way back. But it was closed. I never knew they closed it at night. They don't open until the first train at five o'clock.'

'It's so hard to take in all at once.' Florence looked at Hughie. 'Her dead, and the four lads in jail, and Rosie God knows where. It doesn't seem as if it could have happened in such a short time . . . and all because a well-dressed man with a smooth tongue spoke to Rosie outside a Catholic church. . . . Fantastic, isn't it, that everything began at that point?'

'Oh, I think you can trace it back earlier than that, Florence.' Hughie moved his closed fist over his mouth.

251

'In fact, you could start at the moment Rosie was born when Hannah determined to make her into a lady, her kind of lady. Or the day Hannah stopped in the middle of her washing and took her to the typing school. Oh, there are many points where you could start. You could even go back to the day when Hannah was born, or the day when she landed with her mother from Ireland . . . or perhaps the real point from where all this started was the day when she went to work on Brampton Hill. The grandeur of number eight fascinated her and it was her life's aim to imitate it. But she was a poor mimic was Hannah, she was always a poor mimic.' He began to rub one shoulder with his hand as if to smooth away a pain.

Florence stood up now, saying, 'Lie down for a couple of hours, Hughie; I'll try to get him to do the same. There's going to be a busy day ahead.'

Hughie nodded to her. 'Yes, yes,' he said, but when he had the room to himself he began pacing the floor, still rubbing his shoulder. Then as he was about to pass the couch he sat down suddenly on it and, swinging his feet up, he turned his face into the pillow. It was many a long day since he had wanted to cry, but he wanted to cry now. Not for Hannah. No, no, he was no hypocrite. He could say he was glad she was dead. But he wanted to cry for Rosie who would have to carry her death. All her life till she died she would have to bear the weight of her mother's death. For they would saddle her with it, every one of them. 'If it hadn't been for our Rosie,' they would say, 'me Ma would've been alive the day.' Yet their blame would be nothing to the weight of her own conscience.

And where was she now? Perhaps sitting in some

all-night lorry driver's café, or getting a lift south. But wherever she was he had the feeling she was far away and that he would never see her in his life again.

It was about half past six when Dennis put his head tentatively round the door to ascertain whether Hughie was asleep, and seeing him sitting up on the couch he whispered, 'I'm just off to catch the first bus.'

Hughie, getting to his feet, said, 'Tell your da I'm sorry, and if there's anything I can do later on in the morning, standing bail or anything, he's just got to say, because if the money in the drawer is half burnt it'll have to go through the Bank before it's valid again, you know.'

Dennis nodded dully. 'I'll tell him,' he said. 'Florence is asleep, I'm letting her lie.'

'Yes, let her lie. So long, Dennis.'

'So long. . . .'

Florence was still asleep when, at half past eight, a knock came on the door, which, opened by Hughie, revealed two small boys.

'Are you the cobbler, mister?' said the taller of the two.

'Yes, sonny,' Hughie nodded at them.

'Well we want wor boots. We've been to the shop umpteen times an' it's shut, an' we went to t'other house and it's shut an' all. An' we went t'other day to the house where you live, an' the wife chased us, but me ma sent us back this mornin' an' the man there told us to come here and tell you.'

'Didn't you see a notice in the window telling you to go next door?' asked Hughie.

'Aye, we did. Aa told ya. We pummelled that door an' all, but there's nobody their neither.'

'Come in, out of the cold,' said Hughie, 'and wait till I get me things on.'

'What is it, Hughie?' Florence came to the bedroom door, blinking the sleep from her eyes as she looked at the boys, and when he explained their visit, she said, 'Oh! You'll have to go then. Sure you feel up to it?'

'Yes, I feel perfectly all right.'

'What time did Dennis go? I didn't hear him.'

'He caught the first bus. . . . Come on,' he said to the two boys as he tucked his scarf inside his coat and pulled on his cap, and together they went out.

'Did you go round the back lane at all?' he asked them. 'Mr Cullen's got a big yard there, that's where he works. Perhaps that's why he didn't hear you.'

'We didn't know there was a back-way,' answered the elder boy, 'an' the man from farther up said that the joiner was in bed anyway with rheumatics. But that was just this mornin' when we was knockin' again.'

In the bus the smaller boy turned up the bottom of his shoe and said, 'Me sole's been lettin' in all week.'

'I'm sorry,' said Hughie, and he was sorry. He knew he should have written to Lance Briggs, who would have been along like a shot after he had finished at the factory and seen to things, but Lance wouldn't have come on his own, not before this afternoon when it had been arranged he should take over, because he would be too afraid of appearing pushing.

When they reached the shop he stretched up and felt for the key on the back of the hopper. It surprised him when it wasn't there, and the thought did flash through his mind that perhaps Rosie hadn't been able to reach it. He didn't ask where else she would have put it but thrust his hand into his jacket pocket and took out a key ring. He had always kept a spare. When he opened the door the boys followed him into the shop and the small one said immediately, 'There they are,' as he pointed to one of the shelves.

'Oh, your name's Ratcliffe,' said Hughie, looking at the ticket on the boots. 'You're Mr Ratcliffe's boys?'

They nodded, and then the younger one put in again, 'Me ma's always sayin' to me da it's too far to bring mendin', but me da says you're cheaper and better than the Co-op.'

Hughie was forced to smile. 'That'll be fifteen shillings,' he said.

When the boys counted the money out to him he looked down at them and asked, 'What would you do with fifteen shillings, eh?'

They screwed up their faces at him.

'I'm leaving the shop,' he said, 'there's a new man taking over on Monday, but tell your da the work'll be as good and as cheap as ever. Now here . . .' He took the ten shilling note and handed it to the older boy, saying, 'Give that ten shillings to your ma and tell her to get something nice for your teas, and split this atween you.' He then handed him the two shilling bits and a shilling.

'Ee, mister! You sure it's all right?'

'Of course it's all right.'

'Me ma mightn't believe us.'

'That's true.' He nodded at them. 'Wait a minute.' He pulled a loose pad towards him and wrote on it, 'I've given your boys the boot money back.' Then he signed his name.

'You won the pools, Mister? Is that why you're givin' up?'

'Well something like that.' He nodded at them, and with a hand on each of their shoulders he turned them about and pushed them towards the door.

'Thanks, mister.'

'Aye, thanks, mister.'

'Mind how you go.'

'Aye, mister.'

They didn't mind how they went, they went running and skipping down the icy hill, and Hughie watched them for a moment with a sort of envy before turning into the shop and closing the door. As he did so he noticed the paper lying in front of the window, and, picking it up, he saw it was the notice he had given Rosie. So she had been here, or Jim Cullen had. Well, anyway, he'd have to stay this morning, until Lance turned up in case anybody came for their boots. There were about fifteen pairs of shoes and boots to be collected and about the same number to be repaired. He should have got in touch with Lance before now; he didn't know what he had been thinking about.

He went round the counter and entered the back shop, and what he saw transfixed him for a moment in horror.

Rosie was lying on the bed chair. He knew it was her by her hair and her figure; he would never have been able to recognize her by her face.

'Ooh! Ooh! Ro-sie.' He groaned out the words as he moved slowly towards her, and, dropping down by the

256

side of the chair, he put out a trembling hand to her face. As he did so she opened as much of her eyes as she could. The whole expanse of the upper part of her face was black, swollen and distorted, while her mouth, that tender once laughing mouth, was now a shapeless bloody mass. Her lips were fixed apart and showed a gap where two or three teeth were missing.

'Oh! Rosie, Rosie.' He lifted up her hand, which too was bloody and dead cold.

When he saw her lips trying to move and the narrow slits of her eyes close in pain with the effort, he gabbled, 'Don't don't. Don't move, don't say anything; lie still.' He got to his feet and looked about him as if not sure what to do. The room was like death and she was wearing nothing but the dress he had seen her in the night she first came home.

'You'll be all right, you'll be all right.' He was still gabbling. 'Just lie still.' He rushed to the stove and lit it and put on the kettle; then back to the oil stove and, lighting that turned it to its full extent. Coming to her again, he bent over her. Then saying to himself, 'What am I thinking about?' He tore off his coat and covered her with it. Dashing into the shop, where hung an old coat and an overall on a peg, he snatched these down and came back to her. Gently he raised her feet and folded the coats about them. Then kneeling by her side again he brought his face down to hers and asked very quietly but urgently, 'Who did this to you? Tell me, Rosie. Who did this to you?'

When for an answer the slits of her eyes closed again, he said, 'When I find out who's done this I'll kill them. I swear to God I'll kill them. . . . Aw, Rosie.' He put

257

out his hand to her hair, but so light was his touch that she didn't feel it.

When the kettle whistled he jumped to his feet and mashed a pot of tea, but before he poured the rest of the hot water into a basin he had to take the towel and wipe his face. Last night . . . or this morning it was, he'd had to stop himself from crying, but now he had been crying and hadn't known he was. It was many, many years since he had really cried. It was the day Hannah had cornered him up in the attic and told him that he had fathered Moira's child. She had beaten him black and blue where it didn't show, and nobody knew except him, and her, and Moira. It was from that time he'd had a room to himself . . . the box room, in which you could turn round and that was all.

When he brought the bowl and flannel to her side he was afraid to touch her face, until her lips making a stiff motion she spoke his name, 'Hughie.'

'Yes, Rosie, what is it?'

'I'm . . . I'm v-very cold, Hughie.' He could just make out the words . . . 'Me hands.'

'Put them in the water.' He lifted one hand and put it in the dish that stood on the chair, and taking the hot, wet flannel, he wrapped it around the other hand.

He left her for a moment, to pour out a cup of tea, which he brought to her, saying, 'Try to drink this.' But when he put the hot cup to her lips she started and gave the first real movement since he had come into the room.

'Oh, I'm sorry, I'm sorry.' He was all clumsy contrition. 'I should have thought, I should have put more milk in it. Look, I'll pour it in the saucer.' But when he put the tea in the saucer she couldn't swallow it and it

258

ran down the side of her mouth and over the dried blood and on to her dress.

'Rosie.' He hovered above her. 'Look, you're in a bad way. 'I'll . . . I'll have to get a doctor. There's one just lives two streets away. If I slip out now I'll catch him afore he finishes his surgery. Look, I'll go now, I won't be five minutes. Lie quiet now. All right?'

When she made no move he turned from her and hurried through the shop, just as he was, without cap, coat or muffler, and, locking the door, he pelted down the hill, across the road, and didn't stop until he reached the doctor's surgery. . . .

'A young girl been beaten up?' said the doctor. 'By whom?'

'I don't know.'

'Funny.' The doctor didn't say this but his look said it for him. 'I'll be with you in a minute.' He left Hughie, and when he returned carrying a bag, he said, 'We'll go now,' and led the way to his car. A few minutes later he was looking down at Rosie.

'How did this happen?' he asked her gently.

She made no effort to answer, just an almost imperceptible movement with her head. His hands were tender as he touched her face, and his voice was equally so as he said, 'I'm afraid you'll have to go to hospital, my dear.'

She made another movement, and now her eyes turned in Hughie's direction.

Hughie, too, thought with the doctor that she should go to hospital; that was, until he remembered that Hannah was in hospital . . . in the mortuary. There was only one hospital in the town. It wasn't possible that

Rosie would be long there before she found out about her mother.

He found himself stammering, 'I don't think she wants to go to hos . . . hospital, doctor. She'll be all right at her brother's. If you would just tell me . . . tell me what to do.'

The doctor moved slowly away from Rosie. He moved into the shop as though he was still walking in the same room, and Hughie followed him.

'Her lip will have to be stitched inside.' The doctor looked at Hughie. 'There's nothing much can be done to her face only apply an ointment. That will take time. But she's suffering from shock, and she should go to hospital.'

Hughie looked down at his own twisting hands, and then he said, 'Her mother committed suicide this morning, doctor. She was taken to hospital. She,' he motioned towards the room, 'she doesn't know. There was a fight, a . . . a family row. If she knows what has happened to her mother she'll blame herself . . . because, well' – it was difficult for him to say what he had to say – 'well, in a way she was the cause of the . . . the row . . . you see?'

'Yes, yes.' The doctor's brows moved upwards. 'Yes, I see what you mean. She'll be all right at this brother's?'

'Oh, yes, yes. And I'll be there.'

'Are you a relation?'

Hughie's eyes flicked downwards again. 'No, but I've lived in the same house with her since she was born.'

'Have you any idea how she really came by this?' The doctor touched his own face. 'As you said earlier, it looks as if she's been beaten up. Can you throw any light on it?'

'No, no.' Hughie shook his head. 'Except . . . well, there's a man she's been connected with. He could have done it, but . . . well, it's the time factor. I understand she left home after twelve last night. He could have been waiting for her, but I just don't know. And then there was a woman . . . she was with her at the club earlier on. . . .'

'Oh, that isn't a woman's work.' The doctor paused before moving back into the room and said under his breath, 'If she'll name who did it, he's in for a nice quiet stretch.' He flicked his eyes towards Hughie and his words were scarcely audible as he asked, 'Was . . . was she a good girl?'

Hughie returned the doctor's glance without blinking. 'Yes,' he said definitely. 'Yes.'

The doctor's brows moved upwards again and then he asked briefly, 'Good looking?'

'Beautiful.'

'Hmm! Well, let's hope that this will leave no mark outside or in. But only time will tell that.'

Yes, thought Hughie, as he followed him back in the room, only time would tell that. And then he found himself replying, as it were, to an inner voice, saying, 'Well, she is a good girl, she is.'

It was odd how the mind worked.

Dennis came slowly out of the bedroom and into the hallway where Florence and Hughie were waiting for him. He looked more shaken now than when he had returned in the early hours of the morning from the

261

hospital. He glanced from Florence to Hughie, then swung his head sideways, and with it held at an angle he passed them and went into the room.

'Terrible, isn't it?' Florence went to his side.

He did not answer her but drew his hand around the back of his neck; then looking up at Hughie who had come to stand in front of him, he said. 'You know who did it?'

Hughie shook his head. 'She didn't say.'

Now Dennis looked from one to the other of them again, and his lips moved, but he didn't speak until he turned his head towards the window. Then he said, 'Me mother.'

No exclamation came from either Florence or Hughie, and Dennis said no more. The situation had gone beyond discussion for the moment. . . .

Nor did they bring the topic up during the hours that followed. Dennis related in a somewhat desultory fashion that the lads had been allowed bail and their case adjourned until a week come Monday because of the circumstances of their mother's death; that Ronnie MacFarlane was still in hospital but would likely be out in a day or two; also that there were a few lines of Stop Press in the *Fellburn Observer*, which Dennis said, would keep the appetites whetted until the full account came out next week. And all the while Rosie lay sleeping in the bedroom. She would sleep, the doctor said, for around twenty-four hours, and this would be the best medicine for her.

It was on Sunday afternoon just as the light was fading that Dennis made a statement which startled Hughie. It was a bold statement, and apropos of nothing that had ever been discussed between them. 'You're in love with our Rosie, aren't you?' Dennis said.

The question actually brought Hughie out of his chair, and he stood looking down at Dennis while the bones of his jaws moved backwards and forwards; then, he said, 'What makes you think that?'

'Look, come off it, Hughie. Don't stall. If I'm wrong, well I'm wrong, but it isn't the day or yesterday that I've known how you felt about her; at least,' he jerked his head, 'I felt sure I was right. Anyway if I'm wrong about that, well I must be wrong about lots of other things too. . . . But it's true, isn't it?'

Hughie turned his back towards Dennis and walked to the window and looked out on to the slush-strewn road.

'How many other people think they know how I feel?' he asked in a tight voice.

'Florence.'

'And all the lads I suppose?'

'No. No, it never entered their heads, I'm sure of that. . . . But . . . but she did.' Dennis did not say, 'Me mother.'

'Yes, she did.' Hughie inhaled deeply; then turning and coming back towards Dennis he asked, still in a tight, stiff fashion, 'Well what difference does it make?. Why had you to bring it up, Dennis . . . ? It's no good.'

'Sit down, man. The trouble with you . . .' Dennis nodded rapidly up at Hughie, 'the trouble with you is you don't know your own worth, you never have. Sit down.' He jerked his hand towards the chair, and when Hughie sat down he leant towards him, saying earnestly, 'Take her away with you, Hughie, take her out of this.'

263

'Aw, Dennis, talk sense. Do you think for a moment she'd come with me?' His voice ended on a high derogatory note.

'Yes I do, and so does Florence. Women sense these things quicker than men. Florence feels that you'll have little persuading to do, specially now.'

Hughie beat his knuckles together as he repeated, 'Especially now when she's at a disadvantage, eh? If she did say she would come I'd always know she took it as a last line of escape.'

'Well you want to help her, don't you?'

'Yes, I want to help her.'

'Then do it just because of that.'

Hughie got to his feet again. 'She'd never come.'

'Well, you won't know until you ask her, will you? And you'll be in no worse position if she refuses; you were going away on your own, anyway, weren't you? Don't you think it's worth a try . . . ? Think about it, there's plenty of time.'

'Do you think so?' Hughie turned and looked at Dennis over his shoulder. 'I mean about time, an' I don't mean in my case but in hers. I think the quicker she gets away from this town the better, because if she hears about her mother God knows what effect it will have on her.'

'Well then, there you are.' Dennis was also on his feet now, but Hughie brushed the conclusion aside with, 'I'm thinking about arranging for a holiday for her so that she can get away as soon as she gets on her feet. She needn't know about a thing. It isn't likely that the lads will come here, is it?'

'No, it isn't likely; but don't you be such a blasted

264

fool, man. And what will happen to her on her own at some guest house or hotel? She wants someone near her who knows all about her. There's a strong sense of home in Rosie, it's in all of us; that's why she came back. I would have done the same in her case; in fact I've been doing it for years. Even when I knew there'd be a row as soon as I put my nose in the door, I had to go home every now and again. Rosie will never survive on her own . . . and I don't like to think what she will come to if she's left on her own . . . you know what I mean, don't you?'

Hughie made no answer but started to walk about the room again, until Dennis asked, 'Is there much more to do to the caravan?'

'I don't know.' Hughie paused in his walk. 'Old Jim's in bed, I hear . . . I . . . I think I'll take a dander over now and see how far he's got.'

Dennis nodded at him. 'Do that,' he said. 'And if he's not up to it I would get somebody else to finish it. The funeral's on Wednesday . . . I'd get away before then if you can.'

'Aw, but . . .' Hughie turned, his hand out, protesting, towards Dennis, and Dennis making the same gesture back said, 'No aw buts. Go on, man and get that bit settled; and who knows but the rest will fall into place.'

Rosie became fully awake by seven o'clock on the Sunday evening. She was shuddered into awareness by a voice echoing down a long corridor. It was her mother's voice and she was running away from it. Her shuddering moved the muscles of her face, and the pain brought her hand up sharply to her head. She opened her eyes as wide as she could and saw Hughie sitting by her side.

'I've . . . I've had . . . an awful dream, Hughie.'

'You're awake now; you're all right, Rosie.' He took hold of her hand and smoothed it gently.

'I thought . . . I thought for a moment she . . . she was dead.' Like Dennis, she hadn't said 'me ma'. The words came through the misshaped mouth in a whisper. 'It . . . it was a terrible dream.'

Hughie's hand had become still, and with it his whole body, while his pores opened and he began to sweat; and now he said, his voice shaking just the slightest, 'Don't let it worry you, it . . . it was just a dream. . . . How are you feeling?'

She looked at him, then made a small movement with her head. 'Awful, Hughie,' she said. 'Awful. My mouth's so sore.'

'That's the stitches,' he said. 'You'll feel better soon.'

'Will you stay with me, Hughie?'

'As long as you want, Rosie.'

And he stayed with her until an hour later when, after another dose of tablets, she went to sleep again. . . .

On the Monday when Florence asked her if she would like to get up for a while she seemed a little taken aback, for she felt she hadn't the power to move, but with an effort she sat up in a chair.

But on the Tuesday morning she got up and dressed, putting on once again her blood-stained suit. But she did not leave the bedroom. Now she could move her lips a little but the whole of her face felt more painful than ever, and when she caught sight of it in the mirror it was

266

impossible for her to believe that she was looking at herself. She stared at the black, blue and yellow contorted mass, at the shapeless lips and the black gap where her teeth had been, and she said, 'Oh God! Oh God! How could she.' Yet hadn't she always known that her mother was capable of all kinds of cruelty? That was why her lavish generosity towards her had always frightened her. Her mother's giving had been a kind of insurance which one day she expected to pay off in such a way that the name of Hannah Massey would be enhanced.

If she had come home and told her she was going to have a baby she would have gone mad, but it would have been a controlled madness, for she would have arranged for her to go away until . . . the disgrace was over. And she would have comforted herself with the thought that 'her poor innocent child was took down'. Looking back now, Rosie knew that if she had told her mother the real truth Hannah might have wanted to kill her; and she would, without doubt, have told her to get out, but still she would have kept everything under control. The men would have known nothing about it. And when she didn't come home again Hannah would have declared to her family, 'Well, that's daughters for you. You bring them up on the best and then they do well for themselves and don't want to know you.'

But the unforgivable thing in her mother's eyes was that her sin had been made public. She had destroyed her, she had said, meaning that she had blown up the ivory tower of eight Brampton Hill.

Florence came into the room now and Rosie, looking

at her through the mirror, asked pitifully, 'What am I going to do, Florence?'

Florence put her arms about her, saying, 'In a few weeks it'll be back to normal. The doctor says there won't be any marks, the split was inside your lip. Don't cry, my dear, don't cry. You're more than welcome to stay with us, you know you are. . . . But . . . but . . .'

As she floundered, the sound of a door opening caused her to exclaim, 'If that's Hughie I'll just slip out for a bit of shopping and get back before Dennis comes in. Will you be all right, dear?' She bent over her.

'Yes, Florence, thanks.'

'Now don't cry, everything will be all right, you'll see.'

When Florence reached the kitchen Hughie was standing warming his hands over the boiler. He turned at her approach and asked quickly, 'How is she?'

'She's up.' Florence shook her head. 'She was at the mirror and I thought she was going to pass out; she's upset. And who wouldn't be? How did you find things?'

'Oh fine; the fellow will be finished the night. Everything's ready, I can start anytime.'

'I, Hughie?' Florence repeated. 'Not we?'

Hughie rubbed his hands over the top of the boiler. 'I haven't got the nerve, Florence, and that's the truth.'

'But you want to help her, Hughie, don't you?'

'Of course; but there's other ways than asking her to come with me, when . . . when she's at this low ebb.'

'It's the best thing that could happen to you both, Hughie.' Florence was standing close to him. 'You could make her happy, I know you could. And she could make a different man of you. Not' – she put out her hand and

268

touched him – 'not that I want you any different, but you know what I mean, Hughie. Inside, you'd feel different, self-assured. . . . No more timidity.'

'Oh, I know fine well all about that part of it, Florence.' He drew his breath in. 'But it seems like taking advantage of her. . . .'

'Aw!' Florence gripped his arm and shook him. 'You make me wild, Hughie . . . Well anyway, go on in with her now. I'm going out to do a bit of shopping.'

'Oh, I'll run you there . . . Look.' He drew her to the kitchen window and pointed. 'I called at the garage and picked it up. Everything's in shape.' He pointed towards the Land-Rover out on the road, and Florence said, 'Good, good. But the shop isn't ten minutes away.'

'But you might slip, it's all slushy.'

'I never slip. Have I slipped yet? Go on,' she pushed him and hissed at him, 'and do something.'

A few minutes later Hughie nervously knocked on the bedroom door, but when he entered the room and saw Rosie sitting by the bed his face brightened, and he said cheerily, 'Well, that's more like it . . . how do you feel?' Then without waiting for her answer he went on, 'You're bound to feel mouldy for some time but you're up, that's something.'

When he sat down opposite her she looked at him for a moment before saying, 'It's Tuesday today, isn't it, and you were going yesterday.'

'Oh, things weren't quite ready. Old Jim Cullen had rheumatism and couldn't finish the caravan.' He smiled.

'You won't be going then . . . not yet awhile?'

'Well' – he dropped his head to one side and looked towards the floor – 'everything's ready now. There

269

wasn't really much to do, and Jim didn't mind me getting another fellow to finish it. The roads are still a bit slushy but I've just got to drive the lot to the airport. I've decided to have it taken to the other side by air ferry. Amazing to be able to do that, isn't it?' He lifted his head and glanced at her as if to confirm that she agreed with him on the wonders of aviation.

She was staring fixedly at him through the swollen narrow slits of her eyes. 'When are you going?' she asked.

'Well . . . well . . .' He had his hands joined and was rubbing the palms together. 'Well I could leave to-morrow, but you've got to give a little notice for the plane and things, you know.' He nodded at her. 'I'm going to phone the night; I just may be lucky and get a booking.'

'I'm . . . I'm going to miss you, Hughie.'

He did not say, 'I'll miss you, too,' but said in a small voice, 'Will you Rosie?'

She remained very still, just looking at him. And he returned her gaze as he said, 'Well . . . well you know, there's . . . there's an alternative, Rosie. You needn't miss me.' Now his head jerked and his voice had a nervous gabbling sound as he rushed on, 'I'm no good at this, I'll put it all wrong. The whole thing is, I . . . I don't want to take advantage of you, but it isn't the day or yesterday that I've wanted . . . well . . . Oh, Rosie. . . .' He closed his eyes, then shading them with his hand he murmured, 'I want you to come with me . . . but only for a time, until you're better and on your feet again. I . . . I won't make any claim on you, don't think that, or . . . or think you will marry me or anything like that.

You can be just as free as you are now, but if you came with me you would . . .' He stopped when he felt her hands on his, and as he gripped them he rose to his feet, saying, 'You would, Rosie?' There was awe in his tone.

For answer she moved her head in the direction of his arm as if searching for some place to rest it.

He had held her for only a second when the front door bell rang, and his body stiffened before he whispered, 'Let them ring.' As he pressed her gently to him the bell rang again, and he looked down into her face now and said, 'It couldn't be Dennis has forgotten his key, it's too early for him. Anyway, the back door's open.' When the bell rang for the third time he smiled at her, saying, 'I'd better see.' But before he moved away he brought his eyes on a level with hers, and looking into them, he said softly, 'Aw, Rosie,' and the words were like a passionate endearment.

He didn't hurry out of the room, but walked as he felt, in a relaxed fashion. He was warm inside, glowing as with joy. He had never experienced joy before. Then as he crossed the hall to the front door the kitchen door opened and he was confronted by Broderick.

If the devil had risen up out of the floor he couldn't have been more startled, not only because of the unexpectedness of Broderick's presence at this particular moment in the house, but also at his changed appearance, for he was not looking at the spritely, virile man of sixty-two but at an old, stooped, haggard man, with pain-filled eyes.

'Anybody in?'

'No. Well, I mean Florence has gone out shopping, Broderick, and . . . and Dennis isn't back yet from school.' He pushed past the older man, drawing him back into the kitchen, saying, 'I'll make you a cup of tea, you look cold. Sit down, Broderick. I won't be a minute.'

Broderick came and stood by the table. 'Don't make any tea for me,' he said; and then he asked, 'Is Rosie here, Hughie?'

Hughie had been half-turned towards the sink, and now he swung round and asked, 'What makes you think that, Broderick?'

'Oh, just somethin' that Dennis let slip last night when him and Jimmy were going at it. Jimmy was blaming her for Hannah's . . . mishap,' he did not say death, 'and Dennis then told him the rights of the case. An' when it was told, well, it wasn't like Ronnie MacFarlane had made out; and we . . . the others saw that, but Jimmy kept on and then Dennis . . . well, Dennis said that Hannah had done her best to take Rosie along of her by . . . by beatin' her up . . . I couldn't, I wouldn't believe it, not at first, 'cos, well, she loved her . . . she . . . she thought the sun shone out of her.' His head was moving slowly from side to side now and he muttered something to himself that was inaudible to Hughie. Then looking at him again, he said, 'Dennis says she's gone back to London.'

'Aye, yes, that's right, Broderick, she . . . she went back to London.'

'She went back knowing her mother was dead and to be buried the morrow.'

'She didn't know, Broderick, she was in a bad way. The doctor said it was best not to tell her, it might affect her.'

272

'But she'll have to know sometime, better sooner than later.'

'The doctor didn't see it like that, Broderick.' Hughie's voice was soft. 'He . . . he agreed . . . I mean said, it might affect her mentally if she was to know . . . all her life. And . . . and . . .'

'Then she might never know because she'll never come back.' Broderick pulled in his lower lip between his teeth. 'She was more sinned against than sinning as I see now. I'm not one of those that is blamin' her for Hannah's going; there's many things that helped towards Hannah's going. She was a strange woman was Hannah.' He nodded his head. 'A strange woman, but a fine woman; a strong woman, but strange. Me life's finished without her, the pin's gone.'

'It's early days yet, Broderick.'

As Hughie finished speaking the sound of soft foot-steps in the hall made him start towards the door, but before he reached it Rosie pushed it slowly open and Broderick gaped at the figure for a full minute before realization came to him, and then he lifted his hand and covered his face.

'I . . . I thought I heard your voice, Da.' The words were uneven and thick as if they had their shape coming over her lips. 'I thought you might go without . . . without . . .' She didn't finish because Hughie's voice cut in, saying, 'I'm sorry, Broderick, I . . . I thought it best.'

Broderick took his hand from his face but kept his head lowered as he moved forward, and as his hands groped for hers, he muttered brokenly, 'Aw, lass. Aw, lass.'

'Oh, Da.'

'Your face . . . you poor face. Aw, my God, lass.'

'Don't worry, Da, it's all right, it'll . . . it'll get better.' But even as she said this she didn't believe it ever would get better. At least not so that she would be able to recognize herself as she once was. But through the trembling hand that held hers she realized that her father was in need of comfort much more than herself at this moment. And as his shoulders began to shake with the compressed weeping within, she whispered, 'Aw, don't, Da, don't. It's all right: I tell you it's all right.'

He drew away from her and rubbed his face with his hand, and as he looked at her again his eyes focused on her mouth and he muttered, as if he could almost feel the agony of the moment they had been knocked out, 'Your teeth, lass. Oh, your teeth.'

She said brokenly, 'Don't worry, Da, please.' Then, 'Come and sit down for a minute, Florence'll be back soon.'

'No, lass, no, I've got to go. I've . . . I've business to see to. . . .'

As he said this his eyes were drawn to Hughie and he answered the message in them by omitting to state the type of business that called him away; instead, he said to Rosie, 'What are you thinkin' of doin' with yourself, lass?'

It was Rosie who now looked towards Hughie, and when she turned to her father again she did not lower her eyes as she answered his question, in a minimum of words, 'I'm going with Hughie, Da.'

The effect was to startle Broderick, bringing his mouth agape, and his back straight as if the words had injected him with aggressive life. As he turned towards Hughie

274

it was as if Hannah herself had entered into him, and for a moment Hughie thought he was going to be attacked, at least by a spate of words, accusing, derogatory, spiteful words. Then as Broderick, drawing in a deep breath, turned from him and looked at Rosie again the spirit of Hannah seeped out of him and he asked, quietly, but tersely, 'You know what you're doin'?'

'Yes, Da.' She cast a glance in Hughie's direction, not towards his face but to him as a whole.

Broderick, turning towards the sink, gripped its edge and let his body fall towards it, as if to rest for a moment; then straightening himself, he said in a hopeless tone. 'I'd better be off.'

'Da!' The appeal brought him round to her, and after looking at the face that had filled the last twenty-three years of his life with pride and on which now there was left not one recognizable feature, he clamped his teeth down on his lip and, thrusting out his arms, drew her to him.

'Oh, Da! Da!'

'There now, there now.' They stood close for some moments, then, after passing his hand over her hair, he pressed her gently from him, saying thickly, 'Wherever you go, lass, I pray that you have peace . . . and . . . and happiness. Goodbye now.' He lifted her hand and held it to his face for a moment before pushing her away.

Silently, and with her head deep on her chest, she turned from him and went out of the kitchen; and when she was gone Broderick moved towards the back door, and he stood facing its blankness as he spoke to Hughie. 'I've got nothing against you, Hughie,' he said. 'I never have had, but I'll say straight to you now, I wish from the bottom of my soul this wasn't happenin'. But as it is, it's thankful to God I am she's where she is at this minute, for if she'd known of this there'd have been more than one burial the morrow. Rightly or wrongly she would never have suffered it. Her first daughter an' her last. No, she'd never have suffered it in this world.'

When no word came from Hughie, Broderick raised his head and looked back at him, saying, 'I'm not blamin' you, I'm not blamin' you. As a man I understand. Nevertheless, you must grant it's an odd situation.'

'I do grant it, Broderick, but in me own defence I'll say what I've said before. Karen wasn't really my doing; if ever there was a rape that was it. But with Rosie, well . . . I'll admit to you now, I've sat in the corner of your kitchen for the last few years just so that I could look at her, or be there when she came, and that's the truth. I've always said to meself that I didn't make the break because I hadn't any guts; the other excuse was that I wanted a family, to be a member of a family; but what I really wanted was to be near Rosie. . . . But' – he lifted his hand towards Broderick – 'I never had any hope, don't think that. Not in my wildest dreams did I have any hope of one day having Rosie, that would have been too fantastic, and she wouldn't be coming with me now but she's in a jam, at least that's how I see it. I'm not going to hold her to anything, Broderick.'

'You're not marrying her then?' The question was sharp.

'Not unless she wants it. When she gets on her feet again it'll be up to her.'

'You're a strange fellow, Hughie, a strange fellow. Are you staying in the country?'

'No, Broderick, I'm going abroad as I planned.'

'To stay there?'

'Aye, to stay there.'

'Then I don't suppose we'll meet again, and I'll never see her again.'

'You never know, I can't tell you that, Broderick. Anyway, you might decide to take a trip.'

'Not this side of the grave. . . . One last thing . . . what if she finds out her mother's dead and how she died? The world's a small place; a chance word and she'll know it.'

'I'll meet that emergency when it comes, Broderick. In any case, she'll be in a better state of mind to face up to it than she is now; but if I can help it she'll never find out.'

Broderick opened the door, and pausing before he stepped into the street, he said, 'It's a queer business. . . . Well, there's nothing more to say then. I wish you goodbye, Hughie.'

'Goodbye, Broderick.' Hughie waited for the old man to extend his hand, his own was half wavering forward, but when Broderick made no move in this direction Hughie said, 'I'd like to say thank you, Broderick, for the kindness you've shown me over all the years.'

Broderick now looked straight into Hughie's face and he kept his concentration on him for fully a minute before he said, 'I could say that you've shown your thanks in an odd way, Hughie, but when I've time to reflect I might be thinkin' it's the best thing that could have happened to her, for God knows when a lass takes one step down the ladder there's plenty of willing hands to help her to the bottom. Goodbye, Hughie.'

277

'Goodbye, Broderick.'

Not until Broderick had disappeared round the corner of the street did Hughie go in and close the door, and then he stood with his back to it, his eyes tight shut and one hand inside his collar gripping it hard. He felt exhausted, as if he had been struggling physically with an opponent; and he had, and not only during the past ten minutes, but for years past. But now he had won. No, no, not quite. Perhaps it would be months ahead before he would know for sure, but he'd be content to wait. He was used to waiting, he'd had a lot of practice. But this period of waiting would be different. He'd be waiting as a man waits, not as a mouse in the corner of a kitchen. The thought brought him from the door straight upright on his feet. He squared his shoulders and lifted his head and went out of the room.

It was ten o'clcok the following morning and they were ready to go. Everything that had to be said had been said. Now, with brotherly awkwardness, Dennis held Rosie to him, saying, 'Forget everything as I said and enjoy your life, Rosie.' He bent his head forward under the deep fur hood which covered her face, and gently he put his lips against her discoloured cheek.

'Thanks, Dennis, thanks for everything.' Her voice was unsteady.

Now Florence was standing before her. Her hands adjusting the hood, she said, 'This is the very thing, you can hardly see your face at all. But if anyone gets curious, just do as I said, tell them you were in a car accident.'

'It's so good of you, Florence, I'll send it back.'

'You'll do no such thing. But when you can get about yourself get another coat; this' – she touched Rosie's sleeve – 'would fit three of you. I was mad to let him go shopping on his own.' She cast a tender glance towards Hughie. Then putting her arms about Rosie, she pressed her close as she whispered, 'God bless you.' They were strange words coming from Florence, who didn't believe in God, only in man.

And now Florence was enfolding Hughie in her embrace and was crying unashamedly; then pushing him abruptly from her she said, 'Go on, get yourselves off this could go on all day. We won't come to the car, the less attention drawn to your going the better.'

Hughie and Dennis were now gripping hands in the open doorway. Both were evidently deeply disturbed and Hughie had difficulty in speaking. 'We'll all be together again and before very long, I know. Anyway,' he moved his neck upwards out of his collar, 'you'll be hearing from me later in the day.'

'Aye, aye,' said Dennis, 'phone us from the airport.'

'Oh, may be afore that. So long, Dennis.'

'So long Hughie. You know what I wish you.' The hands gripped for the last time, and then Hughie, holding Rosie's arm, led her to the waiting car, and before they reached it the door of the flat closed behind them.

Hughie hoped that Rosie hadn't noticed this for it might set her wondering at the peremptoriness of it. It might appear as if they couldn't get rid of her quickly enough. But Dennis and Florence were now, he knew, scurrying into their clothes to be ready when the taxi called to take them to the house for the funeral.

But apparently Rosie hadn't noticed anything unusual.

Getting into the car, she settled herself down, and as it began to move cautiously forward she did not turn and take one last look at the flat, but from the depth of her hood kept her eyes directly ahead. She was so full now of a mixture of emotions that she felt the slightest move would cause her to break down. There was on her mind an oppressive weight. Oddly enough the weight did not seem to be connected with what had happened to her in London. Strangely she found she wasn't thinking of that any more. Somehow it had been wiped out by the blows her mother had showered on her; it was, she knew, the thoughts of her mother that were weighing on her, encasing her. And she felt sad, so terribly sad with the knowledge that when she left this town she would never see her father again. She had no regrets about never seeing her mother again.

Hughie was talking now, rapidly, nervously. 'It'll be better when we get on the main road, it'll be clearer. We should be at the airport in two hours, but I'm giving meself four just in case. It was lucky about the booking, wasn't it? That's because there's not so many travelling across this time of the year. I've got to make a call before we leave the town, Rosie. I've got to go to the bank. I might be five or ten minutes. You won't mind?'

'No, no, Hughie.'

'Look,' he was nodding to the road ahead, 'how would you like to sit in the caravan time I'm in there? You could lie down, the curtains are drawn. How about it? You're supposed not to ride in the caravan, but what odds.'

'I . . . yes, I think I'd prefer that, Hughie.'

'We'll stop at yon side of the road. You know,' he

made an effort to laugh, 'I only want an excuse for you to see inside. You've never seen it yet.' He glanced towards her and saw the movement of the hood. She did not turn her face towards him.

They stopped on a quiet road at the top of the park and Hughie unlocked the caravan door, and when Rosie entered, her surprise brought the first touch of lightness to her voice. 'It's wonderful, wonderful, Hughie. I never thought it would be like this, it's . . . it's like a house.' She turned to him now, saying, 'Oh, Hughie,' but he did not look at her. Instead, going to the settee opposite an actual fireplace in the middle of the caravan, he said, 'Lie on this one, will you, it'll make the balance better. The end one there,' he inclined his head, 'might tip it up at the back a bit and . . . and I'm not yet used to the feel of her.'

When she sat down saying, 'I'll just slip me boots off,' Hughie said, 'Oh, don't bother about that.'

'Oh, but I must, they're dirty.'

As she took her boots off and laid them aside he smiled at her. It was an appreciative smile. She would look after nice things, would Rosie. When she was lying down he put a rug over her; then squatting on his hunkers and bringing his face level with hers he said, 'Do you know what I'm going to do?' He sounded excited, like a young boy. She made a small movement with her head. 'I'm going to see the bank manager. I'd arranged with him to send the cheque to Dennis the morrow but I think now it's too long to wait, so I'm going to have him send it by special messenger. He'll do that for me. I've never given them anything, in kind I mean, not a thing, and being human they might just wonder, so I'd like to do

281

this afore we go!' He raised his brows at her. 'There's one thing I'm sorry for, an' that is I won't see their faces when they get it. Anyway it'll be nice to think of the bairn being born in a nice little house, their own house.'

'Oh, Hughie.' She put out her hand with the intention of touching his cheek, but before it reached him he had risen to his feet. 'Better be making a move,' he said; 'I'll need all the time I've got to get to that airport, not being Stirling Moss.' He turned away laughing. Then from the door he nodded to her. 'All right?'

'Yes, Hughie, I'm all right.'

Starting up the car once more he gulped in great draughts of air. It had all been easier that he expected. For he had a horror on him of someone stopping them and saying to her, I'm sorry to hear about your ma, Rosie. It would be just like the thing, he thought, if it happened almost at the last minute. He felt easier now she was in the caraven.

He was in the bank less than ten minutes and he was smiling wryly to himself as he emerged. How smoothly the wheels of life ran when you had a little oil to grease them with. A special messenger would be at Dennis's at one o'clock. Dennis had only the morning off from school so he would be home by then, but if he wasn't home the messenger would return again at half-past four; the letter had to be delivered personally.

As he stepped briskly across the pavement to the car and caravan he knew that he wouldn't be able to relax or get rid of this jittery feeling until they were out of the town, because he knew that his future life, and that of Rosie's, depended on her not knowing that Hannah was dead.

He had gone some distance when he stopped the car again, and getting out and opening the caravan door, he looked towards her, where half-risen, she was leaning on her elbow. 'We're nearly out of the town,' he said, 'but there will be Craig Hill to go up and that's pretty steep; it might be a bit frightening for you if you found yourself up on end. Would you like to come in the car again?'

'Yes, yes.' Hastily she pulled on her boots and he helped her out of the caravan and into the car.

'All right now?' he asked as he started up. 'Comfortable?'

'Yes, very comfortable.'

'You warm enough?'

'Yes, it's lovely, I can feel the hot air around my feet.'

'Yes, the heating's good. By! The cars these days have everything.' He spoke as if he had owned cars that hadn't quite everything. 'Would you like the wireless on?'

'Not unless you want it, Hughie.'

'No, I don't want it. Well now, there's only one more set of traffic lights and we'll be away.'

The traffic lights were against them. In front of them was a small van. It was somewhat to the left of Hughie's bonnet, obscuring the view and the traffic coming from Dean Road. But he wasn't concerned with the passing traffic, he looked to where his route lay straight across the road and up the hill. That was, until he saw Rosie lift her right hand reverently to her brow and a chill passed over him that brought with it a sickening dread as he watched her making the sign of the cross. The hood turned towards him and from the folds of it she whispered, 'It's a funeral.' He stared back almost mesmerised into her sad distorted face; he knew the words she would be saying to herself: 'May the souls of the faithful departed, through the mercy of God, rest in peace. Amen.' He remembered vividly scenes, right back down the years, of Hannah stopping whenever she saw a funeral and blessing herself and repeating the words, and the children with her following suit.

A fear born of premonition paralysed him until he found himself leaning forward and fiddling with a switch on the dashboard of the car. And now his voice almost croaked as he said, 'Rosie, I wonder if you'd mind getting down and looking just under your seat – there's a tool tray there. Would you pull it out and get me a screwdriver?'

'Yes, Hughie, yes.'

The motor-drawn hearse passed slowly before the van and came into view, and as he looked at the coffin under its canopy of flowers his whole stomach seemed to turn a somersault. It was as if his bowels had run to water. He knew who lay there before the first car came into sight. In his mind he saw her struggling to get out and at him. He felt sick, sick enough to want to vomit.

In the first car he made out the black-coated figures of Jimmy and Broderick and Arthur, and . . .

'Is this it, Hughie?'

He jerked in his seat as he looked at the screwdriver in Rosie's extended hand.

'No . . . no, no, Rosie; it's . . . it's a smaller one than that.'

As she bent her head he lifted his again. A second car had passed, and now in the third one, there was John, and Betty and a man he vaguely recognised as Michael from Cornwall.

He had just caught sight of Dennis and Florence in the next car when Rosie said, 'There isn't a small one, Hughie.'

'Hand me the tray up, will you, Rosie?' He could not keep his voice steady.

As she handed him the tray he exclaimed on a deep tired note, 'Oh bust! The lights are changing. Just leave it, I'll do it when we get to the top.' He fumbled at the gears, grating them before he got the car moving again. He had the urge now to go into top gear and race up the hill and out of the town. His whole body was trembling. God! If it hadn't been for that van in front, she must have seen them. There was somebody, somewhere, he thought, on his side. For that to happen at the fifty-ninth minute of the eleventh hour and yet not come off, assuredly there was somebody on his side.

When they reached the top of Craig Hill he was glad enough of the excuse to stop, and as he examined the knob of the screen wiper he said, 'I think it'll do, it only wanted a twist.'

When she made no remark he looked towards her, but she was looking out of the window.

From the top of Craig Hill there was a full view of Fellburn. The town lay between two hills. The other rising on the far side was the famous Brampton Hill, with its long gardens reaching down to the river. Away in the distance, towards the head of the valley, were the shafts of the two dominating pits, and significantly separating them a sloping stretch of ground, which when clear of snow was a landmark which still remained

285

white . . . it was Fellburn Cemetery. As Hughie stared towards it he saw nearing it a thin black line sharply depicted against the snow. It was weird, weird. It was as if she was watching him to the very end. As he hastily went to start the engine again Rosie's hand came on his, and it caused him to jerk his head towards her. 'We're leaving Fellburn, Hughie,' she said.

'Yes, we're leaving Fellburn, Rosie.' And the quicker the better, he added to himself.

'I don't ever want to see it again, Hughie. . . . Not that it's ever done anything to me, but I just don't want to see it again.' She didn't say to him, I don't ever want to come home again, I don't ever want to see me ma again. These were sentiments that couldn't be put into words. You just covered them up with the name of a town.

'Well, you won't ever see it again if you don't want to, Rosie.'

Her hood had slipped back and was showing her hair, bright and unspoilt above the distortion of her face. As Hughie's eyes lifted to it, she turned her face slightly to the side. 'There's something I'd like to tell you before we leave, Hughie,' she said. 'Before we start out so to speak.'

'Aw now,' he put in quickly, 'there's no need to tell me anything more, Rosie. Don't distress yourself further . . . please. I don't want to know. . . .'

'. . . Not that I would have come away with you even before this happened?' She touched her cheek with her fingers.

'Rosie!' He turned slowly but fully round in his seat. 'Do you mean that?'

'Yes, yes. That's . . . that's why I talked to you the other night. I didn't know why I wanted to tell you until after I had told you, and then coming . . . coming on top of the London business I couldn't trust myself or my feelings. I thought I wasn't the capable judge of what I wanted. And . . . and I also want you to know I would have felt the same if . . . if you hadn't come into the money. . . . Believe me on that above all things, Hughie.'

'Aw, Rosie.' He lifted her hands and pulled them inside his open great-coat; then bending slowly forward he let his lips touch hers for the first time. It was a touch without pressure and had the gentleness of a salve on her tight painful skin. Yet it had the power to break through the dead weight on her mind, shattering it, leaving her feeling light and faint with an overwhelming sense of relief, and the touch seemed to exhilarate him. The cloak of meekness he had worn for years disintegrated. His eyes shining, he looked at her a moment longer; then swiftly grabbing the wheel he put in the clutch and swung the car into the middle of the road. But no sooner had he done this when a terrific blast of a horn made him pull the wheel sharply to the left again. As a huge lorry passed him and a big head came into his view, shouting, 'You askin' for trouble, mate?' all he could do was stop the car yet once again.

And now, leaning over the wheel, his hands gripping the top of it, his voice trembling he said, 'I never looked in the mirror.' He glanced swiftly towards Rosie to see what her reactions were to his obviously bad driving, and when he saw her actually attempting to laugh his body jerked with a spasm. Then again it came, until, his head going back, he burst into loud body-shaking, relieving mirth. Looking down at her, he gasped, 'What odds, Rosie, what odds eh? Let them all shout. It won't be the last mistake I'll make before we reach the end of the line. Who do they think they are, anyway? "You asking for trouble, mate?" ' He was mimicking the lorry driver. 'Yes, I'm asking for trouble, mate. Lead me to it.'

Now, Rosie was really laughing, and it was a painful business, as her hands pressed against her cheeks showed, and she cried, 'Oh, Hughie! Don't. Don't.'

He was still laughing when he gripped the wheel once again and started the car. He felt a god, able to cope with any situation. He could make the woman he loved laugh: even under these circumstances he had made her laugh. He had won. He hadn't to wait until months ahead. He knew inside for a certainty now he had won, and he cried with the whole of his being, 'I've won, Hannah Massey! I've won!'

THE END

THE FIFTEEN STREETS

Catherine Cookson

PATHWAY

CONTENTS

AUTHOR'S NOTE

The characters in this book are entirely fictitious and have no relation to any living person.

Although the setting is Tyneside and several place names have been used, 'The Fifteen Streets' are imaginary.

Owing to difficulty in comprehension by the uninitiated, I have not adhered to the Tyneside dialect.

CHAPTER ONE

THE BROTHERS

'Hannah, drop that an' come an' see. The O'Briens are at it again . . . blue murder! Come on. Come upstairs, you can see better from our top window.'

Wiping the soap suds from her arms, Hannah Kelly hastily lifted the lid of the wash-house boiler, scooped off the grey scum with an enamel mug, dabbed the contents of the boiler with a stick, then ran out of the wash-house and across the backyard, thinking as she did so, 'Eeh, I haven't got time for this . . . And our Joe warned me.'

She caught up with her neighbour as she was opening the stair door.

'Who is it this time? The old man?'

'Yes.'

'Who's he at? Dominic!'

'Aye.'

'Are they drunk?'

'Are they ever owt else?'

They scurried across the kitchen to the front room, and automatically took up their stations, one at each

297

side of the window, bodies close to the wall, heads held slightly to the side against the mesh of the Nottingham lace curtains, their arms wound tightly in their aprons.

'My God, what a mess, Bella!'

'He must have thrown them two pictures out since I came down for you.'

'Eeh, God Almighty! It's a shame. Just as Mary Ellen was getting things pulled together again.'

'Look' – there was glee in Bella's voice – 'there they are at the window throttling each other. Christ!' she exclaimed as something came hurtling through the window into the street, 'which one missed that, I wonder?'

'Eeh! he's thrown the pot through the window. Oh, Bella, that'll bring the pollis. God Almighty, it's awful! It's enough to bring on the bairn . . . she's at the worst time, on eight months.'

'Best thing that could happen. Who wants a bairn at forty-five, I ask you? She should have been more cute. Anyway, she wouldn't listen to me. I told her I could get her a bottle of white mixture from our Harry's Emma, who scrubs the wards up at the grubber; the nurses would have given it to her. It would have skited everything out of her.'

'Well, you know she wouldn't do that, she's a Catholic, Bella.'

'Catholic, be damned! They tell 'em to have bairns, but do they bloody well keep them? I'd like to see any priest tell me I must have bairns. Do you know what I'd say?'

Hannah chuckled. 'I've a pretty good idea ... Look, there she is, there's Mary Ellen. She looks like death.'

They both became silent and watched the woman below picking up the two picture frames from the road. The loose glass splintered about her feet as she shook the frames, and as she shooed some children away from the broken chamber, Hannah remarked, regretfully, 'Pity about that. It was a boody one, too.'

Unblinkingly they watched the woman edge her way indoors, with neither a glance upwards nor to the right or left, although as they knew, she was fully aware of the watchers. Only the children were on the street, staring silently until the door closed, when they drew nearer, and some daring spirits, braving the glass, hitched themselves up on the high window sill to get their faces level with the hole. But as they did so the blind was dropped, and Hannah exclaimed, clicking her tongue, 'She shouldn't have done that – dropping the blind right down before dark – it's the sign of a death. It'll be the bairn, likely.'

'Damn good job too. Better if it was her old man though, in case he lands her with another.'

They turned slowly from the window, and Hannah said, 'By, that wouldn't have happened if John had been in; he'd have put a stop to that . . . Funny, isn't it, Bella, that the old man doesn't go for John.'

'Not funny a bit. He's afraid of him, if the truth was known. Old O'Brien and Dominic are both alike, full of wind and water. That's why they fight . . . By God! I wish I was in Mary Ellen's place for five minutes. I'd lay those two sods out with the poker! She's soft, that's what she is, soft as clarts . . . Are you going to stay for a cup of tea?' she added. 'I'll put the kettle on, it won't be a minute.'

'No, lass, I'm not half through, and it's getting on for dark.'

Bella glanced sideways at Hannah. 'Should you come across Mary Ellen – you see her more than I do – and she tells you what it was all about, knock up.'

'Aye, I will. But there's small chance. She's close, is Mary Ellen. You know that.'

'I know she doesn't like me. Thinks I can't mind me own business.'

And she's right there, thought Hannah.

'And anyway, I'm not the same colour as them,' went on Bella nodding her long horse-face. 'Me St Patrick's Day's colour's blue. Wait until next Thursday week when Dominic's wearing his shamrock. There'll be skull and hair flying then. The fifteen streets won't hold him . . . My God, remember last St Patrick's Day? That was a do, eh?' She laughed at the memory.

'Eeh, Bella, I must be off.' Hannah unwrapped her mottled arms, and banged out the creases in her coarse apron.

'Well don't forget to knock up if you hear owt.'

'I won't.'

Hannah went down the stairs, walking sideways in case she slipped, as the stairs were too narrow for her feet encased in an old pair of men's boots. By the time she reached the bottom she had also reached a decision: she wouldn't tell Bella Bradley what she heard, if she heard owt at all. Too nosey was Bella, by half. She'd rather keep in with Mary Ellen, narrow as she was. At least she minded her own business. And her Joe warned her only last night against Bella Bradley. He said he'd bash her face in if he found her upstairs again – he was nettled after hearing what she said about their Nancy not being all there. He knew Nancy wasn't all there, but it maddened him to hear anyone say it. More so now that Nancy was growing up . . . Hannah sighed. What would become of Nancy? She didn't know. And anyway, there was no time to think now, the washing had to be finished.

Across the road, in number 10 Fadden Street, Mary Ellen O'Brien worked in the semi-darkness behind the drawn blind. She adjusted the block of wood under the chest of drawers – the leg had been kicked off during the last row – and screwed in the knob of the top drawer. She picked up the grey blanket and patchwork quilt from the floor and spread them again over the lumpy bare mattress on the iron bed. She pushed the wicker table back into the centre of the room, and stood leaning on its weak support, breathing heavily. Her eyes, dry with the pricking dryness of sand, looked round the walls. They were quite bare . . . Well, they would remain so. The only two pictures in the house were now gone. Never again would she try to build up. She had told herself, if they went this time it would be the last.

She looked towards the closed door, which led into the kitchen. She knew that beyond, on either side of the fireplace, they'd be sitting, spent. Their rage and passion flown, they would be like the two halves of one body, accepting each other now that the conflict was over for a time.

She lifted her apron and wiped the sweat from her forehead. If only they weren't so big . . . like giants. She hadn't dared go between them this time because of the bairn . . . She put her hand on the raised globe of her stomach and felt a movement. It brought no sense of feeling to her other than that of apprehension. Why, oh why was she to have this all over again? Hadn't she been through enough in her time? During the twenty-six years of her married life she had given birth to eleven bairns, and only five were alive, for which she thanked God. What she would have done with thirteen in these three rooms only the Almighty knew.

A pain through her breast made her gasp, and she covered it with her hand, lifting up its weight. Last year this time they'd been flat . . . flat for all time she'd thought, for it was ten years since Katie was born. Practically every year since she was married she'd been dropped, but from Katie there'd been nothing. The pain shot through her again, and she remembered such a pain from the past. It was before John was born. She was as strong as a horse then, as small as she was, and she enjoyed the feeling of the pain, anticipating the tugging of the young mouth on the nipples . . . if it lived. It did live, and it was John . . . John, who had never given her any trouble. Oh, if they were all like John, and, at the other end of the scale, Katie. Funny that these two should be alike and the others so different from them. Dominic was different from the day he was born, the year after John. She had always been slightly afraid of Dominic, even when he was a child. It wasn't that he alone suffered from the O'Brien rages, for they all did, except Katie. It was rather that there was something fiendish about Dominic. It showed in everything he did, in his teasing, in his laughter, and especially in his good-looking face. Like John and Mick, he took after his da for his looks. But although they all took after their da Dominic and Mick were better looking than John. When she looked at her eldest son she had the feeling that the features which made

303

the other two good looking made him ugly, and in some strange way this pleased her. To her mind it separated him entirely from them. It was his nose that made the difference, she supposed, with that funny little nob on the side of the nostril. He got that when he climbed the dock wall to get some coal that bad winter. He slipped and his nose was cut on the broken glass set in the top of the wall. The cut did not join properly and gave his face a quaint look from the side. But it wasn't only his nose; John's eyes were different from the others. They were large and brown too, but a different brown . . . dark and kind. That was it, they were kind, like Katie's.

She sighed and rubbed her hand gently round and round her breast. Then, hearing a shout coming through the kitchen from the back-yard, she moved her head impatiently — she never thought of Molly unless the girl made herself felt by sight or sound. Molly was . . . well, she couldn't place Molly. She was of a too apparent mixture of them all, and so had no individuality of her own. She was swayed, first one way and then the other; even her rages could be deflected by a stronger will. No, Molly would be no heartache, for she aroused no feeling.

Mary Ellen straightened her shoulders and refastened the top button of her blouse over her straining breasts before walking towards the kitchen door.

It was no use standing here thinking; thinking got you nowhere. It was close on five o'clock and John would be in at half past. She'd have to get on with the tea . . . Thank God they fought in here and not in the kitchen. They might have knocked the pan of broth off the hob, and there was nearly fourpennorth of vegetables in besides a twopenny scrag end . . . Well, if you searched hard enough there was always something to be thankful for.

As she expected, her husband and son were sitting one each side of the fireplace, their brows puckered over half-closed eyes. Shane's grey hair was standing up straight in tufts; there was blood on the hair near his temple, and his high cheek-bones were showing blue under the tightened skin. At the first glance she saw that his rage wasn't entirely spent, for the muscle was moving in his cheek as he clenched and unclenched his teeth, and his limbs, as always, were jerking with the nerve tick. His knees, in their reddened moleskin trousers, were wide apart, and his feet were crossed below his hands, which were gripping the seat of the wooden armchair. His body looked as if it was still ready to spring . . . No, his rage wasn't spent yet, because he was sober. He'd had only two shifts in this week and had tipped the money up. But Dominic had a full week. For three weeks now he'd worked full weeks. Not that it made much difference to her – she was lucky if she got ten shillings out of him. She often had to meet him at the dock gates to get even that . . . or send Katie. But Dominic's rage was spent because he was drunk and happy.

She took Dominic by the shoulder and shook him. 'Here! Get yourself to bed.'

He lifted his head and smiled crookedly at her, cracking the dried blood on his mouth as he did so. He looked at her out of one merry, brown eye, the other being hidden behind a curling lock of light brown, youthful hair.

'All right, old girl.'

He rose obediently to his feet, and some detached part of her marvelled for the countless time at his docility towards her when he was in drink. Why was it she could manage him when he was drunk? She even found herself liking him in this state. She had no fear of him in drink, when he spoke civilly to her, often with a touch of affection. But it was strange that even in drink she could have any affection for him now, for she remembered the look in his eyes during these past weeks when they lit on her stomach . . . ridicule, scorn, and something else . . . a something for which she could find no word. She pushed him before her into the bedroom, her head coming just to the bottom of his shoulder blades. She always wondered, when close to them, how she gave birth to such great men.

Dominic sat down with a plop on the side of his bed and began to laugh. 'If he wasn't my old man I'd have knocked him stiff. But I'll break his bloody neck the next time he interferes with me. I didn't ask to be set on the ore boat — they want the young 'uns down the holds.'

He fell back on the bed and lifted up his legs, and Mary Ellen immediately swung them down again. She took off his boots and loosened his belt, then unbuttoned his trousers and tugged them off his legs, leaving these looking particularly ludicrous in their tight long pants. Never in all the many times she had pulled trousers off them had she yet been able to conquer the feeling of revulsion. Husband or son, it was the same.

She heaved him up by the shirt front and dragged off his coat. Then she let him fall back on to the bed. She threw the quilt over him and put his coat on top of it, and lifting his trousers quietly from the floor, she put them across her arm and went out, through the kitchen, past her husband, who now sat hunched up over the fire, and into the front room, where she turned out the contents of the trousers pockets on to the table.

There was a half-sovereign, two two-shilling pieces, and four pennies. The half-sovereign he would have to stump up for his board, so she put that back into the pocket again, together with a two-shilling piece. The other two-shilling piece and the coppers went into a little cloth bag that dangled from a pin fastened to the inside of her skirt. It already held tenpence. She had taken to this device of the bag when Shane came back from the Boer War, because he lifted every penny he could get his fingers on for drink.

She went back to the bedroom and quietly placed the trousers over the bed rail, and as she returned to the kitchen the window was darkened by a distorted bulk, and a gentle tap-tap came on the door.

Mary Ellen sighed. As inevitably as the calm which followed the storm would come this tap-tap on the door after any disturbance in the house. She often thanked God for an upstairs neighbour such as Peggy Flaherty. Many a one, placed as she was above the noise and fighting that was almost part of the weekly routine, would have done more than object, she would have brought the pollis; and after a number of such visits they would have been in court and likely turned out of the house. Peggy was a bit queer; still, as God knew, there were worse states than being queer. But today, Mary Ellen felt tired, and even Peggy's well-meant sympathy was an irritant. She opened the door, and would have smiled, if she could, at the quaint tact of this fat, dirty woman.

'I was after warming meself up with a mouthful of stew, Mary Ellen, an' I said to meself, "I'll take a drop below, it'll stick to Mary Ellen's ribs." ' She proferred the basin, full of a lead-coloured liquid, with darker pieces of matter floating about on its surface. 'Are you all right, lass?' She peered at Mary Ellen through her short-sighted eyes, looking for a black eye or other evidence of the fight.

'Yes, I'm all right, Peggy. And thanks for the soup.'

'Oh, that's all right, Mary Ellen . . . You'll drink it, now, won't you?'

'Yes, yes,' Mary Ellen hastily assured her, wondering whether Peggy was suspicious of the fate of her proferred balms. She would have to be very hungry, she thought, before she ate anything made by Peggy's hands in that menagerie upstairs. Before he died, Charlie Flaherty earned his living in many ways. At one time, he worked for himself as a tally man, and when payment was not forthcoming, took the equivalent in kind; so two of the three rooms upstairs were stacked from floor to ceiling with an odd assortment of things, not one of which Peggy would part with, ranging from a stuffed baby crocodile to a collection of books, out of which Peggy was wont to say 'she got the extinsive iducation' she possessed. She spread more false knowledge round the fifteen streets than it was possible to imagine. Many of the inhabitants would have sworn that Henry VIII was Queen Elizabeth's husband, and that England once belonged to the Irish before William the Conqueror came over and took it from them. For the sum of a penny she would write a letter; for a little more, give advice on how to deal with a summons, or a case of defamation of character, or assault. Often this advice, if faithfully carried out, would have got the worried seeker a sojourn in jail. It was strange, that although she was said to be odd and barmy, her advice was still sought. Perhaps it was because it was known that on these pennies she mainly relied for her existence. There was an unspoken feeling in these streets, which, if translated, would have implied . . . you save someone the workhouse and you'll never land there yourself.

'God and His Holy Mother preserve us this day, the trials we have! Is there anything more I can do for you, Mary Ellen?' went on Peggy.

'No, I'm all right, Peggy, thanks.' Mary Ellen looked at the basin in her hands, hoping to convey a hint that she would like to go in and make a start on the soup.

But Peggy did not notice this move; or if she did, she refused to take the hint; for she had something weighty to say. Leaning forward, she whispered, 'Did I ever tell you, Mary Ellen, Mr Flaherty's cure for all this?' She nodded towards the closed scullery door.

Mary Ellen, suppressing another sigh, said, 'No, Peggy.'

'Iducation! No man would fight, he said, once he had iducation. And he knew what he was talking about, for he got about among the gentry, you know, Mary Ellen. It was his theory that once a man got iducation he wouldn't raise a hand to his wife. He might, being a human being, get a bit irritated and say, "Retire to your room before I kick your backside!" or some such thing, but to lift his hand . . . no!'

'There may be something in it.' Mary Ellen again looked at the basin. 'Sure you haven't left yourself short, Peggy?'

'Not at all. Not at all. Anyway you go now inside, and don't talk any more; and get that down you, it'll put a lining on your stomach. And remember, if you want any advice you know where to come.'

She shuffled away, and Mary Ellen closed the door . . . Don't talk any more, and, Retire to your room before I kick your backside! If there was a laugh left in her she would have laughed; but she would remember them, and some night by the fire she would tell them to John, and they would laugh together.

John came in at half-past five. He hung his cap and coat, together with his black neckerchief on the back of the kitchen door, then sat down on a box in the tiny square of scullery and loosened the yorks that bound his trousers below the knee. Before washing his hands in the tin dish that was standing on another box he looked into the lighted kitchen and smiled towards the three children sitting at the table. Only Katie returned his smile, her round, blue eyes sending him a greeting.

Mick called, 'Got anything, John? Any bananas or anything?'

And he answered, 'Not tonight; we're still on the grain boat.'

When John came to the table, his mother set a plate of broth before him, out of which a series of bare ribs stuck up, like the skeleton of a hulk. The smell was appetising, and the eyes of the three children focused on the plate.

Mary Ellen exclaimed harshly, 'Get on with your bread and dripping!' and almost simultaneously each bit into his own inch-thick slice of bread.

She placed another plate on the table and said to her husband, 'Your tea's out.'

Shane turned from the fire and stared at the plate, and from there to his son and the other three. His body started to jerk, first his head, then his arms, and lastly his right leg. His words too, when they came, were spasmodic and heavy with bitterness: 'Served last now, am I? It's a difference when you're not bringing it in. You've got to work or you don't eat . . . not till everybody else is finished.'

John put his spoon down and stared at his father: 'I'll wait until you're done.'

His mother signalled wildly to him from behind her husband, and pointed to the bedroom.

John read her signal, but continued to stare at his father, until Shane's eyes dropped away and he growled, 'It's them young 'uns — I was never set down before me father.'

His head jerked to one side as if he were straining at a bit, and Mary Ellen said quietly, 'Don't be a fool! Get your tea.'

'You want to start, you do!' Shane sprang up from his chair, kicking it to one side as he did so. 'It only needs you to start. Belittling me before the bairns! That's a new tack.' He towered like a swaying mountain of rage over the short unwieldly figure of his wife.

Mary Ellen took no notice, but went on cutting bread on the corner of the oil cloth which covered the table, and the children continued to eat, their eyes fixed on their plates. Only John kept his eyes on his father, and Shane lifted his blood-shot gaze from the top of his wife's head to meet John's again. He stared at his son for a moment, his compressed lips moving in and out. Then he swung round, grabbed his cap from the back of the door and went to go out: but as he reached the back door he paused and cast his infuriated glance back into the kitchen again: 'The next bloody thing'll be: There's the door . . . Get out!'

He kicked savagely at the box holding the dish of water. There was a clatter and a splash; the door opened and banged, and only the clink of his heel plates becoming fainter down the yard broke the silence in the kitchen.

When they could be heard no more, Mary Ellen moved. She went into the scullery and, bending down with difficulty, began to sop up the water from the hollowed stones.

Dimly, with a mixture of pity and understanding, her thoughts followed her husband . . . Dominic getting drunk on his earnings . . . John coming in from work. Both of them on full time, and him with only two shifts in. He was getting on and he couldn't work like he used to, and the gaffer picked the young and strong 'uns. His strength was failing – she'd noticed that. Drink and hard work and wet clothes that were often frozen to his skin were at last taking their toll. He seemed to retain his strength for one thing alone . . . if only that would slacken with the rest. It must sometime. Then God, let it be soon.

'I'll help you, Ma.' Katie was on her knees by the side of her mother.

'No! Get up out of that. That's the only clean pinny you've got!'

'Well I haven't got to go to school the morrer.'

'Doesn't matter. Get up out of that.'

'Here!' – John stood above her – 'let's have it.' He held out his hand for the cloth.

'Oh get out of me road, the both of you!' Her voice pushed them back into the kitchen, and she went on bending and wringing out the cloth. Who did they think did all the other work, the washing, the cooking, the scouring, the humping of the coal, bucket by bucket from the back lane into the coal house because now she couldn't throw the shovelfuls through the hatch?

She partly soothed her irritation by saying to herself: 'You know John's always telling you to leave the coal until he comes in. Yes, but how can I' – her irritation refused to be soothed – 'with people waiting to get their washing out!' She flung the cloth into the bucket. Oh, she felt so tired. If only she could see a way out of all this . . . if only the bairn was born! Yes, that was the main stumbling block. Once that was over everything would be all right; she would cope, as always.

She went into the kitchen again and said to Mick, 'Go and empty the bucket and wash it out, and bring some clean water . . . See you wash it out, mind!'

Mick's mouth dropped, and he muttered, 'Aw! Why can't she do it?'

He dug Molly in the side, and she cried, 'Look at him, Ma! Stop it, our Mick!'

John took the rib of bones from his mouth: 'Your mother spoke to you.'

'Me ear's bad' – Mick placed his hand over the side of his head – 'it's been running all day.'

'You going out to play the night?' John asked.

'Yes.' Mick scowled at the table.

'Then empty the bucket.'

John went on picking his bone, and Mick clattered from the table, while Molly sniggered into her pinny.

'You'll laugh the other side of your face in a minute, my girl,' said Mary Ellen. 'Get those dishes washed.'

'Then can I go out to play?'

'Who you going out to play with in the dark, you're not going to run the streets?'

'We're going in Annie Kelly's wash-house; her ma's had the pot on, and it's warm. Annie has some bits of candle, and we're going to put them in bottles and play houses and dress up.'

'Play houses and dress up,' Mary Ellen muttered to herself. Aloud, she said, 'And burn yourselves to death! . . . Well, and only half an hour, mind. And you can take Katie with you.'

'I don't want to go, Ma; I've got to do some homework.'

'What!' the mother and John lifted their heads and stared at Katie.

'You got your sums wrong?' asked John, in surprise.

'No.' Katie shook her head and tried to repress a smile, but her eyes grew rounder and her dimples deeper as she looked at their straight faces.

'Then why have you to do homework?' John asked; 'you never have before.'

'I've got to learn something. Miss Llewellyn asked me to . . . '

'She's Miss Llewellyn's pet, everybody says she is . . . I hated Miss Llewellyn. I was glad when I was moved up.' Molly wet the tip of her finger on her tongue, and in this way she secured a number of crumbs from the table. When she had put them in her mouth, she swung round on Katie, saying, 'You didn't tell me ma Miss Llewellyn gave you a penny the day for learning your poetry first, did you? Nelly Crane told me . . . so!'

The smile vanished from Katie's face, and Mary Ellen looked down on her daughter in surprise, the daughter who was the only one of the family to take after her. She could see this child, as she herself once was, plump and bonnie and open-handed. It was unusual for Katie to keep anything.

'Did she give you a penny?' she asked.

Katie neither moved nor spoke, but her eyes, as they looked back into her mother's, became glazed, and she cried out within herself, 'Oh, our Molly! our Molly!' Now it was all spoilt – the wonderful, wonderful thing she was going to do was spoilt. The Easter egg . . . the real Easter egg in a real box, tied up with a real silk ribbon, was lying in fragments about her! And the picture of herself handing it to Miss Llewellyn was lying with it.

That penny had brought her secret hoard to five-pence. For three weeks she had kept John's Saturday penny and the two halfpennies her mother had given her. Today's surprise penny had meant such a lot, for she had only another month or so during which to get the remainder of the shilling.

Her mother became blotted out by a mist; then she felt John's big hands drawing her to him and pressing her against his knees.

When he bent and whispered in her ear, 'Are you saving up to buy a present?' she experienced the feeling she had felt before that John was in some way connected with God and the priests, because he knew everything.

She nodded her head against the bottom of his waistcoat, and he whispered again, 'Your teacher?'

At this she gasped and pressed her face tightly against him. John exchanged a glance with his mother, and a smile flickered for an instant across her face.

'I think you must be the cleverest lass in the school,' John went on.

Katie brought her head up swiftly and stared at him. 'Why, that's what Miss Llewellyn says! She says . . . she says I'm advanced and I must work at nights and . . . and read a lot.'

'There you are. There you are. Miss Llewellyn knows. She knows when she's on a good thing. What have you got to learn the night?'

'Oh, I already know some of it, the end bit,' she laughed. 'Listen. A man named Shakespeare did it.' She stood back from his knee, threw her long black plaits over her shoulder, joined her hands behind her back, and said:

'There take an inventory of all I have,
To the last penny; 'tis the king's: my role,
And my integrity to heaven is all
I dare now call my own. O Cromwell, Cromwell!
Had I but serv'd my God with half the zeal
I serv'd my king, he would not in mine age
Have left me naked to mine enemies.'

John stared down on her face, which was illuminated by the feel of the strange words on her tongue, and Mary Ellen stared at the back of her dark head. Then their eyes met, reflecting the glow of her words, which were unintelligible to both of them . . . But Katie had said them . . . their Katie . . . the only one of them who had ever wanted to learn. With a swoop, John lifted her up and held her on his upstretched hands. Her head was within a few inches of the ceiling, and he laughed up at her: 'Will I push you through to Mrs Flaherty?'

'Eeh! No, John. Eeh, our John, let me down.'

She wriggled on his hands, anxious to get away from the ceiling and the proximity of Mrs Flaherty and her weird house.

As he lowered her to the floor John laughed, 'You'll soon be cleverer than Mrs Flaherty, and then everybody will be coming here and saying, "Please,

Katie O'Brien, will you write me a letter?' and you'll say, "Yes, if you give me sixpence." '

'Oh, our John, I wouldn't! I wouldn't ask for sixpence.'

He bent down to her and whispered hoarsely, 'Oh yes you would, if it would get your teacher a present.'

She slapped his knee playfully, then turned her face away to hide the tell-tale glow.

Molly banged the mugs into the cupboard; she banged the door as she went out; then her voice came through the keyhole:

'Miss Llewellyn has a swellin',
An' I'm not tellin'
Where Miss Llewellyn
Has a swellin'.'

John turned quickly away from Katie's outraged face, rubbing his hand across his mouth. But he could not rub the laughter from his eyes, and Katie turned on him, her voice full of hurt surprise: 'Oh, our John, you're laughing! Our Molly's awful . . . Miss Llewellyn hasn't got a . . . She's lovely, she's beautiful. She wears a lovely white blouse with a frill at her neck, and her hair's brown and shines all over the place. And Mr Culbert's after her. Cathleen Pearson says he wants to marry her.' Katie's voice broke: 'She's beautiful . . . she's beautiful.'

John sat down by the fire and pulled her on to his knee, cradling her in his arms and soothing her: 'Of course she's beautiful, of course she is. And who's Mr Culbert when he's out?'

'He's . . . he's a teacher at St Jude's.'

'Is he? Is he? Well, he can be the Prime Minister for all I care. But you know what I'm going to do? I'm going to this Mr Culbert, and I'm going to say, "You going to marry Miss Llewellyn and take her away from teaching our Katie? You are . . . like panhacklety!!" '

'Oh, our John, you're awful!'

Laughing, she scrambled up and stood on his knees and flung her arms about his neck, endeavouring to strangle him with her small strength.

'Here! hold on.'

'Eeeh!' – she drew her face back from his – 'you haven't got to say that.'

'What, hold on?'

'Yes. Miss Llewellyn says you've got to say, "Wait a moment," or, "Stop a moment." '

'Do you hear that, Ma?' He winked at his mother, who was now sitting at the other side of the hearth mending a pair of moleskin trousers.

She gave a flicker of a smile and went on adjusting a patch. What was it about these two bairns of hers that brought her such strange joy? To see them playing together like they were now seemed to make up for all the heart scolds of life. She still thought of John as her bairn, although he was twenty-two and six foot one. He would always be her bairn, her first bairn. There were some who said you loved all you gave birth to. Fools! You couldn't love even two alike. Even those two opposite, she loved one more than the other, but she couldn't tell which.

Her mind returned to concrete things, and she said without looking up, 'The front window's out.'

John did not reply, but after a moment put Katie on the floor and, taking a box of matches from his pocket, went to the front room.

Katie was about to follow him, when Mary Ellen said, 'Get on with your homework, hinny.'

It was some time before John returned, and still he said nothing. He sat down on his chair again and took off his boots and put his stockinged feet on the fender, and sat staring at the kettle singing on the side of the hob. Presently he took a loose Woodbine from his pocket and lit it . . . Would it never end? Would life go on like this for her until she died?

He cast a glance at her bent head. The hair was grey, yet coarse and strong, springing from the centre parting and refusing to be drawn flat into the knob behind; but the face beneath was deeply marked with lines. They ran in puckered furrows across her forehead and bit deep from her nose to the corners of her mouth. The mouth in repose, as it was now, looked despondent, without hope. Could you wonder at it! And there was this other thing to happen. And her so little, not much bigger than a bairn herself.

He shifted suddenly in his chair. What could he do? He was helpless. If only he had a decent job, if only he hadn't been pushed into the docks. Well, where else could he have gone? If a lad wanted to make money at fourteen he had to give up all idea of being apprenticed to a trade. It was the same in all the places: Palmer's shipyard, the steel works, the chemical works. Now he'd be a dock labourer for the rest of his life; and he would never earn enough money to make any noticeable difference to her life. Did his father ever feel like this, feel this sense of frustration and helplessness? That's why he drank as he did. And Dominic? Ugh — he made an involuntary gesture with his hand as if wiping his brother away — that swiller!

He lifted his feet up to the side of the pan hob and sank deeper into his chair. Drink was a funny thing once it got you. He was drunk only once, and could still remember isolated parts of the feeling. It happened the first week he was on capstan work. He had been promoted from hatching at two-and-six a shift and now felt a man. After being paid off, he was walking out of the dock gates with the men when one of them, nodding towards the line of public houses filling the street opposite, said, 'Comin' over?'

He felt flattered, and went with them into The Grapes. He remembered the feeling of his stomach swelling and the continual belching of wind, and his mouth becoming fixed open in a wide grin. It was this grin that was partly the reason why he did not touch the drink again, for he brought the picture of himself over into his sober consciousness, and in it he saw the face of his father when in drink, as he had seen it since he was a child, with the large full-lipped mouth stretched wide, conveying not the impression of geniality but of imbecility. And his cure was completed by knowing, on waking up in bed undressed, that his mother had done for him what she did for his father. It was some time before he could entirely rid himself of the feeling of shame and humiliation when he thought of himself being undressed by her.

There were times when he wanted a drink badly – like today, when his throat felt clogged tight with dust – unloading grain was a dry job. He had gone across to the horse trough outside the gates and filled the iron cup four times. Some of his mates called, 'Cheap that, John.' 'Aye, and no headache the morrow,' he replied. They no longer asked him to join them.

A crescendo of snores came from the bedroom, and he shifted his position again. There was something he wanted more than a drink, and that was a mattress. Could he put it to her now? He looked towards his mother. She'd had enough for one day, he told himself, without anything more to worry about. But when a series of spluttering coughs terminated the snores, he said, 'There's a pitch boat due in shortly; if I get set on her, it'll mean extra. Could you . . . get me a mattress with it?'

'A mattress!' Mary Ellen stopped sewing and looked at him. 'A mattress?'

He turned his head to the fire again. 'I want you to put Mick in the bed; I'll sleep in the cupboard.'

'Oh lad' – she joined her hands together over the patch – 'you can't sleep on the floor. And anyway, the cupboard isn't big enough, it barely holds Mick.'

'I can leave the door open.'

The sadness seemed to sink from her eyes into her body, shrinking it still further. She turned her gaze to the fire, and her hands lay idle . . . There was no way of getting another bed into the room, even if they could get one. And for John to lie in the cupboard! She shook her head, not knowing she did so.

The cupboard in the bedroom ran under Mrs Flaherty's front stairs; its total length was five feet, and he wanted to sleep in that! If the door was open, it was cold and draughty, even in the summer; if it was closed, it was naturally airless. She often worried about Mick having to lie there . . . but John! And his feet would extend over any mattress – they did through the bed rails, both his and Dominic's. But that wasn't the floor.

She looked at him and saw by the way his face was set that he meant to do it, and if she didn't get him the mattress he'd lie in the cupboard in any case, on Mick's bag of straw. She sighed, and her hands began to work again.

There was no sound in the kitchen except the sound of Katie's pencil and Dominic's muffled snores, until Molly rushed in the back door, crying, 'Ma! do you know what?'

'Make less noise!' Mary Ellen said.

'But Ma, there's somebody moving in next door the morrer.'

'Wash yourself and get ready for bed . . . Who told you that?' Mary Ellen asked.

'Mrs Bradley told Annie Kelly's ma, and Annie Kelly told me.'

'Then if Mrs Bradley said so, it must be right.' Mary Ellen rose, pulled the table to one side to get at the wooden couch beyond, and began to make up the girls' beds, one at each end.

'Get your things off, hinny,' she said over her shoulder to Katie.

The two girls undressed in the scullery, all except their boots and stockings. These they took off, sitting on crackets before the fire, chatting to each other now quite friendly. Katie sat next to John, her bare feet on the fender sticking out from under her patched, flannelette nightie.

John's fingers moved slowly through her hair. And when the bedroom door opened and Dominic lurched into the kitchen he didn't lift his eyes from the paper he was reading.

Dominic stood near the table, blinking in the gas-light. He yawned, running both his hands over his head; then pulled his belt tighter before coming to the fire. He shivered and sat down in the seat vacated by Mary Ellen, growling to Molly as he did so, 'Move your carcass!' He ran his tongue round his dry lips, shook his head in an endeavour to throw off the muzziness, and stretched out his hands to the fire.

'Any grub?' he asked, without turning his head.

'There's broth,' his mother answered from her bent position over the couch.

Katie looked past Molly to her brother's face. It looked huge and frightening, with the dark stubble around his chin and up the sides of his cheeks, and the darker marks of the dried blood stand-ing out around his mouth. When he hawked in his throat and spat at the bars, she drew her feet sharply beneath her nightie, nearly falling off the cracket as she did so. John's hand, still on her head, steadied her, but he did not take his eyes from the paper.

Dominic saw her frightened glance, and a twisted grin spread slowly over his face. He leaned back in his chair, and after a while Katie's toes came from beneath her nightie again. Her feet were cold, for the steel fender was well below the bottom red bar of the fire. She lifted one foot up above those of Molly, to wriggle her toes in front of the lower bar. There was a hiss, a splatter, and Dominic's yellow saliva was running over her foot.

As she hid her face from the sight and pressed her mouth to stop herself from being sick, she felt John springing away from her. His chair was kicked back, and she flung herself to the floor by the bottom of the fender, lying along its length, pressing close to its brass bars to keep clear of the pounding feet. Molly had sprung to the couch, where she now sat huddled. And before Mary Ellen could reach them John's fist swung out and Dominic reeled backwards and crashed into the cupboard door.

Mary Ellen flung herself on John, crying, 'Lad! lad!' She beat his chest with her fists in an endeavour to push him back: 'John lad! John lad! For God's sake!'

John did not look at her, but gathered her flaying hands in one of his, and tried to push her aside. But she kept in front of him by pressing her body against his, calling beseechingly up to him, 'Lad! Lad! John, lad!'

His face was bereft of colour; his lips were drawn back from his teeth, and his eyes were like black marble. Through her body she could feel the waves of anger running through his; her breast was pressed against his stomach, which shook with the elemental forces demanding release.

'Holy Mary, Mother of God, Mother of God!' she cried. 'No more the day, lad!' She took no heed of her other son, standing with his fists at the ready behind her; Dominic, she knew, wouldn't fight John unless

328

he had to, for in John he had more than his match. No, it was John she must stop. 'John, lad – John! I can't stand any more this day. Oh, Jesus, Mary and Joseph, you know I can't stand no more the day.'

She felt a great intake of breath coming into his lungs and the rumbling thunder of the words as they were released from his throat: 'I warned you what would happen if you did that again!'

Relief swept through her; he had spoken; she could manage him if he spoke.

He spoke again, and his words now brought a faintness over her; the child in her womb seemed to stop breathing. The words fell into her inner consciousness, to be remembered as would those spoken by a prophet have been, for, like Katie, she felt that John was near the priests and God, for what he said was mostly true. And he said now to his brother, 'One of these days I'll kill you.'

There was no threat in the words, only a quiet certainty.

CHAPTER TWO

A DAY OF BONNY LASSES

Poverty is comparative. There were those who did not live in the fifteen streets who considered the people living there to be of one stratum, the lowest stratum; but the people inside this stratum knew that there were three different levels, the upper, the middle, and the lower. All lived in 'houses' either upstairs or down; but in the lower end each house had only two small rooms, and upstairs or down the conditions were the same — the plaster on the walls was alive with bugs. These might only appear at night, to drop on the huddled sleepers, but that strange odour, which was peculiarly their own, wafted through the houses all the time, stamping them as buggy. No-one went to live in the lower end unless he was forced. To the middle and upper fifteen streets the bottom end was only one step removed from the workhouse, for its inhabitants were usually those whose furniture had been distrained or who had been ejected from their former houses for non-payment of rent.

There were three nightmares in the lives of the occupants of the middle and upper fifteen streets. And these were linked together: they were the bums, the lower end, and the workhouse.

In the middle houses there were four rooms ... boxes, generally, but boxes that were divided, giving privacy of a sort to one or two extra beings. The upper end had only three rooms to each house, and these were either up or down. Here, water was not carried from the central tap in the back lane but from a tap at the bottom of each yard. This stamped the area as selective, automatically making it the best end.

But even into this stratum of the fifteen streets no-one had ever been known to arrive with their furniture in a van. A flat lorry, yes, or a coal cart; at worst, a hand barrow, after dark. These were the three general modes of removal. But a van! a proper one, bearing the words 'Raglan, Furniture Removers, Jarrow-on-Tyne', never.

The street was out to watch with as much interest as if it were a wedding, or a funeral, or, what was more common, a fight. The three O'Brien children had a grandstand view: they stood in a row beneath their front window sill, and behind them, in the room, were the elders, Mary Ellen, Shane, Dominic and John. The sons stood one at each side of their mother and father. They were standing together as a family for once, joined by the common interest, watching in silent wonder as each piece of furniture was carried into the house next door. They had not seen furniture like this before. There was the big, bright, round table, with the thick single leg and bunchy feet like claws; there was the suite of patterned plush, with ball fringe all round the bottom of the couch and chairs; there was the big clock, nearly six feet high; and there was the bed, a wooden one painted white, with pictures on the panels; there were two other beds, but these were of brass. Yet these were outstanding too, for they were neither chipped nor battered. That was not all. There were carpets, two of them, besides a load of rugs one man could hardly shoulder. And the road was strewn with all kinds of things that rent Mary Ellen through with envy; a feeling she thought she was past this many a year. But then, she had never seen owt like this before in the fifteen streets . . . or anywhere else: the mahogany plant stand, with its looped chains, the large china flower pots, the clothes basket full of coloured china, and the little mangle, which looked like a toy but which she knew wasn't. Who were these folks who could own such things, yet had come to live here? It didn't make sense somehow.

She glanced up at John to see what effect all this was having on him, and her eyes left him quickly and travelled down his gaze to the street again. He was looking at a lass who had just come out of the house. Mary Ellen wasn't sure if she was a child, a lass, or a woman.

John, staring at the girl over the brown paper that covered the hole in the window, was being puzzled in much the same way; the girl on the pavement was as shapeless in form as Katie, showing no evidence of either hips or bust. Judged on her figure, she could be a child; and her face too had something of the immaturity of the child in it. Yet it was old. No, not old – he rejected the word – wise, that was it . . . and bonnie too. Yes, she was bonnie, that pale skin against the dark hair. The hair was unusual in that it hung loose about her head. Cut short, boyish fashion, it was like a dark halo. He was curious to see more of her, and, as she turned to speak to the old man with the white hair, who was directing the unloading, he unconsciously bent forward.

Whatever she said brought a smile from the long, serious face of the man, and she smiled in return: and John knew them to be related; it was as if the same light shone from them. It illuminated their faces, and seemed to convey a ray of light even to himself, for he found his face relaxing into a smile as he watched them. He wondered who they could be. Was the man her da, or her grandda? And the little lad running to and fro was evidently one of them, for he had the same pale skin and dark hair.

As John considered the fine furniture and their fine clothes, his smile faded. The old man was wearing

333

a suit and a collar and tie, as though got up for a do, and the girl, a blue woollen dress with a little woollen coat of the same colour. It looked neat and trim and was as unlike anything the lasses of the fifteen streets wore as John could possibly imagine.

The two removal men were struggling to get a chest of drawers through the front door. It was the biggest chest John had seen in his life; it was taller than himself. He could see only one of the men, who was bearing the weight of the bottom end and was stepping backwards and forwards under the other's directions. John knew what had happened. The front door did not lead directly into the front room, but into a tiny square of passage. The other man had got his end stuck in this passage.

The old man's assistance was to no avail; and John watched the girl glance about her at the dark, huddled figures blocking the doorways. Then her eyes came to the window and met his. For a second they looked at each other, and he noted the surprise and curiosity in her glance, and realised in a flash that to her he must appear as if he was standing on something to look over the brown paper. Humorously he thought: I'd better show her it's me all the way. I'll give them a hand with those drawers . . . and damn the tongues! He turned, to find Dominic, who was nearer the front door, looking at him with eyes full of mirthless laughter. Dominic slowly hitched up his trousers, buttoned his coat, then went out into the street.

With a feeling of frustration mixed with anger, John watched Dominic speak to the girl, and saw her look sharply from Dominic's face to the window as if to reassure herself there were two of them. Then she smiled on Dominic, and he bent his broad back under the chest, taking the weight off the men, and in a few minutes they all moved into the house.

John and Mary Ellen turned from the window and went to the kitchen. Nothing had escaped Mary Ellen; she had followed the desire of her son and felt Dominic interpret John's thought and use it against him. She said, 'Come and finish your dinner, lad, it'll be kissened up to cork.'

Taking three plates out of the oven, she called to her husband. Shane, looking mystified and his head jerking, came to the table. 'Must be bloody millionaires,' he said. 'Know who they are?'

'No,' she answered. 'I know nowt about them.'

The meal was eaten in silence. Once or twice Mary Ellen glanced at John, but his face was closed, telling her nothing. She got up to clear the table, and muttered impatiently when a face was pressed against the window and a voice called, 'Can I come in, Mrs O'Brien?'

Mary Ellen's brows knit together, but she answered pleasantly, 'Oh, it's you, Nancy. Yes, come in.'

A girl of sixteen sidled into the room. Her face was flat, almost concave, and her nose and eyes seemed to be lost in its centre, as though a force were sucking them in. The expression was serious and earnest, like that of a child struggling to be impressive. She began with quaint ceremony, 'Hallo, Mrs O'Brien.'

And Mary Ellen answered kindly, 'Hallo, Nancy.'

'Hallo, John.'

John turned from the table and said, 'Hallo, there, Nancy.'

'Hallo, Mr O'Brien.'

Shane growled something, keeping his eyes directed towards his plate. And Mary Ellen, thanking God that the rest of the family weren't in to lengthen Nancy's usual formal greeting, said, 'Sit yourself down, Nancy.'

Nancy sat down, and John said to her, 'Still like your place, Nancy?'

'Yes, John,' she answered; 'I've nearly been there a month now.' It was a curious defect of her speech that her mouth never closed; her lips refused to meet, so her voice sounded nasal, like that of someone with a hare lip.

John answered tolerantly, 'Yes, you have, Nancy,' knowing that the time she had scrubbed and cleaned in the Fitzsimmons outdoor beershop was nearer to four years than four weeks – time had no place in Nancy's mind. Her body gave the impression of uncontrolled strength; her long arms hung out from the short sleeves of her coat, a brown, faded thing, and her boots looked too small for her big feet.

John said kindly, 'You look very nice the day, Nancy.'

She smiled at him, stretching her face; then, preening herself and dusting down the front of her coat with her red hands, she said, 'This is a new coat. Me ma bought it. And these boots too. And I've got a silk dress, with a sash. And I'm going to get a hat with a feather in.'

Shane's chair scraped back and he went to the front room. Mary Ellen looked after him for a moment – he never could stand the senseless prattle of Nancy. She went into the scullery to wash the dishes, glad that John was in to cope with Nancy should she start laughing . . . Oh, Nancy's laughter! Mary Ellen shuddered. She thought she was afraid of nothing on earth as she was of Nancy Kelly's laughter – it put the fear of God in her. But John could manage her – he always had; he made her think she was like other lasses. She could sense John's pity for Nancy; it was like her own, but without the strain of fear that ran through hers.

She heard Dominic coming up the backyard, whistling. He was pleased with himself for outwitting John, she supposed. She hoped to God he did nothing more to aggravate John's feelings; the sick premonition of last night was still partly with her. She was more afraid of John's rages than of either Shane's or

Dominic's, for his were stronger, being made more fierce through sober justification.

Dominic came in and surprised her by closing the scullery door and so shutting them off from the kitchen. He stood near her as she bent over the dish, and said softly, 'Any chance of you lending me the money to get me clothes out?'

She looked up at him, her hands still in the water. 'I've only got the rent. You put your suit in, you'll have to get it out.'

'I'll give it to you back next week.'

'I haven't got it; I only have a few coppers left for the gas over the week-end.'

Dominic's suit had been in pawn for more than a month, and he had made no effort to get it out, even on his full shifts. Without it he was tied to the house and spent his Sundays in bed, for by some unwritten law no-one went out of doors on a Sunday dressed in their working clothes. Even if a man possessed a shilling to 'get a set in', he never showed his face inside a public house unless he was 'tidy'.

Strangely enough, Mary Ellen realised it wasn't tomorrow Dominic was thinking of, but tonight, and that new lass next door; although how he'd had the nerve to ask such as her out, she didn't know . . . But then she did. Dominic had the nerve for anything if he wanted it badly enough. She said cuttingly, 'Why don't you ask one of your cronies for it?'

He cast her a sidelong glance, in which she saw the sharp, questioning look – he wondered how much she knew. She knew more than he thought she did, to her sorrow. There was a certain woman of the docks, Lady Pansy, so-called because of her style in her heyday when she entertained nothing less than a chief engineer. But times had changed, and with them Lady Pansy's figure and face. Although she couldn't claim big money now she still liked her men young and strong, and Mary Ellen knew that all the money from Dominic's full shifts was not spent on drink – the thought made her sick – and the woman was as old as she was, if not older!

If Mary Ellen's refusal dampened Dominic's spirits, he hid it successfully, for in the kitchen he was extra hearty, forestalling Nancy's greeting by giving an imitation of herself.

'Hal-lo, Nan-cy!'

'Hallo, Dominic.' Nancy wriggled on her chair.

Dominic went and stood over her: 'What's this I'm hearing about you, Nancy? They tell me you're courtin'.'

'Eeh! who told you that?' The girl wriggled in agitation. 'Eeh! I'm not . . . am I, John?'

John said nothing, but left the table and took a seat by the fire. He knew where Dominic's teasing would lead.

'Well, that's what I heard,' Dominic went on; 'I thought you were goin' to wait for me. Nice one, you are.' He pulled his belt tighter in feigned annoyance.

'Eeh, Dominic! I haven't got a lad, I haven't. I don't let them come near me. If they touch me, I yells I do.' Her face gathered itself into a troubled pucker.

John thrust the poker between the bars and raked savagely – he knew that Dominic's tactics were more to madden him than to tease Nancy.

Dominic laughed, and went on, with mock seriousness, 'Let's get this settled. When are me and you goin' out for a walk, eh?'

Mary Ellen came hurriedly into the kitchen: 'I think you'd better be going home now, Nancy, your ma will be wondering where you are.'

As Nancy stood up, Dominic said softly, 'I'll get another lass, mind.'

And Mary Ellen cried, 'That's enough of that! Get away home now, Nancy.' She turned to the girl and led her, trembling, to the door; but before they reached it, it opened, and Hannah Kelly herself stood there.

'Oh, this is where you are' – she looked unsmilingly at her daughter – 'I guessed as much. Go on, get yourself over home.'

Nancy slid by her mother, and Hannah came in and closed the door. Her manner was conspiratorial. 'Well, what d'yer think, eh? D'ye know who ye've got next door, Mary Ellen?'

Mary Ellen shook her head.

340

'My God! Ye'd never believe. They call this the Irish quarter, but what with the Jews and the ranters . . . and now this! Well, my God, I ask ye!'

'What are they?' asked Mary Ellen bluntly.

'Spooks!' Hannah's head came forward, impressing the word.

'What!'

'Spooks. He's called The Spook in Jarrow and Howden and round there. Remember a bit back when the Irish navvies burnt a hut down and the pollis had to get the man away? Well, that was him. He was givin' a service or somethin'.'

Mary Ellen turned and looked from one to the other of her sons, who were now both listening to Hannah Kelly with interest.

'Dorrie Clark knew who he was the minute she set eyes on him, and she was tellin' Bella Bradley that when she was delivering once in Jarrow, he came in and wanted to lay his hands on the woman. That's what she said . . . lay his hands on her! Did ye ever hear owt like it? To ease her labour, he said, because she'd been in it four days.'

Mary Ellen looked distinctly shocked. 'Did she let him?'

'Did she hell! Ye know old Dorrie. She said she kicked his arse out of the door. And she would an' all, full of gin or not. But my God, there'll be the divil's figarties around these doors before long! Mark my words; ye'll see.'

341

Mary Ellen was evidently disturbed. She looked from one to other; then she addressed John, 'What d'you make of it?'

John turned away, and went to the bedroom, saying, 'I don't know; they looked all right to me.'

Hannah laughed and called after John, 'Mind yerself, John lad, that she don't lay hands on you. They say the lass is as bad as the old man.' Then turning to Dominic, she said, 'And you there, ye've soon got yer leg in.'

Ignoring her jibe, Dominic asked: 'D'you know what the old man works at?'

'Now that's another funny thing' – Hannah pointed her finger at him – 'he's the Mr Bracken that has the boot shop in Jarrow.'

The three of them looked from one to the other, and the same question was running through their minds: 'Why did a man who owned a boot shop come to live in the fifteen streets?'

In the bedroom, John pulled the wooden box from beneath the bed and took out his suit. It was too creased to wear, so he knew it hadn't been in the pawn; had it been in his mother would have pressed it ready for him. Taking a dirty raincoat from the back of the door, he stood pondering a moment whether he should change his black neckerchief for a white muffler, but decided against doing so. He would keep it for tonight, when he would be going to the Shields to have a look round the market and

342

perhaps go to the second-house somewhere. Now, he was just going for a walk.

He did not bother to change his working boots, but went into the kitchen and finding his mother alone, asked, 'Will you put an iron over my suit?'

'Yes, lad,' she replied. 'Are you off for a walk?'

He nodded. 'Where's Katie?'

'Here she is, coming up the yard,' said Mary Ellen.

'Want to come?' he asked her.

'Oh yes, John. Yes!' In her excitement, Katie hopped from one foot to the other.

'Not with hands and face like that,' he said. 'What have you been up to?'

'Playing shops ... I won't be a tick; wait for me.'

Mary Ellen was already pouring the water into the dish; and after a few minutes Katie, her face shining and a round straw hat lying straight on the top of her head, was walking down the yard with John.

He took her hand, and they went along the cobbled back lane to the main road.

'Where shall we go?' he asked her.

'Oh, the country, John. Up the country!'

'Simonside?'

'Yes. Oh yes, Simonside!'

The day was cold and clear, with the wind blowing straight in from the sea. The sky was high above the housetops and above the towering cranes, which

343

reared up inside the stone wall edging the road opposite the fifteen streets.

John looked up at the white tufted clouds moving swiftly across the sky, and said, 'Look up there. They look like a fleet of white brakes off for a day's outing, don't they? I bet they're off to the country, too – Morpeth or some place.'

Katie chuckled. This was one of the many reasons why she loved going walks with John – he made up stories about everything. She glanced up at him, her eyes twinkling: 'I bet when they come back they'll be singing, like the people do on the brake trips:

"Aa'm back to canny auld Jarrer,
A hip, a hip hooray." '

She giggled, and John tilted her hat over her eyes, saying 'Saucy piece!'

They walked by the side of the wall for some way, until they came to the chemical works and the tram sheds. Then, further on, as they passed a narrow cut, bordered on one side by the end of the chemical works and on the other by the railings which fence in part of the Jarrow slacks, John asked her, 'Do you want to go down the slipway?'

Katie shook her head quickly and shuddered.

'What are you frightened of?'

'It's that black mud – it's deep, and if you fell in you'd never get out.'

'But the tide's up now, and there might be a little boat moored there . . . All right, all right,' he laughed when Katie shuddered again; 'but you never used to be afraid of the slipway.'

She didn't say that Mick had dragged her down there and pretended he was going to push her in. He had held her over the stone coping, and she had gazed, petrified, at the silvery black, slimy mud sloping away from just below her face to the narrow stream of water at the bottom, running slowly beneath its shot-coloured oily surface. She didn't dare tell her mother in case John got to know, for then he would have gone for Mick.

They came to the Jarrow slacks at the point where they were open to the road. The water was lapping just below the bank, a few feet from the edge of the pavement. The large, square stretch of water was covered with timbers, roped together in batches, right up to the gut.

There was a permanent way, starting below the pavement and reaching to the gut, running through the middle of them. It consisted of logs, a foot wide, lashed end to end and to each side of posts driven in at intervals over the stretch. In parts, the logs were black and rotten and looked as safe for foothold as a loose rock on the edge of a precipice. But children were playing on them with happy unconcern, jumping from them to the roped timbers. Some children were far away over the timbers, laying flat along

345

the edges, trying to rake in pieces of wood that were floating by. And the sight of them brought back the past vividly to John. How many times had he perilously stood on the end timbers, near the edge of the gut, and waited for the tide to come in, bringing with it its drift wood. Often, for weeks on end, this wood was their only source of warmth, but often again, they had to do without the warmth whilst he hawked the sack of wood around, trying to sell it for twopence. He seldom succeeded; coke was the best sell. If he followed the coke carts from Jarrow right into Shields he could pick up as much as two bucketfuls each trip. Pieces would roll off the cart as it jogged along, especially when it crossed the tram lines. He'd get twopence for the coke, and if he could follow the cart three times, that meant sixpence. But he rarely completed the third journey, for his legs became so tired. He remembered the melancholy feeling that would settle on him as he followed the carts. It seemed to be worse when the sun was shining ... That was an odd thing he hadn't entirely grown out of — he didn't like the sunshine. For years this feeling vaguely puzzled him. Then one day the reason was made known to him. The sunshine, he discovered, showed up his surroundings. It brought a queer kind of pain to him. On a dull day, the docks, the coal dust, the houses, the rattling trams, and the people all seemed to merge into one background; but when the sun shone, there they all were, standing out in relief, dirty, stark, tired; and in some odd way it hurt him . . . The feeling was coming on him now, and he tried to ignore it, for it always made him start thinking; and when he thought, he got mad at things. As his mother said, thinking got you nowhere.

Katie plunged him further into the trough by exclaiming, 'You know, when I grow up, John, I'm going to be a teacher.'

He squeezed her hand and said, 'I bet you will too . . . headmistress!'

A teacher! Would Katie's dreams ever be fulfilled? He couldn't see it happening. She would go into a place at fourteen like the other lasses, and the bright eagerness would die. Her dreams, like his own when a lad, would be lost in the fight for food . . . It was funny, but that was all life amounted to . . . working life out to keep it in — working for food and warmth; and when the futility of this was made evident, blotting it out with drink. What did it all mean, anyway? What was living for?

When in this state of mind he always asked this question. The priests had one answer; but that had long ago ceased to satisfy him. Now he was asking himself another question: Had he to stay round these quarters until he died? He wasn't happy around here, yet when he moved out of this quarter, as he was doing now, up into Simonside, the lonely feeling became intensified and he felt lost, and some part of

347

him wanted to get back again into the fifteen streets, into the docks, anywhere but near these grand houses that stood back from the Simonside bank, with their drives and large gardens. He couldn't understand why his sense of loneliness should be greater away from the life that was irking him.

He was being daft, he told himself – just daft. He should get himself a lass. That's what he needed. He was twenty-two and he'd never had a lass. He had never kissed a lass, not even in a bit of fun. Katie was the only one he kissed. He knew there were one or two in the fifteen streets who would come at his nod, but he hadn't nodded. His flingings and tossings in bed at night had equalled Dominic's, and many a time he promised himself to ask Jenny Carey or Lily McDonald to go out on a Saturday night; but with the light of day he forgot about them.

Lately, Dominic hadn't tossed so much. And once or twice John had been tempted to seek his cure; but then again, the temptation vanished with the light.

'Look, John,' said Katie; 'there's Father Bailey.'

The priest was coming down the drive of one of the big houses, and he waved to them, calling, 'Hallo, there.'

John stopped and said, 'Hallo, Father.'

He wouldn't have stopped had it been Father O'Malley; but then, Father O'Malley wouldn't have called 'Hallo, there.' At best, he would have inclined his head slightly. Not even if he knew you hadn't been to mass would he speak to you on the street; he would wait till he had you indoors, then raise the roof on you. But Father Bailey was different. Even when he was chastising you for not going to mass he was nice about it.

'Are you going for a walk, the pair of you?' The priest smiled, first up at John then down on Katie; and not waiting for an answer, went on, 'It's just the day for it. You know, John' – he took a step backwards – 'I believe you get taller.'

'It's the clothes, Father; they've shrunk.'

'Well, there may be something in that, but I've always had the idea I came up to your shoulder. It must have been just an idea.'

He turned to Katie. 'And now, Katie O'Brien, what honours have you been gathering on your head this week? Do you know we have a clever girl here, John? Every week I hear something about Katie O'Brien. She's the top of her class for this, that, and the other. It'll be teaching the teachers she'll be in the end.'

'Oh, Father!' Katie O'Brien lowered her head and blinked at her boots.

The priest patted her straw hat. 'I'm just on my way up to the fifteen streets; I'll look in on your mother. How is she, John?'

'Oh, just middling, Father.'

349

'And your da, and Dominic?' There was a question in the priest's eyes.

They held John's, and he replied gruffly, 'Things don't change.'

'Oh, you're wrong there, John; every minute of the day they're changing.'

'Yes? Well I haven't noticed it.'

Father Bailey patted Katie's hat again, but still addressing John said, 'We never do. But look ahead, John . . . Shall I be seeing you at mass tomorrow?'

'I don't think so, Father.'

'Oh! This'll never do. Not at all, at all! I'll have to come and have a crack with you soon. But I must be off now. Enjoy your walk, both of you. Goodbye. Goodbye.'

'Goodbye, Father.' 'Goodbye, Father,' they said, and continued their way up the Simonside bank, past the little school and into what was termed the country, a few fields with hedged lanes between. If you didn't turn round and look back you could imagine there were no docks, no pits, no drab grey streets; and if you could stretch your imagination you could visualise these fields with their straight rows of tender green going on for ever.

'Shall we walk to the Robin Hood?' Katie asked.

'It'll be too far for you,' said John.

'No, it won't. I could walk miles and miles.'

She skipped on ahead of him, leaving him with his thoughts – thoughts of the priest; of this lonely feeling; and of the lass next door. His mind dwelt on the lass: Would he like to take her out? Good God! he'd never have the nerve to ask the likes of her, even if she were free — she was different somehow . . . Then why was she living next door? . . . There was no answer to this. And Dominic, he wouldn't be backward in asking her. But no! surely he wouldn't have the cheek, the state he was in with drink, and that woman. Yet why did he go out and give them a hand? It wasn't with any idea of helping, but to speak to the lass . . . Anyway, why was he thinking about all these things that didn't matter a damn! Hadn't he other things to think about? His mother in her trouble; and the house with hardly a whole stick standing.

But the sun and the wind were changing his mood — he didn't want to think, he only wanted to wander here in this quiet road.

He took off his cap and let the wind play through his hair. He ran his hand through it, and felt the freedom of being uncovered out of doors. It was such a relief to walk with his cap off, and no-one would see him here so it didn't matter, for it was another unwritten law that a woman did not go out without a hat or a shawl covering her head, nor a man a cap.

Katie came running back to him, exclaiming, 'Oh, John, your hair looks just like Miss Llewellyn's with the sun shining on it! It's all brown and shiny.'

351

'What!' he exclaimed. 'Miss— Don't be silly.' He ruffled it more.

'It is though.'

'Go on with you!' He took her hand and pulled her to his side, and they walked on until they came within sight of the Robin Hood, then turned towards Simonside again. Katie sang hymns, school songs, and rhymes, one following on the other without pause, while John walked along in strange contentment, listening to her.

They were nearing the top of the bank, where it dipped to the docks, when her singing ended abruptly and he felt her hand tugging on his. He looked down on her upturned face. It was alight with pleased surprise – her eyes were wide, sending him a mute message. Wondering, he followed her gaze, and saw a woman coming towards them, a young woman. She was taller than average, and wore a brown cloth coat with a full skirt. It was nipped in at the waist and gave emphasis to her bust. She carried her head high, and her hat, which was green and had a brown feather curling round its brim, appeared like a crown set on the top of her head.

As she came nearer, John became aware of her hair. It fell over her ears in soft folds, and when he noticed the colour, he connected it with Katie's excitement and thrust his cap on his head. Good God! Miss Llewellyn – and she not much more than a lass. And he'd thought she was getting on . . . well, in her thirties. She was looking directly at Katie and smiling.

He looked beyond her, but to his horror she stopped as she came abreast of them and said, 'Hallo, Katie.'

'Hallo, Miss Llewellyn.'

John felt Katie's fingers opening and shutting within his palm.

'You are a long way from home.'

'Yes, Miss Llewellyn.' Katie was breathless.

John gave a sidelong glance at the bent head – he could dare this because she wasn't looking at him. He had never before been so close to such a face. Katie said she was lovely. Katie wasn't far wrong. The skin of her cheeks was a soft, creamy pink, the nose was short, and in striking contrast the mouth was wide and laughing.

When she turned her eyes on him, he switched his away; and he fumbled in the pocket of his coat for his red handkerchief as she said, 'You're John, aren't you?'

He felt his eyes forced back to her, to look her full in the face, and for no reason he could understand he began to tremble inside – almost, he felt, like the jerking of his father's limbs, only invisible. He was painfully conscious of the cap on his tousled hair, of his dirty raincoat, of his neckerchief, and of his big boots, with their leather laces showing numerous knots. His Adam's apple moved swiftly, and he swallowed, but no words came.

And she went on, 'I've heard such a lot about you.'

Her voice, too, was like none he had heard before. Like her face, there was laughter playing around it. Was she laughing at him? Very likely.

He knew she was, and though he felt it was kindly laughter the hot colour flooded his face when she said, 'I don't suppose you know, but you are a combination of Prince Charming and God to a certain young lady.'

He thought quickly, as he found himself doing at times, and spoke before he could stop himself: 'Neither of them would be flattered. And if the last one hears of it there's not much chance of me getting up there.'

Her laugh rang out, joyous and infectious, and to his utter surprise he found himself laughing with her.

Katie stood looking up from one to the other. She did not join in with their laughter, her happiness was too profound – Miss Llewellyn laughing with their John!

When he thought of it later, he was surprised at her next remark – and her a Catholic and a teacher too – for she said, 'I don't suppose that will worry you very much. I should take the heaven you're sure of.' Her words seemed to confuse her slightly and the tinge of pink grew deeper in her cheeks.

He made no answer, thinking that if this life was her idea of heaven he'd bet on the one up there. The wind swirled about them, and she turned her back to it, leaning slightly back and holding her hat on with both hands. Then she terminated the meeting by saying, 'Well, I'll see you on Monday morning, Katie,' and to John, 'I'm glad I've met you in the flesh, for now when I listen to your sayings being recorded I'll be able to place them. Goodbye. Goodbye, Katie.'

'Goodbye, Miss Llewellyn.'

'Goodbye.' John did not turn immediately away, but watched her bending against the wind, the coat pressed against her legs. And he saw that she wore shoes and that her ankles were thin. He turned away, and Katie, walking close by his side, sighed. They looked at each other and smiled secretly, then walked on in silence, until John asked, 'You don't tell her all I say, do you?'

'No. Oh, no!' Katie lied firmly. And in the next breath she exclaimed, 'Isn't she lovely!'

He stopped and looked towards the docks, and Katie went on, 'And isn't it a lovely day!'

'Grand.' The word seemed to answer both her questions.

Far away in the distance he could see the masts of the ships, disembodied things, seemingly borne on air. He looked up at the sun, and for the first time in his life felt glad to be out and under it. He thought of the lass next door and of the lovely lass just gone, and he said, more to himself than to Katie, 'Yes, it's a lovely day; a day of clean wind and far mast-heads, and bonnie lasses.'

Katie stared up at him. Oh, their John was wonderful, the things he said! A day of clean wind and far mast-heads, and bonnie lasses! It was like . . . well, not like the poetry she learnt at school . . . and yet it was. Oh, and Miss Llewellyn had seen him! She had seen how wonderful he was.

Mary Llewellyn, walking briskly away in the opposite direction, was smiling no longer. Her face was thoughtful, and her eyes sad. So that was John. Poor soul! Poor soul!

CHAPTER THREE

ST PATRICK'S DAY

Mick led the Catholics, not because he was the eldest but because he was the biggest. At the top corner of Fadden and Blacket Streets he marshalled his gang, twenty-five in all, and saw that they were supplied with weapons. He made sure that the innocent-looking paper balls dangling from lengths of rope or string each had a good-sized stone in its centre. About twenty yards away, at the corner of Whitley Street, the Protestants were gathering, and their leaders were doing much the same as Mick. This was to be the climax to the day's badgering and cornering of individuals and isolated groups, of swinging the paper balls round the heads of victims, whether Catholic or Protestant, and asking the terrifying question, 'Are you blue or green?' Pity help the individual who had the courage to defend his colour to the opposite clan, for he was often hit until he was sick or rescued by some indignant passer-by.

Mick's gang were protesting loudly that it wasn't fair, for the ranters had three separate gangs – the churchies, the chapelies, and the odds, the latter group consisting of Jews, Salvationists, and a Quaker.

Mick exclaimed loudly that three lots were nowt, for they'd bash all their bleeding heads in. Adroitly he spread out his men in the form of an arrow, placing the bigger boys at the head.

He took a long time over this, for he was enjoying his momentary power and the admiration of the younger children swarming on the top of the stackyard wall that hemmed in the ends of the fifteen streets.

Someone began to sing the hymn:

'Oh glorious St Patrick, dear Saint of our Isle,'

and all the children on the wall took it up:

'On us, thy dear children, bestow a sweet smile;
And now thou art high in the mansions above,
Oh glorious St Patrick look down in thy love.'

The ending was the signal for the advance, both sides moving slowly towards each other. Then, with a rush, there was a swirling of balls, and there were screams and cries of 'Long live Ireland!' 'Up the shamrock!' in which were mingled 'England for ever!' and 'God save the King!'

Hard blows were struck by the arrow heads. But

they had learned no lesson from last year; so their balls became entwined, and many combatants had to stop and free them, and whilst doing so a number of them laughed, especially if their enemy happened to be a pal on the other three hundred and sixty-four days of the year. And so the fight became spasmodic, lacking the ferocity of the earlier battles; it became a mêlée of half-hearted punches and pushes. And the jeering from the mixed supporters on the wall became derisive.

Mick realised there was something lacking. He fell back with his side and engaged in a battle of vituperation!

'Protestant, Protestant, you dirty lot,
Yer backside's blue and yer nose all snot!'

to which the Protestants replied:

'Catholic, Catholic, ring the bell,
When you die you'll go to hell.'

It was all very half-hearted – the excitement seemed to have died in the completion of the preparations.

Mick felt a definite sense of disappointment and feared the flatness of the fight might be put down to his leadership, and that Big Geordie Flannagan might be picked to take his place. He looked round for some sign that would be the means of leading him to fresh applause. And like manna from heaven he found it. Standing solitary at the top end of his own back lane was the boy from next door . . . the spook's lad.

The boy was looking from one group to the other with evident curiosity. His face looked all eyes, and Mick was quick to detect a gleam of fear in them. With the true instinct of a leader, he first of all planned to cut off the enemy's retreat. So he called three of his best men to him, and in a few words told them what he intended doing, and despatched them down Fadden Street with orders to come up the back lane. A few more whispered words to other members of his gang, and they stopped yelling and stood looking towards the boy.

As soon as Mick saw the three outriders coming up the back lane he called out loudly, 'Look! There's the spook!'

After a moment's hesitation the word was taken up, 'The spook! The spook!' Those on the other side stopped their abuse and they too turned towards the boy, whose face had blanched. He did not turn and try to escape down the back lane, for he knew, from the laughs behind him, that that escape was cut off. Instead he tried to think of what his grandfather had told him to do when confronted with hostile thought, but terror swamped any thinking.

Fascinated, he watched the two opposing sides

converging on each other and the children swarming down from the wall. They began to form a solid mass before him, and he listened to shouts that weren't new to his ears:

'His da's a spook!'

'Me ma says he's a divil.'

'Me ma says if you bless yersel' when you pass him he can't do you any harm.'

'Me da says the priest put a curse on him an' he was kicked out of Jarrer, an' he'll wither away.'

'Mr Roberts, our minister, says they're evil and we mustn't have any truck with 'em.'

On and on it went, not loudly or angrily, but steadily and defiantly, and in some faint way the boy detected fear of himself in their voices. Yet he knew what that fear would make them do. It wasn't the first time he had been in a similar situation, but he found that repetition did not make him more brave.

Mick too was aware of the fear. The crowd of them would do nothing, he thought, just call the spook names and perhaps throw a stone or two, until some woman came out from her backyard and scattered the lot of them. He wanted a chase, some life in the proceedings.

Again he gave instructions to others of his gang, who sped away to block the ends of the streets, all but the last one. Then he yelled out to the crowd, proclaiming himself leader and a man of fair play,

361

'Give him a chance . . . Let him away! Give him a start!'

Molly, who was standing near him, whispered, 'Where you goner chase him?'

'The gut,' he whispered back without looking at her, for his eyes were now fixed on those of the boy.

The boy was shivering in stark terror; he knew what this chance meant; it meant running, running, running until his whole body sobbed and his trousers became wet. And he knew that long after the fear would have passed the feeling of his wet trousers would remain. But it was either running or being stoned here.

A gap appeared in the crowd and Mick's voice yelled, 'Come on, spooky! We'll give you a start.' He was leading them all now, the Catholics, the Protestants, the Chapelies and the others. He kept yelling, 'Let him through! . . . Come on, spook. We'll give you ten for a start when you're through.'

There was a whirling in Mick's blood when he saw the boy begin to move, and a stream of saliva trickled from the corner of his mouth. The boy, his face the colour of dirty dough and his eyes stretching the skin, came abreast of Mick. He would never reach the gut, Mick thought – he was too small. They would drag him there.

Suddenly he threw his arms out wide, a signal that no-one must move and shouted, 'One!'

362

At the sound the boy became galvanised. He shot away, and Mick, when he noted the speed with which the boy ran, quickened his counting, almost choking with suppressed glee when he saw the boy's maddened terror on realising the exits of the streets and back lanes were blocked.

'Ten!' was a scream in Mick's throat. He was off, ahead of the milling, screeching children. They stumbled into each other, kicking and pushing to get a clear road. Some left the main chase and ran down the streets, knowing that this would be the quickest way and that they would pick up the chase again on the main road, the word had been passed, 'To the gut! To the gut!'

Among those who diverted was Molly. She sped down her own street, her hair and legs flying. And she almost cried with vexation when she saw her mother step from their front door.

'Here!' Mary Ellen caught at Molly's arm, almost unbalancing herself. 'Have you gone mad? What's all the screeching for?'

'Aw! Ma, let go.'

'Get inside!' said Mary Ellen.

'Aw! Ma, I'm goin' with our Mick.'

'With Mick? What's he doin'?'

'He's . . . he's . . . They're chasin' the lad next door to the gut.'

Mary Ellen brought her hand across her daughter's ear with a crack. 'Get yersel' inside — I'll gut you!

A big lass like you running mad with a lot of lads!'
She pushed Molly before her through the front room,
calling, 'John!'

John came out of the bedroom asking, 'What is
it?'

'It's our Mick . . . he's chasing the lad next door
to the gut. There's dozens of them running mad!'

'Are you sure it's Mick?'

'Ask her.' Mary Ellen pointed to the snivelling
Molly.

When John looked at Molly she hung her head,
and Mary Ellen said, 'Go and see what he's up
to, lad; for if the pollis catches him at anything
down there they won't give him another chance,
after catching him loosening the timbers that time.'

'Why are they chasing the lad next door, are they
playing at something?' John asked Molly.

'No,' Molly muttered into her chest. 'It's because
he's a spook.'

John hastily put on his coat and left the house;
and as he went out into the back lane he bumped
into the girl from next door. She was running, and
gasped, 'I'm sorry.' She smiled faintly at him and ran
on again.

He did not speak, but hurried after her. He guessed
where she was going . . . someone must have told
her. Children were straggled along the road; most of
them, frightened by the thought of the gut, especially
as it was getting dark, had given up the chase.

One bold spirit addressed John: 'Your Mick's goin' to push the spook into the gut, Mr O'Brien.'

John knew that between Mick and Dominic there was only the difference in years; the cruelty was already fully matured in Mick, and he was quite capable of doing what this boy said. He set off at a run and caught up with the girl before she reached the short cut leading to the gut. Shortening his step to suit hers, he said, 'Are you looking for your brother?'

She nodded, but did not speak; and John again had the impression of age. There was a similarity, he noticed, between her expression and that which was more often than not on his mother's face ... This wasn't the first time she'd gone to her brother's aid — by God, he'd break that young rat's neck!

'You go back, and I'll see to them,' he said to her. But she shook her head.

As they turned down the cut, the shouting came to them, and John sprang away from the girl and ran on ahead.

With the intuition of the young, his coming was noted and the boys crowding round the disused boathouse on the edge of the gut gave the cry, 'Look out! Scatter!'

The size of John looming out of the gathering dusk and the fear of being caught and held responsible gave aid to their legs. They made for the opening near the boathouse, and like dots of vapour they disappeared across the disused ground adjoining the slacks.

John pulled up at the slipway. There was no sign of the boy. Likely, he had taken refuge on the wall round the corner. The wall supporting the slipway turned sharply at right angles, bordering the gut for a considerable distance, and ended abruptly where the gut was deepest, for the swirling tides had by slow degrees loosened its large granite stones, and many of these now made only a row of pin-points in the mud. The wall was just above ground level and was eighteen inches wide on the top, but from its back edge arose a six-foot fence of stout sleepers.

John walked sideways along the wall, pressing his back against the sleepers, and as he turned the corner he saw the boy and Mick.

The boy was standing up against the last sleeper of the fence, Mick was lying flat along the wall; and there was no sound from either of them, except the whack of the stick as Mick hit at the boy's legs, trying to dislodge him into the black, oozing mud. So lost was Mick in the relish of the moment that he did not hear John's approach. The first he knew was the sound of harsh breathing over him; then he was whipped to his feet and for one sickening second he was hanging in mid-air over the mud. John brought him to his feet and shook him until his head rolled on his shoulders.

'Get home and stay there! If you're not in when I

get back it'll mean twice as much when I find you.'

Mick clutched at the sleepers to steady himself, and growled, 'You hit me and I'll tell me da.' Then he retreated hastily along the wall, and John went on to the boy.

In the dim light the white face shone at him, and he said soothingly, 'It's all right, sonny, it's all right.'

The boy did not answer, and John said, 'Come on, give me your hand.'

But the boy still did not move; he seemed petrified into dumbness, and his fingers held on to the sleeper as if glued to it. The wall ended directly below this sleeper, and the rising tide was already creeping towards its fallen stones.

As John unbent the boy's fingers he saw that they were bleeding, and he wished for the moment he would have Mick under his hands. When he picked him up the boy lay stiff across his arms like something frozen hard. The girl was standing at the corner, her face as white as her brother's, and she clutched at them both, saying, 'Is he all right? Oh, David, are you all right?'

'Steady!' John said. 'Let's get off here.' And she went before them along the wall to where it met the ground.

As John put the boy down she drew David into her arms, crying, 'Oh, my dear, what have they done?'

The boy shuddered, and his body fell against hers, and she soothed him, saying, 'There! There! . . .

We'll go home – Grandfather will soon be in and everything will be all right.'

But when she took his hand to walk him up the bank his legs gave way beneath him, and he fell forward. John picked him up again, saying, 'You'd better get him to bed.'

As he strode up the road with the girl trotting by his side and holding on to her brother's ankle, he thanked God that most of the people were indoors having their tea and that the corners of the streets were deserted by their usual batches of men, for he felt self-conscious in doing this rescue act.

The door was open and the house lighted just as she had left it; and as John passed through the front room and into the kitchen he had the impression that his home next door was a hundred miles away. He became conscious of his big, dirty boots on the carpet, and when he laid the boy in a chair, drawn up to the fire, the comfort of it was conveyed to him by his hands sinking beneath the boy into the upholstery.

The girl ran into the bedroom, and returned with something in a glass. David drank it, then asked, in a thin, small voice, 'How long will Grandfather be?'

'Not long, darling.'

The girl was kneeling by the chair, and John, looking down on her, repeated to himself, 'Not long, darling.' Never before had he heard the word spoken, except in derision. How strange these people were.

He was turning to go, saying, 'I hope he'll be all right. My brother will be dealt with,' when the girl sprang to her feet.

'What are you going to do to your brother?' she asked. 'Thrash him?'

'What else?'

'Oh please!' her words tumbled over one another – 'Please don't do that! It won't do a bit of good . . . not the slightest, just the opposite.'

John frowned down on her in perplexity: 'What do you expect me to do? Let him off? He might have killed the lad there—' He nodded towards the chair.

Her eyes, set deep in her white face, looked black and enormous, and she began to plead with him as if her life depended on it: 'But he didn't! You must talk to him, point out where he was wrong . . . Will you? . . . Please. But don't thrash him; you'll only thrash it into him.'

'Thrash what into him?' John's brows drew closer together.

'The fears, the inhibitions . . . all the things that drove him to do what he did.'

John stared at her. What was she getting at? Was this part of the spook religion? She was strange, not in sayings alone, but in her looks; her curveless body, like a lad's, was as attractive as any bulging bust and wobbling hips.

He turned away from her and went towards

369

the kitchen door, but she hastily blocked his exit: 'Please! . . . Oh!' – she closed her eyes and moved her head from side to side – 'if only Grandfather was in he'd explain so much better than me . . . But you mustn't thrash him.'

Looking down into her strained face, John saw that for the moment, the thought of Mick being thrashed had entirely eliminated the worry for her brother – she was like no-one he had met before . . . she was really in earnest that Mick should be let off. But he knew Mick, and she didn't, so he said, 'Do you think he would understand a talking-to? No. The only thing Mick and his like understand is the thick end of the belt across their . . . ' Somehow he couldn't say 'arses' in front of her, so he ended lamely, 'You see. You don't know them.'

'Oh, but I do,' she said, smiling faintly, trying to override his last remark; 'I've known dozens of Micks. Look—' She put out her hands and caught hold of the lapels of his coat. The gesture was almost childish in its naturalness, and he looked down at her hands, then at her face close beneath his own; and an odd sensation passed over him . . . Hannah Kelly said, 'Mind she doesn't lay hands on you, lad.' But this wasn't the kind of laying on she was referring to. If a lass of the fifteen streets laid hold of him, there would be a particular meaning to it; they would lark about a lot before she did this though, and afterwards his arms would go round her. He

370

had seen the process enacted at the corner ends and in dark places in the back lanes. Often, when a lad, he watched the climax with an envy that dissolved into loneliness. And now here was this lass with her hands on him, and the sensation he was experiencing was almost one of reverence, similar to that which he at one time felt for the Virgin . . . But he didn't want to feel reverence for her, or any other lass. She was fetching and he wanted . . . He lifted his hand and covered one of hers — it wasn't much bigger than Katie's, but it was different. His blood began to warm with the feel of her, and he smiled slowly. Her soft, curving mouth was just below his, and as he watched it move, it fascinated him. He wasn't fully aware of the words it was forming until she stepped away from him, taking her hand from his and saying, 'If you had to treat a dirty wound, you wouldn't rub more dirt into it, would you?'

Still on about Mick . . . He came to himself, and said thickly, 'I'm sorry; I'll have to deal with him as I think fit.' A feeling of bewilderment and frustration, mixed with annoyance was filling him; and he passed her, saying gruffly, 'He'll have to take what's coming to him.'

It was with relief he entered his own kitchen. Here were people and things he could understand . . . and manage. Going straight to the wall by the side of the fireplace he unhooked the razor strop.

371

'Is the lad all right?' Mary Ellen asked.

'Just,' John answered briefly. 'Come on' — he motioned with his head to Mick.

'I'm not comin'. I'll tell me da!'

'Go canny, lad,' Mary Ellen said to John.

Go canny. Here was another one. 'Go canny!' he rapped out at her with unusual irritation. 'Do you know he nearly killed the lad! As it is he's practically sent him out of his mind. It's as well for you you got hold of Molly when you did, or you'd have something more than a thrashing on your plate the night. Go canny!' He flung round from her and pointed to the door.

Mick began to snivel and cried, 'Ma! Ma, don't let him!'

Mary Ellen turned from Mick to the fire, and John seized him by the collar and pulled him to the door, there to meet Dominic coming in.

Dominic looked from one to the other before eyeing John through narrowed lids: 'What you at? Playin' boss of the house again?'

'You mind your own damn business. If you'd had a little more of it there might have been an improvement in you!'

Mary Ellen hastily broke in, addressing herself to Dominic, 'He's nearly killed the little lad next door.'

After a moment, during which he glanced from one to the other, Dominic stepped aside, and John pushed Mick before him down the yard and into the wash-house.

Mary Ellen found herself staring at Dominic; she couldn't quite take it in; he was sober, solid and sober; and it St Patrick's Day! And added to this surprise was another; for when he took his cap off she saw that he'd had a haircut . . . a proper one; his thick, brown, curling hair was neatly trimmed up the sides, making him, even with the dust of the ore on him, look more attractive. He hadn't come in to tea and she imagined him to be in the bars; but he must have been having a haircut!

She went to the oven to take out his tea, a plate of finnan haddock, but he said, 'I don't want that yet.'

With further amazement she saw him wash himself quickly, take off his yorks and change his coat. He was banging the dust from his trousers as he hurried past her to the front room.

'Where you off to?' she asked.

Dominic paused a moment, and the expression she hated, a mixture of scorn, cocksuredness and craft, came over his face. His eyes flicked over her, and her throat contracted with dislike of him. He said heavily, 'Where d'yer think?'

She stood still, listening to him going out of the front door, and between Mick's howls out in the backyard, she heard the knocker of the next door banging. Her fingers moved nervously back and forth across her lips . . . How would it work out? Candidly she wouldn't care if Dominic left home tomorrow and she never set eyes on him again, but there was no such luck as that happening; he was here and he was going after that lass. It would have been bad enough had she been a Protestant – that was something you could lay your finger on – but what these people next door were was something beyond her ken, something dark and mysterious, something not far removed from the devil; for whoever heard anyone connected with God daring to say they could cure people! Even the priests wouldn't dare. And then another strong point proving their ungodliness was all their fine things. God didn't shower gifts on those He loved – He pointed out the road of poverty to them. Father O'Malley could be hard, but he was right in some things; if you got your reward here, then you could make sure it wasn't from God.

From last Saturday, when they moved in, she had made up her mind to have no truck with them. At odd times she had stopped working and found herself listening to the girl singing. The first time she had heard her she was shocked; she felt it was indecent somehow, almost as bad as if she had seen her walking naked, for it wasn't like a woman singing to a bairn, nor yet over her poss-tub, but was high and clear and without restraint. And the morning she heard the singing before breakfast she was bewildered; for even if you had something to sing about

374

you wouldn't do it before breakfast, unless you were prepared to cry your eyes out before supper . . . No, she wanted no truck with them. Yet here was John saving the lad and braying their Mick, and Dominic in next door pouring sympathy over the lass in his best manner. And he had a best manner, Mary Ellen knew; but she also knew it was an impossibility for him to keep it up. Well — she again fastened the errant button of her blouse and momentarily lifted the weight of her body — that was as far as things were going, if she could help it . . . not one of them would darken this door!

She crossed herself swiftly and murmured, 'May the Lord bless us and preserve us from all evil, and bring us to life everlasting. Amen.'

CHAPTER FOUR

THE CONFLICT

Mary Ellen's temper was fraying thin. The weather was bad enough with the rain pelting down and the wind howling as if it was December, but to have them all in the house except Mick and Molly, who were at school, was too much. Neither John nor Dominic had been set on this morning; a mail boat had come in with a cargo of fruit, but the gaffer had given the work to the men who had not been set on the recent boats. It was bad enough that they were off work, but to have them all stuck round her like this was too much of a good thing. And what was more, she was feeling a little sick with the heat of the oven and the smell of the dirty working clothes put to dry all round the kitchen . . . If only this other business were over. She was tired of it all — her body was so bairn-weary. She was feeling now that things were getting beyond her.

Even Katie could draw no kind word from her, and she pushed her to one side to get to the oven, saying, 'Get out of me way, bairn.'

Katie was home from school because her boots leaked; and her eyes were streaming, not only as the result of a cold but with crying. She hated to be off school, more so now than ever, for Miss Llewellyn had said that if she worked hard she could sit for an examination, which might be the first step on the road to her becoming a teacher. She had tried to tell her mother, but Mary Ellen snapped at her, and even John did not seem interested.

She looked towards him now. He was sitting in the corner on the far side of the fireplace mending her boots. He had put odd pieces of leather on the soles and was now cutting up an old boot to get enough leather to sew across the slits. She returned to her book, the only one she possessed, a Grimm's Fairy Tale, and she knew each word by heart.

The front-door knocker was suddenly banged, and without waiting she went to answer it. It had been knocked twice already this afternoon, once by a tally man and once by a man begging. The beggar wasn't pleased when she brought him a slice of bread. He bent it up and put it in his pocket, and her mouth watered, for it was new bread from a flat cake just out of the oven; it was a long time till tea-time, and she had got out of the habit of asking for bread between meals for she remembered times when they all had bread at tea-time except her mother, and she was frightened that this would happen again.

It was Mrs Bradley at the door, and she asked, 'Is yer ma in?'

Katie said, 'Yes.'

'Then tell her we're gathering for poor Mrs Patton's wreath . . . Here, take her the paper.'

Katie took the paper and went into the scullery to her mother. 'It's Mrs Bradley — she's gathering for flowers, ma.'

Mary Ellen's lips set in a tight line as she read down one side of the list and half-way down the other . . . shillings, sixpences . . . only two or three threepences. She gave a sigh, and lifting up her skirt took fourpence from the little bag and handed it to Katie, together with the list.

As Katie passed John he asked, 'What's that for?'

But before she could reply, Mary Ellen called, 'Go on, you, Katie,' and Katie went on to the front door. Mary Ellen knew that John didn't hold with gathering for wreaths, but what could she do . . . and that Bella Bradley collecting!

John knew what he would have done . . . the gathering for wreaths had always irked him. They would collect as much as two pounds and spend the whole lot on flowers, when the widow, if it was a man who had died, was more often than not destitute, and within a week the bairns would be crying for bread. They knew this only too well, the women who took it on themselves to gather, yet they still bought flowers to show respect for the dead. He

378

snorted and banged the hammer on the last, sending a pain through his knee. It made him mad! He knew that, even if there was no insurance money, besides collecting for the flowers they would collect for cabs, to make the dead look decent. They didn't collect for the hearse. No, that could be ticked, to be paid off at so much a week. But the undertakers weren't so ready to tick cabs. And if it was for one of the Irish, the relatives would pawn, beg, borrow or steal, but they would have a bit of a wake. It was all crazy! And yet he understood from his mother that the funerals were nothing like they used to be, for in her young days, she told him, she longed for the Irish to die so she could go to the wake with her mother and have a good feed.

What had she put on the list, he wondered. Whatever it was, by this time next week they would be glad of it; for if they were not set on there wouldn't be a penny in the house.

Many things were beginning to make him wild. And on a day like this, tied to the house, he had nothing else to do but think. Lately he had been feeling the desire for someone to talk to, someone who could answer questions. Once or twice he tried to talk to Father Bailey, and endeavoured to have the material in his mind formed into concrete questions; but when he was with the priest he found it was no use – he knew what he wanted to say but couldn't get it out.

His mother was always saying thinking got you nowhere; you must have faith and rely on that. Faith! He looked at her now, pounding a great piece of dough, the second batch of bread she had baked today. What had faith done for her? She could hardly get her arms into the bowl for the roundness of her stomach. He took his eyes from her. Where would they put the bairn when it came? He'd have to try and rig up something out of boxes — the clothes basket that had served them all as a cradle was done long since. He pulled his legs up hastily as Dominic made to pass him on his way to the bedroom.

Mary Ellen called after Dominic, 'Don't lie on that bed with those boots on, mind!' but the only answer she received was the banging of the door.

John settled himself back against the wall: he always felt easier when Dominic was out of the room. He had finished one boot and was preparing the thread by rubbing it with tallow for patching the other when he heard his mother give a startled mutter. She was looking out through the kitchen window, and she exclaimed, 'I don't want them in here!'

As she rubbed the dough off her hands, there came a knock on the kitchen door. Katie was about to open it, but Mary Ellen said, 'Hold on. I'll see to it.' When she opened the door, there stood the old man and the girl.

'Good afternoon, Mrs O'Brien.' It was the old

man who spoke, and his voice was as kindly as his smile; but Mary Ellen would not allow it to make any impression on her. She didn't reply, but stared at them fixedly, the door held firmly in her hand, while he went on, 'I thought we would just come round and get acquainted. And also ask you to thank your son for helping my boy last night.'

Mary Ellen's eyes darted to the girl. She was wearing a waterproof coat with a hood attached, and from under it she smiled at Mary Ellen, like a child who was asking to be liked. They were barmy, Mary Ellen thought. Their Mick had nearly done for the lad, and here they were, coming to thank John! They weren't all there, either of them – they couldn't be. She wanted no truck with them. She was aware that the old man was becoming drenched, but that was his look-out; they weren't crossing the doorstep.

She was saying abruptly, 'That's all right. It was our Mick's fault, anyway,' when she felt her hand taken from the door, and John stood there, saying, 'Won't you come in?' It wasn't often she got angry with John, but now it took her all her time not to turn on him.

The old man said, 'Thank you. Thank you. Are you by any chance the Mr O'Brien I owe so much to?'

Pushing two chairs forward John said, 'Take a seat.' He did not look at the girl, but went on, 'It's us should be doing the thanking. Not many people would be taking it like this.' Then he turned to Shane: 'This is my father.'

Shane reluctantly took the proffered hand and muttered something, and his head, which had been still, began to jerk.

The old man, seeming not to notice the lack of cordiality, said, 'My name's Peter Bracken. And this is my granddaughter, Christine.'

Shane nodded, and after a short silence that was broken only by the scraping of chairs, he turned to Mary Ellen, now vigorously pounding the dough, and said, 'I'm off to see if there's anything in.' He pulled his steaming coat off the rod that ran under the mantelshelf, and with a final nod towards Mr Bracken, he went out.

Mary Ellen watched his huge figure slumping down the yard. Off to see if there's anything in at this time of the day! It was just to get out of the way; he hated to talk to strangers at any time. There was a faint wreath of steam still hovering about the shoulders of his coat as he disappeared into the back lane. It brought a tightness to her breast, and she murmured to herself, 'Shane, Shane,' as she was wont to do years ago when her pity was mixed with love. And the feeling made her more resentful towards the pair sitting behind her. Now he'd be wet to the skin, and his twitching would go on all night.

She knew she was being very bad mannered

standing with her back to them, but she couldn't help it; yet she found herself listening to the girl talking to Katie. They were talking about the book, Katie's voice sounding broad in comparison with the girl's, which was quiet and even and without dialect. And then she found herself listening to John. He was talking more than she had heard him do so before. He was talking to the old fellow about the docks and the kind of boats that came in and what they brought . . . iron ore from Bilbao, black fine ore from Benisaf, the heavy ore from Sweden that made the steel, esparto grass for paper, prop boats from Russia, with the cargo stacked from one end of the boat to the other to make the tonnage. As if the old fellow would want to know all that! She had never heard him talk so much about the docks before. He went on to speak of the unloading as if he had been down the holds all his life, instead of just two years. What had come over him? Perhaps he was doing it because she was offhand with them. Well, he knew she wanted no truck with them; and they were a thick-skinned pair to sit there knowing, as they must know, that they weren't wanted.

'I suppose you are always kept busy, Mrs O'Brien?'

She started, and was forced to half turn her body and look at the old man, and to answer him civilly: 'Yes, most of the time I'm at it.'

'You must find it very hard looking after such a big family. And I mean big,' he laughed.

'Well, you've got to take what God sends.' Immediately she felt she had said the wrong thing, giving him an opening to start his ranting, but to her surprise he didn't take it.

He stood up, saying, 'Well, we mustn't delay you — I just felt I would like to make your acquaintance, Mrs O'Brien.'

Mary Ellen turned from the dish, again forced to respond, this time with a smile. It was funny, but they seemed all right. Was this spook business just an idle rumour? People were in the habit of making a lot out of nowt.

She returned the girl's smile too, but when she saw John, silent now, looking at the lass, the smile froze on her face. She didn't want any of that kind of truck, not for John she didn't . . . Dominic could do what he liked.

There was another knock on the front door, and this time she had to tell Katie, who was hanging on to the girl's hand, to go and open it.

Christine spoke directly to Mary Ellen for the first time. 'Will you let Katie come in to tea, Mrs O'Brien? It's rather a special occasion, it's Grandfather's birthday.'

She cast a smile, full of light, on the old man, and he said, 'Sh!'

She answered, 'No, I won't. Do you know how old he is?' She was speaking to John now, looking up into his face.

John's eyes twinkled, and he answered seriously, 'Twenty-six.'

They all laughed, except Mary Ellen.

'You're just sixty years out!' said the girl.

'You're not eighty-six!' Amazement brought the words out of Mary Ellen.

'Yes, that's what I am, Mrs O'Brien.'

Mary Ellen stared at the straight, lean body of Peter Bracken, at his unlined face and deep-set eyes, shining like black coals. The only sign of real age was the white hair, and he was eighty-six. Fear of him overcame her again. You didn't reach eighty-six and be like that, not naturally you didn't. Shane was fifty-seven, and he was old. She had known men live to eighty, but they ended their days in bed, or on sticks. No, her instinct had been right at first . . . there was something funny about them, something beyond her understanding; and she wanted no truck with them.

She was brought from her fear by the sound of footsteps accompanying Katie's through the front room. Who on earth could Katie have let in now!

The small, black-clad figure standing in the open doorway soon informed her. She gasped at the sight of Father O'Malley. His presence always meant a rating for something or other. Today it would be Katie off school and Mick being kept from Mass last Sunday. Oh, she'd had enough for one day! And there were these two still standing there, not smiling now but staring at the priest as if they were struck.

'Good afternoon, Father. Will you take a seat? It's dreadful weather; you must be wet.' Mary Ellen was doing her duty. At the same time, she noticed the half-inch thick soles on the priest's stout boots, and chided herself for thinking: It'll take some water to get through them.

John spoke next: 'Good afternoon, Father.'

'Good afternoon,' said Father O'Malley, in his thin, tight voice; but he looked neither at Mary Ellen nor at John, for his eyes were fixed on those of Peter Bracken.

Noting this, John said, 'Mr Bracken's a new neighbour of ours, Father.'

The priest did not answer, and Peter Bracken said, quietly, 'Father O'Malley and I already know one another.'

'What is this man doing in your house?'

Mary Ellen knew the priest was addressing her, although he did not look at her. She shivered and said hesitantly, 'Well Father . . .'

'Order him to leave at once! And forbid him the door in future.'

Mary Ellen twisted the corner of her apron and turned towards Mr Bracken and the girl. But before she could get the words out, John broke in sharply, 'Hold your hand a minute! Me da's not in, and next to him I'm head of this house, such as it is, and I'm telling no-one to get out, Father.'

The priest swung round on him, his eyes almost

lost behind their narrowed lids and the double lenses of his glasses: 'So you are head of the house, are you? And you will take the responsibility on your soul for associating with this man?'

'I know nothing against the man.' John's face was as set as the priest's.

'You don't?' Father O'Malley raised his eyebrows. 'Then you're about the only one in these parts who doesn't. I will enlighten you. This man is an enemy of the Catholic Church . . . '

'That is not true! I'm an enemy of no church . . . '

Father O'Malley cut short Peter Bracken's protest, and went on: 'Why, I ask you, is a man of his standing living in a quarter like this? Because he makes it his business to live among Catholics so he can turn them against the Church.'

'I live wherever there is fear and poverty, and try to erase it.' The old man's face was no longer placid; it was alight with a force and energy that gave the impression he was towering above them all.

'Do you know what this man has dared to say? Only that he has a power equal to that of Christ!' Father O'Malley's eyes bored into Mary Ellen's and then into John's. 'In fact, he says he is a Christ!'

John, his eyes wide and questioning now, looked to Mr Bracken for denial. But none came.

'You know you are twisting my words!' cried the old man. 'What I maintain is we all have the power to be Christs. If we are made in God's image and likeness, then it stands to reason we are part of Him; our spirit is pure God material. The only difference between my spirit and God's is the size of it – the quality is exactly the same. That is what I preach. And the more I become aware of my spirit, the more I get in touch with it, the more God-like things I can do ... And I have done God-like things—' Mr Bracken pointed at the priest: 'You know I have! And it is this very proof that upsets your slavish doctrine.'

'Silence!' Father O'Malley's voice was like deep and terrible thunder.

Mary Ellen clutched at the neck of her blouse, and Katie hid her face in the folds of her mother's skirt; the bedroom door opened and Dominic came into the kitchen, but no-one took any notice of him.

The priest's voice dropped low in his throat. He addressed himself to John. 'Are you asking for any more proof than that?'

Before John could answer, the girl spoke, 'My grandfather will give him proof – he will show him his own power, and free him from you and your like. It is not God's will, as you preach, that he or anyone else should live in poverty and ignorance all his days. If they were made aware of their own power they would throw all this off.' She flung her arms wide and took a step towards the priest. 'You would stop them from thinking – for once they think, they question. And they mustn't question,

388

must they? They must accept! It wouldn't do for them to realise there's no purgatory or heaven or hell but what they make themselves!'

Before John's eyes there rose the picture of Miss Llewellyn leaning back against the wind, saying, 'Take the heaven you are sure of.' Then his mind was brought back to this slip of a girl facing up to a man like Father O'Malley; not only facing up to him, but attacking him. What she was saying was quite mad, but she had courage.

The thought saddened him; it might be the courage of fanaticism, and she looked too sweet and girlish to be imbued with fanaticism.

The old man drew her back to his side, saying, 'Be serene, Christine. Remember, anger poisons.'

Father O'Malley's voice cast a deadly chill over the room as he said, 'The day is not far hence when you will rot in hell for your blasphemy!'

'The day is not far hence,' took up Peter Bracken, 'when your sect, if it does not throw off its dogmatism and learn toleration, will be fighting for its life; for there are seeds in the wombs of women, at this moment, that in thirty, forty or fifty years' time will shake the foundations of your preaching. The minds of people are moving. They are searching for the truth — they are reading. And what are they reading first? — the very books that are forbidden by your Church, for the first question the groping mind asks is: Why have these books been forbidden?'

Father O'Malley looked as if he was about to choke – black anger swamped his face. After a silence, tensed to breaking point, he addressed Mary Ellen, 'I leave you and your conscience to judge. And remember, I am warning you . . . disaster and damnation follow this man. If you wish to save your immortal soul and those of your family, throw him out as you would a snake!' His eyes burned into Mary Ellen's for a second, and then he was gone. And the banging of the front door shook the house.

It occurred to John that Father O'Malley had ignored him because he stood up to him; it was noticeable that the priest concentrated on his mother because she was afraid. He looked towards her. She was leaning on the table with one hand; the other was held under her breast tight against her heart. And she was shivering.

Dominic spoke for the first time: 'Don't take any notice of him; he thinks he's still in Ireland.' His words weren't spoken to his mother, but to the girl. But she did not return his glance, or answer him, for she was staring at Mary Ellen.

Into this tense atmosphere came Mick. He entered the kitchen, his head on one side and his hand over his ear. 'Ma, me ear's runnin' and it's ach . . . ' He stopped short at the sight of Mr Bracken and glanced quickly from him to John.

No-one moved for a second until Peter Bracken exclaimed in an exalted voice, 'Mrs O'Brien, I will show you! Your boy has earache, probably an abscess. I will cure it. Through the great healing power of God I will cure it.'

He made a step towards Mick, and in a moment the kitchen became quickened into life. Mary Ellen flung herself between them, intending to grab Mick to her, but Mick, thinking of last night and taking Peter's cure to mean much the same thing as when his mother boxed his ears, saying, 'I'll cure you!' sprang away from them both. Mary Ellen made a wild grab at the air, overbalanced and twisted herself to clutch at John's hands that were outstretched to her but missed them and fell on her side on to the mat.

Mary Ellen knew, almost as she fell, what had happened. The blinding pain, like a red-hot steel wire, starting in her womb and forcing itself up through her body and out of her head, blotted out even itself in its transit. When next she felt it she was lying on the bed – the pain was filling all her pores and forcing out sweat. She opened her eyes and looked up into John's face. She wanted to say to him, 'Don't worry, lad. Don't worry,' for his face was like death, but she could utter no word.

The hot wire was boring again, identifying itself from the other pains by an intensity that no previous labour had brought to her. It left no room even for fear when she realised that that Bracken man was near her; nor did she feel any element of surprise when she heard him saying, 'I'll go in and work at her head through the wall. Take her hand and don't let go.'

Mary Ellen felt her hand being taken between two soft palms, and she did as she was bidden when his voice came directly to her, as if through a thick fog, saying, 'Hold on to Christine, Mrs O'Brien, and the pain will go.'

As the pain forced her knees up and her head down into her chest, Mary Ellen gripped the girl's hand. And when she next regained consciousness she knew she was not on the bed but above it, lying on a sort of soft platform, and the girl was still by her side, while Hannah Kelly and Nurse Snell were working on somebody lying on the bed. And then the doctor came, not the shilling doctor, but Doctor Davidson from Jarrow, and she wondered vaguely who would pay him. He reached up and took her hand and tried to unloosen it from the girl's, but as he did so Mary Ellen felt herself dropping down into that contorted mass below her, and she clung on like grim death to the soft hand. She heard him say, 'You're Peter Bracken's granddaughter, aren't you?' There followed a silence. Then his voice came again, 'Well, there are stranger things in heaven and earth than this world dreams of; and I won't despise your help, because I'm going to need it.'

She lay for years on the platform with queer

sensations passing through her body, and the next voice she heard was that of Shane, muttering, 'Mary Ellen, lass, Mary Ellen.'

She knew he was crying, and she wondered at it. She thought of the time when he loved her and she loved him – it was all so long ago. What had happened since? Nothing. He still loved her, but she loved Katie and John. But they didn't love Shane – he had no-one but her. What would happen to him when she died she didn't know – and it didn't seem to matter.

It was odd, but rather nice, lying here thinking untroubled thoughts. She hadn't to get up and see about the baking or washing or meals, or, what was more important, money. She had an ache some-where, but she couldn't lay her finger on it. And she was conscious of smiling when the doctor reached up and, lifting her eyelid, exclaimed, 'Odd, very odd.'

The next voice that came to her was Father Bailey's. It was nice to have Father Bailey near; he brought a feeling of comfort. And as he made the sign of the cross and touched her lips, she felt a great happiness. She saw him standing at the foot of the platform and smiling, not at her, but at Mr Bracken, who, she felt, was standing just behind her head. Father Bailey was saying, 'God's ways are many and mysterious. He has made these ways and only He can judge them.' She heaved a great sigh and fell into a kind of sleep, thinking,

393

'Yes, we are all one.' It was the answer Christine Bracken had given to Father Bailey.

The gas in the kitchen was turned low. It flickered up and down and spurted out of a little hole in the bottom of the mantle. In the dim light John knelt before the fire, taking out the ashes. He raked them slowly and quietly, and was glad of their warmth on his hands, for in spite of a good fire, he felt cold. It was the chill before the dawn, he thought. Was it only twelve hours since all this started? It seemed many lifetimes to him. And what it must be like for Christine, sitting in that one position by the bed, he could not imagine. He thought of her now as Christine – the night had joined them in a relationship that seemed to him to be stronger than any blood tie; he had wrapped a blanket about her and taken off her shoes, and put on her slippers. He had been next door for them, and had to find them himself, for the old man was sitting facing the wall and appeared to be asleep. He had taken her cup after cup of tea, and when, stiff with cramp, she could not hold the cup, he held it for her. Once she leant against him and he supported her with his arm. And an hour ago, he had tried to withdraw her hand gently from his mother's, but the result was the same as when others had attempted to do this – Mary Ellen's fingers became like a vice around those of Christine. His mother had been on the point of

394

death, he knew, her life reduced to a mere flicker, yet whenever her hand was touched it held all the strength of vital life in its grip on Christine's. The doctor had said it was touch and go: 'I've done all I can,' he said. 'I'll be back first thing in the morning.' And looking hard at John, he asked, 'Do you believe in spiritual healing?'

John answered simply, 'I'm a Catholic.'

'So am I,' said the doctor. 'And I'm dead against it professionally and otherwise . . . yet . . . ' He had stopped abruptly, buttoned his coat, and said, 'Good night. We'll know more in the morning.'

Father Bailey had left the house without saying anything, his face set and thoughtful.

Shane's reactions when he saw the girl sitting there were surprising to John. He had come back into the kitchen and stood looking down into the fire, his body strangely still. 'I don't care who keeps her alive – it can be the divil himself,' he said, 'as long as she doesn't leave me.'

He had turned and looked quietly at his son, and John realised that beyond the drinking and the fighting there still remained in his father a deep feeling for his mother. It surprised him and at the same time brought him closer to this man, whom at times he almost despised. A little while ago he had managed to persuade him to lie down – Dominic was already in bed, having retired there shortly after twelve. He had stood with the others round his mother when they thought she was breathing her last, but when she continued to breathe he said there was no point in the lot of them staying up, and anyway he'd have to be out early to see if he could get a start.

John knew that he, too, would have to be at the docks by six o'clock. There was a prop boat due in, and he might get set on – not that he liked prop boats, for there was no piece work – you received four shillings a day, and no overtime; but that would certainly be better than nothing, for with his mother bad, money would be needed now more than ever before.

Although he'd had no rest he did not feel tired; the training of working forty-eight hours at a stretch as a young lad when on tipping had hardened him. He thought nothing of working all day and all night to discharge an ore boat, and the men liked him in the gang. He could set the pace, and the pace meant everything when the quicker the discharge was done the sooner the men were paid. He looked at the clock . . . half-past four. There were many things that should be done before he left the house; so he proceeded to tidy the kitchen, shaking the mats and sweeping the floor – his mother would want them to be dependent on neighbours as little as possible, kind as they might be.

He was setting the table for breakfast when Hannah Kelly came from the front room.

'I'll go over home a minute, lad,' she whispered, 'and get our Joe up. Then I'll be back.'

He thanked her, and asked, 'Do you think there's any change?'

'I don't know . . . perhaps there's a little – she seems to be breathing easier. Funny about that lass, isn't it?' She looked questioningly at John. 'Mary Ellen hanging on to her like that after saying she wanted no truck with them.'

John made no reply.

And after a moment she whispered again, 'She's had me scared stiff, sitting so still. 'Tisn't natural. What d'ye make of it? And what are ye going to do if it goes on any longer?'

'I don't know,' he said.

Hannah shook her head: 'It's rum. Makes ye put yer thinking cap on, don't it?'

He nodded slowly, and she said, 'Aye well, there's queer things happen in the world. We'll know this time the morrer, likely.'

After Hannah had gone, he stood staring before him. What would happen to them all if his mother should die? She was the axis around which they revolved. Molly would soon be leaving school, but she would be less than useless to run this turbulent house. He looked down on her, lying in the corner of the couch. Her mouth was open, and even in sleep she looked what she was, feckless. Now if Katie were older . . . What! The thought shocked him. Katie work and slave after the lot of them! No. Let her have a better start than that, even though it be only in service. But his mother wouldn't die. Somehow they wouldn't let her die.

He classed Mr Bracken and Christine as 'they' when he thought of them in their strange and eerie capacity of healers; but as Mr Bracken and Christine, he thought of them as kindly folk, and in Christine's case, as bonnie and taking.

When he went quietly from the kitchen into the front room to replenish the fire, he saw them as he had seen them last – his mother, lying straight and still and curiously flat, with one arm outstretched to that of Christine, who was sitting close to the head of the bed; only this time there was a difference – inches separated Mary Ellen's hand from Christine's.

Christine smiled faintly. The smile seemed forced on to the chiselled whiteness of her face, her eyes looked vacant, like the hollowed sockets in a sculptured head.

John bent over her, whispering anxiously, 'Are you all right?'

She tried to broaden her smile, but the effort seemed too much, and she fell against him. He glanced at his mother. She was breathing evenly now, and a faint tinge of colour had crept into the greyness of her face.

Christine whispered, 'She's asleep . . . it's over.'

She sighed, and her body pressed with gentle heaviness against him.

'Come into the kitchen,' he said.

'I can't yet. I've . . . I've got cramp. I'm stiff. In a little while.'

She sounded sleepy, and for a moment he thought she had fallen asleep.

Hannah Kelly came into the room again, and exclaimed softly, 'She's let go then.' She peered at Mary Ellen. 'She's better. Ye'd better get away to bed, lass,' she said kindly to Christine.

Christine, in an effort to rise, almost lost her balance, and John put his arm about her and supported her to the kitchen, followed by Hannah's quizzical glance and raised eyebrows. 'Aye, well,' she soliloquised, 'ye never can tell where blisters light. But my God, won't Mary Ellen go mad!'

John sat Christine on a chair by the fire, and stood helplessly watching her as she slowly started to cry. It was a gentle crying; the tears welled up from their source, spilling over the dark, thick fringe of lashes on to her cheeks, then down on to her clasped hands.

'You're all in,' John said. 'Come on, I'll take you in home.'

Like a child, she placed her hand in his, and he drew her to her feet.

'The cramp . . . it's still there' – she tottered as she stood – 'my legs don't seem to belong to me.'

In the flickering light of the gas, she looked up at him and smiled through the tears. 'It's been a strange night, John.'

He nodded silently. He wanted to thank her for what, in the back of his mind, he felt that she and her father had done, but to say 'Thank you for saving my mother's life' would be to accept the strange and terrible power that was assuredly theirs, and some part of him was afraid. It seemed ridiculous that this slip of a lass could be anything but what she looked . . . a fetching, boyish-looking girl.

Christine sighed and said, 'Everything would have been perfect if the baby had lived. Will your mother be very upset?'

He couldn't answer for his mother . . . nor for himself, for he felt she would be shocked at his thankfulness that it was dead.

She swayed, and again he put his arm about her and led her to the door. Her legs gave way beneath her, and she clung to him saying, 'It's only temporary. In the morning I'll be all right, but now all my strength has gone.'

Stooping swiftly and saying, 'This is the best way then,' he lifted her up into his arms. She offered no resistance, but sank against him, her head on his shoulder. One of his hands was under her breast, and he saw the curve of it as her blouse and petticoat pouched, small, not much bigger than Katie's, and the sight of it brought no more excitement to his blood than the tiny mound of Katie's would have done. Some part of his mind wondered at this. His other hand was below her knees, and his face, as it bent above hers, was close enough for kissing. He could have dropped his mouth on to the lips and told himself it was in gratitude. And she too perhaps would have accepted his excuse. And it would have been a start. It would also have fixed Dominic. But he did nothing, not even press her close. Perhaps it was because he was worried about his mother, but he might have been carrying Katie, for his feelings were not aroused above tenderness. Vaguely, he was irritated by this. The night had brought them together in one way, a way that was deep and would be lasting, he knew, but it wasn't the way of a fellow getting off with a lass; it was a way that had missed his body and touched something beyond.

As he carried her into her own kitchen, she stirred and opened her eyes, and her hand came up and touched his cheek. And she whispered, 'You're so nice, John . . . so good.' And he knew that he would have started something had he kissed her, because she liked him in a way perhaps that hadn't gone past her body.

CHAPTER FIVE

THE COMIC

Katie moved the parcel on to her other hip. It was heavy; but not as heavy as the weight inside her; the weight was leaden. To go to the pawnshop with any parcel filled her with shame; to walk up the dock bank, under the knowledgeable stares of the men idling there against the railings caused her throat to move in and out; and to meet any of her schoolmates on the journey made her want to die; but when it was John's suit she was carrying every tragedy of the journey was intensified a thousandfold.

When her mother asked, 'Will you go down to "Bob's", hinny?' Katie had stared at her, speechless. She wanted to say, 'Our Molly should go, she's bigger,' but she knew from experience that Molly always got less on the clothes than she did, and generally too, she lost something, the ticket, or worse still, a sixpence. And because her mother looked so thin and white when she asked her she remained silent, and watched Mary Ellen go to the box under the bed and take John's suit out.

It seemed such a shame that it was John's, because he had started work only that morning. They all had, after being off weeks. But there was nothing in the house now to make them a meal, and although they would get subs, her mother was relying on these to pay the three weeks' back rent. Katie felt that once the rent was paid, her mother would look less white.

Going through the arches into Tyne Dock she met Mrs Flaherty.

'Oh, ye're not at school the day?' Peggy greeted her.

'No, I was sick.' Katie stared up into the half-washed face, criss-crossed with wrinkles, and her tone defied disbelief.

'Oh, that's a pity, it is. Ye shouldn't miss your iducation. Some day, when ye're old enough, I'll lend ye one o' me books; they'll iducate ye like nothing else will. When ye're old enough that is.' She snuffled and caught the drop from the end of her nose on the back of her hand.

'Thank you.' For as long as she could remember Katie had been promised one of Mrs Flaherty's books, and the promise meant nothing to her now. She said, 'Ta-ta, Mrs Flaherty,' and walked on, the parcel now pressed against her chest and resting on the top of her stomach.

Although she thought impatiently that Mrs Flaherty was always on about education, she wished her mother was a bit like her. She had almost given

403

up talking to her mother about the examination and what Miss Llewellyn said, for her mother didn't believe Miss Llewellyn meant what she said — last time, she had stopped her talking, saying, 'Oh, hinny, you mustn't take so much notice of things; your teacher's only being nice. The examination she's on about is likely the one you have every year.' And when Katie had sat quietly crying, Mary Ellen said to John, 'Look, lad. I can't go down to the school and see what she keeps on about, I only have me shawl; will you go?'

'What! Me? Not on your life. Now that's a damn silly thing to ask me to do, isn't it! What could I say to the headmistress?'

'Well, will you go and see her teacher, then?'

John had just stared blankly at his mother, then picked up his cap and walked out of the house.

Katie thought the only one who understood was Christine. She liked Christine nearly as much as she liked Miss Llewellyn, but not quite. Life had taken on an added glow since Christine came into it; for Christine made her pinnies and dresses out of her own old ones. She gave her and Molly nice things to eat, too; and she had even given them money, real money, half a crown each. But only twice, for when they took their half-crowns into their mother the second week she made them take them back.

Katie could not understand her mother's attitude of not speaking to Christine and her grandfather.

She allowed her and Molly to go next door, but Mr Bracken and Christine had never been into her house since that terrible day some months ago when their mother was taken bad. John and Dominic, too, went next door; and she often sat on John's knee while he and Mr Bracken talked. They talked about funny things, one of which stuck in her mind: Mr Bracken said you could have anything you wanted if you only used your thoughts properly . . . There were so many things she wanted, but she wanted above all to be a teacher. Should she do what Mr Bracken told John, lie on her back with her arms outstretched and think of being a teacher until she felt herself floating away? Eeh no! she'd better not, for there were some people who said Mr Bracken was the devil. He wasn't; but anyway, she'd better not do it.

She always had a queer feeling when Dominic was next door when she would wonder if he were trying to do what he was doing that night she went in unexpectedly. He had Christine pressed in the corner and was trying to kiss her. Her blouse was open, and the ribbon of her camisole was loose. Katie knew that Christine was frightened, for she held on to her until Dominic went out. Then she told her not to mention to John what had happened; and Katie only too readily promised.

At last she reached the dark well of the pawn-shop, and listened, her eyes wide and sad, as Bob said, 'Only three-and-six, hinny. It's getting a bit threadbare.' He turned to a woman and asked, 'Will you put it in for her?' And the woman nodded, taking the penny Katie offered her. Katie wished she were fourteen, then if she had to come to the pawn she wouldn't have to pay somebody for putting the stuff in — a whole penny just for signing your name! It was outrageous, and she disliked the woman intensely for being so mean as to take the penny.

As she was leaving the shop with the money tightly grasped in her hand, Bob said, 'I've got something here that might interest one of your brothers. It'll fit nobody else round these parts. It's a top coat, and it's a bobby-dazzler. Ten shillings, it is. And I only wish I had what it cost when it was new. Tell one of them to have a look in.' Katie said she would.

She went on to the butcher's, and from there to buy a gas mantle. In Mr Powell's, she stood waiting while he hunted for the box which contained the turned down mantles. His search took him into the back shop, and Katie was left alone standing before an assortment of comics. They were arrayed on a sloping counter: *Rainbow*, *Tiger Tim's Weekly*, *Comic Cuts*, and others. Her eyes dwelt on them longingly. It was weeks and weeks since she was able to buy a comic. She would likely get a penny off John on Saturday. But Saturday was as far away as Christmas, and there stretched before her the rest of the afternoon and the long, long evening. And she

406

daren't ask her mother for even a ha'penny out of the suit money. On the front of *Rainbow*, the Bruin boys were up to their games again: the tiger, the parrot, the elephant, and others, were playing one of their naughty pranks on Mrs Bruin. And inside the comic, Katie knew, would be the story of the little girl who was really a fairy and worked magic. Her eyes darted to the back shop. All she could see was Mr Powell's feet on the top of a pair of steps. Her hand went up and touched the *Rainbow*. It hesitated for a second, then with one swift movement, the *Rainbow* was inside her coat, and for the first time in her life she found herself wetting her knickers. The combined horror was too much for her. She ran out of the shop, down the dock bank to the arches. She did not stop to look inside her coat; her sin had already obliterated the joy of the comic. She was a thief! She had stolen! Mr Powell would miss the comic and put the pollis on her track; her mother would be taken to court and her face would become white again, and all at school would know . . . Miss Llewellyn would know!

Standing over the gutter, under the high, bleak arches, she vomited, and the comic slipped down from beneath her coat and became fouled with the sick.

There was a long row of boys and girls waiting to go into confession, for tomorrow was the first Friday in the month, on which day they all attended communion. They nudged each other and fidgeted whilst bending over in grotesque positions in supposed prayer. They whispered and passed sweets, and showed one another holy pictures; yet there was no noise at all, so practised were they. It was three weeks since Katie was last at confession, the longest period between her confessions she could remember. Although the chill autumn air was filling the church she felt hot and sick. She had been sick a number of times since the day she took John's suit to the pawn – she refused to think of it as the day she stole the comic. But now she had to think of the comic, for she was about to make her confession.

A teacher, not Miss Llewellyn, came and moved a row and a half of children down to the pews opposite Father O'Malley's box, which were singularly bare of penitents. This left Katie the next to go to Father Bailey. She was filled with a mixture of relief and fear, relief that she had escaped Father O'Malley's judgment, and fear that her turn was upon her.

A small, dark shadow emerged from one door of the confessional box, and Katie stumbled in. But for the faint gleam of a candle coming through the mesh from the priest's side the box was black dark inside.

'Please, Father, give me the blessing for I have sinned,' she began. 'It is three weeks since my last confession.'

'Go on, my child.' Father Bailey's voice was like a soft balm falling on her.

'I have missed Mass once.'

'Through your own fault?'

'No, Father. It was me clothes; me ma wouldn't let me come.'

'Go on, my child.'

'I have spoken in church and I have missed me morning and night prayers.'

'How often?'

'Three times . . . no, four . . . perhaps a few more, Father.'

'Why?'

' 'Cos the lino's all cracked and it sticks in me knees when I kneel down.'

The priest made a noise in his throat and said, 'To strengthen your soul it is important that you say your prayers – prayers are the food of the soul like bread is the food of the body . . . You understand, my child?'

'Yes, Father.'

'Then under no circumstances should you starve your soul.'

'No, Father.'

'Go on.'

But Katie couldn't go on. Her clasped hands, pressed against the elbow rest on a level with her face, were stuck together with sweat. The confessional box seemed weighed down with the smell of incense and mustiness.

'Is there anything more?' the priest asked.

'Yes, Father.'

'Well then, what is it?'

Silence followed his question. And after a moment he went on: 'Don't be afraid, my child; there is nothing so terrible that God won't forgive.'

'I stole.'

The priest's hand was taken away from his cheek and his face turned towards the mesh, and Katie looked up into two white bulbs. Then the hand was replaced again.

Katie shivered during the silence that followed; she felt her sin had been a shock even to the priest.

'What did you steal?'

'A *Rainbow*.'

'A what!' The hand was dropped again.

'A comic.'

The priest coughed. 'Now, my child, you know how it hurts our Blessed Lord when you do anything like that.'

'Yes, Father.'

'And will you do it again?'

'No, no. Never, Father.'

'No, I know you won't. And if you could find a way to pay the shopkeeper for the comic it would put everything right, wouldn't it?'

'Yes, Father.'

'Now, for your penance say one Our Father and ten Hail Marys, and tell Our Lord that never again will you hurt Him; and He will forgive you. And don't forget to kneel when you are saying your prayers, in spite of the lino; for remember the nails in the cross.'

The priest made the sign of the cross and said the absolution, whilst Katie murmured, 'Oh, my God, I am very sorry I have sinned against Thee, because Thou art so good and by the help of Thy Holy Grace I will never sin again.'

'Good night, my child, and God bless you,' said Father Bailey. 'And worry no more; He understands.'

In a holy daze, Katie walked out of the box, and in the same state she said her penance, kneeling in the corner of the dark church, straining her eyes up to the statue of the Virgin and the Child, knowing that her sin was wiped away. And on walking out of the church, there was John, standing under the lamp. It all seemed part of God's Grace. She ran to him and flung her arms about him, crying, 'Oh John! Oh John!' as if she had not seen him for years. Then she asked, 'Are you going to confession?'

'No,' John said; 'I was passing and I thought I'd wait for you.'

She knew this wasn't true; he never had to pass this way; he had come to meet her because she was crying when she left home. She seemed to have been crying for weeks. She knew that her mother and John were worried about her, for she couldn't tell them why she cried. But now she was free again — the dreadful weight was lifted from her.

John, looking down into her bright face, wondered what had wrought the change. He said teasingly, 'Has Father Bailey given you a pair of wings?'

'Eeh, our John!' She shook his arm as she walked by his side. 'But Father Bailey is nice, isn't he? He's so nice he makes me want to cry.'

'Well, in that case, I'll tell him to go for you the next time I see him, for you've done enough crying lately to last you a lifetime.'

Katie did not speak for a time. And then she said softly, 'I won't be crying any more, John.'

'You won't? Well, that's something to know. Why have you been crying so much lately, anyway?'

There was a longer silence before she replied, 'I stole.'

Her statement came as a shock, stunning him for a while.

'You what, Katie?' he asked.

'I stole, and I was frightened. It was a comic from Mr Powell's. And now I've been to confession and Father Bailey says it's all right.'

'You stole a comic from Mr Powell's?' There was incredulity in John's voice . . . Mick and Molly could thieve; Dominic and himself could lift things from the dock, although his own lifting was a fleabite compared with Dominic's — Dominic filled his trousers from the yorks up with grain, and sold it to anybody who kept hens; the only thing in that line he himself brought home was a few green bananas for the bairns, or an odd bit of fruit from burst boxes. Nevertheless, they all did it; but that Katie should lift anything seemed monstrous to him. It might only be a comic, but everything needed a beginning. 'Have you done it before?' he asked.

'No, only that once!'

'Why did you do it?' The question was ridiculous; as if he didn't know why she had done it!

'I hadn't had a comic for weeks, and I hadn't a ha'penny.'

'If you want a comic, ask me. Don't ever do that again, will you?' He stopped and looked down on her.

Katie couldn't see his face clearly, but she knew by his voice that he was vexed, more vexed than Father Bailey had been. 'Oh no, John, I'll never do it again . . . never.'

Yes, she could say that now, but there would be times, many times, when she would be without a ha'penny . . . and he too. What would happen then?

They walked on in silence, and he told himself it was only a kid's trick . . . Yes, it might be . . . any kid's, but not Katie's. It was this blasted, soul-shrivelling poverty, where a bairn was driven to steal because she hadn't a ha'penny! The thought persisted that because she had done it once she would do it again, and that by the time she left school and was ready for a place she'd be a dab hand at lifting. And then there'd be more scope. Nothing big perhaps; just a few groceries, an odd towel, or a hankie . . . Oh, he knew what would happen . . . Well, it mustn't; not to Katie, anyway. He must try and get more work, or different work, or something. He must see that never again would she be short of a ha'penny. But would that solve the problem?

He slowed his pace, and Katie, silent and apprehensive, glanced up at him. Suddenly he stopped again and said, 'What about this exam your teacher's on about? What have you got to do?'

She peered up at him. 'Miss Llewellyn says that if I pass this examination I can do pupil training after I'm fourteen; and do another examination, and perhaps then I may be able to . . . to go to . . . a college.' The last word was whispered, and John whispered back, 'A college?' He sighed, and they walked on again. It was fantastic . . . College! Yet why should it be? What did Peter Bracken say, not only say but lay down that it was a law? Anything to which you applied your thought you could bring into being. Peter had urged him again and again to put some of his methods to the test, but he had laughed at him, saying, 'No, Peter, I'm a Catholic; a poor one, I admit, but nevertheless that's my religion, and I'm trying nothing else.'

But Peter had said, 'This has nothing to do with religion, John; it's merely using your thought in a proper way.'

Well, here was a test . . . Could he think Katie to a college? It sounded as daft as if he had said he would think her into being the Queen of England. Yet hadn't Peter given him proof of his power of concentrated thought? His mother was living proof. And she was aware of it too; that was why she never spoke of it, or to Peter; to her simple mind it was something too terrible for probing.

Peter said that once you set your mind and heart on something and concentrated on it day after day, things came to your aid in what seemed a mysterious way but which was simply your positive thought reaching out into the realm of all thought and making contact with its own kind.

John did not profess, even to himself, to understand half Peter's words, let alone their meaning, but this much he could, perhaps, believe . . . if you wanted a thing badly enough you could get it. But as Peter warned, beware of what you want, for sometimes that which you felt you wanted most could, in the end, wreck you.

Well, it would certainly be to Katie's good if she became a teacher, and he couldn't see that wrecking anyone. It was a wild and almost impossible dream, yet he would will it. But first he must know what he was up to. He would go and see Miss Llewellyn.

For the third time he stopped. Was he mad? Go and see that lass! She'd scare the yorks off him. Well, he wouldn't wear yorks. No, he wouldn't. To Katie's astonishment, he hurried on again, and now she had to run to keep pace with him.

Only Mary Ellen was in when they got home, and Katie stood listening to John with an astonishment equal to that of her mother's as he said, 'Look, Ma, there's fifteen shillings' — he placed the money on the table — 'I was saving it up towards a suit. I want you to pay the seven-and-six off that top coat and get me a new shirt . . . one with a collar.' He did not look at Mary Ellen when saying this, for never before had he asked for a shirt with a collar; it had always been a striped flannelette one and a new muffler. 'Get a good one,' he added, 'about five shillings. And get me a cap too, a grey one, darkish.'

'What's up, lad?' Mary Ellen asked quietly when he had finished.

'Nothing much.' He turned and smiled at Katie, and punched her playfully on the side of the head. 'I'm going to see her teacher about that examination, as you asked me, and I want to be decent.'

CHAPTER SIX

THE VISIT

John stood sheepishly before Mary Ellen: 'Now if you tell me I look like the silver king I'll not set foot outside the door.'

Mary Ellen didn't proffer to tell him anything, she merely continued to stare at him. Who would have thought that a coat and a collar on his shirt would have made such a difference. He looked like a ... well, like one of those adverts in the *Shields Daily Gazette* ... no, better; there's never been a coat like this in Shields, she was sure. And anyway, the name inside the pocket said London. He was big enough, God knew, but the coat made him look even bigger. It was not shaped like those she was used to seeing, but hung full and was as thick as a blanket, with a check lining of fine flannel. A thrill of pride surged through her. Why, he could pass for a 'big pot'. His boots were shining as they had never done before, and the grey cap matched the dark, heather colour of the coat. She said, with a poor effort of offhandedness, 'You'll do. Mind, don't forget to take your cap off when you go in.'

'Now what do you take me for! I'm not a numbskull altogether.'

'No, lad, I know,' she said apologetically. 'Anyway, you'll likely not find her in . . . Saturday night and all. Why you couldn't go in the daylight, I don't know.'

'You know fine enough. Imagine me going down the street like this; the place would be out.'

Breaking the silence of her admiration, Katie burst out, 'They would have thought you were going to a wedding and shouted, "Chuck a ha'penny out." '

'Yes, they would that,' he laughed. 'Well, here I go. And if that Miss Llewellyn doesn't fall on me neck and say, "Oh, John, you look lovely," I'll skelp her face for her.'

He left them both laughing, Katie rather hysterically, her face buried in the couch.

Now he was outside in the dark street the jocular ease of manner he had assumed before his mother fell from him. He walked swiftly, passing people he knew but who failed to recognise him, and of whom he felt one or two turn as if puzzled and stare after him.

When he reached the dark stretch of road beyond the sawmill, he slackened his pace and, like a child, fingered the coat. He brought the lapel up to his nostril and sniffed. There was a faint aroma of tobacco mingled with another smell . . . not scent . . . he couldn't place it. He could only think it was a swell of a smell anyway. But now he must forget about the coat and think of what he would say to Miss Llewellyn. God, what an ordeal! Would he be able to speak to her alone, or would her family be there? Had she a family? He supposed so. Anyway, as his mother said, being Saturday night she might be out. Likely with that Culbert fellow. But it was early, not six o'clock yet, so there was a chance he'd catch her. If he didn't he could try again on Monday, which would give him another chance to wear the coat. He chuckled to himself: 'I'm like a bit of a bairn, and as frightened.'

Katie had told him where the house lay on the outskirts of Simonside. She said he would know it, for it had a lawn in front and two gates, and that one of the gates had a wooden arch over it. He found it all too soon; it stood by itself, lying well back from the road. There was a light in an upstairs window, and the only light downstairs came through the stained glass of the front door. He stood at the gate looking towards the house until the sound of approaching footsteps, which had the ominous tread of a policeman, gave him the impetus to walk up the short drive.

His ring was answered by a maid, a little slip of a thing, all starch and black alpaca down to her feet. Very much like Katie would be if this didn't come off, he thought.

The maid spoke first, after having peered at him. 'Mr Llewellyn's not in.'

He almost laughed. They could titivate her up, but they couldn't titivate that accent; it was the broadest of Tyneside.

'Neither is Mrs Llewellyn,' she said, and was on the point of closing the door on him when he found his voice.

'It's Miss Llewellyn I want to see.' He smile at her; he could be at home with her, anyway.

'Oh.' Her eyes grew wider, and she opened the door further. 'Well, you'd better come in. She's upstairs; she's just got back.'

John stepped past her into the hall, and she went to open a door to the right, then changed her mind, saying, 'Eeh no, you'd better wait in here.' She crossed the hall, passed the foot of the stairs and went down a short passage. And when he followed her she ushered him into a long, narrow room, at the far end of which a fire was burning.

She left him, only to return before he had time to look round. 'I forgot. What's your name?' she asked.

A great desire to laugh came over him. It could be Katie . . . no, Molly; Katie wouldn't have forgotten to ask the name.

'O'Brien.'

'O'Brien,' she repeated. Then, seeing the twinkle in his eye, her face refused to be uniformed like her

420

body and she smiled broadly. 'I'm new, I've only been here a week.' She hunched her shoulders. 'I'm always putting people in the wrong rooms. This is Miss Mary's.'

She disappeared, and he stood, cap in hand, looking around him. Well, he was inside, in Miss Mary's room. So she was a Mary, like his mother. And she had a room to herself . . . not a bedroom either. He thought the Brackens' furniture wonderful. Then what could he say of this room?

As he gazed about him, the room took away the ease and self-possession the little maid had momentarily given him. It was a melody of colour. He had never imagined colour as part of a room — good, strong furniture, yes, but the colour never got beyond a shiny brown. Here there was russet and green, gold and white. The room was carpeted to the walls with green. Green curtains hung across the entire wall at the further end of the room, and a russet-covered chair and couch were standing crosswise before the fire. Half of one long wall was taken up with a low bookcase, on top of which stood a number of china figures, gentlemen in ruffles, ladies in crinolines, their delicate colourings reflected in the dark surface of the wood, on which they endlessly danced or bowed. The yellow tone was supplied by early chrysanthemums, rearing with frosty elegance from a tall glass vase standing on a round table . . . And then the white tone. He found his eyes drawn to this, and he walked a few steps towards it. It was a statuette of a woman, dead white and completely nude. The trailing hair covering part of one breast and falling across her stomach and over her womb only emphasised her nakedness. She was standing on an inlaid box by the side of the green curtains and reached just above his waist. She was about two feet tall, but she filled his entire vision, seeming to become alive before his eyes. In the back of his mind, he knew that she was indecent and should not be in a good Catholic home, especially a schoolteacher's.

As he heard the quick, muffled footsteps descending the stairs, he almost sprang back away from her into the centre of the room again, and faced the door. Mary Llewellyn came in smiling, and as he looked at her he wondered at his nerve in daring to come and see this woman. Never before had he come into contact with anyone like her, and he was struck dumb. She seemed to move in a radiance. Did it emanate from the softness of her eyes or from the tenderness of her lips, or from the quick movements of her hands as she spoke? He did not know — he knew only that she was different.

'Hallo, Mr O'Brien.' Like her eyes, her voice was warm; and a slight catch of huskiness in it added to its charm. 'You wanted to see me? Come up to the fire and sit down.'

He followed her, his eyes fixed on the piled coils

of her hair, and his inarticulateness was passed over in the process of sitting down.

He sat, half in the big chair, his cap in his hand, and she sat on the couch, across the hearth from him. She was wearing a blue dress with a dark red belt . . . she was like her room, full of warm, embracing colour.

'I suppose you've come to talk about Katie?' she smiled at him and waited.

'Yes.' The voice didn't sound like his own; it was as if he were shouting in a large, empty hall.

'I'm so glad you have, for I should like to know your plans for her . . . Would you like her to become a teacher?'

'Yes.' Damn! Couldn't he say anything but yes! She would get the impression he was nothing but a numbskull.

'I'm glad of that. I know what to do now – I'll speak to the headmistress about her. Even if she only becomes an uncertified teacher, it would be something, wouldn't it?'

'Yes. Oh yes.' Was he a fool altogether? Yes, yes, yes. Why couldn't he be himself and say something, badly as he might express it?

There followed a silence, during which their eyes met and held. Hers were the first to drop away, and he felt she was embarrassed by his staring . . . perhaps annoyed. She leant forward and stirred the fire, and he suddenly began to talk – to straighten matters, as he put it to himself.

'I'm a poor envoy.' He wasn't sure if this was the right word, but he liked his placing of it; and he went on, 'There is so much I want to say about Katie, and so much to ask you. There's nothing I want more in the world than for her to become a teacher, but . . . Well, it's like this. You can guess how we are . . . ' he substituted the word 'situated' for 'fixed' – 'You can guess how we are situated. It's no good pretending, is it?' Without being aware of the transition, he was at his ease, talking frankly as he would have done to someone who knew all there was to know about him. 'There won't be any money to help her as far as I can see. If it's going to mean money, well, I'm afraid . . . ' He lifted his shoulders expressively. 'If it was left to me and I could earn it I would, but I'm rarely on full time.' This was coming down to earth with a vengeance, he thought. So much for his coat.

Mary was leaning back against the couch now, and she too, as she listened to him, was thinking about his coat. Remembering how she had seen him before, she had expected to find him dressed in much the same way. The coat so altered his appearance that she hardly recognised him as the same person; he looked rather handsome. Well, not handsome. There was something too rugged about his face for it to be handsome. Attractive? Yes, he looked very attractive. His eyes, particularly, were nice, especially when he smiled. It was strange what a difference clothes could make, outwardly at any rate. Yet the first time she saw him, she remembered imagining how he might look if he could dress like Gilbert. It seemed odd now that she should have met him the day she refused Gilbert . . . Suddenly she thought, I like him; he's nice – he's like Katie in a way.

She stood up hastily, saying, 'I haven't had any tea. Perhaps you'll have a cup with me, and then we can talk the whole thing out. Excuse me a moment.'

She gave him no time to refuse, but hurried away; and when she reached the door she turned, saying, 'Would you care to take off your coat? . . . you'll feel the benefit of it when you go out; it's nippy tonight.'

John stood up, staring down the empty room. This was a contingency for which he hadn't bargained. Against the coat, he knew his suit looked cheaper and shabbier than ever . . . Well, she was no fool to be taken in by the coat – no doubt she had guessed he had come by it second-hand. He took it off and laid it with his cap over the chair. Then he stood on the hearth-rug looking down at his suit, and a determination was born in him: this was the last suit he'd ever get from a tally man. The coat had told him one thing: there were clothes that were made to fit a man. And he'd have them. How? He didn't know; but have them he would. If one rig-out had to last him a lifetime; he'd be dressed decent for once.

And she had asked him to stay and have a cup of tea . . . tea with Miss Llewellyn! It was fantastic.

He ran his finger round the inside of his collar; it felt tight against his neck. He glanced into the mirror over the mantelshelf, and hardly recognized himself; the soft glow of the light seemed to make him look different. Or perhaps it was the collar . . . And that was another thing . . . never again would he wear a muffler at the weekends, and perhaps not at nights either.

He had just sat down again when she came in with a tray; a silver one, with a teapot and jug on it. As he would have done to relieve his mother from carrying anything, he got up and took it from her. She smiled her thanks, and brought a little table, and set it between the chair and the settee, and he placed the tray on it.

The maid came in carrying another tray, which Mary took from her, saying, 'All right, Phyllis, I'll see to it.'

With a sense of unreality, John watched her pour out the tea. She had set a little table at his hand and told him to help himself. The bread and butter was so thin he could have put the plateful in his mouth at once. He watched Mary double her piece in two, and followed suit, refusing her offer of jam, for that would mean too much palaver.

And so, like one in a dream, he took tea with Miss Llewellyn, and listened with only half his mind while she talked of Katie. He was thinking of this room and of her and of the strangeness of the whole thing ... They were sitting here alone together, having tea, just as if ...

He was startled back to the full import of what she was saying by hearing her repeat something he had said weeks ago: 'A day of high winds and far mastheads, and bonnie lassies.'

She laughed at his startled expression, and said, 'Now, when I find phrases like that in Katie's composition, although I know she's a clever child, I don't think she's that clever. Nor when she writes this: "The morning sky was massed with white clouds, like brakes ready for a day off." '

He felt the hot colour flooding up from his neck, and she asked, 'Have you tried writing these thoughts down and working them into something?'

'Writing them down?' he repeated. 'Me? Good Go ... lord, no.'

'Why not?' she said. 'Burns did, and many others. I think you should. I was sorry when I had to make Katie scrap the composition in which she stated that ore on her tongue and sweat in her hair and bleeding nails meant gold on a Saturday and roaming round the market, hemmed in with the smell of tallow and the flapping of skirts.'

Now his face was scarlet, and he said, 'I'll have to be more careful of what I say ... You see, we go for walks—' He stopped.

427

'You should write them up, you know,' she put in; 'a lot of what Katie repeats has poetry in it. Why don't you try?'

He had been leaning back in the chair, quite at ease. He still leant back, but he was no longer at ease. His face drooped into a sadness, which conveyed itself to his voice, together with reproach and stark frankness as he said, 'I can't even speak properly.'

'Oh, please don't say that!'

It was Mary's turn to flush now. She stood up, and taking his cup, refilled it. 'You don't speak differently from anyone else. And that has nothing to do with putting your thoughts to paper.'

'I've been told there's such a thing as grammar.' There was a touch of bitter sarcasm in his voice.

'Yes, but that comes . . . you learn as you go.'

He made no reply, and she, too, became silent, furious with herself for being a tactless fool. He had been so at ease, with quite a charming naturalness, and she had to bring up such a suggestion as him starting to write, of all things! But on the other hand, she was perfectly sincere in all she said, for some of the things Katie repeated were surprising in their poetical content. But be careful of what you are about, she warned herself. Don't put into his head ideas that will make the life he has to lead more obnoxious to him. Remember, you are not talking to Gilbert.

She glanced at the clock . . . half-past six. She

hoped Gilbert wouldn't put in one of his friendly visits; visits that were, she knew, manoeuvred by her mother.

John, noting her glance, said rather flatly, 'Well, I'll think over what you've said. I'd better be going now . . . Saturday night isn't a very convenient time to call.'

'No, no' – she put out her hand as if to press him back into his chair from the distance – 'you haven't finished your tea yet, and I'm not going out again. And anyway,' she laughed in a renewed effort to put him at ease – 'there are many things I want to ask you. Who, for instance, are Mr Bracken and Christine? Oh, Christine's wonderful!' She gave an imitation of Katie, closing her eyes and screwing up her face. 'You see, I get them every morning – while Katie is walking with me to school.'

John laughed with her. 'Our Katie's a chatterer. They are the people who live next door.'

'And Christine has a wonderful house, and cooks wonderful food, and has wonderful clothes . . . Oh, she's wonderful!'

John's laugh rang out, free and unrestrained now – her imitation was so like Katie when describing anyone. 'I'm afraid Katie thinks a number of people are wonderful. Not that she isn't right,' he added hastily, realising that sitting before him was, to Katie, the most wonderful of them all.

Mary, looking intently at him, wondered if he was

in love with this Christine, about whom she heard so much. Katie talked of only two people, John and Christine; before, it was only John . . . Our John said this, Our John said that . . . and the child had managed to convey a picture of someone quite out of the ordinary. Mary knew that the O'Briens were poor; not just clothes-poor, but of the poor who did not always eat well, which was a different and more potent kind of poverty; but the child had made this John emerge as someone untouched by poverty, an independent being, living with yet not of them. Then lately, to this worship was added that of this Christine . . . Christine and John, Christine and John.

How was it, Mary wondered, that some girls got men like this to love them, big kind men with a sense of humour as he had. At their first meeting, she'd thought he was to be pitied, but now she saw that she was wrong – he was intelligent and entertaining, the latter without making any effort to be so. He was certainly better company than Gilbert, even if he lacked Gilbert's taste in literature and art . . . or perhaps, because of it. Being a big man, like her father, was he attracted to small women, she wondered. This Christine, according to Katie's description, was apparently small. So was her own mother, small and helpless. Helpless! The word brought a cloud over Mary's eyes, for she had come to recognise that beneath her helpless

430

exterior her mother was pure granite; and to live in peace with anyone like her meant submerging oneself entirely. When she was young, her happy, loving nature did not question her mother's tyranny, and it was easy to accept 'Mother knows best'. How different her life would have been had she stood against her; for now her art study would have been finished. And who knows where it would have taken her — London — even Paris. Because her mother considered it wicked to draw bodies with no clothes on, she obediently put clothes on them. And again, when her mother said she would never make an artist . . . and anyway, artists weren't nice people . . . she subdued her natural talent becoming a schoolteacher, not through necessity, but because her father insisted she should have an occupation. But during these last few years had come a change, until now a state of undeclared war existed between her and her mother. The request to have a room of her own began it, and the refusal to be pushed into marriage with Gilbert Culbert, the son of her mother's old friend, widened the breach. And when, answering some inner urge, she bought the statue, and her mother demanded that it be removed from the house, the breach was further widened.

Lost in her thoughts, she did not notice that they were sitting in silence. How strange. She could never sit in silence with Gilbert. She lifted her gaze from her hands and found John looking at her, not intently, but rather reflectively. She smiled, and he blinked and roused himself.

'Are you interested in boats?' she asked. 'I mean the building of them.'

'Well, I know nothing about the building of them. I only know I get certain feelings when working in them. A feeling of friendliness for some and dislike for others. I suppose it has a lot to do with their cargo . . . and,' he laughed, 'the sweat in my hair.'

She laughed with him and asked, 'Would you like to see some models my father has made?'

'Yes, I would, very much.'

'Come into his workshop, then.'

She rose and went down the length of the room, and John followed her towards the green curtains. Before she drew them aside she gently moved the box and the statue. He watched her steady the statue with her hand, and it occurred to him as being strange that the statue no longer looked indecent but rather lovely . . . very like what she would be . . .

He was red in the face when she looked up at him, and she said hastily, almost apologetically, 'I came across it in an antique shop in Newcastle. It's an octoroon. I don't suppose you know any more than I did what an octoroon is; but, on looking it up, I found that she is the offspring of a quadroon and a white person, and a quadroon is one part negro and three parts white. Sounds very complicated, doesn't it?'

They were standing regarding each other now. Her hand was on the curtain and her face was unsmiling, and in her eyes he fancied he detected an appeal. For what exactly, he didn't know. But he said, 'I think it's very beautiful.' He, too, was unsmiling. And when she answered simply, 'Thank you,' it almost appeared as if the compliment had been meant for her. She turned swiftly and opened the french window, and stepped into the conservatory. He followed, going through a door close by and into the workroom.

It was in darkness, and she said, 'Just a moment. There are matches here, I'll light the gas.'

She gave an impatient exclamation as the box fell from her hand, and when, instinctively, they both stooped to retrieve it, causing them to collide and she to overbalance, his hands naturally were thrust out to steady her, and in the darkness he supported her . . . for one brief second his hands held her arms, and in that second the thing was done – the fuse that might have smouldered and died was fanned.

When the room was plunged into stark light from the double burner, John was still standing near the door. Mary did not speak for a moment, and when she asked, 'What do you think of them?' he moved slowly into the room and began to look round. There were dozens of models of small craft, set in stocks, on the shelves. In amazement, he asked, 'Your father made all these?'

'Yes. And most of them he's built full-size and sold. Do you recognise Mary, the tug?'

It was with genuine astonishment that he exclaimed, 'Your father's Llewellyn the boatbuilder then!'

'Yes. Didn't you know?'

He shook his head. He had never associated Llewellyn, the boatbuilder, with Miss Llewellyn the teacher. He knew Llewellyn by sight, as most of the dock men did. He had a little boat-building yard, tucked away on the side of the river. It still went under the name of Haggart's Yard, and it was known that Llewellyn worked in it as a lad by the side of his father. But that hadn't suited young Llewellyn; and he and his father built a boat on their own and sold it. It was said they built it in their backyard. That was a start, and eventually, when old Haggart died, and his own father too, Llewellyn bought the yard. He was known as a rising man . . . And he was her father!

With this knowledge, she again assumed to him the unapproachableness of an hour ago. How had he the nerve to come here!

When she spoke to him, smiling over her shoulder and saying, 'Come and look at this little yacht, my father hopes to build her some day,' he went to her; but the ease had left him, and he held the model in his hand without making any comment. Her nearness made him uneasy. He suddenly wanted to get away from her and her politeness . . . she

434

would act like this towards anyone, a beggar on the road, even . . . she was made that way, courteous, easy of manner.

'What do you think of it? You have seen lots of boats, but have you seen anything like her?'

She was looking up into his straight face, trying to draw him out again, when a voice from the doorway said, 'Hallo, Mary.'

They both started at the sound of the quiet, even tone.

'Oh! hallo, Gilbert,' she said, and after a pause, added, 'Come in a minute . . . This is Mr O'Brien. Mr O'Brien, Mr Culbert.'

Neither of the men made the usual gesture to shake hands, but inclined their heads . . . John in an abrupt nod, and Culbert in a more leisurely movement. John knew that he was under Culbert's scrutiny, and after his first concentrated stare, he did not look at the man but at Mary; for he was asking himself how anyone like her could take up with a fellow like Culbert, a weed of a man, narrow all the way up, right to the pointed head, over which his thin hair was meticulously brushed.

When Mary led the way back into her room John made straight for the chair over which his coat and cap lay, and she said nothing to delay his departure.

He nodded again to Culbert in farewell, and Mary escorted him to the front door. The feel of his coat

435

about him did nothing to allay his renewed feeling of gaucheness.

'Well, thanks,' he said awkwardly. 'It's been kind of you to . . . to help me about Katie.'

They stood regarding one another, and she too seemed to have lost some of her ease of manner. 'I'll do all I can for Katie, I'm very fond of her. And she's a clever child . . . Good night, Mr O'Brien.'

She held out her hand, and after the merest hesitation he took it. Firm and cool, it gripped his, conveying a sense of breathlessness and urgency. The feeling hung between them; even when their hands parted and he passed through the doorway it was there . . . a breathlessness.

He walked away down the path with her parting words acting like an opiate to his brain. 'If you feel there is anything you would like to know, at any time, please come and see me again.' It was odd, he thought, but she was the kind of person he could ask questions of.

But once out in the cold night air, the old brake of 'Steady your keel' thrust its reality upon him, and he said to himself, 'Well, that's that! It went off all right; Katie's set.'

As he reached the bottom of the Simonside bank, he deliberated whether to go into Shields and the market or walk slowly back home. If he did the latter it would mean thinking and going over every second of the past hour. No. He would go into Shields where there were lights and people . . . But what about being seen in this coat? Well, what about it? It seemed that within the past hour he had lost and regained his self-confidence a number of times, but, each time he regained it, it was stronger, for now he didn't mind being seen in the coat; it was the portent of things to come . . . he would have things . . . his mother and Katie would have things. How, he didn't know; but they would.

His decision to seek company in the shape of crowds did not immediately have the desired effect, and he found himself again thinking of Mary Llewellyn, but with a forced detachment. Fancy a lovely lass like her going to marry that . . . skinny-malink! Well, it was certainly no business of his. She had been very nice to him, more than nice; and she would help Katie; that was the only thing that mattered.

As he entered the first arc of Tyne Dock a well-known figure, shambling towards him, brought him back with a bump to his own world. It was Nancy; and he could hear her snivelling when she was still some distance away.

'Hallo, Nancy. What's the matter?' he asked her.

She hesitated, shuffled off the pavement in uncertainty, then shuffled back when she recognised him. 'Eeh, John. Eeh, John.'

'What's the matter?' he asked again.

'It's our Annie. She left me in the market – she run away, and she had me tram fare. An' me ma said she had to look after me and put me on the tram for me place.'

'Have you walked all the way from the market?' he asked her gently.

'Yes . . . It's our Annie. She run away, she did. An' me ma'll skelp me when I get in, she will, cos Mrs Fitzsimmons said I had to be back to clean the shop out when they closed. An' me ma said our Annie had to put me on the tram.'

John put his hand in his pocket and gave her threepence. 'Now stop crying. You'll be back in plenty of time. There's your tram fare and a penny to buy some bullets. Stand over there' – he pointed back towards the bottom of Simonside Bank – 'the Jarrow tram will be along in a minute.'

'Eeh! I can't get on the tram there, John. There's a bar there an' me ma says I've got to keep away from bars, cos the men come out.'

John could see the tram in the distance swaying towards them. He held out his hand to her: 'Come on, I'll put you on it.'

The tram jolted to a stop, and he helped her up, saying to the conductor, 'Put her off at the corner of Ferry Street, will you?'

As the conductor rang the bell, a figure leant forward from the end of the long wooden seat: 'Why, is that you, John?'

He recognised Mrs Bradley, and answered rather shortly, 'Yes, it's me.'

'Why lad, I hardly knew you . . . Well I never.'

The tram rumbled away, and the last John saw was Nancy showing the coins in her hand to Mrs Bradley. The picture did not remain in his mind an instant, but he was to remember it, and, unimportant as it seemed, it was to assume such proportions that although it happened on this day of emancipation, when he had first worn a fine top coat and taken tea with Miss Llewellyn, its ugly significance was to blot them out.

CHAPTER SEVEN

CHRISTMAS EVE

Mary Ellen hummed softly . . . it was many, many Christmases ago that she felt as happy as she did now. The morrow was Christmas Eve and she was really looking forward to it. She worked at the table in the middle of the kitchen, cutting out pastry for mince pies. Above her head hung a large, honey-combed paper ball, suspended from the paper chains crisscrossed under the ceiling. The kitchen was quiet and warm with an unusual air of cosiness about it. As she worked she planned for the morrow. She'd get up earlier than usual and blacklead the stove before lighting the fire; and then, after she'd got them all off to work, she'd get done and put everything shipshape; then she'd get the dinner ready, and have the afternoon clear . . . to go and get the coat.

Aye, it was a long time since she'd had a coat, a new shawl would have done her; but no, John had a bee in his bonnet, and she was to have a coat for Christmas . . . What had come over him lately? He was the same lad to her, yet somehow he was altered. It wasn't only the new suit he had, although that made him look fine; no, it was in some other way he'd altered. Well, never mind, he was still her lad, and the best on God's earth. If only the other one was like him.

The thought of Dominic caused her to stop humming. Why hadn't he gone away, as he'd been hinting of doing for some weeks past? Then Christmas would have indeed been grand. She knew he had been enquiring after jobs in both the Liverpool and London Docks; anywhere, he had said, to get away from this hole.

When she came to think of it, Dominic too seemed changed. It was all that lass next door she supposed — he was set on her; but he didn't seem to be making much headway. Was John his stumbling block? This was another thing which puzzled her. John was always in next door, and often she heard his laugh joined with that of the girl's. But there it seemed to end. If he were courting her, he was doing it in a funny way; for he never took her out. Pray God he wouldn't either. No, no, that would be terrible if John really took up with her. Well, she wasn't going to think about it; she was going to enjoy this Christmas. She already had a piece of brisket and an aitchbone, and if John went down to the market last thing the morrow he might pick up a duck or something cheap. They sold them off for next to nothing rather than have them left on their hands. By, it'd be grand if he could get a duck! And on Christmas Day they'd have Christmas cake and the rice loaf she'd made. Nobody knew yet, but she was going to put icing on the cake. By, they'd have a grand do.

A tap on the door broke in on her thoughts and she called, 'Come in,' and Peggy Flaherty, after kicking her boots against the wall, stumbled into the kitchen.

'Oh God above, it's enough to freeze your liver! It's at it again, Mary Ellen — won't be able to stir hand or foot outside the door shortly.'

'It hasn't started to snow again, surely?'

'It has so, Mary Ellen. As if it wasn't bad enough with everywhere frozen solid. God's truth, I've never seen anything like it! We'll have to be after watching the tap in the yard, Mary Ellen, or it'll be a dry Christmas in one way we'll be having. Oh, ye're lovely and warm in here, lass' — she wriggled her fat inside her many coats — 'and the smell's good enough to eat. And did ye ever see such a picture of a kitchen, with all those bonny chains!'

'Sit down and warm yourself, and have a pie,' said Mary Ellen.

'I will an' all, for I'm chilled to the bone. I'm just back from Shields. Look' — she pulled three small packages from her bass bag — 'some bits of things for the bairns' stockings.'

'Now, Peggy' — Mary Ellen compressed her lips — 'that's madness, that is! You know you haven't got it to go and buy presents.'

'Why haven't I then? I haven't got a bite of sup to buy for Christmas or Boxing Day, because out of the goodness of your heart ye've asked me down . . . so why haven't I? There they are' — she laid the packages on the mantelpiece — 'we'll say no more about them. There's only one thing I regret, and that is I haven't got it to buy you all something. But business isn't what it used to be; divil the pennorth of advice I've given out this past three weeks. What's the matter with people, Mary Ellen? 'Tisn't as if there were no rows; God alive, they followed each other like flies down at the bottom end last week? If it wasn't for running me clubs I'd be hard set at times; but as long as I get my rent I'm all right. And God's good. There was last week-end I didn't know which way I was going to turn, when, coming up the yard, that blessed lad of yours slipped me sixpence. By, Mary Ellen, I think if ye lost everything in the world and ye'd only him left, ye'd get by . . . Is he courting, Mary Ellen?'

'Courting?' Mary Ellen turned and with a blank face looked at Peggy. 'Not that I know of. Why do you ask?'

'Only I've seen him a number of times, three to be exact, and the last no later than this dinner-time, talking to the same lass. And a bonnier piece I've never seen. And mark ye, she wasn't from around these doors either. Today she had a fur coat on, and the tails hanging from the collar alone must have left a number of poor animals feeling cold around their backsides.'

'A fur coat?'

'The same. Tall she was, and strapping looking. And a voice like the gentry, for I heard her as I passed. And it's me that knows how the gentry talk – ye know that, Mary Ellen – for Mr Flaherty spent his life rubbing shoulders with them. And it's the same process, ye know: as ye can't touch pitch without becoming defiled, so ye can't mix among the gentry without picking up their lingo.'

Mary Ellen surveyed Peggy. 'You must have made a mistake.'

'Not a bit of it, Mary Ellen. John called out to me himself. "Hallo there, Peggy," he said, as true as I'm sitting here.'

Mary Ellen turned back to her baking board . . . John talking to a lass with a fur coat on. Who could it be? And three times. He wasn't a one to stand talking to lasses at any time, only that one next door. She turned to Peggy again: 'It wasn't—' she nodded her head towards the fireplace.

'No. I may be short in the sight, but I'm not that bad. This was a big lump of a lass, in fact she was a woman; and twice the size of that scrag end next door, bless ye.'

Mary Ellen could question Peggy no more at the moment, for there was another knock on the door; it was Hannah Kelly.

She had a coat over her head, and she shook the soft snow off it before coming into the kitchen. 'What weather! The only ones enjoying it are the bairns. Hallo, Peggy. Is this where ye are? By! they smell good Mary Ellen.' Hannah nodded towards the pies.

'Help yourself, lass,' said Mary Ellen.

'Not now. Thanks all the same. I only came over to see you a minute . . . about something.'

Peggy, taking the covered hint with the abundance of her good nature, said, 'I'll off up, Mary Ellen, for I must make a start; I'm up to the eyes upstairs.'

'She never said a truer word,' said Hannah, when Peggy had gone. 'How she lives among that junk, God alone knows. I came over to tell ye about our Nancy, Mary Ellen; but I couldn't do it with her sitting there – she'd be offering me advice, and I'm not in the mood to take Peggy's advice the day.'

'Is anything wrong, Hannah?'

'It looks like it; I've had a letter from Mrs Fitzsimmons about her. She says she's getting more queer every day, and she's getting that way she won't work; she just stands staring at her and says she can't. Ye know, Mary Ellen, that isn't like Nancy. As bad as she is she can do the rough work of half a dozen. Mrs Fitzsimmons says I'll have to bring her home if it keeps on . . . Oh, Mary Ellen, there'll be hell to pay again with our Joe if she's in the house all the time.'

'I'm sorry, lass. But perhaps you'll get her in some place else.'

'Not if she won't work. Ye don't mind me coming across and telling ye, Mary Ellen? Ye've got enough on your plate, I know, without my troubles stacked on top, but ye're the only one I seem to be able to talk to about her.'

'Why, lass, I only wish I could help you.'

Hannah sat down by the side of the fire and stared into the glowing coals for a moment. 'It's an awful thing, Mary Ellen, to know that a bairn ye've given birth to isn't all there.'

Mary placed her hand on Hannah's shoulder. 'We all have our loads, lass; if it isn't one thing it's another.'

Hannah gnawed at her lower lip. 'You and John are the only two who treat her like a human being. I know I don't. Sometimes I can't stand the sight of her. Oh, ye don't know, Mary Ellen, it's awful. But then, when I hear Joe going for her, I get a sort of feeling and want to protect her somehow.' She shook her head sadly. 'Well, the only thing I hope is she doesn't come home till after the new year. Joe's banking on a little bit of a do on New Year's Eve, but it'll be knocked completely on the head if she's home; he'll do nothing then; likely stay out most of the time.'

'She'll be all right,' Mary Ellen persisted, 'don't worry. Look, let's have a cup of tea.'

Mary Ellen bustled about making tea. In the face

446

of the tragedy of having a partly imbecile daughter her load seemed very light. She had poverty and drink to put up with, but not that, thank God. Hers were all right up there.

The two women drank their tea and talked on . . . about Bella now. Hannah wasn't speaking to Bella, for whenever she did Bella made some excuse to come downstairs and ferret out her business. And Bella's constant presence in the house maddened Joe. Mary Ellen could well understand this, for she had no use for Bella Bradley, who was never happy unless someone else was in trouble . . .

As the snow thickened and the light vanished earlier than usual the kitchen was lit only by the glow of the fire – through necessity the gas was never lit until it was almost impossible to see, and Mary Ellen worked on, after Hannah had gone, more by feel than anything else. She began to sing softly to herself – her mother and grandmother had sung the song before her – the simple words expressing the tragedy of at least one phase of their love:

> Love, it is teasing,
> Love, it is pleasing,
> Love is a pleasure when it is new;
> But as it grows older and the days
>   grow colder
> It fades away like the morning dew.

447

Mary Ellen wasn't thinking of the words, or how they applied to her own life, but that she had much for which to be thankful: Shane had not been really drunk since she was bad that time, and his twitching had eased. There had been no row in the house for months either. Well, they said it was a long road that had no turning, and hers had turned.

On these pleasant thoughts the kitchen door was thrust open again. She turned towards it, but could not distinguish who was standing there. It could have been John, Shane or Dominic; but she was expecting none of them for another hour.

'Why can't you light the bloody gas!'

Mary Ellen groped for a piece of paper, which she lit in the fire and put to the mantle, then turned and looked at Dominic. She had seen his face portraying many moods, contorted with passion or anger, drawn tight with cunning; but his expression now was one she had never seen; his eyes were wide and hard, and to her mind, had the thick, dull shine of a beer bottle. He seemed to be spread in a new kind of anger, wide and high with it.

'I want me tea now. I'm going out!'

'Well, get in first, can't you! It isn't ready yet. Can't you get changed and have it with the others?'

'No, I can't! And anyway, you wouldn't expect God Almighty to sit down with me, would you?'

She stared at him. Had he gone off his head? She watched him fling his cap across the table on to the couch, pull off his coat and fling it after the cap. The coat, in its flight, whipped a number of pies on to the floor and sent a cloud of flour off the board.

'Here!' Mary Ellen cried, 'what's up with you?'

He did not answer, but grabbed the kettle from the hob and emptied it of hot water. He also emptied the pail of cold water, and proceeded to wash, the water splashing over the side of the dish and up the wall as he did so.

Mary Ellen cleaned up the mess from the floor; then picked up the kettle and pail and went cautiously down the backyard. The ashes on top of the ice were already covered with a layer of snow. The tap was running in a thin trickle and she stood on the fringe of ice and water, steadying herself against the wall as she filled the pail . . . Always something to spoil things. What was it now?

She hunted around in her mind, but could find nothing. Whatever it was was connected with his work, for he was home early. And him saying, 'You wouldn't expect God Almighty to sit down with me.' Did he mean John? She couldn't fathom it.

When she returned to the kitchen, Dominic was in the bedroom, and she hurriedly cleared the table and set some bread and dripping and mince pies out.

When he eventually came to the table he stared down at the food. 'That's a fine meal for a man, isn't it!' His voice seemed to be torn from his throat.

'Well, you wouldn't wait. I'm going to fry.'

'You're going to fry!' he mimicked raspingly. 'Well, see that you do plenty of it; the big pot'll need it to fill his swelled head.'

Then his anger had to do with John. But how? What could have happened at work?

After having eaten all Mary Ellen had placed before him, Dominic left the house by the front way. As soon as the door banged behind him Mary Ellen went hastily into the room, and stood listening. Then, as she expected, came the muffled knock. He was next door.

She sang or hummed no more but, filled with the old dread, waited for John coming in – she had spoken too soon about her road turning. There was something afoot, and from the appearance of Dominic it was bad.

Katie and Molly rushed in, their hands blue and their noses red. 'Oh, Ma, is the tea ready?' 'And, Ma, our Katie's dirtied her knickers,' cried Molly.

'What!'

Both Katie and Molly burst out laughing at their mother's expression. Molly bringing her head down to Katie's and the two of them pressing their faces together in their mirth.

'Not that way. She slipped on a slide and ended up in some broken ice and slush,' Molly giggled.

'Are you wet?' Mary Ellen asked Katie.

'No, Ma, it dried.'

'Tea won't be for some time yet,' said Mary Ellen.

'Here take a bit of bread and get yourselves out again.'

Mary Ellen pushed a slice of bread at each of them. 'You can stay out for another half-hour or so. Hunt up Mick and bring him back with you.' It would be better, she thought, if she had the house to herself when John came in.

When at last she heard the clanking footsteps in the yard, she stood still facing the door. It might be Shane. The feet kicked against the wall, and the door opened. It was John, not with brows drawn and lips tight, but with an almost childish expression of pleasure on his face. He wasn't smiling — with an effort he was keeping his face straight — but the light in his eyes danced at her. She turned from him, puzzled. It couldn't be that lass with the fur coat. No, how could that affect Dominic?

'Is it still snowing?' she asked, as she bent over the pan on the fire.

John didn't answer, but came and stood by her. 'Anybody in?'

'No,' she said.

He took her by the shoulders and pulled her round to face him, so close that her head had to go back to look up at him. 'I'll give you three guesses . . . What do you think's happened?'

'Why, lad, how should I know?'

'Go on.'

'You've been set on the Benisaf boat.'

John flung his head back and laughed out loud. 'Aye, lad, how should I know? Tell us.'

He stepped back, thrust his thumbs into the lapel of his coat, drew himself up to his fullest height with mock dignity, and said, in the deepest tones of his voice, 'Mrs O'Brien, behold . . . a gaffer!'

A gaffer . . . Mary Ellen could make no comment. Had he gone mad too? A gaffer. Her lad, and him only twenty-two. Why, there was something wrong somewhere. There was only one gaffer over the boats, and he must be a man steady in his years. The old gaffer had died a couple of days ago, she knew, but they couldn't have picked John. It was fantastic. Her face expressed her feelings, and John laughed and said, 'You don't believe it?'

'Well, lad . . .'

'Yes, I know it's hard to take in.' He was suddenly serious. 'I haven't taken it right in meself yet. I couldn't, for the life of me, believe they meant it.'

'Did the men pick you?'

'Yes, they voted for me to take old Reville's place.'

It was customary for the dock men who unloaded the boats to choose their own boss. They also paid him so much a head out of their wages. Most of the unloading was paid on tonnage, and the gaffer's job was to select men for the boat and at the end of discharging collect the money from the dock office, subtract his due and pay out the men. But this alone did not cover his duties, which often entailed taking

452

off his coat and fighting it out with any man who thought he was not getting a square deal, and who said so forcibly. Another thing expected of the gaffer was to provide subs for men who were out of work and advances to those just being set on again.

This was in Mary Ellen's mind when she said, 'But lad, how can you do it? . . . The subs.'

'I've got over that. You know McCabe in the dock office. Well, when I went to tell him he seemed to know how I was fixed, and offered to lend me a few pounds to make a start . . . I'll be able to pay it back in a few weeks. And I won't forget him for it.'

'Lad, don't start on borrowed money. There's the twenty-five shillings for that coat. I don't need a coat; I've made . . .'

'Here . . . that's enough. You're getting that coat.'

'Were all the men for you?' She gazed up into his face; she was smiling now and her heart was racing within her breast. To think her lad had been picked for a gaffer. Oh, the road had turned all right.

'Not all. But the ones that mattered were.' He turned away and took off his coat. She knew he was referring to Dominic, and perhaps Shane.

'Does your da know?'

'Yes. He took it all right.'

She heaved a sigh of relief. Now perhaps Shane would get set on more often. No. She could quieten her hopes on that score – John would more likely be fair to the other extreme.

'Was none of the others after it?' she asked.

'Yes. But none of them were steady.'

Her eyes became misted. They had picked him, despite his years, because he was . . . steady. Her John a gaffer. And Katie set on the road to be a teacher. Oh, God was good.

The tears, gathering in her throat, threatened to choke her, and she turned away and put her apron to her face.

'Here! Here!' John pulled her round, and as his great arms pressed her gently to him a dam burst within her. No sorrow could have broken it; but this happiness was overwhelming, and she sobbed it out, leaning against him.

An hour later, when John saw Christine, he knew that she was already aware of what he had come to tell her; and after she exclaimed, 'Oh, John, what wonderful news! And at Christmas too,' he looked at her closely and asked, 'What's the matter? Aren't you well?'

'Yes. Yes, I'm all right,' she said hastily.

'No you're not, you're as white as a sheet. Has . . ?'

She turned away and picked up a half-dressed doll from the table. 'Dominic's just gone. He told me about you being made a gaffer,' she said.

'Yes, I bet he did; and he'll likely be the first one I'll have to take my coat off to. But that didn't make you look like this.'

Christine sat down by the fire with the doll on her knee, and proceeded to pull a frilled silk dress over its head.

'Look. If he's been up to any of his tricks . . .'

Christine cut him short with unusual curtness: 'He asked me to marry him.' She said it while looking John full in the face; the look was almost a challenge, and he experienced a feeling of guilt. Why, he couldn't fathom; but it was so strong that it swamped his indignation at Dominic's audacity.

'He wants me to go to Liverpool with him; then perhaps abroad.'

'Abroad?'

'Yes.'

'Are you going to marry him?'

'No.' She was still looking at him, the dress was only half over the doll's head. He blinked, and looked away from her down at his feet; and she sighed faintly and resumed the fitting of the dress.

John looked at her again. She was so sweet sitting there dressing the doll; why couldn't he go to her and put his arms about her and kiss her, just as often before he'd had the desire to kiss her? But he knew that, whereas for him it would merely be a kiss, to her it would be the absolute symbol of love. How he became possessed of this knowledge he didn't know, for, as he had asked himself on previous occasions, what did he know about lasses? If she were Jenny Carey or Lily McDonald he would perhaps have

455

kissed her by now and let things take their course, but with Christine he couldn't, it wouldn't be fair. Was it even fair to come in so often? He supposed not, but he liked talking to her and Peter.

The strain that had fallen on them was relieved by David appearing. After glancing round, he asked, 'Has he gone then?'

'If you're staying in take your coat off, dear,' said Christine.

John knew to whom David was referring, he also guessed that Dominic had shooed David out.

'I'm getting a sculler for Christmas, John . . . a real one.'

'No!'

'Yes. Aren't I, Christine?'

The boy's large, dark eyes, glowing in his pale face, always aroused a tenderness in John. He was so thin, and almost girlish in his fragility.

John asked Christine, 'He doesn't mean a real one?'

'Yes. Grandfather has already bought it — it's at the quay corner. David's going to paint it himself and get it ready for the fine weather. Aren't you?'

The brother and sister smiled at each other. John realised that this was another of Peter's ways to eliminate yet another fear from his grandson. The child was highly strung and nervous, and had never quite got over the shock of seeing his parents killed in a collision between a tram and a cab when he was five years old. The episode at the gut no doubt added the fear that the boat was to erase. And the thought came to John, as it had often done lately, that Peter was a splendid man. How could anyone mock at him? By! he wished he'd been there when that crowd of hooligans burnt his hut down. They would have gone along with it.

He looked at the boy standing by Christine's side watching her put the bonnet on the doll . . . They were like a little family of saints, tender with each other, kind to everyone, and forgiving beyond his power to understand. He sat for a while longer watching Christine finishing the doll. Then he said he must get indoors and give a hand, for there were still more decorations to be hung around the walls.

Christine smiled at him as he left: 'I'm glad about your job, John.'

'Thanks. I knew you'd be . . . Tell Peter, will you?'

Christine nodded; and David cried suddenly, 'I'm going to stand at the corner, Christine, and wait for Grandfather.'

The boy chattered loudly as he and John walked down the yard, but outside, in the back lane, he pulled at John's arm and whispered, 'John, can I . . . I want to tell you something.'

'Yes, what is it, David?' John stooped to him.

'It's Dominic — Christine's frightened of him . . . she's always frightened of him. He made me go

457

out and he said to Christine you wouldn't get her, but he would, some way. You won't let him, will you?'

John remained silent for a moment, looking at the blur that was the boy's white face, which stood out even against the newly fallen snow. It was straining up to him, appealing, pleading. 'Don't you worry, David. Christine will be all right; I'll see to that.'

'Will you, John? Will you?'

'Yes—' John patted David's hand, and the boy seemed satisfied and ran off in evident relief; and John turned thoughtfully into the backyard, to meet Katie coming out of the lavatory.

'Come in here a minute,' he said to her, drawing her into the washhouse and closing the door; 'I want you to do something for me.'

'Yes, John?'

He knew by her voice that her face was eager. 'Look; whenever you hear Dominic go in next door, you run in the other way, will you?'

'Yes, John. But if me ma . . .?'

'You can tell her you are going to return something of David's, a picture book or something.'

'Yes, John.'

'And no matter what he says, don't leave him alone with her. If he makes you and I'm in, come and tell me. You've got that now?'

'Yes, John.'

'Has he ever chased you out?'

Remembering Christine's warning, Katie merely answered, 'Sometimes.'

'Have you ever seen him . . ?' John stopped. 'Well, never mind. You know what to do, don't you?'

'Yes, John.'

Neither Katie nor Molly could remember a Christmas Eve like this one. They had faint memories of being excited at the prospect of hanging up their stockings, and a memory, not so faint, of disappointment at the meagreness of their contents when they opened them; but tonight was different. In the cupboard at the side of the fireplace were parcels, some that John brought in last night, some from Christine, and others. Katie and Molly would make running dives at the lower door of the cupboard, calling, 'I'm gonna open it, Ma! I am! I am!'

Apart from saying, 'You dare,' Mary Ellen took no notice of them. Her face wore a faint smile and her body seemed settled in contentment as her needles flew on the toe of a sock. They were the last few rows of a pair she was knitting for Shane. Why had she thought of knitting him socks for Christmas she didn't know – she could not remember ever giving him anything at Christmas, except the first Christmas they were married. She wouldn't, of course, say that these were for a Christmas box; she would just put them out with his change of clean

459

underclothes. Perhaps he would notice them, perhaps he wouldn't.

She glanced up as John came out of the bedroom, and she had to say to Katie, 'Leave John be, hinny, he's got to go out . . . Stop clambering! you'll dirty his suit.'

'Give me a shuggy before you go. Come on, John, just one,' Katie coaxed.

'Well mind, just one . . . that's all.'

'You're worse than she is,' said Mary Ellen as John sat down and crossed his knees and stuck a foot out.

Katie clambered on to the foot, and he held her hands as he hoisted her up and down. And she giggled and shouted, 'But say it! You're not saying it!'

'Give over, Katie, John's got to go out! You'll be packed off to bed, mind . . . Oh, what's the good! You're worse than she is,' Mary Ellen exclaimed, as John began to chant with each movement of his foot:

> Father Christmas soon will come
> Laden with all treasures.
> I would like a boat to sail,
> A rocky horse with a bushy tail,
> A farthing or a spade and pail;
> Katie wants a big, fat . . . dol-ly.

After the final heave, Katie fell off his foot,

laughing, and John's eyes were drawn, for a moment to Molly. She was standing to one side, smiling, yet wistful. He suddenly realised he'd never had much time for Molly, and, scatterbrain as she was, she felt it. He saw it in her face now as she stood there. Impulsively, his hand went out and he pulled her to him, saying, 'Come on, you big soft lass,' and, laughing and giggling, she sat on his foot.

'Well I never. What next, I wonder!' Mary Ellen's tone was half laughing, half derisive.

Molly wasn't so easy to lift as Katie, and before John was half-way through the rhyme she had tumbled off on to the floor, where she lay, clasping Katie, helpless with laughter.

Mary Ellen, trying not to allow her gaze to linger on this son of hers, who was looking so grand, said, 'Get yourself away, lad, or else I'll not get them to sleep the night. And if you should see Mick, send him in.'

John put on his coat, saying, 'Well, expect me when you see me – I may have to follow the men to Newcastle to get the ducks. It's six you want, isn't it?'

He left the house with his mother joining in with the laughter of the children. The sound made him happy. There was something different about this Christmas . . . Well, so there should be. A gaffer! He breathed deep of the icy air. But it wasn't that alone. There was a difference both inside and outside

461

the house. Perhaps the difference lay in himself; life at last seemed to be opening.

He walked briskly to Tyne Dock, and stood waiting for the Shield's tram. The snow plough had been out, and the space opposite the dock gates had the appearance of land on which the grab had been at work; pale grey mounds lined the pavement, and the hurrying figures, passing in and out of the lamplight and the light from the bars, looked jet black against them. Some iron ore men, still in their working clothes, came out of a bar and hailed John: 'Why, man, you look as if you've had some money left you. Pinched our wages already? Or has the North-Eastern left you a prop boat?'

'Aye, they offered me one for Christmas, but I told them what to do with it: "A Benisaf or nothing" I said.'

There was loud laughter at this. 'I bet you did too! Well, a happy Christmas, and many of them,' they called as they moved away. 'And see we have full shifts for full bellies next year, mind.'

'Many of them,' John answered.

As he watched their unwieldy figures disappear into the darkness, he felt a thousand miles removed from them. They were good enough fellows in their way, but with one thought dominating them all . . . plenty of work, which meant plenty to eat and drink, or the reverse process. But somehow he didn't feel of them. It wasn't just since he had been made a gaffer, he had been feeling like this for some time past. Was it since he had got this coat? He didn't know; something had changed him . . .

The aisles of the open market were congested with buyers, and the shouts of the stall-holders were deafening. John saw that it would be hours yet before the stuff was sold at anywhere near his price. Ten or eleven would be the time to come back. So he walked down King Street, debating whether he should go to the second house at the Empire or the Tivoli. To whichever place he went, he couldn't go in the threepennies, not in this rig-out. It would mean the sixpennies, or even the ninepennies. That was one drawback of being dressed-up.

'Hallo, Mr O'Brien.' Mary Llewellyn stood in front of him, her arms laden with parcels.

'Good evening, Miss Llewellyn.'

They were blocking each other's path and that of the other pedestrians as, after the greeting, they stood mutely surveying each other, surprise showing in both their faces, as if this was the last place one would have expected to find the other.

'Did you ever see such a crowd?'

'No, I never have.'

John hadn't noticed the crush before, but now they seemed to be hemmed in on all sides.

'Are you doing your last-minute shopping?' she asked him.

'No . . . yes . . . Well' – his eyes twinkled – 'I'm

hanging around until they give the ducks away in the market.' And as he said it, he wondered why it cost him nothing in pride to admit such things to her.

They laughed together, and one irritated shopper exclaimed, 'If you want to stand laughing your heads off clear off the flags and let people pass.'

They pulled long faces at each other, and Mary said, 'I suppose she's right.'

'Can I carry some of your parcels to the tram?' John asked.

'Well, I wasn't going home yet. But it would be a help if you'd relieve me of some of them for a time; I have a little more shopping to do.'

He took the boxes from her and stacked them under his arm. Then they turned towards the market again, John walking slightly ahead of her to make a way.

Laughing gaily, she left him outside while she went into a linen shop, and he stood gazing into the window, seeing nothing. He knew that this night was different. There was magic about it; in the cold and the snow, in people's faces, and in meeting her. Strange, up till a few months ago, he had never set eyes on her. But since that night he had been to see her they had run into each other a number of times, mostly when he was coming from work; yet she didn't seem to mind his working clothes. The first time they met, it was she who stopped and talked, just as if he were all got up instead of being covered from head to foot with splatters of wet clay. He had been working on a boat from Sweden, and the ore was embedded in lumps of clay, which made the digging and picking heavy and dirty.

After these meetings, he never allowed himself to think, using his mother's formula ... thinking got you nowhere. She was interested in Katie, and through Katie, kind to him. That was that. But this meeting, like everything else on this Christmas Eve, was different. She had asked him to carry her parcels, and he was standing waiting for her as if he was her ...

'I won't ask you to carry this one.' She was standing by his side, and he stared at her, not speaking; her face, under her fur-trimmed hat, shone at him like a star. For one brief second, the street and the hurrying crowds vanished, and she was alone in a vast emptiness, shining, and for him.

His face was unsmiling and his voice deep in his throat as he asked, 'Have you time ... would you care to go to a variety show or the pantomime?'

He waited, tense and unthinking as her smile faded. The expression in her eyes changed a number of times in as many seconds, but not once did they portray annoyance or amusement.

'I should love to.' She turned away from him, and he fell into step by her side, thinking now, as he had never thought before: Had he gone mad? What of the Mr Culbert? It was Christmas Eve and perhaps she was expected at home for a party or something. What in the name of God had made him ask her! And what about money? He had five shillings of his own . . . would that do? . . . Yes. Somehow, he knew she wouldn't expect too much. But again, what in the name of God had made him do it! It was the last thing on earth he would have thought of doing . . . Or was it? Hadn't he often wondered what it would be like to take someone of her stamp out? Yes, but just as one dreamt dreams, never for one moment expecting them to happen. The funny thing was she hadn't refused. She hadn't been merely polite, either; she seemed quite sincere when she said, 'I'd love to.' Well, now he must put his thinking cap on. They would have to go in the very best seats, and she'd have to have some bullets. Bullets! he repeated scornfully . . . chocolates. Get a little box . . . A box! No need to go mad altogether. She wouldn't expect it anyway. He pushed his shoulders back. Expected or not, he'd get a box.

'Do you think there's time for me to make a telephone call?'

They were standing outside the Empire, and for a moment she drifted from him into the class that made telephone calls.

'Where do you have to go? The post office?' he asked.

'Yes; I won't be more than five minutes.'

'Of course. Come on.' He shouldered his way

through the crowd. Class or no class, she was going out with him, this once anyway. And he'd do the thing properly; it would be something to remember.

In spite of her fur coat and rinking boots, Mary shivered as she waited in the telephone box. It had happened as she hoped it might. But where would it lead? . . . There was time enough to ask that later, she told herself. What she had to do now was to smooth things over with those at home.

She gave a gentle sigh when she heard her father's voice say, 'Yes. Who is it?'

'It's me, Mary.'

'Mary? Why, where are you? What's up? You should be home by now; we're nearly ready.'

'Look, dear. I won't be home . . . not until . . . quite late.'

'But where are you? You know you can't do that, Mary; we're going to Gilbert's! Look lass' – he cut her short as she was about to speak – 'it's Christmas, and we want things to go peaceable like. Where are you, anyway?'

'Shields Post Office.'

'What's made you change your mind?'

'I . . . Well, I met a friend.'

'But it isn't right. You know what a state this will put your mother in.'

'I never wanted to go. I've told her so all along. She shouldn't have accepted for me . . . Look, Father, can't you see what Mother is trying to do?'

467

'Yes. I know, I know.'

'Well then, why should you want me to go? And anyway, it isn't fair to Gilbert. She's giving him the idea that I can be coaxed round, and I can't.'

'Who's your friend?'

'Oh, you . . . you don't know him.'

'It's a man then?'

'Yes, it's a man.'

'Well, this is going to be a lovely evening for me.'

Mary laughed softly. 'It's yourself you're thinking about.'

'Well partly.' There was a chuckle. 'You'll be for it tomorrow, mind. And somehow I did think this was going to be a peaceful Christmas.'

'It's the loveliest Christmas I've ever known. Goodbye, dear.'

'Here! Mary . . . look, who's this fellow?'

'We may talk about him later.'

'Mary . . . you'll go to Midnight Mass? For God's sake don't miss that, or there'll be hell to pay.'

'We'll see. Goodbye. Wait. Do you want to know something?'

'What is it?'

'I like you, Mr Llewellyn.'

Laughing, she hung up the phone, and almost ran to join John.

Mary Ellen yawned. She wished John was in, and then she'd go to bed. She leaned back and glanced

468

up at the clock . . . ten-past eleven. Had he managed to get a duck?

She sat with her chair drawn up close to the fire, her feet on the fender, her skirt tucked up on to her lap, exposing her short legs to the dying ashes. The house was quiet, only Shane's and Dominic's snores alternating with each other's from the rooms. Behind her, the girls lay curled up under the thin brown blankets and a heap of coats; and, at each end of the mantelpiece hung their packed stockings, together with one for Mick.

As she yawned again, she heard the muffled pad of footsteps on the yard, and, pulling down her skirt, she got up to open the scullery door as John quietly lifted the latch of the back dór.

Stupefied, Mary Ellen gazed at him; then, in a whispered exclamation, said, 'In the name of God! have you bought the market?'

John laughed softly as he lowered a great parcel on to the table, followed by a stone brown paper bag and a square box. 'You'll never guess what it is . . . it's a turkey! And this is a bag of fruit. And there's bullets in that box.' He spoke softly and rapidly.

'A turkey! But where'd you get the money, lad?' Mary Ellen looked closely at him. If she didn't know differently she'd have thought he'd had a drop – his eyes were shining, like coals . . . Perhaps it was the frost.

'We . . . I waited till the last thing, and I got him for four bob.'

'But what's all this other?'

'Fruit.'

'A stone bag of it!' Mary Ellen looked amazed. 'Are they specked?'

'No, I should say not.'

John did not look at her. He had taken off his cap and was combing his hair. 'Miss Llewellyn sent them for the bairns.'

Mary Ellen stared silently at his profile. Miss Llewellyn.

John turned to her, putting on his cap again. 'I'm going to Midnight Mass at Jarrow. I'm getting the last tram up.'

Miss Llewellyn and Midnight Mass. Her lad going to Midnight Mass with Miss Llewellyn! It was funny but she'd been thinking about Midnight Mass earlier on this evening, feeling the need to give thanks for all her good fortune at this Christmas time. It was years since she had been to Midnight Mass, and in spite of her tiredness, she'd thought: For two pins I'd go to Midnight Mass if John was in. She would have worn her new coat, although it wouldn't have mattered about going in her shawl; there'd be mostly shawls and mufflers there anyway. And she'd imagined herself kneeling as she used to do in the aisle, or even on the altar steps, wrapped about in the thick, incensed air, full of hushed rustle, so full would the church be.

And for a brief hour she would really feel the Child was being born and be one with Mary in her travail.

But John was going to Midnight Mass, and he was going with Miss Llewellyn. She knew now the reason for the light in his eyes.

John tried not to show undue haste, but there was only a few minutes before the tram would pass the bottom of the street, and she would be on it. Already it was late, and perhaps they'd not get in the church. He did not want this to happen, for he had the desire to kneel at Mass with her, not only because it would mean being with her another hour or more, but because to go to Mass with a lass had a subtle meaning, which neither needed nor could be defined by words.

The four hours they had been together seemed to spread back down his lifetime. There seemed no moment when he had not watched the expressions dancing over her face like shadows in a garden, nor a moment when he had not been carrying her parcels or buying her chocolates, or when he was not sitting with her in the dark and laughing with her at a pantomime; or when there was a second in his life when she did not urge him to remain quiet while the stallholder, in desperation, brought his final and unmovable price of eight shillings a turkey down to four shillings! or when had he not watched her taking her choice of fruit, bananas, pomegranates, oranges, apples, pears and nuts. And

471

now they were going to Midnight Mass, and there would be no tram back. They would have to walk all the way from Dee Street, in the centre of Jarrow, to the heart of Simonside. It would be a long way for her, and difficult walking, for the pavements were sheets of knobbly grey ice; and it would be a long way to walk without touching each other. She might have to take his arm – he thought of it as 'link' – Miss Llewellyn and him linking!

A surge of feeling that demanded some form of expression swept through him, and, stooping, he kissed Mary Ellen swiftly on the side of the brow. Without a word, he was gone. And Mary Ellen stood fingering the place his lips had brushed . . . Her lad had kissed her . . . for the first time since he was a tiny bairn. And because he was in love.

She had been worried lately, thinking he was struck on her next door, and had wondered where it would lead, for she doubted, if he took her, there'd be much happiness for him; not that she had anything really against the lass, only that terrifying religion of hers. God knew there was no happiness came out of a mixed marriage. With a Church of England one it would be bad enough, but with a Spiritualist! . . . And yet, as awful as that possibility seemed, he would have had a little show of happiness in a way, whereas now there was none for him that she could see. For what was the obstacle of religion compared with the obstacle of class? Had he gone mad? And that Llewellyn lass, too? Where did they think it would lead? Her da was a boatbuilder; and a docker, even a gaffer, would be so much midden muck to him. They had a fancy house, with even a lavatory inside, so Katie said, and kept a parlourmaid and a cook. Was the lass mad? There was no-one better than her lad, no-one in the wide world, but he was a docker and from the fifteen streets. And that lass must know nothing could come of it . . . She was struck by his size and his ways, and she would shelve him when the novelty wore off. And what would it do to him? She thought of his eyes when he had come in, and slowly she sat down by the fire again and stared into its rose-grey embers.

CHAPTER EIGHT

NEW YEAR'S EVE

It was a good thing New Year's Eve fell on a Saturday, John thought, for it meant one day less holiday. They would start work on Tuesday, the ones, anyway, who were sober enough. He wanted work, and more work. If he had his own way he'd carry on, night and day, for three parts of the week; he'd make them throw the stuff out of those holds as it had never been thrown out before. He wanted money. God, how he wanted money.

He sat before the fire, dressed in his working clothes, tense with thinking. Shane sat opposite him, sober and sullen; he'd been drunk only once during the holidays. This was a record. Was he turning over a new leaf? John wondered, or was it because he was forced to realise that the more he drank the more he twitched? But twitching or not, tonight he'd likely have a skinful. What would she say to this house and the lot of them? Would she take them as she took him? That was too much to ask. Whereas last Saturday night he thought he'd never known

474

a moment in his life without her, now, across the vast space of time since he last saw her, he could not even recall her face clearly. Again and again he tried to visualise her; but always her face ran into a blur. Even when he attempted to recapture the wonder and the ecstatic feeling of achievement as, with her on his arm, he walked past the fifteen streets, huddled and sleeping under the star-carpeted sky, the feeling would slither away. It was strange, too, but he could not actually remember how he left her. What did they say to each other? Nothing much. They were quiet on the journey back; all the laughter and fun had been left in Shields market. As they walked up Simonside Bank, he had asked if she were tired, and she had replied that she'd never felt less tired. Yet she sounded sort of sleepy when she said it . . . But there must have been more than that said. One thing he knew he hadn't said: 'Can I see you again?'

Why hadn't he, when it was foremost in his mind during those last few minutes with her? But foremost, too, had been the thought of money. He couldn't really ask her out unless he intended taking her somewhere. Well, he could have taken her out tonight.

All this morning he was hoping he would run into her as he came home from work. And when he didn't, he told himself it was the best thing that could have happened; there were many things he could do with those extra few shillings – his mother would know what to do with them. So perhaps it was all for the best — he moved impatiently in his chair. Perhaps . . . there was no perhaps about it. What was he aiming at, anyway? Was his brain softening, just because of that one night? If he were to see her again, what would it lead to? So intense was the urgency of the question that he almost spoke aloud. You are going stark, staring mad! Look around, and ask yourself what you and she can ever be to each other . . . even if she does like you . . . He was on his feet, staring down into the fire; she likes me all right, I know it. She more than likes me . . . she feels the same as I do.

Mary Ellen could remain silent no longer; John's drawn, twisted face was wringing her heart. Shane was dozing now, and she whispered, 'What's up, lad?'

'Nothing. I'm going to have a wash.'

He went quickly into the scullery, and as he washed himself Mary Ellen gazed sadly at his back. She knew this would happen — she knew there'd be no happiness in it for him. She wanted to go to him and in some way comfort him; but her mind was lifted from him to Molly.

Molly's screeching voice came from the back lane, and Mary Ellen knew she was fighting again, for she was hurling rhymes at someone's head:

Annie Kelly's got a big fat belly,
And her belly wobbles like jelly.

My God! that lass nearly fourteen and yelling things out like that. Mary Ellen pushed past John and opened the back door.

'You, Molly! come in here!'

Molly was having her last word: 'You wouldn't do much for God if the divil was dead, Annie Kelly. You're mean, so you are. Poor Nancy!'

'Come in here!' Mary Ellen hauled Molly over the step. 'You can thank your lucky stars your da's dozing,' she whispered fiercely, 'or I'd bray you!'

'Well, I was only sticking up for Nancy,' Molly snivelled. 'She's been sent back from her place, Mrs Fitzsimmons won't have her. And Annie wouldn't let her play with us; she punched her.'

'Sent back from her place,' Mary Ellen repeated to John. 'That means the do's off.'

'Damn good thing, too,' John answered shortly. 'They'll be yelling out for the money before the new year's in a week.'

'It'll likely be spent now, lad, in any case.'

The door opened again, and Katie rushed in breathless.

Mary Ellen hushed her: 'Be quiet, hinny! And close that door, the cold's enough to cut you in two.'

'Ma, can I go with Christine? And Molly too? There's a big stretch frozen hard, past Cleveland Place, and everybody's going there to slide . . . proper sliding. Christine's got proper sliding skates with knives on the bottom. And there's a man there with a fire selling roast taties . . . Oh, Ma, can we go?'

'Go on, Ma, let's.' Molly joined her plea to Katie's.

'What about it cracking?' Mary Ellen asked John. 'Will it be deep?'

'It won't crack in this frost.'

He was drying himself, and asked Katie, 'How does Christine know there's skating? Has she been?' He hadn't seen Christine since Christmas Day, and then only to wish her a happy Christmas and to thank her rather sheepishly for the tie. He knew now why he hadn't kissed Christine, and the knowledge made him strangely embarrassed in her presence.

'Yes,' answered Katie. 'She was there yesterday, her and David. She says they're going to have a big fire on the bank the night to light the ice up.'

'How far past Cleveland Place is it?'

'It's in Roper's Field.'

'You'd better give it a miss,' said Mary Ellen; 'you'll slide the boots off your feet.'

'Not any sooner than with sliding in the streets,' said John.

'But it's them falling through I'm afraid of.'

'Don't worry,' he said; 'I'll take a walk up and have a look.'

He went into the bedroom and started to change hastily. Roper's Field . . . off the Simonside Road. There was just a chance she might be there.

In the kitchen of Cumberland Villa, the two maids

478

were standing near the partly open door, straining their ears.

'Hear anything?' asked the cook.

'Not a word,' replied Phyllis. 'And the way the missis looked I thought she was going to explode. I bet you anything you like though she'd heard about that fellow.'

'I wouldn't believe a word of it,' said Cook. 'And I'd be careful what I was saying if I was you. Miss Mary walking out with one of the O'Briens! Huh! I'll believe that when I see it.'

'I tell you our Doris saw them in the market, and our Doris knows them both as well as I know you. She was standing behind them, and she said they were laughing and talking together like . . . well, like a couple who was walking out . . . Sh! Listen.'

Phyllis's elbow stopped the cook's retort. 'There!' she hissed. 'Get an earful of that. Have you ever heard the missis go off like that before? What did I tell you?'

In the drawing-room, James Llewellyn was appealing to his wife: 'Look, Beatrice, leave this to me.' He spoke gently and soothingly; the jocular brusqueness, which was his usual defence against her, was gone from his tone.

'Too much has been left to you, and look at the result!' She turned from him, and again addressed her daughter, with quiet tenseness now. 'No wonder you wouldn't tell me who you were with on

479

Christmas Eve! It is to your credit that you were ashamed.'

Mary stood with her elbow resting on the mantelpiece; her face was half turned from her mother, and she stared unseeing into the fire, her attitude belying the anger that was filling her body.

'You must have lost every spark of decency. You never, at any time, had a proper sense of what is correct. But this! Have you any idea how I felt when Florence Dudley told me they saw you in the Empire with a . . . docker?' Beatrice Llewellyn spat out the last word, her thin nose and delicately chiselled mouth almost meeting over it. Her large pale blue eyes showed depths of purple, and her expression was weighed with actual hate as she looked at this girl whom she had come to think of as being by her but not of her. This last disgusting episode proved only too conclusively from which side she had inherited her qualities. 'Will Dudley says he comes from the fifteen streets and the family are notorious,' she ended.

Mary faced her mother, and her tone was infuriatingly quiet when she said, 'Of course they are. Anyone within a three-miles radius of the fifteen streets knows that. If you didn't shut out every unpleasantness from your life you would have heard it before . . . One of the main things for which they are notorious is hunger. Dwell upon that the next time you're preparing for the Dudleys coming to dinner.'

Beatrice Llewellyn stood aghast – never before had Mary dared to address her so. 'They are poor because they drink and gamble. And you! You are a slut! You were out with that man until three o'clock in the morning. Do you think it won't be all round Jarrow and Shields by now?'

'I hope so.'

Mary's stillness seemed to lift the tension to breaking point. Her father cried, 'Here, lass! Here, that's enough!' and Beatrice Llewellyn perpetrated what was to her mind unforgivable . . . she screamed. 'You low creature!' The words seemed to emerge from the top of her head. 'You're utterly debased. I shall have Father O'Malley to you. Yes. Yes. I shall . . . Leave me alone!' – she tore her arm from her husband's soothing hand, and flung like a small tornado out of the room.

During their twenty-six years of married life, James Llewellyn had never seen his wife lose control; this was the first show of sincere passion he had witnessed, and it left him, not only shaken, but worried. Usually she tried gentle tears and studied silences, alternated with the persistent reiteration of her point. But for Beatrice to lose her dignity meant this affair had indeed struck home.

'You've done it this time.' He came to the fireplace and knocked out his pipe against the bars. 'You know, lass, it was a bit of a shock.'

'To you too?' Mary asked sharply.

'Aye . . . yes. It's no good saying one thing and thinking another. But when Will Dudley got on about seeing you with one of the Big O'Briens I could have punched him in the face. Although he put it very nicely, I could tell it had afforded them a good topic of conversation all the week, and that was why Florence Dudley was so anxious for us to drop in this morning. When your mother came down-stairs with her I thought she'd collapse . . . How long has it been going on, lass?'

'It hasn't been going on, as you call it; that was the only time.'

'Oh . . . Well' – there was a measure of relief in her father's voice – 'and are you . . . Well, is it finished?'

'I don't know.'

'You don't know! What do you mean, lass?'

'I mean that if it rests with me it won't be finished.' Mary turned towards him, nervously rubbing the palms of her hands together. 'I haven't seen him since, because he never asked me.'

James Llewellyn stared at his daughter. His lass, who was the best-looking lass for miles, and who could have her pick, was in love. Even had she not practically put it unashamedly into words, he could see it in her eyes. She was in love with this dock worker, John O'Brien; and not in the light-hearted way that lassies fell in love, but in an earnest, stub-born, painful way, a way that would leave a mark

482

on her, however things went. Well, he wasn't going to stand by and see her make a hash of her life, and say nothing. This was one time her mother was right. 'Now see here' — he planted his feet firmly apart and pointed his finger at her — 'you know which side I've always been on, don't you? You know that life would have been much easier for me if I'd taken your mother's part all along.'

As his fingers wagged at her, Mary thought: he's nearly as big as John, and he has the same clumsy movements, a sort of endearing gaucheness. All the money in the world won't polish him. Anyway, he was once a dock worker himself, so why can't he understand about this?

'But I want you to understand, lass,' James Llewellyn went on, 'that I'm with your mother in this.'

'You'd rather see me married to Gilbert then?'

'I don't want you to marry anyone you don't fancy ... But yes' — he thrust out his head — 'yes, I'd rather see you married to Gilbert than carrying on with this business. At least you wouldn't starve ... Oh, Mary' — his large leathery face crumpled — 'stop while there's time. You don't know what you're running yourself into. Lass, I hate to say it, but I've seen those O'Briens rolling from one side of the arches to the other. I even remember the mother, years ago, a little body, standing outside the bars with the bairns clinging round her, trying to get a few shillings out of her

483

man before he blued the lot. I tell you, lass, they're noted.'

'He doesn't drink.'

'That's what he says.'

'He doesn't, Father.' There was a fierce ring in her voice. 'And he's not just a docker either; he's been made a gaffer.'

'What! Did he tell you that? How old is he?'

'Twenty-two.' Her head was thrust up in defiance, daring him to say, 'So he's younger than you.'

But what he said was, 'He's a damned liar! There's no fellow could be made a gaffer at twenty-two. Thirty-two would be more like it. He's stuffing you, lass. Can't you see?' He was angry for her.

'No, he's not. Anyway, it should be easy for you to find out.'

'Yes. Quite easy. But even so, if he is a gaffer, what's that?'

Mary did not reply but stood looking at him, her eyes wide and sad, for she too, was asking herself the same question . . . He was worth something better than that.

To James Llewellyn, she looked at this moment pathetic, and he could never remember his joyous, laughter-loving daughter looking this way. Taking her by the hand, he said, 'Hinny' – using the endearing word that was banned in the house because of its commonness – 'I only want your happiness. What do you think I've worked for all these years? To leave you comfortable. Look, my dear, tell me you'll drop this.'

The tears gathering in her eyes obscured her vision. Why, oh why, did they think money could buy off or replace a feeling that was made of intangible stuff? Money and love were on two different planes . . . Yet were they so divided? Love needed money for its existence. Without it, more often than not it died, as the body, wherein it was housed, fought and struggled for life. Yet if the chance were given her, would she risk the survival of this love that seemed to be eating her away? Oh yes, yes. The tears spilled on to her face. 'I can't. If he asks me out again, I'll go.'

She watched her father leave the room and close the door after him with painful slowness . . .

Mary was sitting in her own room, crouched over the fire, when the dinner bell rang. She made no move to carry out its summons. Nor, as the time went on, did anyone come to enquire why. Never before had she felt so unhappy, and she couldn't see the unhappiness lifting; it stretched on and on into the future, for the only person capable of dispelling it was as class-conscious as her mother. She felt now that Christmas Eve had been merely a lapse of John's, and that during the quiet walk back from Jarrow he was already regretting it; he had left her with scarcely a word. Every dinner-time and teatime of this past week she had fought with herself not to stroll casually down through the arches, presumably on her way to Shields, in the hope of encountering him. But some hard core of pride said no . . . she wouldn't scheme to trap him into asking her out; if he wanted to see her he would find a way; and there was always the post.

What a New Year's Eve! She got up and wandered about the room. If only she could see him for a moment, run into him accidentally, as she had done last Saturday night . . . But wouldn't it have been better had they not met at all – not last Saturday, but in the first instance. He attracted her that first night he sat in this room, and she had been unable to get him out of her mind since.

The memory of that meeting brought back the niggling envy of Christine . . . Was that girl something to him? Was she the reason why he hadn't asked her to repeat the evening? She didn't know . . .

She went upstairs and put on her outdoor things, for she felt that were she to stay indoors any longer she would scream, as her mother had done this morning. Remembering her mother's voice and look, she realised that whether she pursued this business to its height or it merely fizzled out, the last supports of the barrier that had been erecting itself for years between them were hammered home today, and their combined lifetimes would not be long enough to break it down.

Standing on the bank at the edge of the field, John

486

looked down in amazement on the scene. He had witnessed nothing like it before. The field, which dipped into a shallow valley, had every appearance of a lake, and there was scarcely a yard of its surface which had not its moving figure. Very few had skates; the main sport seemed to be concentrated on the long single and double slides. On the double slides young men and girls crossed hands, skimming away with enviable balance towards the centre of the ice. Children had their slides nearer the edge, and were watched by spectators, who outnumbered the skaters. Some of the young lads were already getting the bonfire going. The air was filled with laughter and shouting, the smell of burning wood, and the thick, comforting smell of roasting potatoes. The faces of the crowd seemed alight with a newborn joy.

The feeling of mass gaiety puzzled John. It was this whiteness; it had gone to their heads and caused a madness. The drabness of life was lost under the spell of its gleaming sparkle, and the people seemed to be deluded into thinking this clean, white world would remain – their house roofs were white, their window sills, their doorsteps. The docks and the ships, too, lay buried under the clean illusion – even on the top of the highest mast there was a virgin white cap of snow, fast and secure and promising to remain for ever. There would be no tomorrow, or the next day, when the gutters would be choked with brown slush, the roads become rivers, and the houses grey again, and they themselves grey and blue, feet wet, bodies shivering. It was cold now; but this was a dry cold, which quickened the blood, freed the perception and brought all the instincts to the surface, giving to each person an awareness of his existence, which demanded of the body that it be used, now, at this very time.

As he stood there John began to feel something of this mass joy. The whole scene, which seemed to have been dropped from another world, where only light laughter existed, bewildered him, and part of him realised that it was out of place in the realistic grimness of this area.

He watched Christine gliding gracefully in small circles near where Katie, Molly and David were sliding with other children. She looked little more than a child herself, a dark, elfin, slip of a child.

Christine caught sight of him, and waved and beckoned him on to the ice; but he shook his head and waved his hand in refusal. And after a while, she glided to where he stood on the bank.

'Isn't it wonderful! Come on . . . I'll pull you.'

'Not on your life,' he laughed.

He was relieved that there was no stiffness in her manner, for it must have been evident to her that he had avoided seeing her during this past week. She looked very fetching, standing below him with a red tam-o'-shanter on the back of her head, and for a fleeting second he felt a regret that it was not she who was filling his mind and body at this moment, for then things would have been plain sailing.

'A big thing like you afraid of the ice!' she called up to him, teasingly.

'You'd be more afraid if you got me on there and I fell on you.'

'I'll risk it. Come on. Come on, John' – the pleading was in her eyes and voice.

He shook his head: 'I've a number of other ways of making a fool of myself besides that.'

Christine saw that it was no use trying to coax him; nevertheless, she stood for a time gazing up at him. Then, without further words, she turned and skimmed away again.

John continued to watch her and the children, but between times his eyes would search the field. Although the light was fading he could still see the further bank, and he thought it would have to be very dark to prevent him from picking her out from the crowd. He noticed Katie leave the long line of sliders and walk quickly towards him.

'What's the matter?' he asked. 'Are you tired, or after a hot tatie?'

'Our Dominic's along there, John. He's watching Christine.'

John remained silent, and did not turn to the spot Katie indicated but looked to where Christine was still whirling unconcerned. 'Is he all right?' he asked; which meant, was he sober.

'Yes, he looks it . . . and . . . and he's got a collar and tie on too.' Katie's eyes fell to John's collar and tie, then to his new coat; and she added, with awe in her voice, 'He's got a new coat an' all, John.' Her eyes were round in amazement – the advent of any new clothes in the house was something to dwell upon, for in most cases their approach was awaited for weeks. As late as last night Dominic had no new clothes, yet here he was, all dressed up.

John's mouth moved into a twisted grin. Dominic wasn't to be outdone then. The buying of new clothes would be all to the good if it kept him off the drink; but John knew only too well that someone would have to whistle for the money for the coat. He glanced casually now in Dominic's direction. Yes, there he was, practically head and shoulders above the crowd, and even from this distance and the little John could see of him, the difference in his appearance was noticeable.

Momentarily John's attitude towards his brother softened, and he wondered if Dominic's feeling for Christine was anything like his own for Mary. But his wondering was definitely only momentary . . . He would have gone about it in a different way if it was . . . and he still paid visits to 'Lady Pansy'. Moreover, his love for Christine, if it could be called such, had instilled her with nothing but fear.

He bent down to Katie: 'Don't forget what I told you about keeping with Christine.'

'No, John, I won't.'

'No matter what he says on the way home, don't you leave her, mind.'

'No, John.'

'Go on then, on your slide; I'll be here for some time yet.'

Groups of lads and lassies on the banks had started singing. 'Keep your feet still, Geordie, hinny' vied with 'Cushy Butterfield', and 'Bleydon Races' with 'Auld Lang Syne'. But now the careless mad pleasure of the scene was dispelled for John, for Dominic was there. His presence acted like a pressure forcing out the ease from his body and the quietness from his mind, and replacing it with antipathy, which was the only true bond between them.

As the daylight of the last day of the year faded, the twilight seemed to urge on the gaiety. The bonfire was well alight now, sending up showers of sparks through the grey dusk into the far-reaching blue beyond. John found that after looking towards the fire for a time the skaters on the ice appeared like dark, scribbled lines on a white canvas. He closed his eyes and pressed his eyeballs with his fingers. And when he opened them, there she was, standing not a yard from him.

When he was a child, his mother, if she had a

piece of toffee for him, would say, 'Shut your eyes and open your mouth and see what God will send you.' He had shut his eyes, and look what God had sent him.

He took a slow step towards her – Dominic and all he stood for was gone, and the magic and madness of the scene was upon him fully now. No subterfuge need be used on a night like this; truth was easy, and desirable.

'I wondered if you would be here.'

At his words, her face, which had been set and strained, fell into a smile; not her usual, light-flashing smile, but one holding a tinge of sadness.

John did not detect the sadness . . . sadness and this girl were as apart as the earth and the sky. To his mind, she spelt radiance, to his body, magnetism; she was ecstasy and joy. But he had only plain words with which to speak: 'Have you ever seen anything to equal this around these parts?' He did not take his eyes from her face, but indicated the ice with a movement of his head.

'Never. It's like something you'd see in Switzerland.'

Her eyes, playing over his face, made him drunk with feeling; all the barriers between them were being swept away on a swift moving tide. The need was upon him to touch her, if only her hand.

'Have you been sliding?' he asked.

'I haven't any skates.'

'What about using our feet? It seems popular.'

'Here?' She pointed to the entwined throng below them.

'No. Let's go round to the other side; there are fewer people there, and if we fall there'll be less to laugh at us.'

Mary made an almost imperceptible motion with her head. The action was more pointed than words in its acquiescence.

They turned together. Then stopped. It was the red tam-o'-shanter that brought itself to John's notice. Without it, Christine, at that moment, would have been merely another face – even Katie was just part of the crowd.

Christine and Katie stood hand in hand below them, silent and staring.

'Why! Hallo, Katie.'

'Hallo, Miss Llewellyn.' Katie's fat, rosy cheeks were very like the proverbial apples as she smiled.

'Are you having a lovely time?'

'Yes, Miss Llewellyn.'

'And did you have a nice Christmas?'

'Oh yes, Miss Llewellyn. Oh, lovely! And thank you, Miss Llewellyn, for the presents and all the lovely fruit.'

Mary's eyes were forced from Katie's to the girl in the red hat. The girl was staring at her; her eyes, dark and enormous, seemed to glow with a purple gleam. Even in the dusk, their light was penetrating, and Mary felt it stripping her. It was an odd sensation.

It was almost as if the girl was looking into the very depths of her heart and finding there things of which even she herself was not aware.

When John said, 'This is Christine,' the girl, with a lightning movement, whirled Katie round and away, and in a moment they were lost in the moving figures and the dimness.

The situation had suddenly become awkward. Why had Christine dashed off like that? He knew fine well why! His neck became hot. Then a surge of relief swept over him . . . thank God he had never made up to her! He was free in that sense, anyway . . . free for Mary. Oh, the daring, the audacity, the madness of it!

He turned towards her again, and this time the sadness in her face was clear to him. She too then had seen how Christine felt. He must make it clear to her that there was nothing in it.

'What about the slide?' he said.

Without answering, she turned from him, and they threaded their way among the crowd.

'Christine's a nice girl,' he began lamely.

'Yes, she looks it.'

They were forced to step apart to make way for a group of running children, and when they came together again, he continued, 'I don't think she'll ever grow up though. She's . . . well, she's just like Katie.'

She looked at him and smiled, a small, understanding smile. He smiled back at her, and they walked on in silence.

The far bank was almost deserted, the crowds having been drawn to the light of the bonfire and the man with the brazier and the roasting potatoes. The ice, too, was not so smooth here, for tufts of grass broke the surface.

'Shall we chance it?' He held out his hand, and she took it and stepped from the bank on to the ice. 'Single or double?'

'Single I think, for a start . . . You go first, I haven't been on the ice for two years.'

'Two years! It must be at least eight since I was on a slide . . . Well, here goes.' He ran and started to slide; wobbled, steadied himself, and wobbled again; then, with a suddenness that found every bone in his body, he sat down on the ice with a heavy plop.

With a sureness that spoke of past schooling, she reached him as he was getting to his feet. He was laughing, and said, 'Good job you weren't behind me.' And when he felt her hands gently dusting his shoulders he prolonged his own banging of his clothes to shake off the loose snow.

'Shall we try again?' he asked.

'If you like,' she said; but there was little enthusiasm in her voice.

'Do you want to slide?' He was facing her now, their breaths were mingling and their eyes holding. The words were a question that did not mean what it asked, and she answered with a candour that seemed to be of the very essence of the day.

'No.'

He reached out and took her hand, and they walked carefully towards the bank again.

'Would you . . . would you like to go for a walk? Or what about Shields?'

'Not Shields. Let's go for a walk.'

They walked down the narrow lane and on to the main road without speaking. Being a country road it was unlit, and in spite of the snow covering it, it appeared black after the glare of the fire-lit field. The darkness gave him courage, and he unclasped her hand and drew her arm through his, entwining his fingers through hers and holding them close to his coat. They walked on in step, and as he felt her hip moving against his he became conscious of the stillness between them, a stillness that seemed to be waiting only for the right moment to burst into sound . . . sound that would bewitch and delight him, because it would be her voice telling him what he wanted, above all things, to know. But as they walked on, it seemed to him as if the silence would never be broken.

When, of one mind, they turned down a side lane and stopped and faced each other, he told himself that never before had any man felt for a woman as he felt for her. But now the moment had come he seemed paralysed, and even the potency of his feeling could not lift him over the barrier to her. It was she who opened the way, with such words that flung barriers, prejudices and classes into oblivion: 'Oh, John, if you don't tell me I won't be able to bear it.'

There was a second of wonder-filled time before his arms went about her, not gently, as he had imagined them so often doing, but savagely, crushing her into him until he could feel her racing heart pounding against him. He did not kiss her immediately. His lips travelled the whole surface of her face before they reached hers, but when they did, their bodies merged and rose, above the snow and ice, above their separate lives, away from this earth to some ethereal place where time is not. When, swaying together, their lips parted, it seemed to them both as if they had actually fallen into another era of time, so much did they know of each other.

'Mary.'

She did not answer but leaned upon him, moving her face against his.

'I love you.'

Her arms tightened about him.

'I'm mad . . . I shouldn't say that.'

'Oh beloved.'

Beloved . . . a woman had called him beloved . . . him! This beautiful woman, this girl, this . . .

'How is it you can care for a fellow like me? Mary! Oh, Mary!'

Her reply was smothered against him. And when he would have again begun deprecating himself her fingers covered his mouth. 'You're the finest person I know – there is no-one to come up to you.'

She cut short his protest: 'John, let nothing ever separate us, will you?' Her voice was earnest. 'Nothing, nor no-one. Promise. Never.'

The urgency in her voice stilled him – it was almost as if she was pleading with him. That she should be asking to let nothing separate them seemed fantastic.

Taking her hand gently from his lips he said, 'It's me should be putting that to you. What do you think will be said when this gets about? Will you be able to stand it?'

Her answer was the covering of his mouth by hers with such passion that all the longing, all the loneliness of his life, all that was drab and tawdry, vanished. Her love for him raised him to a new level of self-esteem.

'Oh, Mary, my love . . . my dear . . . do you know what you mean to me? Do you know what you stand for?' He was gentle now, holding her face between his large hands, peering at her, seeing each feature in his mind's eye: 'You're beautiful.'

'I couldn't be too beautiful for you.'

Her words were like notes of tender music, borne on the white wings of the snow. He shook his head slowly at the wonder of them. 'I don't know how you can love me . . . you who have everything. I'm ignorant, and I'm ashamed of it. Mary' – his voice was shy – 'will you teach me?'

'Oh, my dear, you don't need . . .'

He stopped her, 'Yes, I do need. And you know I do. I never want you to be ashamed of me.'

'John . . . John, don't.'

His humility brought the tears to her eyes, as he went on, 'And there's my folk. It isn't that I'm ashamed, only . . . well, I suppose you've heard of our family. There hasn't been much chance for any of us; my mother slaved all her days, and . . . and my father and brother . . .'

'Sh!' She leaned gently against him, stroking his cheek as a mother would soothe a child.

She murmured something, and he whispered in awe, 'What?'

And she repeated, 'It's a case of Ruth and Naomi.'

But still he did not understand, yet although the words held no meaning for him, her tone conveyed a deep humility, and he was filled with wonder.

CHAPTER NINE

NANCY

The home-made paper chains lay in a jumbled heap on one side of the table, the three bought ones lying neatly concertinaed by themselves together with the honeycomb ball. These would do for another year, Mary Ellen decided, if she could hide them somewhere. She had never before been so late in taking down the decorations; it was 5th January, and she was just escaping bad luck by taking them down today, the morrow would be too late. But it had been nice to leave them up till the last minute, for they carried on the feeling of this wonderful Christmas and New Year. By! — she stopped in her work to look out of the kitchen window to the roofs beyond, where the last of the snow was sliding in a grey mass into the gutter — she had never known such a time. The stuff they'd had to eat! And Shane being sober, even on New Year's Eve; and no rows in the house. There was Dominic's surliness, of course, but she was used to that and had not allowed it to spoil things. And anyway, he was out most of the time . . . all night, once.

This business of John's troubled her at times; but what could she do, for he said nothing. He was going about looking like a cat with nine tails. She hoped to God something would happen to make it last. But how could it – him and Miss Llewellyn! Where would it end? . . . Well, she wouldn't worry – everything else was going fine; the coal house was full of coal and the bairns were rightly set up with clothes, the last, thanks to them next door – the thought of thanks took shape before she could stop it – well, anyway, they had been good, no matter what they were. She'd wished time and again she could go and thank them, but she was unable to bring herself to do so. The fear of them still held her, and she couldn't face them, so she had sent her thanks by the bairns and John. The fear had strengthened in an odd way too during these past weeks, for Mick's ear had stopped running for the first time in two years, and Shane . . . Why was it, after all these years, Shane had eased off the drink and his twitching had lessened? Did he find himself lying on a platform above the bed with Peter Bracken's hands moving over him? My God! She shuddered. It was the first time she had admitted to herself the influence of Peter Bracken on her the night the child was born. She put her hand inside her blouse and felt for her rosary, which she had taken to wearing round her neck of late.

Staring out of the window, she said her beads: Hail, Mary, full of grace, the Lord is with thee. Blessed art thou amongst women, and blessed is the fruit of thy womb, Jesus . . . She had gone through two decades, when she saw the backyard door open and Hannah Kelly enter the yard.

Hastily, she fastened her blouse.

What did Hannah want so early in the morning? . . . There was something curious about her walk: she couldn't have had a drop already, surely. She watched Hannah fumble with the latch of the kitchen door, and when she came in and closed the door, and stood with her back to it, Mary Ellen exclaimed, 'Why, lass, you're bad! Come and sit down.'

Hannah shook her head and murmured, 'Oh, Mary Ellen!'

'What is it? Is it Joe?'

Hannah again shook her head. She tried to speak but the words refused to come, her mouth opening and shutting like that of a fish.

'What is it then? Nancy?'

Hannah's eyes drooped and her head fell on her chest.

'Tell me, lass. What is it?'

'Dear God, dear God,' Hannah said, and her voice sounded small and lost, and she looked like a bewildered child in spite of her long, bony frame. 'I may be wrong. Will you come over with me,

Mary Ellen, and see? I came the back way, for Bella Bradley's on the lookout.'

'Is Nancy ill?' Mary Ellen asked, taking her shawl from the back of the door.

Hannah made no reply but went out, and Mary Ellen followed closely after her . . .

Nancy was in bed, lying well down under the clothes, and Mary Ellen, as she entered the bedroom, could see only her eyes. They held an odd look, a mixture of wariness and cunning, an expression not usual to their dullness.

'Hallo, Nancy,' said Mary Ellen.

But Nancy did not reply with her usual normal address; she just stared from one to the other.

Hannah, stripping the clothes from her, said, 'Lift up your nightie!'

With her eyes still darting from one to the other of the two women, Nancy complied. The nightdress was short and tight, and she had to drag it over her hips.

Mary Ellen gazed at Nancy's stomach. She knew now what Hannah suspected, and she exclaimed to herself. 'Oh, Jesus, don't let it be.' Nevertheless, to her eyes there was nothing really to justify Hannah's suspicions, and she looked across the bed to Hannah: 'Lass, what makes you think . . ?' she said.

'She's past her time, and I've seen nothing; and I think that's what Mrs Fitzsimmons twigged. And her being sick and not working.' She spoke as if

Nancy wasn't there. 'Stand up!' she said harshly to her daughter.

Nancy lumbered out of the bed, still with her nightdress held above her stomach. And now Mary Ellen thought she could detect a small rise. But still she would not believe this thing possible; nobody in their right senses would dream of taking a lass like this.

'Look, lass' – she turned to Hannah – 'it may only be wind. Or perhaps a growth,' she said hopefully.

Hannah, her eyes dead in her large, round face, turned away and walked into the kitchen.

'Put your clothes on, hinny,' Mary Ellen said to Nancy; and the girl immediately pulled her night-dress over her head and began to dress.

In the kitchen, Hannah was sitting dejectedly at the table, and Mary Ellen said, 'Get her to the doctor's lass. Take her now. It may not be what you think, and it'll set your mind at rest . . . Anyway, it can't be that.'

Hannah, in dismay, turned and stared into the distances beyond the kitchen walls: 'It's that all right. I'll take her, but I know.'

'Have you asked her anything?'

'Yes, I asked her if a man had touched her, and she wouldn't answer. And that's a funny thing in itself, for she always says right away, "No, Ma, when men speak to me I run away." And then again, twice last week she disappeared. I had Annie out looking for her for three hours on New Year's night, and she found her round by St Bede's Church. She had come across the salt grass, but she wouldn't say where she'd been . . . Oh, Christ . . . Christ Jesus!' Hannah burst out. 'What's going to happen? Joe will kill her. And if he finds out who it is there'll be murder done. Oh, Mary Ellen, what am I going to do?'

'Here, steady yourself, lass. Come on, get up and put your coat on and take her now.' She pulled Hannah to her feet. 'You'll catch him if you go now.'

While Hannah was putting on her coat, Mary Ellen went into the bedroom where Nancy was still laboriously dressing: 'Hurry up, hinny, your ma's waiting.'

Mary Ellen found she couldn't look at the girl . . . If she were going to have a bairn and had kept quiet about the man, then there was some part in her that was sensible, Mary Ellen reasoned. Unless, of course, she was too afraid to say anything. But now that she came to look at her, the lass looked less afraid than she had ever done.

She bustled Nancy into the kitchen: 'There you are then, lass' – she was addressing herself to Hannah – 'get yourself off . . . And remember, whichever way it goes, don't worry. You can't help it; the blame can't be laid at your door, you've done your best.'

She watched them walking down the street, wide

apart, like strangers, Nancy humped and shuffling, Hannah as stiff as a ramrod; and a sadness settled on Mary Ellen, the beginning of a long, long sadness.

John hurried out of the docks . . . Friday night and the first week of the new year over, and six boats discharging at the same time. He had just come from the weigh beam after paying off half the men. It was a strange sensation standing at the weigh beam with his pockets full of money and handing each man his due, and feeling that although he was young enough to be a son to three parts of the men they liked him, and trusted him to give them a square deal. As he left the last arch and passed the bottom of Simonside Bank he glanced through the darkness to the curving incline, and the thought that within the next hour he would be hurrying up there brought a leaping and tingling to his blood. The nights of the past week had been like glimpses of paradise – was there anyone in the world as beautiful and as sweet as her? Where was there a woman of her standing who would take him as he was? He had no notions about himself. Eight years in the docks had not filed him down, but roughened him. The only saving grace, he told himself, was that he was aware of it and would do his best to remedy it. He would have to if he were ever to feel worthy of her, even to the smallest degree. Moreover, another thing he would have to

506

do was to find a better job. It was impossible for him to remain in the docks . . . even as a gaffer, for it would take more than a gaffer's wages to support her in the way to which she was used. Almost every night of the past week, after he had left her, his main thought had been that he must better himself; and he had worked it out that there was no chance for him in the North, nor yet in England . . . America . . . the Mecca of the Tyneside Irish loomed before him like a lodestar. If she would have him he would go there. Perhaps she would go with him right away . . . No; not for a moment would he consider that. When he had made enough money he would send for her. Not for one day of her life would she live differently because of him . . . And then there was his mother and Katie. If he went to America he'd be able to send them money too. For look at the wages you earned out there! And it wasn't all moonshine. The Hogans from High Jarrow were doing fine, he'd heard; the father and four lads all in regular work, and sending for the rest of them this year. And there was that young Stanley Tapp, who went out and had his lass follow him. So why shouldn't he, with his strength and fitness, make a go of it! There was no job he couldn't tackle. Yes, that's what he'd do. But he'd have to wait a while before he put it to her; he couldn't ask her anything yet; it was too soon. Had he been loving her for only a week? It seemed now as though it had been going on for years. And each time they met the knowledge grew stronger that she loved him with an intensity that almost matched his own. This coloured his life, and lifted him to the heights whereon he saw himself wrestling a mighty living out of the world and giving her, not only the things that she was used to, but such things to which even she had not aspired.

He was whistling as he walked up the backyard, but stopped before he entered the house; his mother wouldn't have whistling in the house, it was unlucky. She was standing by the table, and before her, on the mat, stood his father and Dominic with their bait tins still in their hands. Shane's lower lip was thrust out, and he was saying, 'The swine should be crucified!'

'What's up?' asked John, loosening his muffler.

'It's Nancy,' said Mary Ellen, looking down at her feet.

'Nancy? What's wrong with her?' John took off his coat and rolled up his sleeves before reaching for the kettle from the hob.

'She's going to have a bairn.'

John's hands stayed in mid-air. 'She's going to what!' His brows met over the exclamation.

'It's true. Hannah's had her to the doctor. She's nearly out of her mind.'

Turning slowly, John looked from his father to Dominic, and back to his mother again. Nancy Kelly going to have a bairn! It was utterly incredible. He thought of her face as it really was without the veil of his pity covering it . . . the loose, repulsive mouth, the beady eyes, and the pushed-in nose. How could any man touch her, unless he too 'wasn't all there'.

Mary Ellen was saying, 'And the funny thing is, she's gone . . . odder' – she couldn't say 'brazen' to the men – 'I can't keep her out of the house.'

Although Mary Ellen was filled with pity for Hannah and the girl, she had found the day trying beyond description, for when Nancy wasn't standing leaning against the stanchion of her own front door, staring across the street towards the house, she was knocking at either the back or the front door. Mary Ellen felt she could not say anything to Hannah as yet, for Hannah was distraught, not only with her daughter going to have a child, but at the change in her. It was as if now, with life moving within her, some part of Nancy had become activated into normality . . . a crude and shocking normality to the women, for she seemed proud of her achievement and was determined to show it to her world. Subconsciously through the years, she must have taken in, with perhaps a feeling of envy, the arrogance of the pregnant women standing at their doors, their arms folded across the bulks of moving life. And she may have laughed unknowingly at their jokes as they patted the tiny flutterings of their aprons, saying with raw wit the old, threadworn joke, 'Lie down, yer father's not workin'!'

Whatever had happened, she was now . . . brazened, and Mary Ellen's pity was turning to irritation.

Dominic sat down by the fire – he hadn't spoken – and Shane and John still stood regarding Mary Ellen.

'This'll send the little bantam clean off his head.' It was Shane who spoke, and he was referring to Joe.

As Mary Ellen was about to make some reply, the back door opened and Nancy sidled in.

'Look, Nancy!' Mary Ellen exclaimed sharply; 'get yourself away home.'

But Nancy, who never to Mary Ellen's knowledge had disobeyed a command in her life, simply ignored her. Instead, she came well into the kitchen and stood looking from one to the other of the men. They all stared at her, Dominic out of the corner of his eye. And when Nancy met his gaze, she flung herself round from him, showing him her back, like a child in the huff, and amidst silence, she walked towards John, and smiled her grotesque smile as she placed her hand on his sleeve.

'John.'

Tears almost came into John's eyes as he looked at her: God, but it was awful! Yet above his pity there arose a feeling of revulsion against her. Some subtle change in her was making itself felt – she was no longer the child.

She said again, 'John;' and he was about to say something to her when his head was jerked up by the sound of choking.

It was Dominic; he had risen from his chair, his body quivering with waves of shut-in laughter. Mary Ellen and Shane were staring at him. He lumbered past them and threw himself on to the couch, where he sat leaning back, facing them, his face working with glee.

Staring wide-eyed and questioningly at her son's contorted face, Mary Ellen was wondering what in the name of God had come over him.

Suddenly Dominic could control himself no longer, and his laughter filled the house. Bellow rolled on top of bellow. But as he rocked himself back and forth his eyes never left John's, and the implication was lost on none of them. He waved a helpless hand, encompassing Nancy and John. And John's voice rose above Dominic's laughter, almost deafening them, as he cried, 'You bloody swine!'

With one movement he flung Nancy aside and sprang for Dominic. At the same moment, Shane and Mary Ellen threw themselves on him. Dominic got up, his laughter gone now: 'Let him fight, the dirty bastard! Come on!' He tore off his coat and made for the back door.

John's rage sent Shane and Mary Ellen spinning away from him, and he was after Dominic; but as he crossed the step, Dominic's fist shot out and caught him full in the face: yet so little did it affect John in his rage, it could have been Katie's hand.

After the light of the kitchen, the backyard appeared black, and for a time they struck at each other blindly. But soon their fists met the other's body with quickening and sickening thuds.

'For God's sake, stop them!' Mary Ellen cried to Shane. She tried to push past him into the yard, but he barred her way, saying, 'Let them have it out.'

'No! No! He'll kill him. John'll kill him! For God's sake stop them!'

A small crowd was now gathering at the yard door, and the windows on the far side of the back lane were being thrown up – the cry had gone round, 'The O'Briens are at it.'

The one showing the least concern was Nancy; she stood against the kitchen table her arms folded on her stomach and a silly smile flicking her face.

The sight of her thus was too much for Mary Ellen. She darted back into the kitchen, and taking Nancy by the shoulders, pushed her through the front room and out into the street shouting, 'Go on! Go on, you young trollop, you! And don't darken these doors again!'

Back in the kitchen she tried once more to push past Shane, for blood was flowing freely now. It was running from John's mouth and from Dominic's eyebrow, and their shirts were wet with it.

Peggy Flaherty's voice came from the upstairs window, crying, 'Stop it! Stop it, you lads! Stop it, the pair of you. John, where's your sense gone? Do you want to break your mother's heart? Behave like a gentleman, can't you! Oh, if only Mr Flaherty was alive!'

Mary Ellen, through Shane's arm, could see the dark bulk of Peggy hanging half out of the window.

Peggy cried down to her: 'Mary Ellen, are you there? Will I throw some slops over them?'

Mary Ellen made no answer, for she was now staring at the lass from next door. Christine had come into the suffused light, paused for a moment near the battling figures, then walked right between them.

John's fist was travelling towards Dominic's body, and Mary Ellen closed her eyes tightly, for the girl's face, as she confronted John, was in line with it.

Only the sound of gasping breaths came to Mary Ellen. She opened her eyes slowly, and they were apart, with the girl standing untouched between them.

Christine lifted her hands and pushed John towards the kitchen door, where Mary Ellen pulled him over the threshold.

Then Christine turned to Dominic. He was leaning against the washhouse wall now, wiping his face with his shirt sleeve. He paused and looked at her, and said pointedly, 'This is one time I'm fighting in the right.'

'Fighting was never in the right.'

'No? Huh!' – he spat out some blood, then went on wiping his face – 'not even when your wonderful John gives Nancy Kelly a bairn?'

There was a rustle among the crowd about the yard door. The whispers linked, forming a wave; then broke again, as one person after another darted away into the blackness . . . John O'Brien had given Nancy Kelly a bairn!

When John at last arrived at their meeting place, Mary wasn't there, and his feelings became a mixture of sick disappointment and relief . . . relief because of the uncertainty of her reaction when she saw his face. She would, he knew, be full of sympathy, but would she think that he was indeed one of the 'Fighting O'Briens', fighting for fighting's sake? – he'd be unable to explain why he had fought. So he walked towards her house, keeping on the far side of the road, and when he came opposite the gate he stood well back in the shadow of a hedge, and waited, wondering what construction she had put on his non-appearance.

The house was lit up, and occasionally a shadow darkened the blinds, but the shadow could have belonged to anyone.

How long he stood there he did not know, but

a clock somewhere in the distance, struck the hour, and he guessed it was nine o'clock. And as he was making up his mind to move away, the front door opened, and she was there, silhouetted against the light. But not alone; a man was with her, and from his thinness, John knew him to be Culbert.

John's nerves tensed as he watched them standing talking, and his teeth grated when he saw Culbert's hand take hers. But she remained still and Culbert moved away, and the door was closed.

After standing for a while longer, John walked slowly away. He was cold, and his eye was paining, and the whole of his face was stiff and sore. Now the import of Dominic's wild laughter rose to the fore of his mind again; and with it came a paralysing sense of fear. Fear was the least of John's emotions – he could not remember ever having known real fear; he had been scared, but being scared had no connection with this weakening feeling of fear. What if it got around, what Dominic had suggested? God! he couldn't stand it. Anyway, people wouldn't believe it. Him take Nancy Kelly! . . . But wouldn't they? The lot around the fifteen streets would accuse Jesus Christ himself of it, if they were in the mood to do so. At times, it would appear they were utterly devoid of reason or sense, the rumours they believed and passed on.

As he neared the corner of Fadden Street, the huddled darker blur standing out against the wall told him the men were there. It was usual for them to gather at the corner and crack, and it was their voices which generally proclaimed them. But tonight they were quiet. And as he passed them he knew a mounting of his fear, which almost reached the point of terror when he realised the rumour was already let loose.

A figure stepped from the group and walked for a few steps by his side, then stopped. John stopped too, and the two men peered at each other.

'I want a word with you,' said Joe Kelly.

John did not answer him, for the fear was drying his mouth. He waited, and Joe seemed to be waiting too.

Then Joe brought out thickly, 'What have you got to say?'

'What about?' John parried.

'Come off it, you know bloody fine!'

John made a desperate effort to bring reason and calmness to the fore: 'Look, Joe,' he appealed to the little man, whose face, even through the darkness, conveyed its trouble to him, 'do you, for a moment, think I would do such a thing? For God's sake, man, have some sense! Nancy's always made a set for me because I've been kind to her . . . What do you think I am? I mean no offence, Joe, but I'm not that hard up for a woman.'

'Then why did you take her up the country?'

'Take her up the country? Me?'

'Aye, you! And give her money . . . You might be big, John O'Brien, but I'm going to kick the guts out of you!'

Before Joe could spring to carry out his intention, John's hands gripped his shoulders and pinned him against the wall, while he kept his body bent out of reach of Joe's legs.

'Listen here, Joe Kelly: if there's any guts to be kicked out, I can do a bit of it myself. But before we start that, let's get this straight. The whole thing's a pack of damned lies from beginning to end. You bring me the one that saw me up the country with Nancy; and let's get Nancy herself and ask her.'

'That's the ticket,' said a voice from the group of men; 'give him a fair crack o' the whip. I told you you were up the pole to believe it. Now, if it had been the other big sod . . .'

Another voice was added to that of the first: 'Aye, Joe . . . Ask your lass, and get Bella Flabbygob to face him and tell him herself.'

Joe's writhing body was stilled. 'All right then,' he growled. 'If you've got the face, come and clear yourself.'

John, walking swiftly and tensely by Joe's side, said, 'I don't need to have any face, I've done nothing that I'm ashamed of.'

Thrusting open his back door, Joe cried to the startled Hannah, 'Get her up!'

After one bewildered glance towards John, Hannah went into the bedroom, and in a few minutes returned, pushing Nancy, half awake, before her.

Nancy had a coat about her shoulders, and her long, thick legs stuck out, like mottled props, below her short nightgown. Her feet were bare and not very clean, and the whole picture of her was revolting to John ... That anyone should imagine he could touch a thing like this! The thought made him angry, and momentarily banished his fear. He confronted Nancy.

'Look, Nancy. Have I ever taken you up the country?'

Still only half awake, she blinked at him.

'Have I?' he persisted.

'No, John.'

John cast a quick glance at Joe.

'Now,' he went on, 'have I ever given you money?'

She blinked again. She was a child once more; her new-found self was lost in bewilderment and sleep. 'Yes,' she answered simply.

Joe scraped his feet on the floor as John said, 'Listen carefully now. When did I give you the money?'

She thought a while, then said, 'Up Simonside.'

They all stood silent. Simonside was the country. It was the place for lovers and courting. Hannah drew in her breath, and Joe bit out, 'Want to know any more?'

'Yes. How much did I give you?' John bent towards Nancy.

'Threepence.'

'And what did I give it to you for?'

'For being a good girl.'

Joe snorted and John turned on him. 'I know the night I gave it to her. I met her crying under the arches. Annie had left her in the market and she hadn't her tram fare. She was afraid to stand outside the bar, and I put her on the tram, and' — the face of Bella Bradley peering at him came back to John — 'Bella Bradley was on that tram. It was her who put this into your head.'

'I've no use for that 'un,' Joe said, indicating Bella with a lift of his eyes towards the ceiling, 'but she said she saw you coming down the Simonside bank with her.'

'How the hell could she,' burst out John, 'if she was in the tram and it black dark!'

Joe had no answer to this. He turned from John to Nancy, his look indicating his detestation. Then he flung a question at her that made Hannah cry out and John wince.

Nancy stared back at her father, unmoved by the question itself. She was wide awake now, and she wriggled and flung her head to the side with a new defiance. As Joe, all restraint gone, went to hit her, she screamed and jumped aside like a grotesque animal.

Hannah caught her husband's arm, crying, 'Leave her be, man!'

Then Joe, Hannah and John were struck speechless, for Nancy, standing in the corner, her coat lying at her feet, her long neck thrust forward, was yelling at Joe: 'Leave me alone . . . see, you! You hit me if you dare, see! I'm gonna have a bairn, I am, an' be married . . . Yes, I am. I'm gonna be married when the bairn's born I am.' She tugged her tight nightgown back and forward around her hips, then turned her face towards John: 'Aren't I, John?'

John stood gazing at her; he was dumb and sick. Had she remained the half imbecile child he could have dealt with her, but this new Nancy, full of craft and cunning, filled him with horror. When she came boldly towards him, her hand outstretched, he yelled at her, 'Take your hands off me!' and like someone possessed, he rushed from the house and started to run, with Joe's voice bellowing after him, 'You won't get off with it like that!'

CHAPTER TEN

MARY LLEWELLYN

Her home had always appeared a place of warmth and comfort to Mary, but not up to now had she looked upon it as one of the tentacles of her mother's possessiveness. Mary knew that, in her gentle way, her mother clung like a leech and sucked at one's individuality; and one of her sucking tentacles was the creating of comfort . . . good food, warmth, even the seductive fire in one's bedroom.

After Mary's victory of claiming a room to herself the creature comforts were diminished for a time; if she wanted a fire in this room she had to light it. Yet after a while, Beatrice Llewellyn saw that by pandering to her daughter's ridiculous idea of privacy, a new tentacle could be affixed. But since New Year's Eve, much to Mary's discomfort, this tentacle had been released. No fire had been lit in the sitting-room for a fortnight, let alone in the bedroom, and Mary's enquiry of Phyllis had been answered by, 'The mistress says there are fires in the drawing-room and dining-room, Miss Mary.'

For the first week of the new year it had not irked her, for her evenings were spent with John; and the fireless room was merely something that showed up her mother's pettiness. But for six days now she had seen John only once, and that under such circumstances, she would rather not have seen him at all. Added to this, the striking cold of her fireless rooms seemed to have brought her up against life with a vengeance.

Last night, after having gone fruitlessly to their meeting place, she wrote John a letter . . . a letter bare of pride. She had thrown pride over from the first night he failed to keep their appointment, for each dinner-time since, she had taken a round-about way home, walking slowly through the arches, hoping against hope to meet him. Then today she saw him; but unfortunately only after she had met her mother and father almost at the dock gates. After her father's kindly greeting and her mother's fixed stare, they were walking on abreast, past the gates themselves, when John came out. His abrupt stopping brought them all to a halt; but before she even had time to speak, he was gone, across the road and into the Jarrow tram.

It was only by using all her control that she did not follow him. In the brief moment of meeting she could see something was wrong. He was in trouble, and he had been fighting. His eye was dis-coloured, and there was a scar across his lip. But it was the look in his eyes that shocked her. They were not the brown, kindly eyes of her John, they looked haunted . . . even frightened.

It was disastrous that her mother should see him like this. Mary knew, by her mother's tilted chin and stiff profile, that she recognised him and was showing her disgust. And her father's repeated short coughs spoke, too, of his embarrassment.

Mary stood now in her bedroom, recalling the incident. There was another hour and a half before she would know if her letter had broken this estrangement for which she could find no cause. She pulled her fur coat tighter about her as she sat down by the window and looked out into the black garden. If he did not come tonight what would she do? Her life seemed barren and futile without him, and he had toppled her standards overboard. Up to a few months ago she was sure she knew what she wanted from life: culture, travel, and of course a lovely home. It was true she had never loved Gilbert Culbert, but it was his profession, she thought, had weighed her feelings against him; for she could not see herself going out to work when married, and thirty-seven shillings a week wasn't going to enable her to do the things she had planned, although she knew if she were to make this match there would be considerable help forthcoming from her mother. Yet, compared with John, Culbert was a man of means. But here she was, willing to forgo everything she valued for this man, who would hardly be able to feed her, as her father had so strongly pointed out, apart from supporting her in the smallest comfort.

She was helpless before the power of her feeling. No clear thinking would touch it. Nor did she want it to be touched, for she realised she had found something given to few, a love strong enough to defy convention. And not in the ordinary way; but to defy convention by living under its nose. For that's what it would mean if she, Mary Llewellyn, the boat-builder's daughter, married John O'Brien, the docker.

'Miss Mary!'

Mary started. 'Yes?'

'Your mother says she wants . . . she would like to see you in the drawing-room.'

'Very well.'

Mary turned from Phyllis, whose bright eyes were greedy for more scandal. Mary guessed her own doings were the high spot of conversation in the kitchen, and knew that, because she was associating with one whom they considered to be below their class, she was unworthy of their respect. It showed covertly in their manner, and she upbraided herself for being hurt by it. For this, she told herself as she went downstairs, was nothing to what she would have to put up with – she must get used to scorn, and the scorn of the poor was scorn indeed.

Her mother was sitting in her wing chair to one

side of the large log fire, the heat of which met Mary as she entered the room. Beatrice Llewellyn looked smaller and younger and more fragile at this moment than ever before.

'You wanted me?' Mary halted in the centre of the room.

'Yes.' Beatrice Llewellyn paused, adjusted the lace cover on the arm of her chair, then went on, 'I would just like to ask you, Mary, to conform to the rules of this house if it is your intention to stay in it.'

Mary remained silent; it was like the ultimatum to a lodger.

'You know your meals are served in the dining-room! If you do not deign to have them there with us, then I'm afraid you'll have to eat out, for I'm not having them taken to your room.'

Anyone but Mary would have been deceived by her mother's tone into thinking that behind its even-ness lay forbearance and toleration, but to Mary its studied calmness, in itself, was a danger signal.

'Is that all you wanted me for?' she asked.

'No, it is not all I wanted you for.' Beatrice Llewellyn lifted her eyes from the contemplation of the lace cover and looked straight at her daughter. 'You astound me, Mary. I cannot begin to under-stand you . . .'

'No?' Mary raised her eyebrows slightly and waited.

'I can't think that one, even with your liberal

tastes, can have sunk so low as to continue to associate with a man who is the father of an imbecile girl's child!'

The words glanced off the surface of Mary's mind. She was prepared to hear something against John, she hadn't thought her mother would speak otherwise, and at this moment she was feeling sick with cold and worry; so until, like a boomerang, their meaning rebounded back at her she just continued to return her mother's stare. There was a cause then for the six empty nights and his avoidance of her at dinner-time . . . there was a reason; someone was going to have a baby by him.

What! – her mind jumped clear of its numbness – her John who was clean and loving and kind, whose love, so full of desire, was yet restrained, whose hands, even in their loving, were not the probing, groping hands of Gilbert . . . her John going to father a what!

She repeated aloud, 'What! What did you say?'

'You heard what I said.'

'And you expect me to believe you?'

'No' – her mother's voice took on a note of resignation – 'No, all Tyneside could believe it, but not you. You are so obsessed by that . . . that man, that individual with the brutalised, battered face, whose licentiousness drives him to take a poor imbecile . . .'

'Be quiet! How dare you!'

526

'Don't speak to me like that, Mary!'

'I will! You sit there taking a man's character away ... damning him ... you, who know nothing ... !'

'I take his character away! Can a man have any character who would touch that dreadful Kelly girl?'

'Kelly. You mean Nancy Kelly?'

'Yes, I mean Nancy Kelly.'

'You're mad! No man would ... would go with that girl.'

'She's going to have a child, and you don't for a moment imagine it's an immaculate conception, do you?' Her mother was being unconsciously funny; if only the implications for John were not so terrible Mary would have laughed.

There was scorn in her mother's smile and maliciousness in her voice when she said, 'His exalted position of being a gaffer is in jeopardy too, I understand. For even certain dock men have standards of morals.'

The desire of her mother to hurt her was so palpably evident that Mary was stung to reply, 'Yes, for your sake, I should hope so, seeing that my father worked in the docks until he was twenty. You seem to forget that, don't you. I, in my way, am doing exactly what you did ... taking up with a dock worker.'

Beatrice Llewellyn rose swiftly from her chair – she was no longer calm; Mary had touched a vulnerable spot, and she hated to be reminded that her prosperous husband had ever been other than what he was now. 'There's a coarseness in you, Mary, that disgusts me,' she said sibilantly. 'Your father was never a dock worker; he was apprenticed to a trade, as you well know.'

'What difference does it make?' Mary found she wanted to argue, to keep talking, so that she would not have to think.

But her mother ended the interview by leaving the room. She walked past Mary, her face tight and her blue eyes flashing with vexation, causing the air seemingly to vibrate with her displeasure. Mary did not move — she stood nervously tapping her lips with her fingers . . . Nancy Kelly was going to have a child . . . that dreadful-looking girl who was no more than a child herself. And they were saying John was responsible. So that was why he looked as he did. And that, too, was why he had been fighting. How had he come to be accused of such a thing?

The old saying: There's no smoke without fire, came to her. But she refuted it with her mind and body; and she swung round and rushed upstairs. Yet the thought persisted; why had he been named?

Mary reached their meeting place half an hour before the appointed time. In the darkness of the lane she waited, each moment dragging itself out into seeming hours, filled with dread and anxiety.

Twice she heard footsteps on the main road, but they didn't turn into the lane.

When at last she heard the heavy tread of feet coming towards her, she pressed back into the hedge, fearing lest it was not him. But as the dark bulk drew to a halt, she whispered softly, 'John.'

No answer came to her, and she moved slowly forward, and again she said, 'John.'

In the centre of the lane, he stood out against the starlit night, and she could feel the tense unhappiness holding him down. She reached out her hands and again spoke his name. This time he answered her. His arms went about her, and she was lifted into his embrace and held tightly against him in an unhappy silence. He did not kiss her, but bent his head and buried it against her neck; and his mental anguish engulfed her.

'What is it, my dear?' She purposely asked the question, for she felt he must tell her himself, and in the telling perhaps the strain would ease.

But he said nothing. And so they stood, wrapped close in an embrace that was full of questioning and stress. Then, as if his words had journeyed through many doors before finding a way out and were now tremulous in their release, he asked, 'Mary . . . would you marry me if I had enough money?'

The proposal was so unexpected – it was the last thing she had thought of hearing at this moment. She had imagined he would give some reason for their separation, if not speak of this dreadful other thing. For perhaps a second she remained still. Then she gently took his head between her hands and raised it. His face was indistinguishable in the darkness, but so well did she know each feature that his expression seemed at this moment to be outlined in light.

'Oh, my dear, I'd marry you now, just as you are.'

The question of Nancy Kelly flashed like a falling star across her mind, only to disappear into nothingness; its dreadful import could not possibly touch this man.

'No, no. Never that.' John's arms fell from her, but she held his face tightly, saying, 'Why not, my darling? Why not?'

'Because' – his head moved restlessly between her hands – 'I'll never take you while I'm in the docks.'

'But, my dear . . .'

'It's no use.'

He gently released his face from her hands, and held them tightly: 'I couldn't do it . . . Mary, I'm going away. Will you wait for me?'

'Where are you going?'

'America.'

'America! But John! Oh, my dear' – she pulled him towards her – 'I can't let you go . . . not all that way, not without me . . . John, take me with you. Let's start together' – she was pleading as if for her very life – 'if we are together nothing matters.' She had

530

her arms about him now, and he stood still within their circle, steeling himself against her offer, which for the moment had lifted him out of the terrifying depths of despair and revulsion to life that had almost overwhelmed him during these past few days, and which during that one brief moment had erased the picture of Nancy Kelly from his mind, so that he could no longer see her waiting for him at the corner of the street, or watching the house from her door or front window. His whole life had been coloured darkly by her. He would see her face reflected in the expression of the dock men's covert glances and in the too friendly overtures of a section of the men, who wanted him to know they didn't believe the rumour. The house that, during the holidays took on a semblance of happiness, was now a place of dread, and his mother seemed to have become bent under the load of it. Time and again he had found her watching Nancy from behind the curtains as she, in her turn, watched the house . . . What would his mother do when he was gone?

He jerked his head as if to throw off this additional worry, and answered Mary, rejecting her offer, as he knew he must, but crying out internally at the necessity that drove him to it: 'No, it wouldn't work. I've got to go there and get a start, and make enough money to set up.'

The term set up and all that it implied lifted him back to a week ago, when there was no fear in his life, only the ecstatic feeling of loving her. He pulled her to him blindly and kissed her, and so was lost for a time, until she murmured, 'John . . . listen to me. Now don't get wild at what I'm going to say. But I've got a little money . . . only a little' – she felt his withdrawal and clung on to him – 'Listen, darling, don't be foolish. It isn't much, for I've never bothered to save. It's what my grandfather left me. There's two hundred pounds. We could . . .'

'Mary . . . do you love me enough to wait a year, perhaps two?'

It was as if she had never made her offer. She answered, 'Yes . . . for as long as you wish.'

'That's all right then.'

He kissed her again. Then said, 'I've been making enquiries; I'm going as soon as I can. I went up to see some people called Hogan in Jarrow last night. They've told me what to do.'

'Oh, John' – the huskiness of her voice was deepened by the catch of tears – 'why . . . why all this rush?' And as she asked the question, Nancy Kelly came back into her mind. It was because of this he was going more than anything else. He was running away.

'John, what is it? What's worrying you? Tell me.'

He remained quiet, and she felt the stiffening of his body again. Then he put her thoughts into his own words: 'I'm running away . . . I've been accused of something, and I can't face it . . . Mary' – the muscles of his arms hardened against her soft flesh — 'if you heard something bad about me would you believe it? I can't prove to you that I'm innocent, I can only tell you I am . . . It's about . . . I'm . . . ' He stopped and a shiver passed through his body. He could not bring himself to say, 'I'm accused of giving Nancy Kelly a bairn,' nor could he say, 'I'm as innocent as Christ himself, for I've never had a woman; nor will have until I have you, be it in two years or twenty.'

The cold dark bleakness of the night pressed down on them. They stood slightly apart, and Mary waited for him to go on and voice his misery. But he remained silent. The silence seemed to fill the lane and to widen the distance between them. At last she could bear it no longer, for now she was with him she knew without doubt that he was incapable of committing that of which he was accused, and she cried out, 'You would never do anything bad. Never! Oh, my dear, don't let this thing cause you to make hasty decisions. Don't let it drive you away. Stay and see it out.'

'You don't know what it is they are saying.'

'Yes, I do. I know all about it.'

The silence fell on them again, softly now, filled with reverence.

She knew all about it and she was here! He whispered, 'You know about Nancy Kelly?'

'Yes.'

The wonder of her love and faith coursed like a

533

mountain stream through him, sweeping before it the fear and dread that had been intensified by the thought of her revulsion towards him should the rumour ever reach her. Her name burst from him on a broken laugh that could scarcely be identified from a sob.

She was in his arms, crushed tightly against him, and he was pouring words over her: 'Nothing matters now. I can face anything. I'll make money. We'll start a new life together . . . Oh, Mary, my love, I'm as innocent of what they say as . . . as Katie is. I've always been sorry for the girl. I used to mind her when she was a bairn, and she would come to me when she was frightened . . . She's changed; she's different now. But somehow, I think she's still frightened, and that's why she's made a dead set for me. And it's made them think . . . But what does it matter now? Nothing matters, only you. We'll start life in a new land; and you'll teach me, as you were going to, and make a new man of me.'

She tightened her arms about him . . . She teach him! What could she teach him but the superficialities, whereas he could teach her all there was to know of life.

CHAPTER ELEVEN

ASK AND YE SHALL RECEIVE

The February storm had raged for three days, during which hail, snow and rain was driven against the houses with such force as to almost penetrate the walls. It succeeded through many windows, and some of the people found it as dangerous to stay indoors as to go out and risk the flying slates and toppling chimney pots. But today the storm was lashing itself out. The streets were dry and the sun shone fitfully through the racing clouds.

It shone now on Nancy standing in her doorway. It showed her up vividly to Mary Ellen as she watched from behind her curtains. For the past three days Mary Ellen had seen Nancy only dimly, and appearing more grotesque than ever through the two rain-streaked windows. But now, there she was, as vivid as the picture that was seared on Mary Ellen's mind.

The girl, Mary Ellen knew, was possessed of a devil. This was the only way to account for her laying the blame of the bairn on John without actually saying so, and for her turning on Hannah and standing up to Joe. Mary Ellen knew that she, too, had become possessed of a devil. It entered into her the night Dominic and John fought, and when John stayed out all night, wandering the streets, after Joe Kelly had followed him into the house, demanding to know what he was going to do about supporting Nancy. The devil had frightened Mary Ellen, for he urged her to do Nancy a physical injury, and she prayed constantly to be relieved of all temptation. But from the night her lad told her he was going to America, she prayed no more, and the devil took full possession of her. She watched Nancy at every available moment, and there were times when she actually lifted the sneck of the front door with the intention of making a dash at the girl and tearing her limb from limb.

Nancy stood now scratching her head. She was doing it systematically, working over first one section then another; and Mary Ellen wondered for the countless time how anyone in their right senses could imagine her lad touching that thing . . . But they not only imagined it, they voiced it. Since Bella Bradley had set the ball rolling, at least half the fifteen streets would swear to having seen John with Nancy Kelly in some questionable place.

She could have borne it all, Mary Ellen thought, if only it wasn't driving her lad away. What would she do without him? The day he left the house, it

536

would be as if she were laying him in his coffin, for she would never see him again. It was all right him saying he would send her money . . . he'd want all his money if he was going to marry that lass. And anyway, she didn't want money, she only wanted him. What would life be like when, cooking, washing and mending, she wasn't doing it for him?

She moved from the window and leaned against the wall, and pressed her nose tightly between finger and thumb, meanwhile taking great gulps of air — she mustn't start crying now, it was close on twelve o'clock, and John and Shane would be in soon, it being Saturday. Dominic was already in, sitting over the fire, picking his toes.

In spite of her efforts, tears started to flow. Unless Dominic got that job in Liverpool she'd be left with him and his beastly ways. John never sat over the fire, picking his toes . . . he washed his feet in the scullery. But not Dominic; he'd sit picking at the hard skin on the soles of his feet, or lifting the dirt from his toenails with his fingernails. There was nothing so ugly, Mary Ellen thought, as feet, and none so repulsive as Dominic's, big and broad and well-shaped as they were. She knew, with an overpowering certainty, that once John was gone and she was left to suffer Dominic, the devil would have his way. And there would be no door standing between her and Dominic, as there was between her and Nancy, acting as a deterrent to her uplifted hand. And the devil alone knew what she would have in her uplifted hand. Oh, if only her lad wasn't going to that America. Oh, God, if only something would happen to prevent him! She groaned and rocked her body . . . Ask and Ye Shall Receive. Yes, but there were so many things she had asked of God, and had she ever received them? Perhaps she hadn't asked properly. Or she may not have wanted them as she wanted this one thing. If there was only somewhere she could be alone and kneel down, she'd pray to Him and ask Him. But the minutes alone were few and far between, especially at the week-end . . . But she was alone now. She moved swiftly to the room door and closed it. Self-consciously she knelt down close by it so that she wouldn't be taken unawares if Dominic made to enter, and should anyone happen to glance in the window through the narrow aperture of the curtains it would look as if she were scrubbing.

Almighty God, she began, Almighty Lord of Heaven and earth, grant me this one prayer and I swear unto You that never until the day I die will I miss Mass. Almighty and powerful God, grant me this plea . . . She did not at once voice the plea, even mentally, but searched about in her mind for other words to denote power with which to adorn the name of God. But she could think only of Great and Almighty. She discarded the set prayers — she wanted something more powerful with which to contact Him. So she began again . . . Great and Almighty God, Ruler of our lives, You who can do all things, do this for me I beseech Thee . . . don't let my lad go to America. Make something happen to stop him. Only You can do this, Almighty God . . . only You.

Her joined hands were pressed tightly between her breasts and her chin above them quivered with emotion. As she rose trembling from her knees, Katie's voice called from the scullery, 'Ma! Ma, I want you.'

Mary Ellen smoothed down her hair and rubbed her face over with a corner of her apron before going into the kitchen. She knew Katie must have seen Dominic and would not pass him, fearing lest his fingers were pushed beneath her nose.

Katie was standing in the scullery, trying to tidy her windblown hair before replacing her hat.

'What is it, hinny?' Mary Ellen asked heavily.

Katie whispered, 'Sh!' and pointed towards the kitchen. She pulled the door to, before going on in hushed tones, 'I just wanted to tell you I'm going to the slipway with Christine.'

'The slipway?' said Mary Ellen. And Katie again cautioned her. 'Sh! Ma.'

'What are you going to do there?' asked Mary Ellen softly.

'The boat's there . . . Mr Bracken had it fetched from the quay this morning on a cart. It's all painted up. David did it all himself. Oh, it looks lovely, Ma.'

'It's too windy, hinny, you'll get blown off the wall.'

'I won't go on the wall, Ma. The boat won't be on the wall' — Katie chuckled at her mother's ignorance — 'it'll be in the water!'

After a pause during which Mary Ellen adjusted Katie's hat, she asked, 'Who'll be there?'

'Only Christine and David.'

'Not Mr Bracken?'

'No.'

'Then you'd better not go, hinny. There should be no messing around with boats unless a man's knocking about.'

'But Christine knows all about boats . . . she can row! But anyway, Ma, it's tied up, and Christine's not going out in it, she says it's too windy. She says, maybe the morrow if the wind goes down we'll have a sail . . . there's a sail in it too, Ma!' She looked up at her mother with a mischievous smile. 'We'll take you out for a sail, Ma . . . right to where the big ships are. And the boat'll rock, and you'll be sick.'

The picture of her mother being seasick tickled Katie, and she leaned against her, and put her arms round her mother's ample waist, and shook with laughter as she moved her from side to side, imitating the rocking of a boat.

'Stop it, hinny!' Mary Ellen felt far from laughter, but she smiled at this canny bairn of hers, and she had the desire to fondle her. She took off Katie's hat again and reached for the broken comb lying on the scullery window-sill, and began to comb the top of her plaits.

Katie made a protest, 'Ma, Christine's waiting!' But she still leaned against her mother, and the pressure of her arms tightened about her.

When Mary Ellen replaced the hat she patted Katie's cheek. Then, awkwardly, she stooped and kissed her. Katie's arms came up swiftly about her neck, and she returned the kiss with an ardour that seemed strange in one so young. Kissing was an uncommon ritual in the house, and Mary Ellen said, 'There, there. Now off you go.'

But although she told Katie to go, she still held on to her, buttoning her coat, lifting her plaits from off her shoulders, and yet again straightening her hat. When at last she closed the door after Katie, she stood for a time thinking of her, and the thoughts brought her a modicum of comfort . . . she'd always have Katie. For years and years yet she'd have Katie, and they'd cleave together even more so when John was gone . . . That was another thing . . . Katie had to be told that John was going. What would her reactions be, for John was to her as a god?

A new fear entered into Mary Ellen . . . Would it create an aim in Katie's life, and that aim to be to go to America to join John? She shook herself. This was going too far . . . this is what came of thinking . . . Let God's will be done.

She steeled herself to go into the kitchen and to the oven where a hot-pot was cooking, for Dominic would be still on with his poking — she knew he prolonged it merely to tantalise her. But when she entered the kitchen he wasn't there; and further to her surprise, he came out of the bedroom, pulling on his old mackintosh. He had changed his trousers and was wearing his good boots. And he passed her without a word and went out, slamming the door after him.

Where was he off to in such a hurry? Surely he couldn't have heard what Katie said. If he did hear, he was off now to corner the lass at the slipway. It was quiet there, and nobody to stop him . . . only Katie. Well, Katie was as good as any.

Dominic's chase of Christine had aroused little interest in Mary Ellen of late. Under other circumstances the fact that Peter Bracken had forbidden him the house would perhaps have aroused in her a feeling of shame that a son of hers should have acted in a way to merit such treatment. At times, she did wonder at Dominic's persistence, and wondered too what it was about the lass that made him half demented for her. These past few weeks he had been drinking more than he had done since the Brackens came to live next door; not getting blind drunk, but just enough to arouse his temper and make him more detestable still. He was close on that stage

542

now, having spent the best part of the morning in the bars.

Shane came in, and to her surprise spoke first.

'Lashing itself out,' he said gruffly.

It was some time before she answered, 'Yes, and about time too.' There was a change in Shane that bewildered her; he had almost dropped the drink, and he sat with her at nights instead of going to the corner. It began, she felt, when she was ill . . . or was it when John was made the gaffer? She knew that in his own way Shane was proud of that. And the change was more evident still since this trouble of John's. She felt dimly that he was trying to comfort her for what she was suffering on account of the lad, and dimly also, she felt a bigness in him for doing this, for it was John who had the affection that should have been his.

'Will you have it now or wait for John?' she asked, indicating the dinner.

'I'll wait.'

It was strange that she should ask him this and that he should comply. Not long ago he would have bellowed, 'Who the hell's boss, him or me?'

When John came in she did not glance towards him, for she knew how he would look – his face would be straight and lean; the flesh had dropped from the bones these past weeks; the brown of his eyes would be darker, and in their depths would be a look she could not bear to see.

Mary Ellen's heart lifted towards Shane when, seated at the table, he said to John. 'We got her out in time all right, didn't we?' He was referring to the unloading, and her emotion almost choked Mary Ellen as she realised that her husband was trying to get on a friendly footing with his son; for never before could she remember him speaking in such a way, not only acknowledging John as an equal, but as his superior . . . it was how a man spoke to his gaffer; it was also how a father tried to convey his faith in his son.

John looked hard at Shane, then said quietly, 'You did that.'

They ate on in silence, and Mary Ellen went into the scullery to try to suppress the choking in her throat. As she stood, her hands pressed tightly against her neck, Molly's voice came screaming from the back lane. 'Ma! Oh, Ma! . . . Ma!'

What could she do with that lass? Would she never grow up?

'Ma! Ma!' Molly's voice came nearer.

Was she mad, screaming like that! By, she'd box her lugs for her when she got her inside.

Molly's cries effectively suppressed Mary Ellen's emotion, and she pulled open the back door with an angry jerk . . . She'd give it to her; she'd swipe the hunger off her!

'Ma! Oh, Ma!' Molly tore up the backyard and flung herself on her mother, ignoring the upraised hand: 'Ma! it's Katie . . . Katie and Christine.'

She stopped and gasped for breath as Mary Ellen gripped her shoulders.

'What's happened?' Mary Ellen asked with strange quietness; then called over her shoulder, 'John!'

As John reached the door Molly was gasping out, 'They're in the boat; they haven't any oars . . . It's going round and round down the gut. It was our Dominic; he tried to get in the boat with Christine, and she pushed him back and Katie loosened the rope . . . I was behind the railings watching. Katie wouldn't let me go with her, but I sneaked down, and I saw our Dominic come. Oh, Ma! and David's screaming in the slipway.'

John was running down the yard with Shane on his heels, calling, 'Make straight for the slacks; don't go down the slipway, it'll be in the main gut by now.'

Mary Ellen, with Molly at her side, followed them, whispering as she ran, 'What is this now? What has come upon us now?'

On the main road, passers-by stopped and gaped at the two great men in shirt sleeves tearing along as if the devil was after them, the old man behind the young one, and the little woman and the lass behind the old man.

Someone called, 'What's up? Is it a fire?' But the running men took no heed, and one after another, the passers-by appealed to the woman and girl. And sometimes the girl answered, 'It's me sister ... she's in a boat an' being carried down the gut.'

Children tacked themselves on to Mary Ellen and Molly, and men turned in their tracks to run back down the road towards the slacks.

When John came to the open space of the slacks his heart almost stopped. Without looking towards the gut he knew the boat was there, for the bank was lined with people. At this end of the slacks was the double tram line, where one tramcar had to wait for the other to pass. They were both standing empty, and their drivers were calling to the people, 'We'll have to go'; but none of the passengers attempted to leave the bank.

As John ran down the pavement towards the middle of the slacks where the gangway of timbers led from the bank to the edge of the mud, he had to push his way through the people now pouring out from the streets known as the New Buildings that faced a part of the slacks. He thrust at them with his arms, knocking them aside and calling forth hot exclamations. Those standing on the gangway jumped clear of him, and he took the timbers four at a time. The noise from the bank died down and there was only the wind, on which was borne thin wails, and the squelch of the water between the timbers beneath his pounding feet. Automatically he paused at the cabin, which was mounted on a platform of lashed timbers in the centre of the great square, and grabbed up a long pole with a hook on its end that the timber man used for pulling the timbers together. Now the race was to reach the end of the timbers bordering the gut before the boat came abreast of him. He could see it was being held stationary at the moment; but by what he couldn't tell. If it was stuck on the other side of the gut on the great mud flat that extended to the river then it was almost a certainty that it would be sucked into this oozing morass.

Arrived at the end of the roped timbers, he had to take to the narrow planks that formed a precarious gangway to the gut. Here, he couldn't run, but had to pick his way over the green slimy wood. The pole impeded him still further; and once he slipped and the water swirled about his thighs before he could pull himself up again. He had managed to retain his grip on the pole; and as he regained his footing a great 'Oh!' came to him from the bank. The sight of the boat speeding towards him lent wings of sureness to his feet, and within a matter of seconds he reached the gut.

Clinging to the great post that was the last support of the foot timbers he shouted madly to the approaching boat, 'Grab the pole!' But the wind tore at his voice, carrying his words away from him and them.

The boat was now making swift circles; one second, he would see Katie's face over the gunwhale, her eyes staring in terror, the next he would be looking at the back of her head, her hat still on it. Christine was sitting in the middle of the boat, her arms stretched taut, her hands gripping the sides in a pitifully vain endeavour to steady the tiny craft. She had seen John, for each time she fronted him her eyes held his for the second before they were torn away again.

It was not the wind that was driving the boat down the gut so much as the tide which was in full ebb; the locked waters between the floats of timbers were rushing madly back into the gut to meet the water draining from the mud flat beyond. Added to this, the suction of the cross channel, bordering the sawmill on the far side of the slacks, made the main gut a frothing, boiling mass of water.

As the boat came abreast of him, John bellowed, to the very limit of his lungs, 'Catch the hook, Christine!'

Perhaps she heard him and was afraid to loosen her grip on the sides of the boat, or perhaps his voice became only part of the wind, for when he cast the crooked end of the pole towards the boat it fell close to it, and anyone on the alert could have grabbed it; but the fraction of time during which this could have happened was lost. The boat gave another mad turn and was away, past him. He saw Katie stand up. She seemed to stand perfectly straight and still, and he experienced the odd sensation that her face was floating to him . . . imagination! But it was not imagination when he heard her voice coming to him against the wind . . . 'John! Oh, John!'

The boat was now flung into the vortex of water where the channels of the gut crossed. It heaved and whirled. Then like a ball, held by some mighty hand, it became still, and John saw clearly the two figures, their arms wound tightly about each other, crouched together; the hand was lifted, and the boat like a ball, was thrown up and over.

As John raised his arms to dive, two hands clawed at him and grabbed his belt. He half turned, screaming at the man behind him, but in wrenching himself free he overbalanced and toppled into the water. When his head broke the surface Peter Bracken grabbed his hair, and Peter's agonised voice screamed at him, 'It's no use! It's no use! They've gone. Don't make another.'

Two more hands stretched out and, gripping John's braces, they hauled him on to the plank again, where he lay still with Peter Bracken bending over him. A great stillness was pressing down on him. It was the stillness of the dead of all time. In it there was no regret, no pondering, no desire, no recrimination, no feeling whatever; it was void, because it held no thought.

He looked towards the upturned boat; he watched Katie's hat, mounted on a crest of frothing bubbles, rise and fall, bobbing round and round the swirling boat, like the earth round the sun. Peter Bracken's tearing sobs came to him, and he did not wonder at them. Nor, when he turned towards him was he surprised to see a very old man. Time passed and the receding tide showed the shining mud about the planks on which they stood.

Men were walking cautiously along the planks now. First, Peter Bracken was helped back, and when the men said, 'Come, lad,' John allowed himself to be led back to the timbers, one going before him and one behind, steadying him as though he were a child.

The timbers were thick with men, soundless men. John walked alone now, and they made a path for him. Closing in again after him, they followed him to the bank, where the sobbing and wailing rose and fell like the waves of the wind.

Three people were standing apart at the foot of the bank, and when John stopped and looked at them, the stillness began to lift from him. The first impression to penetrate it was that his father had his tick back worse than ever. This was followed by the painful realization that his mother was a little old woman, and her not yet fifty, and that Molly would never be Katie. They looked at him, and the sobbing on the bank seemed hushed.

Then from the middle of a group of women, David's voice rose, crying, 'Christine! I want Christine!' and the stillness was lifted completely from John; and a name passed through his brain like a tearing flame . . . Dominic!

He threw up his head as if sniffing a scent, and

his eyes swept the crowded bank from one end to the other. But from where he was standing below it, it was impossible to seek out anyone from the broken front line of the crowd.

A path was miraculously cleared for him when, turning suddenly from the agonised stare of his parents, he rushed up the gangway. Across the main road was a rise of grassy ground bordering the New Buildings. He made straight for it. Now he was looking down on the congested road, and there in the far distance, on the very outskirts of the crowd, he saw Dominic's head. It was hatless, and the fitful sunshine was turning the hair to gold. Whether Dominic had seen him John did not know, but as he tore along the comparatively clear ground Dominic's head disappeared; and when John reached the spot, Dominic was gone.

To a woman of the fifteen streets, John said only one word, 'Dominic?' and she pointed to the disused workmen's hall: 'He went round by the back of there, lad.'

When he reached the back of the hall John caught sight of Dominic . . . he was running across the middle of the field used by the chemical works as a dumping ground for their foul-smelling residue. The field was a mass of small mounds, and Dominic was leaping like a kangaroo over them.

As John raced over the field the distance between them lessened appreciably, and when he came out on to the Cleveland Place road, there was Dominic, not twenty yards ahead, disappearing round the corner of the tram sheds.

They were both on the main road now, and the people struggling back to the fifteen streets called to John, 'Stop lad! . . .' 'Give up, lad! . . .' 'What's done's done . . . think of your mother.' And when men's arms went out and tried to hold him he brushed them off like flies.

As they neared the fifteen streets Dominic was lost in the dense crowd awaiting news from those who had been down to the slacks. But John knew that Dominic would make for the stackyard at the top of the streets; here, in the maze of stacked timber he would hope to escape. He was right; he saw Dominic mount the wall and disappear.

John did not jump the wall, but stood on its top – his desire was teaching him cunning. He could not tell which way Dominic had taken, and once on the ground it would be like searching for a needle in a haystack; but from up here he should see Dominic's head as he moved between the stacks.

It was some minutes before John detected it, for Dominic's hair was in tone with the seasoning wood. Dominic had paused to glance behind, and John was off the wall, running swiftly and noiselessly, not in Dominic's direction but to the right of him. Dominic was making for the railway line at the end of the yard and he'd get him there.

John reached the end of the stacks and waited, his eyes darting back and forth to the last three openings — it would be from one of these that Dominic would emerge. He came out of the middle one, running swiftly; and pulled up a few yards from John. His mouth was open and his jaw was moving from side to side. The brothers surveyed each other, John's eyes sending out streams of diabolical hate, while in Dominic's the hate was mixed with fear.

John did not say, 'You killed them . . . Katie and Christine, and now I'm going to kill you,' nor did Dominic say, 'It was an accident'; without any word they closed, and John, like a raving bull, smashed his fists into Dominic's face. From the start, Dominic was handicapped by his raincoat, but fear made him hit back desperately. It also made him aware that he could not stand up to the blows being levelled at him; so he used his knee. Bringing it up sharply, he rammed it into the lower part of John's stomach, and as John bent double Dominic ran back down the opening through which he had come, only to be brought to a stop by the cries of men coming through the jumbled stacks. Assuming that the men were after him, he decided to carry out his first intention of taking to the railway. But when he turned once more there was John, at the opening of the stacks.

Blindly, Dominic rushed at him, using his fists and his feet; but it was as if John had set up a guard of flaying hammers, and soon all Dominic could do was to protect his face with his crossed forearms. He was pinned against a stack, and long after he ceased to fight John's fists pounded him, and he seemed to be kept on his feet only by the succession of lifting blows At last, Dominic's knees gave way and he slid on to his side. John stood above him, gasping; then, using his foot, he pushed Dominic on to his back, and only then did he become aware of the crowd gathered about them.

Exclamations came from all sides. 'My God!' 'Leave him be, lad; he's had enough.' 'God Almighty, I think he's done for him!'

On hearing the last remark, John wiped the blood from his face with a sweep of his hand, and stared down on Dominic . . . Was he dead? No, he mustn't be dead . . . Not this way, this easy way. He was going to die in the gut. He would drag him there, to the spot where they went down, where Katie's straw hat went round and round. The tide would be low, so he'd throw him down the steep incline of mud. He would be conscious and would claw at the mud as it slowly sucked him in. But — he looked up from Dominic and stared glassily at the faces of the men — they would stop him. Yes, if he attempted to do it now. Well, he would beat them; he would take this thing home. He moved Dominic again with his foot . . . He wouldn't let him out of his sight, and in the night he'd get him to the gut. If he had to drag him every inch of the way he'd get him to the gut.

The exclamations came to him again, more shrill now, for the women had joined the men, after forcing open the stackyard gates.

'Oh, Jesus, have mercy on us! he's killed him. God Almighty, it'll be a hanging job!'

It'll be a hanging job! . . . The cry reached Mary Ellen, standing on the outskirts of the crowd, surrounded by a group of women, all with tear-stained faces, and all urging her, in one way or another, to return home . . . 'You can do no good, Mary Ellen.'

'You must think of yourself and Shane.'

'Yes. Shane's lying back there bad, the shock's been too much for him . . . Come on, lass.'

Mary Ellen stood quiet in the centre of them. She wasn't crying, there was no liquid left in her body to form tears. Her body was dry, it had been burnt up, and the flame was now going to her head . . . If these women didn't get out of her way, she'd scream. She must get to her lad. He had killed Dominic, so she must be with him. To her, this seemed to be the end of a long waiting – Katie was gone; Dominic was dead; and there was only John . . . He had done what he said he would do – John always meant what he said. Now there was nothing else to wait for.

Mary Ellen knew that the agony within her was screaming to be set free. The agony was wide and deep, reaching into the bowels of the earth. In an odd way, she felt herself one with the earth . . . the dirt, the mire, and the richness. The scream of agony

555

was tearing around in the dry emptiness of her body, and swiftly, in a spiral, it was mounting to her head. Once it was there, she would be free, for when it escaped from her lips she would feel no more . . . at least, not with any feeling she would recognize; once she screamed, she would be changed for all time, for madness would possess her.

As her mind ran to meet the scream, she heard it. It seemed to lift her and the women from the very ground. But it wasn't her scream; it was Nancy Kelly's. And it was mixed with laughter . . . the terrible laughter. The women covered their ears, but Mary Ellen stood listening. Then she thrust wildly at the bodies hemming her in, and forced her way through the men to the space where John stood, and Dominic lay with Nancy Kelly kneeling by him, pulling at his torn and bloodstained clothes, and crying, 'Dominic! Dominic! Don't be dead! I've kept me mouth shut, Dominic . . . I did what you told me.' She pulled at him, trying to shake life into him again. 'Dominic, you must marry me when the bairn's born . . . I've been a good girl, Dominic, I did what you told me.'

Nothing but her screeching voice could be heard; the crowd was as silent as the stacked piles of wood.

The blood pounded into John's head. Dominic, the father of the bairn! The swine! The god-damn, dirty swine! Reaching down, he grabbed Nancy and flung her to one side. Then he was on top of Dominic, crying out as he beat his fists into the inert, blood-covered face, 'You dirty swine! And you put the blame on . . .'

His words were lost as the men tore him aside. Fighting, they bore him to the ground, and so many held him that only his eyes were free to move.

As one of the men shouted to the others, 'Look slippy there! Get him away, can't yer!' John heaved in an effort to free himself . . . If they got Dominic away they'd hide him. Why didn't he finish him off when he had the chance! He writhed and struggled until the uselessness of his efforts was borne upon him, and he suddenly became still. Well, wherever they took Dominic he'd find him! Oh, Katie! Katie! – he closed his eyes to shut out the men's faces as sorrow overwhelmed him.

When the men released him and he got to his feet, he saw his mother. She was picking at a button of her blouse, her eyes, dead in her white face, staring at him.

When he said, 'I'll find him,' she remained silent; then she turned and walked slowly away, and he followed her; and the crowd closed in behind, like a gigantic funeral procession.

CHAPTER TWELVE

THE AFTERMATH

There was no door in the fifteen streets that was closed to John; for three days he had walked in and out of the houses, into bedrooms, some tidy in their bareness, some a mass of jumbled old clothing and mattresses, and some indescribable in their squalor. He saw nothing of the conditions, he looked only for a concealed form; under beds, in cupboards, in rooms where the sick were lying, and where weary hands would reach out in a vain effort to give him comfort. He spoke to no-one, and he trusted no-one; he knew that in this time of trouble the people of the fifteen streets were united in one huge family to protect him, as they thought, from himself. So he did not search systematically, but after searching the houses at the lower end, he would suddenly double back to the top or middle streets, and houses he had searched but a short time before would be gone over again. No harsh word met him; even if he stalked in on a family eating he would be greeted soothingly.

He had one assistant in his search: Peggy Flaherty. Her fat, wobbling body hugged by coats, she would accompany him at odd hours of the day, most of the time talking away at him: 'Never give up, John. We'll get him yet. By God! we will an' all . . . He needn't run off with the idea he can escape you, can he lad? And he'll not get out of these buildings.'

Often, in his darting from one place to another, he would leave her behind; but she would be guided to the house where he was. And again she would tag along after him, nodding knowingly to the groups of people gathered in the street. Only at night did she leave him alone for any length of time, for then he paraded the main road.

John knew that Dominic would be in no fit condition for days and that it was practically impossible for him, up to now, to have made his escape by the stackyard, for since the breakthrough, the gates were doubly locked, and there remained only the wall as a means of exit that way. So for two nights now he had watched from the main road. The night policeman, on his beat, would stop and talk to him, the darkness wiping away his officialdom: 'Is it worth it, lad? You know what will happen, don't you? You'll get time, if not the other. Anyway, how do you know he's not already gone? By what I hear, he's likely in hospital. If it hadn't been for your sister saying the little lass loosened the boat, we should have been on to him ourselves. And you can count yourself

559

lucky, you know, one of us wasn't on the scene when you got at him. So don't look for trouble, lad, and get yourself home to bed.'

No words had penetrated John's mind since those spoken by the men when they were holding him; and it might have been that he did not hear this advice, for he made no reply. It was as though his mind, so packed with the weight of his sorrow and hate, could take in nothing more. During the first two days he did not actively think of Katie and Christine, nor yet of Mary, whom he felt to be part of his sorrow for all time, for she, in some strange way, was a partner in the guilt he was laying on himself. Because he had allowed the madness of his love to possess him, he ignored the danger in which Christine stood, and did nothing to protect her beyond ordering Katie to act as a buffer to Dominic's advances.

On this, the third day of the search, when the strain was telling on him, in the leaden weight of his limbs and his unsteady walk, and in his burning eyes that would close whenever he stood still for a moment, his mind, strangely enough, was beginning to sort itself out; thoughts were separating and presenting themselves, as it were, before him. He was standing leaning against the wall on the waste ground at the top of one of the streets, where he had paused for a moment during his search; and his hand moved over the three days' growth on his face. His body felt dirty, his inside empty, and his head light. But the thoughts came, one after the other, isolated yet joined: I must stop sometime . . . if only they find them before they're carried out to sea; if I could see Katie once again it might not be so bad. Oh! Katie! Katie . . . My father's done for, he'll not work again. Why am I not with my mother, she needs me? But she understands I've got to find him. She wants me to find him; she hates him as much as I do . . . Why doesn't Peter Bracken look for him instead of yapping, 'Forgive us our trespasses'. Father O'Malley says Peter is the cause of all this, and if my mother and me had done as he commanded this would never have happened.

As if his thoughts had conjured up the priest, Father O'Malley, accompanied by Peggy Flahetry, appeared before him.

'Oh, there you are, lad,' Peggy said. 'And here he is himself, Father . . . Away with you now!' she added to the children who were following them.

Father O'Malley confronted John: 'Come into the house,' he ordered. 'I want to talk you.'

John blinked slowly and made no reply.

'Did you hear me?' demanded the priest.

And after a short silence, during which Father O'Malley waited, and the children sniffed, and a few women added themselves to the group at a respectful distance, the priest went on, 'This has got to stop! Who are you to take God's work into your own hands? He will seek vengeance without your help. He has already shown you what He thinks of you going against His Holy Will – I cannot repeat too often, that had you kept that man Bracken from your house this state of affairs would never have come about.'

'It's hopeless,' Peggy Flaherty broke in. 'Time and again I've told him to give up the search. Oh! it's no use at all.' She proceeded to rattle on, in spite of the priest's gimlet eyes demanding her silence and John's blurred and bewildered stare as slowly the fact forced its way into his mind that she, and she alone, had urged him in his search.

There were murmurs from the women: 'The priest's right. There's been no luck about the doors since that Bracken man came.'

'No! nor will there be!' Father O'Malley threw at them, effectually drowning the more considerate comment: 'Aye, but he's lost his lass too.'

'Come!' Father O'Malley commanded John.

John stood for a while longer . . . the priest and Peggy, and the women, were becoming blurred: he must rest and have something to eat if he intended going on. And so, in the eyes of the women and children, strength was added to the priest's power when John turned and obediently followed him . . .

In contrast to John's ceaseless moving Mary Ellen sat almost immobile in the kitchen. At odd times she would go to the front room and attend to Shane; but she cooked nothing, nor cleaned, and, like John, she did not speak. And if at times she stared at Molly, her face did not show any surprise or wonderment at the change in this daughter of hers; for Molly was 'running the house'. She had screwed her plaits into a tight little bun at the back of her head and she wore her mother's holland apron, rolled up at the band. Overnight, Molly threw off her prolonged childhood; she was not now a girl, but a little woman. And she was spurred on by the praise of the neighbours: 'That's it, hinny, you be your mother's right hand. You must take Katie's place now.' They talked as though Katie had been an elder sister.

Sometimes Molly would stand in the scullery and cry for Katie, while at the same time experiencing a feeling of relief that Katie was gone; for she would never have been needed had Katie still been here; and she was needed – they couldn't do without her. Why, she told herself, she was the only one in the house who hadn't lost her mind . . . except Mick; and he was no help, one way or the other. All he could do was to stand among awe-struck groups of lads, bragging that he knew where Dominic was hiding . . . He didn't! She tucked her apron more firmly about her as she thought that, of all the youngsters, she was the only one who really knew – Dominic was taken into a house at the top of the street when they carried him from the stackyard; but when John started to search they moved him. It was Peggy Flaherty's idea. They did it in the night and John hadn't found Dominic yet.

Thinking of John, Molly looked again at the screwed piece of paper in her palm ... After attending her father, the doctor had said, 'Look, my dear; take heed of what I'm going to say to you. Now do you think you can make your brother John some tea when he comes in and put these two tablets in without him seeing you? Be very careful of them; they are strong and will soon put him to sleep.'

She felt very proud it was she who was asked, for her mother was sitting there and he never asked her to do it. So there was a rising of excitement on Molly when she saw John and Father O'Malley coming up the backyard. She'd make the tea now, and offer a cup to the priest; and perhaps he would bless her and say she was a gift of God to her mother and them all at this time.

But the priest did not bless Molly, nor speak to Mary Ellen, but continued to talk to John, who was sitting with his elbows resting on the table and his hand covering his eyes.

Mary Ellen listened while she looked into the fire. Did he never tire? Would he never stop? Why did he persist that the Bracken man was accountable for all this, when it was she herself who had brought it about? Hadn't she prayed on her bended knees to God, and asked Him to make something happen to stop her lad from going to America? Well, He had made something happen ... John would never

564

go to America now. God was laughing out of the side of His mouth at her, she felt, and He was waiting for the climax between John and Dominic. The regret she felt in the stackyard when she knew that Dominic was not dead had soon changed to a dread that John would find him. By now, he must have been in every house in the place bar one, and if he were not half demented, that one would surely soon present itself to him. She cast her eyes towards the ceiling . . . How much longer would Dominic remain there, hidden amongst the old furniture, the crocodile, and the poss tubs? She felt like his jailer, sitting outside the prison door, protecting him from a vengeance that hunted him. Had the hunter been anyone but John she would have let him in to do his work.

She turned to look at the priest drinking his cup of tea, and she wondered what she would do if he should propose that they kneel down and say the Rosary, for she was feeling hostile towards a God who had done this to her . . . using her own prayers to bring her to grief! Her eyes moved slowly to John — he was drinking his tea at one go. Soon he would be asleep, if Molly had done what the doctor told her. How long would he sleep? Long enough to get the other one away? And when would he go back to work? There would be only him to work now, for it was doubtful whether Shane would do a hand's turn again . . . No. John would never now go to America.

She turned to the fire once more, and her old dominant self made an effort to oust the apathy . . . Get up and see to Shane! it ordered. And that lass is wasting the food trying to cook it. You can't expect neighbours to go on bringing stuff in . . . But the apathy lay heavily on her and she allowed it to settle about her again as a protection.

The priest's voice was going on and on, and she was listening again. He was saying, 'You've been godless for years, and then you wonder why tribulation like this comes upon you. Can't you see, man, you can't defy God and get away with it; the ignoring of His Holy Mass Sunday after Sunday brings its tribulation. Make up your mind to turn over a new leaf . . . Throw off all undesirable companions, and come to Mass.'

The priest's voice was falling to an almost sympathetic tone, it was quiet and even; and, as Mary Ellen listened, the wonder was born in her that he could be capable of such gentleness. As his voice became slower still, she turned to look at him. His eyes half closed, he was leaning across the table, for all the world like someone drunk, and he was emphasizing each laboured word with a wobbly shake of his finger.

Mary Ellen rose sharply to her feet, staring at the priest, her eyes wide and her mouth open. As Father O'Malley lifted his head and slowly comprehended her astonished look, he pulled himself upright . . . What in the name of God had come upon him! This great, great tiredness. He shook his head in an endeavour to throw it off. Holy Mother of mothers, had he caught something? . . . But what could he have caught? Where had he been today? . . . The Flannagans . . . and the child with the suspected sleeping sickness . . . In the name of God, it couldn't be! God wouldn't let his faithful servant suffer such a thing. But he had surely caught something — never before in his life had he felt so tired.

As Mary Ellen began to laugh, the priest rose slowly to his feet. These people! What were they? Ignorant hooligans, who could be driven to do the right thing only by fear . . . Oh, God, don't let this thing fall upon me! he appealed. By the use of my strong will I will bring these people to You . . . Only take this from me . . . that woman laughing! She was mad! . . . He must get home and to bed. He turned and staggered through the front room, with the terrified Molly behind him and Shane, half raised up in bed, following his erratic course in bewilderment and Mary Ellen's laughter becoming dimmer in his ears.

Mary Ellen had no power to stop the laughter; it swelled inside her, like the fire did a few days ago . . . or was it years? It shook every fibre of her body. She held one hand tightly against her stomach and a forearm across her wobbling breasts.

567

John was standing over her, his glazed eyes blinking, and saying, 'Stop it, Ma! Look; steady on.' He was holding her by the shoulders, and her wide-open mouth and grimacing face were doing more to bring back his mind to normality than all the reasoning in the world. It only wanted his mother to go mad to complete the whole thing. 'Look, be quiet!' His voice cracked hoarsely on the words.

'I . . . I can't, lad.' She moved her hands to her sides, where the pain of her laughter was tearing at her. 'The . . . the pills! she p-put them in the wrong . . . c-cup.'

John could not understand what her words were meant to imply. He shook her again: 'Ma! Ma! Stop it, I tell you!'

Shane's voice came weakly from the front room, calling, 'What is it? What is it out there? Why are you laughing? For God's sake!'

Slowly Mary Ellen's laughter subsided, and she gazed up into John's dirty, stubbly face, and for a second her own smoothed out into an expressionless mask before crumpling under the release of her tears; and her broken words, 'Oh, me bairn! me bairn! me bonnie bairn!' cut through John, and completed his awakening.

He put his arms about her, holding her tightly, and her emotion rocked its way through him, and the burning of his eyes became unbearable. Like the rush of water when the main dock gates were opened to admit a ship, the tears came to him too. Silently flowing, they fell on Mary Ellen's brow; and their raining, more than her own, restored her, and set her once again in her rightful place as pivot of the house. And so, as always, they balanced each other.

Mary Ellen's body still shaking and her tears still falling, she drew away from John, and taking his arm, saying, 'Come, lad,' she led him to the bedroom. When he sat on the bedside she lifted up his feet, and as she unloosened his boots he groaned and, turning his face into the pillow, sobbed, with the tearing, heart-rending sobs that only a man in sorrow can cry.

As Father Bailey hurried up Fadden Street he kept telling himself that this was not the time to be amused; tragedy had stalked this street, and was still doing so. But, nevertheless, only the darkness hid the twinkle in his eye and the quirk on his lips. The story the child Molly had brought to him was fantastic ... giving Father O'Malley the tea with the drug in! And him staggering out into the street to be confronted by Peter Bracken, of all people. And then to be taken into Bracken's house! Oh, it was the limit of limits. In the wildest stretches of imagination, Father Bailey could not see his pastor allowing himself to be even touched by the hand of Peter Bracken, apart from being led into his house.

When Peter Bracken opened his door, Father Bailey said, 'You sent for me?'

'I did,' said Peter. 'Will you come in?'

Nothing more was said until they reached the kitchen, and even then not immediately; for the sight of Father O'Malley stretched out on the mat, with his head on a pillow and a blanket covering him, was almost too much for Father Bailey. Father O'Malley looked less prepossessing in sleep than he did awake. He looked, Father Bailey thought whimsically, as though he might be dictating to the sender of dreams as to their type and quality.

Father Bailey suppressed his mirth and left till later the relish this situation would provide, particularly for those times when his superior would be most overbearing . . . Oh, the laughs he would get from this would last him a lifetime!

'How did it come about?' he asked Peter, without daring to raise his eyes from the floor in case this man who was also in sorrow, should detect his mirth.

'I happened to be coming up the street,' replied Peter, 'and found him slumped against the wall near my door. Molly was with him and she told me what she had done. There was no-one about at the time, but I knew that should anyone see him it would be said immediately that I'd put the evil eye on him.'

Without looking up, Father Bailey nodded.

'Or should he have been seen staggering about,' went on Peter, 'some people would have said . . . well, that he was drunk. People only need to see a shadow to create the substance.'

Father Bailey slowly brought his gaze up to this man . . . How many terrible substances had been created from shadows for him! And not a few by the priest at his feet. And yet he had endeavoured to save Father O'Malley from the stigma of drunkenness!

'You can get a cab and take him home,' Peter Bracken went on: 'Or you can leave him here till he wakes.'

Yes, he could get a cab, Father Bailey thought, and take him home. But then again, should he be seen being carried from the house, this man would be blamed for putting some 'fluence on him . . . No; he would leave him here. And please God, he'd be here to see him wake . . . he wouldn't miss that for a bucketful of sovereigns.

'Would it be putting you out,' he asked, 'if he stayed?'

'Not at all,' said Peter Bracken quietly.

'And myself too?' added Father Bailey. 'I have some things to attend to, but I'll come back later if I may . . . And I'd better look in on the doctor who issued those tablets.'

'There's something I'd better tell you,' said Peter . . . 'It was important that John should have taken those tablets' — he nodded down at the sleeping

571

priest – 'for tonight it is arranged that . . . that' – he couldn't bring himself to speak Dominic's name – 'the other one is to be got away.'

'You know where he is then?' said Father Bailey, with interest.

'Yes. But he can't remain there much longer. John will shortly regain his senses, and he will surely guess; for he's upstairs above him in the only house he hasn't searched.'

'Good God!'

'John is too good a man to suffer . . . for him. He must be got away!'

The priest nodded again, and asked, 'Where is he going?'

'I can't tell you that. I can only tell you he'll be put aboard a tramp steamer.'

'Will he be fit to work his passage?'

'Not for a time; but that has been arranged.'

Peter Bracken said no more, but Father Bailey knew that sick men weren't taken, even on tramp steamers, for nothing. And the man before him was the only one around these parts who could supply the money and arrange the whole thing. He shook his head . . . Here, indeed, was a good Samaritan; and under such circumstances as to make the act heroic. He looked at Peter's shrunken figure and at the face, which during the last three days had drooped into deep lines of age, and he said: 'I think you're a very brave and forgiving man.'

The old man turned away, his lips trembling: 'I am not brave; it is that I can bear my sorrow easier than the others, for my child is near me. Death to them' – he nodded towards the wall – 'even with their religion, is a severance that only death can join again. But to me there has been no parting, the main part of her is still with me.'

For the moment, the priest experienced a tinge of envy for this man's faith . . . Here was faith as it should be. Would any Catholic think like this? No, he thought regretfully. Christ Himself was in the blessed sacrament of the altar for them, but their faith was so limited that it could not reach over the boundary to Him . . . so there were few miracles. They prayed to God to come to them, instead of boldly going to Him.

'Can I help in any way?' he asked. 'Is there anything I can do?'

Peter turned to the priest again: 'You can, if you will. John wouldn't suspect you. You could get more tablets and see that he takes them. If the men don't get the other . . . this done tonight, there may not be another chance for days. And then it may be too late.'

Father Bailey looked steadily at Peter Bracken: 'Why are you taking all this trouble over someone who has done you such a terrible injury?'

Peter's eyes closed, and his face set in lines of pain. He had lost the mainspring of his life and hopes, for

573

Christine would have carried on his ideas. She had been brave; more so than him in some ways, for he was vulnerable to jibes — how many deaths had he died these past three days because of the attitude that had been taken towards Christine. It was as if his girl did not count . . . as if she too had not died the same death as the child, even the blame for the tragedy, in some subtle way, had been laid on her, while the perpetrator of it had even come in for a modicum of sympathy from a section of the people, and he himself was more hated and feared than before . . . and his heart was sore within him.

But he answered the priest calmly: 'Because I believe in the Great Plan of Life. I believe all that has happened had to happen. What I am doing I must do, for I feel also that it isn't in the Plan for John to commit a crime and suffer for it. There are other things for him, he has begun to think, and nothing can stop him evolving.'

As if expecting some deprecating remark, Peter's eyes held those of the priest for a moment before he went on: 'I believe he will eventually do something for the betterment of his people . . . I know he will, for Christine has told me; and she knows, for, you see, she loved him.'

Father Bailey's gaze was almost tender, as he looked at this old man, who, strangely enough, held views which were in exact keeping with some of his own; did he himself not always say that the path was all mapped out for each one of us from the day he was born, that the great Creator knew the shape of every pebble to be trodden by our feet. This man was a thinker, and was possessed of a spirit that wasn't un-Christlike. He preached that he was part of Christ in his understanding and in his power, and although the doctrine he taught was divided by insurmountable barriers from his own, nevertheless the essence was very much the same. And he must talk to him; for whether he knew it or not, at this moment his need was great. Father Bailey knew that to extend to Peter Bracken the hand of friendship would be a herculean task; the main stumbling block would be, not so much the difference of their religions or opinions, but the priest now lying on the mat between them; and not him alone, but others of his breed, who with a little learning packing the narrow channels of their minds, set up theories bred of their own enlarged egos and used them under the stamp of the Church . . . Well, this was one time he was going to make a stand. If this man and he could never see eye to eye, they would have gone far if each could respect the other's point of view . . . A flash of enlightening candour through the priest's mind told him that the trying would be his work alone, for this man in his humility was advanced far beyond him.

He put out his hand and touched Peter Bracken's sleeve: 'I'll fix up that lad next door; then perhaps we can have a talk.'

After Father Bailey had gone, Peter, his eyes bright and head raised, stood by the side of the sleeping priest. He spoke as if to someone near: 'You were right, my dear; your going had a purpose. Never could this have come about otherwise. Will you ask all the guides of tolerance to help this man here? I, too, will work on him, that he may become more like him just gone.'

While Peter Bracken was sitting at the head of Father O'Malley the priest jerked violently – it was as if his spirit was up in arms at this outrage. From time to time his lips and cheeks would puff out and emit sounds like 'Pooh! poo-pooh!'

Peter did not smile – it needed Father Bailey to appreciate the humour of the situation.

The tin alarm clock on the mantelpiece showed twelve-thirty. Father Bailey sat looking at it, and from time to time he wondered whether it had stopped. But as he stared, the hand would give a slight movement, and once again he would tell himself that these were the longest three hours he had spent in his life . . . and the oddest. Was there ever such a situation! Here he was, sitting in this kitchen, after midnight, with this toil-worn woman opposite, so still she might be dead; and three cups on the table, the largest holding the white powder already mixed with the milk. And there on the hob was the teapot, stewing its inside out. They would

576

likely all die from tannin poisoning if they were to drink the stuff. Well, pray God there would be no need. Less than half an hour now, and the men would be here and gone, and John could remain asleep or wake up just as he pleased, and no harm done . . . And for himself, he would go next door, where at least there was a comfortable chair to recline in while waiting for the grand awakening, as he termed it, of his superior . . . Was there ever such a situation! There next door was lying the man who was the sworn enemy of all spiritualists, and of Peter Bracken in particular and being tended gently by the man himself.

Father Bailey felt his eyes closing and he was thinking sleepily that it was many years since he enjoyed a conversation like the one this evening . . . a very enlightened man that. Of course, God help him, he was entirely wrong in many of his opinions, but there were some which tied up amazingly with those of the Church. Peter Bracken's idea, for instance, that the spirits, termed guides, and through whom the healing was done, were the good people who had gone on, whom he and all Catholics termed saints. Now that was an interesting point . . . He was awakened, startlingly, by a gasp from Mary Ellen.

They exchanged glances and looked towards the bedroom door; the bed was creaking heavily. There was a shuffling, a short silence, and John appeared at the open door.

It was only two days since Father Bailey last saw John, yet the change in him hurt the priest; he looked gaunt and twice his age.

But now was not the time, Father Bailey told himself, to waste on useless pity. Of all the times John could have chosen to wake up this was the worst; even if he drank the stuff this minute, as strong as it was, it was doubtful whether it would take effect before the arrival of the men.

John shook his head and ran his hand over his forehead. Then he looked dully but enquiringly at the priest.

And Father Bailey said promptly, 'Your father's not too good, John. Your mother called me in.'

John accepted this, and looked at his mother; then from her to the clock . . . twenty minutes to one! The pain of his existence flooded back to him . . . he had slept for hours! They would have got him away then. Well he had to sleep some time. But, oh God, why couldn't he have got him first, then this agony would have been appeased. Now it would go on for ever.

'Have this cup of tea, lad.' Mary Ellen was pouring the black tea into the cup with shaking hands.

John ran his hand round his face and shook his head: 'I'll have a wash first.'

'I could do with another, myself, Mrs O'Brien. Have a cup with me, John, it'll pull you together.'

The priest took the cup from Mary Ellen's hand and stirring it vigorously, passed it to John.

Without demur, John took it and drank a mouthful of the hot tea. He pursed his lips before replacing the cup on the table. Huh! the taste . . . his mouth was dry and thick!

Going to the hearth, he picked up the kettle. It was empty; and the occurrence was so unusual that he shook the kettle, then glanced at his mother. It seemed a symbol of the new life . . . nothing would ever be the same again.

Mary Ellen took the kettle from John's hand, whilst he went to the table and finished his tea. The priest sighed and sat down heavily, saying to John, 'Sit down, lad.'

Docilely, John sat down, as if his being knew nothing of hatred and the craving impulse to destroy.

Mary Ellen passed between him and the priest and placed the kettle on the fire. Then she too sat down, and the silence became heavy; until Father Bailey exclaimed, 'Well, Mrs O'Brien, I must soon be making my way home.' But he didn't move; and into the renewed silence came a soft padding. It bore no relation to footsteps. Mary Ellen and the priest exchanged quick glances, but John went on looking at the kettle, which had begun to hiss softly.

The padding which came from the wall at John's back now passed on to the ceiling. The priest turned his gaze from Mary Ellen and stared into the fire . . . Well, if they made no more noise than that, it would be all right — the old stockings round their boots were quite effective. Another two or three minutes, and it would be over.

The minutes passed, and John stood up and lifted the kettle from the fire, forcing back into himself the urge to be going. What was he idling here for, anyway? In another few minutes he'd be asleep again. And there was still the chance he might find him; for how did they know how long he would sleep. They might have been afraid to risk getting him away. This time he would stay at the bottom end of the streets; it was ten to one he was there, for his cronies were in that quarter.

'That water isn't hot,' Mary Ellen broke in, getting to her feet — in the scullery he would be standing under the staircase and the padding had started again.

'It'll do.'

As he made to pass her, he was brought to a halt by the sound of something falling on to the floor above. It could have been a chair or a box, or any piece of Peggy Flaherty's ménage. Perhaps John would have let it pass as just that had he not looked at his mother and from her to the priest. The apprehension in their exchanging glances was like a revelation to him . . . 'The bitch!' The words were forced out through his clenched teeth — at this moment he wasn't thinking of Dominic so much as Peggy Flaherty. It was as clear as daylight . . .

580

her trailing round with him to throw him off the scent of that swine! What a bloody fool he was! He almost threw the kettle on to the hearth; but when he turned to dash out of the back door he found the priest barring his way.

'Get by!' he said grimly, towering over the tubby figure of Father Bailey.

'Listen, John. I'm not going to get by . . . Now you listen to me!' — the priest stared up at John with as much aggressiveness as was in him to portray — 'you can do nothing . . . you're as helpless as a new-born babe. Get that into that big head of yours. You've just swallowed an excellent sleeping draught, one that would put a horse to sleep. And that's where you'll be in a very few minutes.'

John stepped back and glared at his mother. Mary Ellen, her hands clasped, her eyes dumbly pleading, said nothing. He remembered her laughter, earlier on, and her jumbled words about Molly and the pills, and the queer turn of the priest . . . Now Father Bailey sitting there waiting, with that tale about his father. Why, they'd all hoaxed him like a child! But he wasn't asleep yet. No, by God! not by a long chalk.

He swung up the bucket of water standing by the tin dish and bending, poured it over his head; then towelled himself vigorously. And before Mary Ellen and the priest were aware of his intention he was through the front room.

581

In the street, he ran as he had never run before, round the bottom corner and up the back lane. But when he reached the backyard he found only Mary Ellen and Peggy there. They were standing by the kitchen door, an epitome of the conspiracy against him and of its successful close.

In the moment of his pausing he was made aware of the effects of the drug, for he had the desire to push past them into the kitchen and to sit down. But the desire was swept away and he turned and ran again, for the main road now. However they tried to evade him, eventually they must make for the main road.

A cold drizzle was falling, and already his shirt was wet; but this would keep him awake. There was no-one in sight, as far as he could see, and he stood in the shadow of the wall, scanning the openings to the streets. There was a lamp at each corner, but so far did the streets seem to stretch away into the darkness that he realised he must keep on the move if he hoped to discern any movement from the lower streets.

His lids felt heavy and drooped slowly over his eyes. He stretched them and swore grimly to himself. They had only to play a waiting game . . . they were in there somewhere still, he was sure. How much longer could he fight against this increasing drowsiness?

He had to lean against the wall. Gradually his anger died in him, and all he wanted to do was to lie down . . . Blast them! He started to walk,

582

briskly as he thought, but soon stopped again and leaned against a lamp post. His head was throbbing to the rhythm of approaching horse's hooves. Soon the black shape of a cab rocketed towards him, and ahead of it, on the pavement, he made out the scurrying figure of Father Bailey.

Panting, the priest came alongside John and laid a hand on his arm. He murmured something, but John did not hear what it was. He was looking at the cab, which was now abreast of him . . . and there was Dominic's face! His eyes were turned towards the window. They were sockets of darkness in a white blur. Time seemed to stand suspended, giving the brothers the opportunity to exchange their last looks of hatred. Then something sprang from John and leaped upon the sneering face of his brother. But whatever it was it had no effect . . . the cab rolled on, the bandaged face disappeared. And John, like a child, allowed himself to be led gently away by the priest; he was thinking dimly that all his life there would be a want in him . . . something uncompleted.

CHAPTER THIRTEEN

RENUNCIATION

The under-manager of the sawmill watched John jump the wall; he was waiting for him on the pavement of the main road.

'You know, that's a punishable offence,' he said evenly.

John straightened his cap. 'I suppose so.'

'Well, I don't want to seem stiff' – the man was almost apologetic – 'but it's got to stop. I shouldn't mind if it was just one doing it, but it only needs a start you know, and we'll have everybody living in Jarrow coming out this way, and I leave you to guess what'll happen to the timber . . . It's got to stop you see.'

John merely nodded before moving off; and the man, looking after him, thought 'poor devil'. It was right what they said, he had gone a bit queer. What other reason could there be for him not using the dock gates – for though the sawmill yard might be a short cut to Jarrow, it was difficult of access. Perhaps the lad thought he was still chasing his brother. Well, whatever he thought he was doing now, he'd have to find some other way of doing it but by this wall . . .

John realised this as he strode homewards. But there was no other way to avoid meeting Mary; if he used the main gate sooner or later they would be bound to meet. For four weeks now he had come out by the wall; it cut off the arches and the length of road past the Simonside bank. It did not cut off the gut – no deviation could cut off the gut. At first, he was determined to avoid Mary only until he should feel strong enough to face her; but with each passing day he became weaker, and told himself that in the silence between them the madness would fade and he would not have to see her. Then her letters started to come. Every day for the past three weeks there had been a letter. They were all neatly stacked in his box under the bed . . . and all unopened. With the coming of the first one he knew he must not open it, for the words it held would break down his reserve.

In the long stretches of the night he would think of the letters and what they held, and it would seem as if their substance created Mary herself, bringing her into the room to him . . . at times, even into the bed. He would feel her there, even smell the faint perfume that was hers, and his arms would go out to her, and in pulling her to him he would come to himself and, getting up, would stand on the cold floor, staring out of the window into the black square of the backyard, or up at the piece of sky visible between the houses, and know that Mary and the magic world that she alone could make was not for him – this wherein he stood was his world, this his night view for all time . . . this was his far horizon; this was the limit to all his wild hopes; here in this house he would have to work out his salvation. Sometimes he would lean his head against the window frame and murmur, 'Katie, Katie,' as if asking her forgiveness . . . If only he had never had the idea of making her a teacher! It was his fault, for she was a child and would have forgotten about it. Then he would never have got dressed up to go and see . . . her. And not seeing her, he would have come to love Christine; and the issue between him and Dominic would have been finished earlier, and his Katie and Christine would have been alive today . . . Again, had the Brackens not come next door, and, like a disciple, he had not sat at Peter's feet, lapping up all his mad ideas about the power of thought, this would never have happened.

Well, he was finished with thinking . . . his mother was right – it got you nowhere. There would be no more wild imagining for him. The road he was on held no space for flights of fancy. He had been mad in a number of ways. Between her and Peter he had gone crazy for a time. She even made him believe that the quaint thoughts which came into his head were unpolished gems, holding poetic qualities . . . and Peter, that life held something gigantic for him, that one day he would lead men, not into battle, but out of it . . . out of the battle with squalor into brighter and better conditions. Peter even egged him to take on the job of being a delegate to the Labourers' and General Workers' Union . . . God! how far above the earth he had walked; until that business of Nancy Kelly's! Even then he saw his Mecca in America. But now it was all over. He knew where his Mecca lay . . . in this house, in the fifteen streets and in the docks, working to feed his mother and father and Molly and that other growing Dominic.

Yet as he walked up the road, he knew that it wasn't all over; the hardest part for him was yet to come. He would have to see her and finish it. Far better to make a clean cut than try to keep dodging her. Once it was done, he would feel better; he could not feel worse.

Saturdays were like the opening afresh of a wound; the week-ends altogether were a torture. And now another was upon him. Since jumping the sawmill wall, he knew how he must spend this one . . . he must read the letters! . . .

When he entered the kitchen, his eyes, in spite of himself, were forced to the mantelpiece. There was yet another letter against the clock. He thrust it into his pocket, then washed himself before sitting down to dinner. Shane was already at the table, and John, out of the pity growing in him for his father, answered his questions patiently . . . Yes, the first boat of the year was in from Sweden with Lulea ore, and it seemed heavier than ever . . . yes, there was one due in on Monday from Bilbao.

'That'll mean piece work,' his father said . . . 'five shillings a shift.' He shook his head and looked down at his trembling hands. 'Perhaps if I made a start I would steady up . . . eh, lad?'

'Give yourself time,' said John, knowing that all the time in the world wouldn't put his father back in the docks.

'Yes. Another week then,' said Shane, with pitiable relief.

Silently, Mary Ellen moved between the oven and the table. Into the love she held for this son of hers was creeping a feeling of awe. The letters were creating it. The lass was writing to him every day, yet he was standing out against her. If ever a lad was in love, he was. But he was renouncing her . . . and for them. Where did he get his strength? She recognised him as a man with a man's needs, and her humility ignored the origin of his strength in herself. If only in some way he could have the lass . . . But it was impossible, the house depended on him; they could only live by him.

Here was another Saturday. How she dreaded and hated Saturdays! She seemed to spend her weeks gathering strength to face the Saturdays. Yet life went on. Round the doors, it was back to normal.

588

Already the incident was being referred to as something long past, in remarks, such as, 'That was a Saturday, wasn't it?' or, 'That day the two bairns went down.' The only ones outside the house who still felt the weight of that day were Peggy Flaherty and the Kellys . . . Peggy, because John, as she said, wouldn't look the side she was on. He wouldn't forgive her for duping him, and her fat was visibly disappearing through the worry of it. Her simple soul felt that until she was on speaking terms with John again nothing would be right. The Kellys were affected because now there could be no redress for Nancy. They would be saddled with her child and their scraping to live would become more difficult, while the possibility of yet another Nancy would be growing under their eyes. Mary Ellen, too, often thought of this. In a short while now, the child would be born, and she would be a grandmother. And always there would be Dominic across the street from her . . . from behind the curtains, she would look for the traits to show. She could see herself doing just that all down the years, for there was no possibility of her ever leaving the fifteen streets. Nor did she want to now; all desire for a change had long since left her, and she knew she must see life out to its close here. This did not worry her, but what did was that her lad would have to do the same. She hadn't wanted him to go to America, but that wasn't saying she wanted him to be stuck in the fifteen streets all his life . . . Dear God, no . . .

The meal was over, and while Molly cleared away Mary Ellen, taking Mick's shirt from the top of the pile of mending, cut off the tail and pinned it across the shoulders, before sitting down opposite Shane and beginning to sew.

John came from the bedroom, and looking hard at Molly, asked, 'Did someone call here a while ago? You know who I mean.'

Molly, after staring back at him for a second, hung her head and answered, 'Yes.'

'Why didn't you say?'

Molly turned her head a little and stared down to her mother's lap . . . How could she say to him, 'You were all mad when she came'? She recalled going to the door on the Sunday afternoon and seeing Miss Llewellyn standing there. She had asked to see her mother or father, and Molly had said she couldn't, they were both bad. It felt nice, at the time, to deny something to her one-time teacher, a teacher who had never taken any notice of her; and when she was able to deny her John, saying that he was out and she didn't know where he was, she experienced a definite pleasure. There was no room in her to feel sorry for Miss Llewellyn, who looked pale and bad. She didn't want her here, anyway. She guessed that Miss Llewellyn had clicked with their John, and she was puzzled, yet made bold, by sensing the come-down it was for anyone so swanky to click with their John. And so, after Miss Llewellyn had gone, she forgot about her. And now here was John blaming her, and she didn't want him to be vexed, for the daily aim of her life was that he and her ma would come to like her as they had liked Katie.

When she gave him no reply, John went back to the bedroom. He picked up the letter he had been reading . . . 'Dearest, I felt I must come and see you. Judged by my own sorrow, yours and your people's must be unbearable . . .' She had come here, to this house. Through the open door she must have glimpsed the conditions from the bareness of the front room, yet it had not put her off; nor the fifteen streets themselves. Nothing would put her off. She would go on believing that when he had accepted his sorrow he would come again to her.

He picked up another letter . . . 'Beloved, I understand. I will wait patiently. Each night I go to the lane, and I know that if you are not there there is always the following night, or the one after, or yet the one after that . . .' He ground his fist into the palm of his hand, and getting up, began to pace the floor in his stockinged feet . . . How much could a man endure! Of all the millions of women in the world, this one, who stood out above them, had to offer him a love such as this, a love men dreamed of, and died with it still but a dream. And it was his, it was being offered to him, John O'Brien, of 10 Fadden Street, of the fifteen streets. Yet he must renounce it, and do so now, this day. He must tell her in words that the mad dream was over. He must do it quickly and cleanly; the cut must be made without sentiment; there must be no tender goodbyes, and no holding out hopes for the future. He knew what the future held for him . . . he was a gaffer, and he'd remain a gaffer; and there was not even the remotest chance of her even becoming a gaffer's wife.

John caught sight of Mary before she saw him. She wasn't in the lane but on the main road, walking slowly with her back towards him, and the setting sun cast an aura of white light about her as she moved. He paused and drew in to the side of the road. The sight of her back had taken all the strength and determination out of him — what hope had he then to stand firm when he faced her. It was easy to be brave in a room talking to oneself. There you asked the questions and fired the answers; there were no eyes to bore into your heart and no touch to set the blood racing. In the bedroom he had been brave enough to don his old style of dress; with a grim defiance he had knotted the muffler ends around his braces, put on his old trousers and heavy boots, and lastly his mackintosh and cap. This, he told himself, was getting back to what he really was, and it would make things easier for her; she would have less regret at what she imagined she was losing. But now he wasn't so sure. His decent clothes would at least have left him free of thinking of himself. Fingering his muffler he could only think of her reaction when she saw him like this – well, wasn't that what he wanted? He continued to watch her for some minutes, and his heart defying his head, cried out, 'Mary – oh! Mary!'

As if the voice of his longing had become audible, she turned, and John, knowing that the time had come, stepped into the centre of the path and walked slowly towards her.

Mary remained still, gazing over the distance towards him. She did not see his clothes, only his face. Even from a distance it sent out its lostness to her, and she murmured aloud, 'My dear! my dear!' and with a little cry she picked up her skirts and ran to him. John halted before she reached him, and the resistance needed to stop the automatic gesture of holding out his arms became a pain.

'Oh John! – my dear!' Her hands were on his chest.

He swallowed as if ridding himself of a piece of granite, and said, 'Hallo, Mary.'

'Hallo, my dear,' she smiled at him gently; 'how are you?'

'All right.' He could not take his eyes from her face. She was pale, but she was more beautiful than he had ever seen her, and the tenderness in her eyes caused him to groan inwardly.

'How is your mother?' she asked softly.

'All right.'

'And is your father better?'

'Yes.'

Her eyes fell from his to her hand. Her fingers were softly stroking his muffler. 'I've missed you, dear.'

It was unbearable. No flesh and blood could stand it. He moved brusquely away from her and began to walk; and in a second she was by his side with her hand in his arm. 'What is it, John?'

He did not reply, and she went on, 'Shall we go up the lane?'

He turned into the lane without speaking, his arm hanging straight and stiff under her touch. The action was boorish, but he knew that if he allowed himself one tender move he would be finished. They stopped by the field gate, where they had been wont to lean and watch the moon and make love. Beyond, the after-glow was tinting the field of young wheat with sweeping strokes of pastel colour. John did not lean against the gate but stood staring into the field.

'Talk about it, my dear. Katie would want it so. It will make you feel better.' Mary had withdrawn her hand from his arm, and now she stood by the side of him, waiting.

'No talking would make any difference to that,' he replied tersely; 'but there's something else I've got to talk about.'

She remained silent, and he went on, swiftly now, 'I am not going to America — that's finished. This business has put paid to my father. He'll never work again. And Molly and Mick are still at school. There's no money coming in, only mine.' He turned now and looked at her; the afterglow which was mellowing the world around had no softening effect upon his face. 'Nothing can come of it now – it's no good going on. You understand?'

'No,' she said, 'I don't.'

He moved his head impatiently: 'How can I? What will there be to live on?'

'We could wait . . . you asked me to wait while you were in America.'

'That was different. What could there be to wait for now?'

'Molly leaves school this summer, and your brother will soon be fourteen.'

'And what about my mother and father?'

'There are ways and means. You could always manage to keep them.'

'Out of what?' he almost shouted. It was as if he were fighting her now, and some part of him was shocked; but he went on, 'Where would we live, and on what? – just tell me that.'

She made no answer. And his head dropped, and he murmured, 'I'm sorry.'

'There's no need to be sorry.' She took a step nearer to him, but did not touch him. 'John, look at me.' She waited until he raised his head before going on: 'We love each other. There won't be anyone else for either of us – we know that – so don't let this happen. There is a way out, there must be — there is a way out of everything.'

Peter's words — 'There is a way out of everything. Use your mind and it will give you the solution.' Peter's reasoning, added to the appeal of her voice and the entreaty of her eyes, broke the tension of his body for the moment, and he allowed his mind to clutch at a fleeting hope — could there be some way out? Could the madness be resurrected? Oh the joyful bewilderment of touching her again! Her face blurred before his eyes, and her voice became blended with the evensong of the birds.

'If you'll only listen to me, darling — I don't mind where I live or how I live, as long as I'm with you. We could be married and I'd go on working. John — I'll come to the fifteen streets . . .'

The blur cleared. The mention of the fifteen streets held the power to betray dreams for what they were. No longer did he see the pleading in her eyes. He saw only her well-cut costume, the gold wrist-watch, the ring on her finger with the large amber stone in the centre, the patent leather of her narrow shoes, and the glimpse of grey stockings, which were of silk; and covering all, the perfume which emanated from her was in his nostrils, the perfume whose ingredients lay not in any bottle but in a sequence starting from a scented bath to fresh linen — and she said she would come to the fifteen streets! He laughed inwardly, harsh, bitter laughter, and said sharply, 'Be quiet!

You don't know what you're talking about. Have you ever been inside a house in the fifteen streets?'

'No.'

'It's a pity you haven't.'

'There's no disgrace in being poor.'

'No? I used to think that at one time, but I don't any longer — it's a crying disgrace, but one that I can't alter. But I can do this — I can save you from yourself. You shall never come to the fifteen streets through me.'

'John, darling, listen.'

'I can't listen, I've got to go.' He stepped back from her outstretched hand.

'John, please . . . Oh, don't go like this — John, I love you . . . Don't you see, I can't go on without you?'

The stillness of the field settled on them. Outwardly they appeared lifeless things, fixed in their staring. Then, in spite of himself, he spoke her name, 'Mary.' And like a caress it touched her. But the caress was short-lived, for he went on, 'This has got to be — it's got to finish right now. It's no use going on — no — no!' — he silenced her quietly and with upraised hand. 'All the talking in the world won't make it any different. You'll forget — time will help.'

'It won't — I know that deep within my soul you'll remain with me for ever; I won't be able to forget you — John, oh, John — please! Please let us try to find a way out.' She held out her arms to him, and the humility in their appeal probed a fresh depth of pain in him. But he did not touch them, and Mary made a desperate final effort: 'Katie would have wanted it — she loved to think that we . . .'

'Don't! . . . Goodbye, Mary.' For a second longer he allowed his gaze to linger on her. A lark in the field beyond suddenly rose, singing, from the grass and soared into the dusk of the closing evening. When he saw the mist of tears blinding her eyes, he turned from her and went down the lane.

It was done!

CHAPTER FOURTEEN

WHITHER THOU GOEST

Mary Ellen was puzzled by her own emotions. The sorrow of Katie's loss had not died or faded — it was as poignant as the hour when it happened — but she could bear it now with equanimity because of use. What puzzled her was that it seemed to have moved aside to make room for the sorrow she was feeling for John. Daily she watched him closing up — life seemed to be dying in him. He was becoming the kind of dock man he had never been, even before he had taken to wearing collars and ties. He had not yet taken to drink or lounging at the corners, but he never seemed to get out of his working clothes, and he never moved from the house once he came home from work. Nor did he sit in the kitchen, but spent hours in the bedroom — wrestling, Mary Ellen thought, with himself.

It was a fortnight since the letters ceased, and in some strange way their cessation had brought an added emptiness to her days. With their daily arrival, there remained the hope, however faint, that things would come right for her lad. Now hope was dead, and with it the part of him that had survived Katie's loss was dying too.

What was there to live for now? Mary Ellen asked herself, as she banged the poss-stick up and down in the tub, full of clothes. With no possibility of happiness for her lad and nothing she could do about it, her usual incentive to 'cope' was gone — if only an act of God would finish them all off and leave John free! But God never did things like that — nothing with any sense or reason in it . . . There she was, going again. Her bouts of defiance against God brought her hours of fear and remorse in the night, yet mixed with her fear was a tinge of admiration at her day-time audacity at facing up to Him, and strange, too, was the contradictory feeling of late that she wanted to go to church — not to Mass, so escaping Father O'Malley's censure, but just to sit quietly in church, with no-one there, and perhaps come to terms with God. She did not actually think of it like this — she had not advanced so far in her bravery to do so — but the feeling in her urged that should she go to church and sit quiet she would feel better. The feeling was strong in her now, and she stopped possing and whispered aloud, 'I'll go — I'll go now!' She rubbed her wet arm across her forehead and shook her head, and muttered, 'For God's sake, what's come over you? Have you gone completely up the pole? There's another two hours washing in

600

front of you yet!' She stooped, and lifting the clothes from the tub, began running them into the mangle. There was a series of groans, squeaks and loud jolts, as garment followed garment.

The tub empty of clothes, she dragged it into the yard and poured the water down the sink, and she made no effort to move as the dirty foam swirled about her feet. Rolling the tub back into the washhouse again, she happened to glance up, and met Shane's eyes on her. He was standing at the kitchen window and his face bore the look of despair that covered them all. Although he had made no mention of it for weeks now, she knew that he, too, was continually crying out inside himself for Katie, and also that he was suffering because of the knowledge that through his dependence things were not right with John. She stood leaning over the empty tub for a moment, her eyes gazing down at the water-worn wood. Then, as if she had found a command written there, she hurriedly left the washhouse.

In the kitchen, she dried her arms and combed the top of her hair. Shane watched her silently. Even when she put her coat on he did not question her. With her face turned from him, she said, 'I won't be long.' Then, as if compelled to expose her madness to him, she added, 'I'm going to the church.'

That any woman could leave her washing at two o'clock in the afternoon to go to church must prove, she thought, to a man like Shane that she was mad;

but he made no comment on her extraordinary behaviour. Not until she was going through the front room did he speak.

'Mary Ellen.'

She turned: 'Yes?'

He was groping in his trouser pocket. 'Will you light me a candle?' He handed her a penny and their eyes met over it; and perhaps for the first time in their married lives they felt joined in thought and purpose.

As Mary Ellen opened the front door a pantechnicon passed and stopped at Peter Bracken's, and she saw Peter himself standing on his doorstep. For a space they looked at each other, and she knew that she should go to this man and say some word, for her son had been the means of killing his lass; yet through his lass she had lost Katie. With his very coming here, tragedy had entered her life. Peter's eyes were asking her to speak, but she found it impossible. It was strange that only once had this man and she exchanged words – that day in the kitchen, the day the bairn was born. Before she turned away she tried to send him some kindly message; but whether she succeeded or not she couldn't tell. She hurried away down the street, knowing that she had looked her last on Peter Bracken – he was leaving the fifteen streets and never again would they meet. Why had he come here in the first place? To relieve poverty and ignorance, he said. Oh, God, how happy she would have been in her poverty and ignorance had she still Katie. Yet she could feel no virile bitterness against him, which was strange. Instead, she felt they were sharing the same sorrow, and she wasn't troubled at her manner towards him, knowing intuitively that he understood . . .

The day was dull and the sky low. Inside the church the light was as dim as if it were evening, and the air, as usual, was different from that outside – thick and heavy with the weight of stale incense. At the top of the centre aisle, Mary Ellen, her head bowed, made a deep genuflexion. She did not look towards the altar, where always and forever reposed Jesus in the Blessed Sacrament; somehow she wanted no 'truck' with Him; It was His mother she needed. She went down the side aisle walking softly, as if trying to escape the notice of the Holy Ones standing in their niches with flowers at their feet.

There were no candles burning on the half-moon stand to the side of Our Lady, and she stood in shadow until Mary Ellen lit her candles, one for Shane, one for John and one for herself. Then The Virgin was illuminated, smiling down on Mary Ellen, half holding The Child out to her.

Mary Ellen knew she should kneel and say a prayer, and ask The Virgin about Katie and tell her about John, but she felt very tired and all she wanted to do was to sit. She sat in the end of the front pew, as near as she could get to The

Virgin, and gazed at her, preparatory to speaking about her lad. But as she sat on, her feet resting on the long wooden kneeler and her hands joined in her lap, she found she couldn't think of John. It was as if he and his troubles had shrunk, her mind groping for them in vain. As the flame of the candles lengthened, the smile of The Virgin deepened, and it seemed to Mary Ellen that she moved and hitched the Infant higher up on to her arm as she herself used to do with Katie. The light of the candles grew brighter and brighter as she stared at them, and the church outside the ring of light became darker. A great peace swept over Mary Ellen. It started in her feet with a tingling warmth and coursed through her body, flooding her being with a happiness she could never remember experiencing before, or ever imagined possible. So great was her happiness that it left no room for fear when she saw The Virgin move and gently push someone towards her.

When Katie stood at the end of the pew and, smiling shyly, said, 'Oh, Ma!' Mary Ellen felt no surprise. She leaned forward and gripped Katie's hands. 'Why, hinny, I thought you were – gone.' She wouldn't say 'dead'. And when Katie answered her, saying, 'It was only for a few minutes, Ma. Things went black and then it was over,' Mary Ellen took it as a natural answer, and went on, 'You're not out there then, hinny? – not out in the sea?'

Katie's laugh tinkled through the church, and

she glanced back at The Virgin, and The Virgin's smile broadened. 'We never went out there, did we, Christine?'

Katie turned her head and spoke into the shadows, and Mary Ellen asked, 'The lass, is she with you?'

'Why, of course! We're waiting together – it's nice waiting.'

'Waiting?' repeated Mary Ellen. 'For what, hinny?'

'For the time to come when we should have died, and then we'll go on – we went too soon, Ma.'

'Yes, hinny, you did.'

Now death had been mentioned, a sweet contentment was added to Mary Ellen's happiness – she felt she was with death, and it was a pleasant thing, not only pleasant, but strangely exciting. Her bairn was in it, and was happy. 'How long must you wait, hinny?'

'We don't know; but once it's over we'll start growing again – a different growing, getting ready to come back – won't we, Christine?'

Mary Ellen peered into the shadows but could see nothing, and Katie went on, 'Before we go, I'll come and see you again – and Ma . . .'

'Yes, hinny?'

'Don't worry about John; he's going to be happy, so very happy.'

'How can you tell, hinny?'

'We know about those we love. Go home now, Ma.'

Katie's lips rested on Mary Ellen's and the sweetness

of them pressed down into her being . . . the sweetness like a gentle perfume was in her nostrils when she opened her eyes.

'Katie, hinny—' She put out her hand, gropingly. She could not see Katie, but something stronger than reason told her she was there. She whispered again, 'Katie, hinny,' then looked towards The Virgin. She was as she had first seen her, yet different, for her face seemed to hold the knowledge of all eternity.

Katie and Christine were all right . . . they were with her. It did not enter Mary Ellen's head to question how Christine – the spook's daughter – could be with The Virgin, who, above all others, was a Catholic first and the Mother of God after.

Smiling gently to herself, Mary Ellen left the church. Katie was happy, oh indeed she was happy – and everything was going to be all right for her lad. Katie had said so.

The ghoulish picture of Katie floating in deep water that had filled her mind for weeks had gone – Katie wasn't there – she knew where Katie was . . .

Going homewards Mary Ellen walked with a lighter tread; there was an urgency in her to reach the house and tell Shane, although how she was going to tell Shane about Katie without him thinking her completely mad she didn't know. But Shane needed comfort, and if she could tell him in a sensible way that she had seen Katie she had no doubt that he would feel as she did now. She hurried up the backyard, ignoring the dead fire under the washhouse pot and the mounds of unfinished washing, and entered the kitchen. Shane was there, sitting in his armchair beside the fireplace, while opposite him sat the lass. Mary Ellen had never met Mary Llewellyn, but there was no need for anyone to tell her who this was.

Bright spots of red burned in the dull colour of Shane's cheeks: 'I told the lass to stay – you wouldn't be long.'

Mary rose to her feet and watched the little woman unpin her hat and hang her coat carefully behind the kitchen door. She had not spoken, and Mary began, 'I hope you don't mind, Mrs O'Brien . . . I wanted to talk to you.'

'Sit down, miss,' said Mary Ellen with strange gentleness, 'you're quite welcome. Can I offer you a cup of tea?'

'Please; I should like one.'

Mary Ellen pressed the kettle, which was standing on the hob, further into the fire. At the same time Shane rose, saying, 'I'll be lying down for a while.' He left the kitchen without glancing at Mary – it was as if she had been there always and was likely to remain. The room door closed behind Shane and the two women were left alone.

Mary Ellen, filled with a growing awe and wonder, silently placed the teapot to warm, and unhooked the cups from the back of the cupboard and put them on the table. Oh, Katie, Katie. Can this mean what you said about John's life? She dare not look at the lass in case she should disappear as Katie had done.

'How is John, Mrs O'Brien?'

Mary Ellen was forced to stop in her trotting to and fro and look at this woman, whom her lad loved. She said simply, 'He's not too grand, miss.'

Mary turned her gaze towards the fire, and after a moment asked, 'Do you agree with his decision?' Then before Mary Ellen could make a reply, she turned to her again and went on rapidly, 'Please believe me . . . I understand . . . I know that you have only him now to look after you, and I want him to do that always. But that is no reason why we should be separated – is it, Mrs O'Brien? We care for each other – very deeply, and there is a way out if only he would listen to reason.'

'You can't marry without money, lass.'

'Did you wait until you had money?'

Mary Ellen shook her head. 'This is different . . . you're different. He'd want money to give you a home.'

'I don't want that kind of a home, Mrs O'Brien' – Mary leaned forward and took hold of Mary Ellen's hands – 'the solution is for me to come and live here. I must show him that I can do it. There are always empty houses going, and I could continue my work. Even if I didn't, I have a little money, enough to keep us a couple of years, living simply ... How much is the rent of these houses?'

'Four and tuppence.' Mary Ellen, her hands locked in the soft firmness of Mary's, was trying to measure the cost it had been to her lad to give up this lass, whose charm was already telling on her ... Aye, but it wouldn't work out. She would never be able to stick it here; it would strip her of everything but the capacity to regret ... Yet why should she stick here? Wouldn't John fight with every fibre of his being to take her out of this? That is, if she persisted in coming here and persuaded him to marry ... Peter Bracken's gone, the house next door is empty ... It was almost as if Katie was at her elbow – the voice in her head was Katie's. She remained still, listening to both Katie and the lass.

'Will you help me, Mrs O'Brien? I can assure you that you'll not suffer for it. Please, Mrs O'Brien, do help me. I want to come and live here, somewhere near. He will know nothing about it until it's done. I must show him that I can live here successfully ... will you?'

'There's a house empty right next door, lass.' It was as if Katie had nudged her. 'It was the Brackens' you know ... the lass ...'

'Yes, yes, I know ... Oh, Mrs O'Brien, tell me what to do. Who do I see about it?' In her excitement Mary stood up, and Mary Ellen, her mind suddenly filled with doubt, turned away and mashed the tea.

Would John want to live in a house where the lass Christine had lived? . . . She seemed to hear Katie's laugh tinkling again as it had done in the church. Now it was deriding her superstitions, and Mary Ellen set down the teapot, and turning back to Mary, said resolutely, 'I'll do anything to see my lad happy; although I'd better tell you, lass, it'll be hard for you . . . at the very best it'll be hard going.'

'You doubt that I'll be able to stand it?'

'No, somehow I don't. If you care for him enough it'll keep the iron out of your soul.'

With a sigh that swept the tenseness from her body, Mary sat down again. As she took the cup of tea from Mary Ellen, they smiled at each other and a quietness settled on the kitchen as they sat drinking and thinking, their thoughts in different channels but flowing the one way.

The flat cart was at the door – a clean, respectable flat cart, but the sight of it and its import had prostrated Beatrice Llewellyn. She lay on her bed, faint with rage and self-pity. There was rage, too, in James Llewellyn's voice as he talked to Mary from the doorway of her room, moving from time to time to allow the removal man to pass. He only spoke in the man's absence, talking rapidly to get in all he had to say.

'You'll regret this to your dying day . . . do you hear me?'

'I hear you.' Mary, with her back to him, went on lifting books from the shelves and packing them into a tea chest.

'You don't know what you're doing — you can't! Why, woman, the scum of the earth live in the fifteen streets — he's not a man! No man who could lay any claim to the name would ask anyone like you to go there.'

'He hasn't asked me, he has refused even to see me.'

'And you have so little pride you are going to live there and push yourself on him?'

'Yes, I have so little pride I am going to do just that.'

The man came in and as he lifted the tea chest asked, 'Is this the lot, miss?'

'Yes . . . except the two trunks and the cases in the hall.'

James Llewellyn threw a murderous glance at the unfortunate man as he lumbered past him with the box. 'Have you got the place furnished?' he barked the question at her.

'No.'

'No? You mean to say you are going to live there with those few odds and ends?' He nodded towards the hall.

'I have bought a bed and a table . . . just the necessary things.' Mary kept her face turned from her father. She thought of the problem the buying of the bed had caused — whether to be modest and buy a single bed, or to be true to herself and buy what she hoped would be necessary. She had not asked Mary Ellen's advice about this. It was something she had to decide for herself . . . And was she brave enough to face the comments of her future neighbours? for she did not delude herself into thinking it would escape their notice; and she could practically hear their comments on a single lass buying a new double bed. She knew already that the hardest thing to bear in the fifteen streets would be her lack of privacy.

She had ordered a double bed and by now it would have been delivered. She glanced for the last time round the room, her eyes avoiding her father's. He was standing, black and massive, filling the doorway. She did not mind her mother's censure, but his cut deep into her. She would have gone happily to the fifteen streets had he given her some kind word.

'You'll be the talk of the town — a laughingstock!' He barred her way, and she waited, eyes cast down, until he would move aside.

'I'll not be the first, or the last.'

'Your mother's ill.'

'My mother isn't ill . . . she's merely angry, and you know it.' She lifted her eyes to his. His face was mottled with his emotions, and she could not bear to witness it any longer.

'I must go . . .' She stepped towards the door, but her father did not move. He stood staring at her, his face working, fighting against the softening emotion that was breaking him down – his lass going to live in the fifteen streets! His Mary, who loved colour, and light and laughter, who was so close to him, closer than his wife, who could reason like him and laugh at the same things. She was going to live in one of those wrecks of houses, just to be near that big docker . . . God Almighty! it was unbelievable . . . Yet he had given her credit for being able to reason like himself. Then could she be so far wrong? . . . Was there something worthwhile in the fellow? Worthwhile or not, she had no right to be doing this. She was mad.

'Mary, lass, don't go . . . I'll try to fix something . . . a job or something, for him.' His face fell into pitying lines of entreaty.

She shook her head slowly and put out her hand to him, speaking with difficulty.

'It wouldn't work . . . he'd refuse. This is the only way, to take whatever he has to offer, however small, and make it do . . . Perhaps later—'

'Oh, lass' – he pulled her into his arms – 'oh, Mary, lass!'

They held each other for a moment, tight and hard. Then, thrusting her from him he went hurriedly down the passage, and Mary, trying to stem the flood of tears, listened in amazement to him barking down the drive at the carrier.

'Come in here, and give a hand with these things.'

613

He came back, followed by the man, whom he bewildered with his torrent of orders.

'Get that china cabinet out, and that bookcase. And the couch and chair. Then up with this carpet.'

'Father — no, don't. Listen to me,' she protested, 'I don't want them . . . I must go as I am. It will only make it more difficult. He wouldn't want . . .' She stopped. Her father wasn't listening; he was in a frenzy of action. He passed her, carrying one end of the heavy bookcase, almost pushing the man off his feet, both with his confused orders and force, and she knew she must let him do this for her. However more difficult it would make the work ahead, she must accept these things.

When the room was at last bare, she walked down to the gate, her father at her side. In deep embarrassment they stood facing each other.

'Well, good luck, lass. I dare say I'll find my way to see you . . . what's the number?'

'Twelve Fadden Street.'

'You can always come back, you know.'

'Thanks, my dear.'

'Goodbye, lass.'

'Goodbye.' It was impossible to say more. Blindly she went down the road. The cart on ahead was a blur, and it remained so until she came within sight of the fifteen streets.

All afternoon they worked. They cut the carpet, and

it covered the floor of the front room and bedroom. The kitchen boards were bare except for two rugs, which to Mary Ellen's mind were far too bright and grand for such a room. The things the lass had brought were lovely! She was glad the lass's father had made her take them, for now one of the main problems to the marriage, as she saw it, was removed . . . they were set up. But her happiness in this new turn of events was marred, and it was the statue that was responsible . . . that great white, bare woman, as naked as the day she was born, and standing on a box where anyone at the front door would get an eyeful of her. The lass was respectable, she knew that, and apparently to her mind this naked woman meant nothing except what she was, a statue. But let them about the doors get a glimpse of it, and Mary Ellen knew the result as if it had already taken place. The women would dub the lass 'a loose piece', and from the start her life in the fifteen streets would be suspect. They would conjure up the men she'd had, and her lad would become an object of pity for having been caught, and never would the lass be able to pass the corners of the streets without hungry eyes and low laughter following her. If only she could explain to her . . . but it was a hard thing to explain. Mary Ellen knew she wasn't at her best with words, but actions now . . . yes. If she were to knock the thing flying accidentally . . . She stood looking at it. There wasn't much time left, for John was due any minute now. Molly was on the watch for him at the corner, and the lass was in the kitchen getting her first meal ready. Well, it was now or never. She lifted her hand and swiped the naked woman to the floor. As it crashed, she heard a gasp, and there, standing in the doorway, her face white and shocked, was Mary.

Across the debris they stared at each other. Mary Ellen, her face working, tried to explain. 'I had to do it, lass ... they would think ... the women would say ... They wouldn't understand around these doors ... I want you to have a good start.'

Mary gazed down on the fragments of her expression. The statue had been a symbol of truth to her; a figure indeed of her emancipation from cant and hypocrisy; a symbol of her growing freedom. But now it was gone. Never until this moment had she fully realised what coming to the fifteen streets would mean. She imagined at worst it meant living meagrely. Now she saw that was but a small part of it. To live happily, her life would not only have to be altered from the outside, but from within. Not only her actions, but her thoughts, must be restricted. This little woman had not broken the statue from malice, but from a desire to help her. Some deep knowledge of her own people had urged her to its destruction, and it might be only one of the many things which must be destroyed if she were to suffer this life. Could she suffer it?

'Lass, I didn't mean to hurt you.' Mary Ellen's face was pitiable, and her fingers, as always when she was in distress, picked nervously at the button of her blouse. Had she, with her mad action, destroyed what she wanted most? Happiness for her lad. The lass looked hurt and bewildered. She wanted her off to a good start, but she had achieved just the opposite. She bent her head in an effort to hide the raining tears ... was nothing ever to go right?

When she felt the lass's arms go about her, she leant against her, faint with relief, and felt herself almost a child again as Mary patted her back, saying, 'There, there! It's all right. I understand. I should have had more sense than to bring it. Please don't cry! Just think' – she gave a little laugh – 'if Father O'Malley had seen it!' They both began to shake, small, rippling tremors, which mounted into laughter; quiet, relaxing laughter such as Mary Ellen never thought to laugh again. Oh, the lass would get by. She knew what to laugh at.

They both stopped abruptly when a knock came on the front door, and Mary Ellen opened it to Molly.

'He's coming up the road, Ma.'

'All right,' said Mary Ellen, 'you know what to do. Tell him I want him to come in the front way.'

Without looking again at Mary, she said, 'Well,

lass, I'll get myself away in,' and she went through the kitchen and out of the back door.

In her own backyard she paused a moment. Within the next few minutes she would have lost her lad, for she had no doubt that once he stepped inside that door he would be gone from her and another woman would have him. She wanted his happiness didn't she? Yes, above all things she wanted his happiness. But with it she hadn't thought to feel this added sense of loneliness. Well, she'd have to turn her mind to the others. Shane, for instance, who needed her as never before. And Molly, who seemed to have been born when Katie died. And Mick, who'd need two steady hands on him to keep him from Dominic's path. Yes, she still had a lot to cope with. And her lad would be next door for some time yet — Rome wasn't built in a day.

Left alone, Mary felt unable to move. There were a dozen and one things she wanted to accomplish before seeing him; among them to change her apron and do her hair. But now she could only stand rooted. A few minutes ago she had asked herself if she could suffer this life. What a ridiculous question to ask, when her whole being told her she could suffer no life that did not hold him.

The heavy tread of his steps reached her, and she lifted her head to the sound. All the colour of life, all the essence of the music she had heard, all the beauty she had seen and felt with her soul's capacity, rose in her, and she moved towards the door. Not until she heard the sound of the knocker on his own door did she lift the latch.

It was some time before he turned his head towards her, and then he did it slowly as if afraid of what he would see. She held out her hand, and he moved towards her but did not touch her. It was she who took his arm and drew him over the threshold and closed the door behind them. Walking ahead of her into the room he looked about him, and his face was drained of its colour. He brought his gaze from the fragments of the broken statue lying by the fireside to her face, and he said grimly, 'No, Mary. You can't do it . . . that's how you'll end, like that — broken.'

'Some things are better broken.'

'I'll not let you do it.'

'You can't stop me, dear . . . it's done. Here I am, and here I stay until you have me . . . and after.'

His eyes travelled again around the room, and she smiled gently at him. 'Do you like it?' He made no reply, and she said, 'Come and see the kitchen.'

In the kitchen he stared at a table set in shining whiteness for two. The kettle, startlingly new, was singing on the hob. It caused something to break in him. He closed his eyes, striving to fight the weakness. 'You don't know what you're doing . . . you'll regret it . . . your father should—'

He could say no more. She was leaning against

him, her arms about his neck. The oval of her face was lost in light. 'Hold me, John.'

His arms, telling his hunger, crushed her to him. The faint perfume of her body mingled with the acrid smell of iron ore, and in the ever increasing murmur of his endearments and the searching of his lips her words were lost:

Whither thou goest, I will go: and where thou lodgest, I will lodge: thy people shall be my people, and thy God my God: Where thou diest, will I die, and there will I be buried: the Lord do so to me, and more also, if ought but death part thee and me.

THE END

THE GOLDEN STRAW
by Catherine Cookson

The Golden Straw, as it would be named, was a large, broad-brimmed hat presented to Emily Pearson by her long-time friend and employer Mabel Arkwright, milliner and modiste. And before long it was to her employer that Emily owed the gift of the business itself, for Mabel was in poor health and had come to rely more and more on Emily before her untimely death in 1880.

While on holiday in France, Emily and the Golden Straw attracted the eye of Paul Steerman, a guest at the hotel, and throughout his stay he paid her unceasing attention. But Paul Steerman was not at all he seemed to be and he was to bring nothing but disgrace and tragedy to Emily, precipitating a series of events that would influence the destiny of not only her children but her grandchildren too.

The Golden Straw, conceived on a panoramic scale, brilliantly portrays a rich vein of English life from the heyday of the Victorian era to the stormy middle years of the present century. It represents a fresh triumph for this great storyteller whose work is deservedly loved and enjoyed throughout the world.

0 552 13685 9

JUSTICE IS A WOMAN
by Catherine Cookson

The day Joe Remington brought his new bride to Fell Rise, he had already sensed she might not settle easily into the big house just outside the Tyneside town of Fellburn. For Joe this had always been his home, but for Elaine it was virtually another country whose manners and customs she was by no means eager to accept.

Making plain her disapproval of Joe's familiarity with the servants, demanding to see accounts Joe had always trusted to their care, questioning the donation of food to striking miners' families – all these objections and more soon rubbed Joe and the local people up the wrong way, a problem he could easily have done without, for this was 1926, the year of the General Strike, the effects of which would nowhere be felt more acutely than in this heartland of the North-East.

Then when Elaine became pregnant, she saw it as a disaster and only the willingness of her unmarried sister Betty to come and see her through her confinement made it bearable. But in the long run, would Betty's presence only serve to widen the rift between husband and wife, or would she help to bring about a reconciliation?

0 552 13622 0

THE MALTESE ANGEL
by Catherine Cookson

Ward Gibson knew what was expected of him by the village folk, and especially by the Mason family, whose daughter Daisy he had known all his life. But then, in a single week, his whole world had been turned upside down by a dancer, Stephanie McQueen, who seemed to float across the stage of the Empire Music Hall where she was appearing as The Maltese Angel. To his amazement, the attraction was mutual, and after a whirlwind courtship she agreed to marry him.

But a scorpion had already begun to emerge from beneath the stone of the local community, who considered that Ward had betrayed their expectations, and led on and cruelly deserted Daisy. There followed a series of reprisals on his family, one of them serious enough to cause him to exact a terrible revenge; and these events would twist and turn the course of many lives through Ward's own and succeeding generations.

0 552 13684 0

A SELECTION OF OTHER CATHERINE COOKSON
TITLES AVAILABLE FROM CORGI BOOKS

☐	13576 3	THE BLACK CANDLE	£5.99
☐	12473 7	THE BLACK VELVET GOWN	£5.99
☐	14633 1	COLOUR BLIND	£5.99
☐	12551 2	A DINNER OF HERBS	£6.99
☐	14066 X	THE DWELLING PLACE	£5.99
☐	14068 6	FEATHERS IN THE FIRE	£5.99
☐	14089 9	THE FEN TIGER	£5.99
☐	14069 4	FENWICK HOUSES	£5.99
☐	10450 7	THE GAMBLING MAN	£4.99
☐	13716 2	THE GARMENT	£5.99
☐	13621 2	THE GILLYVORS	£5.99
☐	10916 9	THE GIRL	£5.99
☐	14328 6	THE GLASS VIRGIN	£5.99
☐	13685 9	THE GOLDEN STRAW	£5.99
☐	13300 0	THE HARROGATE SECRET	£5.99
☐	14087 2	HERITAGE OF FOLLY	£5.99
☐	13303 5	THE HOUSE OF WOMEN	£5.99
☐	10780 8	THE IRON FAÇADE	£5.99
☐	13622 0	JUSTICE IS A WOMAN	£5.99
☐	14091 0	KATE HANNIGAN	£5.99
☐	14092 9	KATIE MULHOLLAND	£5.99
☐	14081 3	MAGGIE ROWAN	£5.99
☐	13684 0	THE MALTESE ANGEL	£5.99
☐	10321 7	MISS MARTHA MARY CRAWFORD	£5.99
☐	12524 5	THE MOTH	£5.99
☐	13302 7	MY BELOVED SON	£5.99
☐	13088 5	THE PARSON'S DAUGHTER	£5.99
☐	14073 2	PURE AS THE LILY	£5.99
☐	13683 2	THE RAG NYMPH	£5.99
☐	14620 X	THE ROUND TOWER	£5.99
☐	13714 6	SLINKY JANE	£5.99
☐	10541 4	THE SLOW AWAKENING	£5.99
☐	10630 5	THE TIDE OF LIFE	£5.99
☐	14038 4	THE TINKER'S GIRL	£5.99
☐	12368 4	THE WHIP	£5.99
☐	13577 1	THE WINGLESS BIRD	£5.99
☐	13247 0	THE YEAR OF THE VIRGINS	£5.99